Arcane Call

Path of the Ranger, Book 13

Pedro Urvi

COMMUNITY:

Mail: pedrourvi@hotmail.com
Facebook: https://www.facebook.com/PedroUrviAuthor/
My Website: http://pedrourvi.com
Twitter: https://twitter.com/PedroUrvi

Translation by:
Christy Cox

Edited by:
Mallory Brandon Bingham

DEDICATION

To my good friend Guiller.

Thank you for all your support since day one.

Content

MAP

Chapter 1

Astrid arrived at the foot of the south wall of the Zangrian fortress and crouched, her body against the rock wall. It was late at night, and only the crickets and some distant toad could be heard—besides the hoot of an owl that was not really an owl. She looked down at her clothes. She was dressed in black with the hooded cloak and scarf of a Stealthy Spy. It was similar to the Natural Assassin attire she was used to wearing for the King's missions, although it was a deeper black to make it harder to be discovered.

She adjusted the scarf that covered her mouth and nose. Only her green eyes could be seen, and barely, since she had painted her forehead and around her eyes also in black. She usually did not need paint to hide, but for spying missions like the one tonight it was necessary. So, she had been instructed during her higher training, and so she did now that she had graduated and was back in the service of the realm.

She stood in position, trying to make no noise. She had practiced stealth a lot, both in her training at the Camp and at the Shelter. It was an essential skill in Expertise, and she was an expert at it. A lot better than her comrades and friends. Not even Viggo came close to her subtlety of movement without being seen or heard, even though he was talented. She took pleasure in the fact, and whenever she had a chance, Astrid rubbed it in, only to hear her friend's biting replies.

She looked right and left but could see no one. She glanced up at the battlement above her head. She could not see any guards, although she knew there were at least three on patrol. She had been spying on the fortress for several days and knew where the watchmen were posted, their routines, the time it took them, the changes and when they happened, and the weak points of the castle's security. All part of what a good spy ought to know before initiating an intrusion.

She waited for the right moment, flattened against the wall. She knew it would not take long. A metal sound reached her from the battlement. She looked up and saw the light of two torches. The change of guard was taking place. She watched carefully and followed the course of the two points of light. When they both vanished from sight, she knew the time had come. She took three steps back from the wall, uncoiled the thin but resistant, treated rope she had been carrying around her torso under the cloak, and left it on the ground beside her. The rope was such a dark brown that when she put it down it seemed to vanish. She took out one of her special assault arrows with a hooked tip from her quiver and tied one end of the rope to the end of the arrow.

She knocked the arrow with the rope quickly and silently. Crouching to remain hidden, she raised the bow toward the battlement. It was a special shot, as were the bow and arrow she was going to use. She needed an arched shot, and for that she was using a short climbing bow. It was a special kind designed to release arrows with hooked tips which some Ranger Specialists used, such as Stealthy Spies. Astrid had been practicing with the weapon for a while, and with Ingrid's and Nilsa's help, who were exceptional shots, she had managed to master it.

She concentrated, aimed, and—very gently—released. The arrow flew to the battlement in a strange arc, forced by the bow's design and hampered by the weight of the rope, but it flew as she had expected it to. The shot was good and the arrow went over the edge. She put the bow across her back and carefully pulled on the rope to see whether the hook had taken hold in the rock of the battlement. It seemed to be stuck firmly, so she started to climb up. She did not have much time—the watchmen would soon be passing the point where she was climbing.

As she went up using her feet on the wall and the strength of her arms, she looked up at the sky. A storm was threatening, it was overcast and the moon and stars were covered, making it more difficult for the watchmen to spot her. That was one of the reasons she had chosen to carry out the incursion that night. The other reason was that her target was in the castle. Count Orzentok had arrived two days before and would not stay much longer. She had to act before he went on his way.

She reached the upper part of the battlement and scanned the wall. Her side, the south wall, was clear, but not so the eastern or western sides. There were two guards standing on each side and two more were doing the rounds. She could not see the northern part of the wall since the castle's central building was in the way, even so, she knew there would be two more guards posted and two more on patrol. The northern guard changed after that on the south, so they would soon be doing so. She gathered the rope and coiled it around her torso as if it were armor; it was so light and thin that its weight did not bother her much.

She crawled along the battlement and without wasting a moment, advanced like a water snake at top speed to the right-hand turret. According to her calculations, she had just enough time. At least she hoped so, or else she was going to have a most unpleasant encounter. She reached the round rocky structure right when the door was opening and two guards were coming out. As the door opened, Astrid got to her feet and like lightning stood with her back to the wall behind the door, which hid her completely once it was fully open—exactly what she had intended. The two guards came out and walked to the center of the battlement, chatting and pointing at the sky.

Astrid waited for the voices to move away. She did not understand what they were saying, but she watched them with half her face peeping out from behind the door and guessed they were talking about the storm that was coming. Nothing worse for the watchmen than spending their shift in the rain. She waited one more moment and swiftly and silently came out from behind the door and went into the turret. She waited to see whether any other guards were coming up the spiral stair; but since everything seemed quiet, she went down the stone stairs to the foot of the tower.

Things got complicated now, since she had to cross the courtyard and slip inside the main building of the castle. It was a great square tower with four other round turrets, one in each corner. Castles in the kingdom of Zangria were quite simple. Architecture and design were not Zangrian strong points, which made the mission easier. Complex and overdone buildings were not so good for incursion missions. She had to be careful though, since the Zangrians were quite good at fighting and killing.

She scanned the courtyard, the stables, and inside the walls. Everything looked quiet. She sought the entrance to the main tower building of the fortress. The door was guarded by two soldiers and most likely there were two more inside. It was huge, and opening it was not going to be easy. Doors of that kind were strengthened and weighed about a ton. They were built that way to withstand a siege. When the outer walls fell into the hands of the enemy, the great tower building acted like the last bulwark where the lord of the castle took shelter with his people. The door would be locked from inside and a couple of strong soldiers were needed to move it. Besides, screeches and creaks would accompany any attempt at opening it. Astrid shook her head—this was not the best point of entry. Too many obstacles to clear.

She studied the building carefully. She had done this from the outside, but because the fortress was located on top of a mountain, she had not had good visibility. She did not have a map of the castle either. Sometimes the King's missions were not exactly well organized or planned, as was the case with this one. She heaved a sigh, releasing part of the unease that churned in her stomach. People wondered why Rangers lived such short lives—missions like this were one of the reasons.

"I'm not going to die here tonight," she muttered under her breath. She had too many things to live for. She was not going to lose her life in a badly planned, risky mission, even if Gondabar had entrusted it to her as a direct request from the King. This was not a scenario of the Higher Training, it was a real situation and dangerous. One mistake and the Zangrians would capture her, and if they did, torture and death awaited her. That was the fate of any captured spy, no matter what realm they came from. In fact, she was carrying with her a special lethal poison of almost immediate action which Engla had taught her to prepare just in case she was caught. Then she could put an end to her life and avoid torture. She was not the kind to take her own life though, even if pain and suffering became unbearable. She was grateful to Engla for the quick way out the poison would give her, but she was not going to use it. Her thoughts turned to the poor Elder, who was recovering at the Shelter from the mental accident she had suffered during the Higher Training, and hoped the Elder would recover fully, even if it took time. She felt a pang in her chest, because the same thing was happening to the good giant, Gerd. They had left him at the Shelter, recovering. Gerd had insisted they leave, that they continue with their duties, and that he would soon be joining them. Astrid was hoping it would be so, but she feared her friend's recovery would take longer than they thought.

The Ranger's way of life was dangerous, and that of a spy like her was even more so. But that was exactly what attracted her to the specialty. She had always liked danger and action—too much for her own good, but she could not help herself. Her character had driven her to become a Ranger and then a Specialist. She could not hide that she was pleased being a Stealthy Spy, because she was. She loved it. Although at moments of danger when she was staking her own life, doubts did appear. She took a deep breath; they would soon vanish.

The night watch was marching to the eastern side at a neutral pace. The six soldiers who formed the watch were wearing the characteristic Zangrian colors: yellow and black, with the coat of arms of the castle lord on their backs. The western side of the building was clear. She saw an arrow slit of a suitable size and headed to it flat against the base of the wall, seeking the shadows so as not to be seen. She had always enjoyed walking like a shadow without anyone noticing her. She had trained a lot, and now she was capable of melting with the gloom as if she were not there.

The arrow slit was about twenty-four feet high. The structure of the wall was irregular; they had not been careful smoothing out the rocks they had used to build it with or polishing the wall. It was something that happened in old buildings and was a weakness someone like her could exploit. She took out a small, sharp pick, stepped on a small crack, and with a little momentum hit the rock wall with the pick and took hold. Thus, she climbed up the rocky surface. It was a climb that would be impossible for a soldier, but not for a Specialist like her. Climbing up walls and reaching mountain tops was something they had trained hard at. This fortress wall was much easier to climb than many summits Astrid had climbed already.

Using the irregularities of the wall, and with the aid of the climbing pick—which she used as little as possible to avoid the noise it made—she reached the arrow slit. It was a narrow, long stone window the defenders used to shoot through without being hit from below. Astrid had calculated that it was wide enough for her to squeeze through. She would soon find out. Holding onto the opening with one hand, practically hanging above the void, she got rid of her cloak and dropped it inside. She passed her weapons and belt through the slit, and then it was her turn. She slid an arm and half her body into the opening and felt the pressure of the stone on chest and back. She pushed and put her head in sideways and the pressure intensified. She was trapped halfway in and halfway out. Exhaling all the air in her lungs and pulling with the arm and leg that were already in, she managed to free herself from the narrow window and get in.

She lay there on the floor.

"Phew... that was close..." she whispered in relief. Then she thought of Viggo—he believed himself so good and special—and she grinned. He could never have gotten through with his wider chest. Viggo would certainly try to pass through such a small opening, but his ego would get him stuck and trapped. It would be a terrible end but quite appropriate. She smiled and went on, cloaking and arming herself again as she went into the fortress. She saw a corridor lit with torches. She was in one of the upper levels. She now had to find Count Orzentok's chambers.

She moved along the corridor with stealth—there were no bedrooms or studies on this floor, only war posts and maybe an armory. She went up another level and nearly ran into a patrol doing the rounds of the corridors. Luckily, she was alert and heard the soldiers' footsteps on the rock, magnified by the silence. She hid and waited for the footsteps to pass. She checked the whole area, moving in total silence and alert to any noise. She found no trace of her target.

Astrid headed to the lower levels. Nobles did not like to go up too many stairs in their fortresses, and their chambers were usually on the second or third level, rarely higher up. Advantages of being noble. It also made it more predictable to find her target, which was good for her.

She searched the floor below carefully, since there were rooms there and the last thing she needed was to enter into a hall full of soldiers or any of the Count's people of trust who must be lodged in that area. No one must see or hear her—that was critical for the mission to be successful. It added difficulty to the task at hand, but she was prepared to face such a situation and others even worse. She felt prepared, not only because of her training and experience but because she had matured. She was no longer the young girl who had arrived at the Camp to become a Ranger; she had grown up in all aspects. She was now a Stealthy Spy/Assassin of Nature/Forest Sniper. Something no one else had ever managed to achieve. She was unique, exceptional. She felt so and knew herself to be so. With her trust in this knowledge, she went on.

She went down one more floor and at the turn of a corner she saw two soldiers on guard duty in front of a door. Acting instinctively, she hid back around the corner. That had to be the

Count's chamber, otherwise it would not be watched. There was not usually a guard at soldiers' or even officers' rooms: only of nobles or high-grade militaries. So, this had to be the room Astrid had to get into. The two guards were strong, and for a Zangrian's average height these were quite tall. The Zangrians were as ugly as they were short and strong—a colorful group. What they lacked in height they made up for in girth, which turned them into dangerous rivals, rocky and strong.

The situation was becoming complicated. Not because she could not deal with the two guards; she could easily do so with all her Assassin of Nature's knowledge. Unless they were specially trained soldiers, bodyguards, or special protection forces, which some nobles or high ranked officers did use. That could make things a little more difficult. Even so, there were only two, and she did not expect them to be exceptional fighters, at most experienced. But for her to be in trouble, there would have to be at least five.

But if she did take down the guards, they would realize someone had entered the fortress and that would make the mission fail. This was why Viggo had not been considered. If he had been sent, he would have left a trail of dead soldiers and guards and the mission would have failed before even beginning, even if he, undoubtedly, had come out victorious. This part of the mission had to be carried out by a Stealthy Spy, and no one was to know she had been there. She had to get in, get the information, and get out without anyone knowing about it, particularly the Count and his men.

The fact that this complicated the mission and ruled out Viggo and his assassins' arts—and that she was the only one who could carry it out—filled her with satisfaction. The fact that she could not kill anyone or be discovered excited her. Astrid had been born for these circumstances: for danger, action, and excitement, and the more compromised and dangerous the situation, the more comfortable she felt. She thought about Lasgol and how worried he would be right then, wondering about her fate. The best she could do was to finish her part of the mission and run to his embrace. Everything would be all right then.

From her Ranger's belt she took out two round objects. This time she was carrying potions and components in her Stealthy Spy's belt and not her usual Assassin of Nature's stuff. She looked at the two objects. They looked like chestnuts, only they were not. She pressed the top of each one with her thumb and then took out a wooden container and uncorked it, carefully pouring the contents into the two objects. Astrid knew there would be a sudden strong smell from the reaction of the components with the reactive liquid inside the chestnut containers.

She peeped around the corner to see what the guards were doing. They were staring ahead like two stone statues. Their eyes were wide open, and they looked surly, like most Zangrians. They were not asleep but they did not look very awake either; Astrid had to execute her next move with great care. She checked where the two torches that lit up the corridor were placed and sought the gloomiest spots nearest to the guards. Bending over and with great care, she rolled the first chestnut along the corridor to the gloomy part. The movement made no sound and the guards did not notice anything. She made the second chestnut roll to touch the foot of the nearest guard.

Astrid hid around the corner and waited. A while went by, and suddenly two dull blows were heard. Astrid poked her head out and saw that the two soldiers had fainted. She placed a small black pincer on her nose as a protective measure. The Giant Toppler she had prepared was a toxic preparation so strong that even the Giants of the Ice would drop unconscious if they inhaled it. Or so they said. The best thing about the compound was that it did not let out any smell, which made it valuable to render guards, watchmen, and others senseless without them ever suspecting a thing.

She left her corner and approached the guards; they were knocked out. She sat them leaning against the wall as if they had fallen asleep and slipped down to the floor. When they woke up, after a while, they would think they had succumbed to sleep. Being on duty, this was something unacceptable which would entail severe punishment. They would get to their feet at once and pretend nothing had happened and agree not to ever mention the incident. They would never suspect foul play, since there would be no indications. She finished placing them and took out her special lock picks. She was not as good as Viggo with them, since nothing can compare with growing up in the worst streets of the city, but she managed pretty well. As part of her training as Stealthy Spy she had learned to open all kinds of locks.

It did not take her long to pick the lock. She cracked the door open silently and looked inside. The room was gloomy but it appeared to be spacious. She caught a rhythmic sound coming from another chamber at the back. It was snoring; the Count was sleeping soundly. Astrid opened the door and went in. At a crouch and careful not to bump into anything and knock something over, she headed for the second chamber. The door was ajar, and she glimpsed the Count asleep in a great bed. This was a bedroom with an antechamber.

She retraced her steps and searched the room thoroughly without making noise. If the Count woke up and found her, the mission would be lost. Taking a deep breath to relax, she searched the closets, cupboards, and even a war chest, a difficult task in the half darkness. What she was looking for had to be well kept, but she had better make sure. There was no luck. She went over to a big oak table which must be the Count's desk, with three locked drawers down each side. This would take some time and she started to worry—the guards would wake up soon and she needed to hurry.

She brought out another set of small lock picks, special for this type of lock on drawers or smaller doors. One by one, she carefully picked the locks as fast as she could, but she did not find what she was looking for. Bad news. It was not in the study, so there was only the back room where the Count was sleeping.

Sliding along like a black adder, she reached the left bedside table. The Count was snoring above her. She felt the table carefully and found a drawer, also locked. Nobles were becoming more distrustful every day, something that was going to complicate her life. She kept her cool and took out a third set of lock picks and, as if it were the most natural thing in the world, she opened the drawer while the Count's snores deafened her ears. He felt so close that Astrid looked up to see a lock of gray hair right above her; he was really close.

Suddenly, the Count cleared his throat hard and the snoring stopped. Astrid froze, lying on the floor parallel to the bed with her arm stretched and her hand inside the drawer. She waited—had she been discovered? The Count moved in his bed and she reached for the dagger at her belt. There was a throat clearing sound and the man turned over. The snoring resumed shortly after.

Astrid exhaled in relief; he had simply shifted in his sleep. She was clear. She felt inside the drawer and found what she was looking for. Taking it out slowly, she went back to the outer room. She opened the door to the corridor just a crack to check that the guards were still as she had left them. She looked at the envelope in her hand that she had found in the bedside table. The seal was broken, which meant the Count had already read the information it contained. She unfolded it and read it too. She smiled. It was what she had come to get. She memorized it and put it back in the envelope.

Without waking the Count, she returned to the back chamber put the letter back in the bedside table drawer. She used her lock picks to leave everything just as she had found it—no one could suspect anything. She left the room and went out into the corridor. One of the guards was beginning to wake up. Astrid ran off and turned the corner before the guard came to. She sought the same entry point through which she had come in and went out the narrow window. She climbed down and hid at the foot of the wall, waiting for a good moment to go to the battlement.

Unfortunately, she could not be hasty in her escape. She ran the risk of discovery. Hastiness was the greatest mistake a spy could make; patience was critical, even more than having skill with weapons. She had to move exactly and at the right moment or else she would not live long. She was well aware of this, so she waited for the change of guard, hidden in one of the smaller turrets of the wall.

The right moment came—the guard changed. Astrid counted the footsteps until the guards had left and ran to the point of descent from the battlement. She uncoiled the rope, tied the hook, and started down. Once on the ground she gave a well-practiced pull: the hook came off and the rope fell to her. There could be no trace that anyone had ever been there.

In the middle of the night, Astrid vanished into the shadows of the forest.

Chapter 2

Lasgol was running through a fir forest, leaping over branches and bushes. Ona was at his side, keeping up with him and dodging obstacles with characteristic feline grace. It was a cool morning but with no sign of storms. The sun's rays shone through the branches, lighting up the forest. Lasgol felt in his own element in that environment. After the time spent training at the Shelter, the forest had become an even greater part of who he was. The Specialties of Tireless Explorer, Forest Trapper, and Forest Survivor he had managed to master had granted him a new way of understanding, appreciating, and living in nature around him. He felt that forests and mountains were now his home. It was not that he did not miss his home, which he did, but in the forests he felt happy, happier than before. It was as if he were more in harmony with this environment.

The feeling was strengthened by Ona's presence beside him. His inseparable friend enjoyed journeying through forests as much as he did, even if she preferred the snow-covered mountains. The snow panther had also grown and looked like an adult specimen, although she was not fully grown yet; at least not in Lasgol's eyes. They had left Camu lagging behind because they needed to move quickly through the forest and that was not something he was good at. His size and restricted agility limited him in that kind of environment. Of course, Camu insisted he could cross forests and mountains as well as his sister, but everyone knew this was not so. The bigger he got, and he had grown a little larger, the less agile and graceful he became. After all, he was a reptile, one of ancient ancestry, but still a reptile. He was not made for crossing forests at a run, and this was one large, thick forest.

Lasgol leapt over a fallen tree trunk and smiled, remembering how Camu had insisted on taking over Astrid's mission. He was sure that by using his Invisibility Camouflage skill and his ability to go up walls by using his adhesive paws which stuck to everything, he could get the information. It had taken them a good while to persuade him that even if he managed to get into the fortress without being seen, he would not be able to obtain the information without arousing suspicion. Camu was not exactly stealthy and careful. Besides, it was necessary to read the document, and this was beyond the creature's reach. He could fly but not read, which was curious if one thought about it. Camu had finally given up and Astrid had been put in charge of the first part of the mission. She had done it successfully, and they now had the information they needed. It was now Lasgol's turn: he had to carry out the second part of the mission.

They reached the end of the trees, and Lasgol stopped. He crouched beside the last two trees and scanned the road ahead. As he had been expecting, he glimpsed the column of Zangrian soldiers coming toward him. The road divided two forests—the one where he was hiding to the north and a less dense oak wood to the south. He stroked Ona beside him.

Good girl. Everything will be all right, he transmitted using his *Animal Communication* skill to soothe her.

Ona peeped once, which Lasgol took for a timid 'yes.' The snow panther had sharp instincts and she already sensed trouble.

Egil's plan for the mission is good, he transmitted.

The panther peeped once again.

Trust him and me. Everything will go according to plan.

This time Ona said nothing and rubbed her head against Lasgol's side. Every time the snow panther did this and showed him her affection, Lasgol wondered how it was possible he was so lucky to have her as his familiar. He returned the caress and scratched her head.

The breeze touched Lasgol's face and Ona's fur. It was coming from the north. He remembered how Gondabar had welcomed them as soon as they arrived in the capital, Norghania, from the Shelter so they could explain everything that had occurred during the Higher Training. Sigrid had already sent him several messages explaining, but given the seriousness of what had happened, as leader of the Rangers, he wanted to know every detail. The Panthers had gone to his personal study in the Tower of the Rangers and told him everything they had experienced. Gondabar had asked a thousand questions to which they replied as best they could. The leader had been concerned and regretful regarding the failure of the Higher Training program. He had finally let them leave to go and rest from the journey. He would give them new orders as soon as he received them.

The Panthers were hoping that with the threat of the Dark

Rangers gone; the tense calm with the Frozen Continent, where Asrael and his Shamans of the Ice were trying to gain the leadership and reins of the continent; and with the west of Norghana also calm and recovering from the defeat in the civil war, their next mission would be a simple one: catching outlaws, intimidating some discontent noble from the west or east, since King Thoran had feuds with nobles from both sides and liked to show his power through strength, or something similar. Besides, it should not be too urgent, and they might be able to spend some time in the capital, which was always nice since it was filled with interesting things to discover and enjoy.

They were completely wrong. They had not had time to rest more than one day when they were summoned. This time Gondabar was accompanied by Duke Orten, which they all took to mean that the mission would be complicated and delicate. So it was. Besides being a secret mission for the King's brother, it was in enemy territory. They would have to go into the kingdom of Zangria, to the east of the neighboring realm. Although Norghana and Zangria were not in declared open war, the Zangrian territory was considered as enemy land. The peace between the two realms was fragile and might break at any moment. The presence of a group of Norghanian Rangers in Zangria, in any kind of action, would be considered an act of war and the peace would be broken.

Making use of his bad character and loud voice, Duke Orten had yelled at them to make sure they would not fail or be found out. If they were captured, they would be alone and left to their own fate. The King would not rescue them, and he would deny any knowledge of their presence there. In fact, this mission was Orten's idea, and his brother Thoran most likely had not even wanted to know all the details so he could deny it all in case things went wrong and there was a diplomatic crisis. And things going wrong would mean that the Royal Eagles had been captured or killed, which in the middle of Zangrian territory was an all too real possibility. Gondabar had begged them to be extra careful and discrete and not to risk too much. Orten, on the other hand, had demanded that the mission be a success. He would not accept failure from the Royal Eagles, least of all now that they had received extraordinary training and were consummate specialists.

Lasgol sighed. They had not been able to say a word. Orten

would never listen anyway. He never listened to anyone. So here they were, carrying out the mission and risking not only their lives, but the peace between Norghana and Zangria, since the mission implied an act of war and the Zangrians would interpret it as such. Once again, Lasgol wondered how they always ended up in such messes with so much at stake. At least on this occasion it was not his fault or Camu's. The orders were directly from Duke Orten, so he was the one responsible. It was little consolation, but it was something. What was important was that they managed to carry out the mission without being found out by the Zangrians. That way, they would not be able to blame the realm of Norghana. Just in case, Egil had a plan to deflect suspicions—how could it be otherwise being one of his friend's brilliant plans.

The sound of the yellow-and-black soldiers' footsteps became louder. Lasgol called upon his *Hawk's Eye* and *Owl Hearing* skills and watched their advance. He counted two dozen soldiers marching on foot with a dozen light cavalry leading them. By the standards they bore and the coat of arms on their uniforms, he knew they were part of Count Orzentok's forces. In the middle of the column were two closed, military style carts pulled by strong horses.

It would appear that the forecasts were right, he transmitted to Ona while he checked the soldiers' weapons. The infantry carried metal spears and shields. Since the Zangrians were not very tall, but rather on the short side, the spears evened the fight somewhat when they faced other infantries and were their favorite weapon.

The panther looked at him and growled once.

Yes, it's time to act, he transmitted to her and then checked that the light cavalry was also carrying spear and shield. What he did not see were archers, something he was grateful for. Archers were always an added difficulty hard to counter.

Ona stiffened, her fur standing on end along her back; she growled again.

Go wait for me on the other side of the forest, to the north, Lasgol transmitted to her and pointed his finger to where he wanted her to go.

A moan from Ona told him she was not happy leaving him there on his own.

I'll be okay. I don't want them to see you with me. It would be suspicious. Go north and wait for me. If you see me in danger, you can come to my aid then.

Ona growled affirmatively.

Good girl. Go now.

The panther went into the forest to the north, following his instructions. Lasgol watched her leave and started preparing for what would come next. He went back a few paces until he was hidden in the forest thicket. The column kept advancing toward his position along the road. He put his quiver full of arrows on the ground and his composite bow beside him. Taking out an intensely red, hooded cloak, he exchanged it for his Forest Survivor's, which was green-brown with streaks on one side and snow-white on the other, which helped him camouflage in the forest both in spring-summer or autumn-winter.

He took a deep breath. What he was about to do next went against everything he had been taught by his instructors. That red color was visible a league away inside the forest—it was a totally out of place color in his surroundings. He adjusted his quiver, picked up his bow, and prepared to act. He trusted Egil's plan—he always did, even if this one was quite risky. Lasgol thought again and shook his head; all of Egil's plans ended up being risky. This one would be no different. He concentrated and began to call upon the rest of the skills that would help him in the situation he was about to get into: *Improved Agility* and *Cat-like Reflexes*.

The riders at the head of the column who were escorting the two carts reached the part of the road where Lasgol was waiting. Without warning, he rose, nocked an arrow, aimed, and released against the rider at the head. He hit his shield, the arrow bouncing off the metal and almost hitting the rider beside him. The two soldiers turned toward the origin of the shot and discovered Lasgol in red in the thicket. They started to shout and point at him with their spears. Calmly, Lasgol nocked again and, amid the shouts of alarm, released again against another of the riders. The arrow hit the shield and, like the previous one, bounced off.

The rider at the head of the column ordered the attack against Lasgol amid shouts and arm waving while he watched calmly. The riders charged. Lasgol turned fast and ran away like a deer being chased by hungry wolves. He dodged trees, bushes, and rocks while he headed north. The dozen riders who were chasing him soon realized that going into the forest with the horses was not a brilliant idea. They could barely move in the dense thicket. Lasgol had been expecting this already, and that was precisely why he had chosen that spot to attack.

The riders tried to reach Lasgol, who was getting away easily, navigating the forest at will. He led them deeper into the woods, making sure they could see his red cloaked back at all times. He did not want them to abandon the chase and return to their column, so he revealed himself every now and then, but he maintained a prudent distance he knew the horses could not reduce in there; Lasgol was a lot faster than the coursers inside the forest, and that was what he was going to use against his pursuers. It was lucky the Zangrians were so bellicose and had such bad character, since it made it easier to make them chase after him. By the time they thought clearly, it would already be too late.

He stopped. He turned and glimpsed the twelve men chasing him on their mounts. By their shouts it was obvious they were furious. If they caught up with him, they would likely skewer him with their spears. He had to avoid that. He nocked an arrow and aimed at the leading rider through the trees. The shot would be difficult because of the brush and trees he needed to avoid, and Lasgol was not the best of shooters, so he did not risk it. He used his Gift and, searching in his pool of energy, began to call upon his *True Shot* skill. It was a little risky, since calling upon this skill always took him some time and the riders kept coming toward him. But he had measured the approximate time he needed and the distance he had to maintain, and if he had not made any mistakes the shot would come on time. If he managed to summon the skill—if he did not, they were going to riddle him with spears.

The leading rider spurred his horse through the low brush and pointed his spear at Lasgol while he covered himself with his shield. Lasgol went on summoning the skill, keeping cool, trusting his Gift. He hoped that one day he could call upon his Gift in half the time it took him now, but unfortunately, he still had not managed to improve this yet. He made a mental note to work more on it. The rider was close, and although he felt his inner energy stirring, which meant the skill was going to respond, it still had not. The rider shouted a curse, seeing he almost had Lasgol, but at that moment the skill activated and a green flash ran through his arm. The arrow flew to the point Lasgol had been aiming at: the right arm, the one holding the spear and not covered by the shield.

The arrow hit the man and the rider fell backward off the horse from the impact. Seeing the second rider already on top of him and unable to use the same skill for lack of time, Lasgol decided to use his other skill: *Fast Shot*. He concentrated and searched for his energy. He still had a moment, and he needed it since this one was another skill that did not respond as swiftly as he wished, although he had improved quite a bit. Every time he found himself in one if these messes and needed his skills to escape, he told himself he had to keep working on all his skills and not only try to develop new ones. Danger and the proximity of death were powerful incentives. He promised himself that as soon as the mission was over, he would start working on his skills again.

While all these ideas went through Lasgol's mind at top speed, the second rider almost caught up with him. Lasgol became a little nervous—the skill was taking too long to respond. He tried to calm down, since if he lost focus, he would not be able to activate it. Losing his concentration was the worst enemy while calling upon his skills. Even the ones he used the most and which he invoked almost unconsciously needed a small degree of concentration or they did not activate.

Then, suddenly a green flash ran through his arms and three arrows flew to the rider at lightning speed. The Zangrian managed to stop the first two with his shield, but the third one pierced his defense and plunged into his shoulder. His shield fell to the ground. He reined his horse and looked at Lasgol, who was already nocking another arrow. He drew his sword to attack Lasgol, who aimed his bow at him. The Zangrian rider shouted something in his own language and attacked enraged. But then his sword arm seemed to lose strength, and a moment later he fell off his horse.

Lasgol stopped aiming at him and turned to the next rider within his range, although the man was still at a distance. He called upon his *True Shot* skill, which activated as if he had estimated the timing perfectly, and caught the rider in the left arm, unsaddling him. Without a thought, Lasgol combined this skill with that of *Fast Shot* and caught the fourth rider, who ended up on the ground.

He had been aiming at his enemies' right or left shoulder each time; he wanted to unsaddle them, not kill them. Lasgol preferred not to kill if possible, and besides, they were not at war with Zangria, at least for the time being, so there was no need to use lethal shots.

Besides, Egil had planned to use poison in the attack, so they only needed to wound the riders and the poison would knock them out. It was a powerful numbing mix.

The next two riders dismounted when they saw what had happened and attacked jointly, protected behind their shields. Lasgol aimed and found himself facing an unexpected difficulty. The Zangrians short figures and the forest's tall thicket obscured his vision so he could only see a shield and a helmet among the bushes, complicating the shot. He had not foreseen that they would dismount and attack him on foot. The Zangrians might be ugly and bad-tempered, but they were no fools. He aimed as they came toward him, but he did not have a clear shot. He sought a better position, saw a large bush, and hid behind it. He took out two traps he carried ready in his backpack and placed one on each side of the bush.

He stood and peaked over the bush and saw the two soldiers coming at him with their spears ready to run him through. He crouched and used his *Trap Hiding* skill, making the two traps invisible. He rose again and released twice against the soldiers, but he only hit the shields they hid behind to protect their advance. He crouched again and stepped back from the bush and waited for the soldiers to reach him.

Suddenly, the tips of both spears pierced the bush, seeking to kill him. Lasgol had already stepped back. The soldiers thrust their spears through different points of the bush, seeking flesh to stab. Lasgol waited at a crouch—he wanted them to think he was hiding. The soldiers suddenly attacked, one on each side of the bush, first with their spears and then their shields. They both stepped on the traps before realizing where Lasgol was, carried by their own impulse. There was a metal sound and sharp spikes came up from the ground, piercing the soles of the two soldiers' feet.

Lasgol took a few more steps back. The soldiers turned to him amid shouts and curses in Zangrian. They started to go after Lasgol, who continued to withdraw. They had not taken more than ten steps when they both fell to the ground. Lasgol had prepared the traps by pouring the numbing poison on the spikes. He checked—they were knocked out—and raised his gaze. He saw the other half dozen riders turning back toward their column on the road.

That was not how it was supposed to go. The whole cavalry should have followed him so he could lead it to the other side of the forest where Ona was waiting for him. He wrinkled his nose. Plans always suffered deviations. He would have to correct this one, or the rest of the plan could go down the drain.

He ran after them.

Chapter 3

Nilsa lifted her head and scanned the thicket. She was hiding south of the road, inside the oak wood. The shouts of the Zangrians left no doubt, Lasgol had already begun the assault on the convoy. She went to the edge of the wood with her bow ready. She was also wearing red, like her friend, so she had had to hide deep within the forest until that moment. If she had been spying in those clothes, she would have been discovered and that would have endangered their plan.

She raised her bow and nocked an arrow in a swift movement. She was posted halfway up the column which had stopped when the cavalry had raced after Lasgol. She glimpsed three officers in the column: one at the front who was shouting orders at the top of his lungs; a second one between the two carts and a third one at the rear. They were easy to spot, they shouted and gestured and their helmets were different, more pointed than the soldiers.'

She was nervous. What she had to do was complicated and she was finding it hard to keep calm. She was always nervous, it was the way she was, and in a way, she liked being like that, it made her different and special. She did not know anyone like herself. She had met other Rangers and Guards who were a little nervous and restless, but not as much as she was. But at times it was counterproductive, as on this occasion. She had been working a lot on controlling her nerves and on being less clumsy, which was nothing but a consequence of the uncontrolled nerves she had. She would never admit it openly, since Viggo would immediately mock her and with all the effort she was making, the last thing she needed were the jokes of their dumbass friend.

She breathed through her nose. She filled her lungs and then let the air out slowly. She always did this when she wanted to relax; repeatedly. Then she held her bow hard so the touch of the wood of her weapon would finish calming her. She almost always managed to relax this way; not that it lasted long, but it was a small triumph which Nilsa enjoyed every time she was successful. Small victories in life, especially those that were hard to achieve ought to be enjoyed;

she knew this and valued it. She was well aware that she had to keep working until she could master her nerves and clumsiness, and one day she would; of this she was certain. What she was not so sure was when, or whether all her efforts would yield the fruit she wanted. It was one thing to want something and work toward it. And a very different thing that the work would be the right kind in order to obtain what she wanted in the end.

She shook her head; this was not the time for such thoughts. She had to focus on her task and not fail. Her comrades counted on her and she was not going to let them down. She focused on the three officers, watched them for a moment and then aimed at the one furthest away, the one at the rear of the convoy. She waited to have a clean shot. The officer was not moving from his place but he was gesturing a lot, and the soldiers around him, although not breaking their double line formation, were also restless. She took a deep breath and narrowed her eyes to fix her sight on the exact spot she wanted to hit. Curiously, when she was about to release, she never felt nervous; not for quite a while, which made her an excellent shot, particularly in the long range. She did not know why, since the moment of release was the most critical moment and most tense, but she found quiet in sighting the target and hitting it squarely.

She released the arrow, which flew through the trees and hit the officer's arm. With a look of horror, the Zangrian looked at the arrow and for a moment he seemed to be in shock because he did not react. Nilsa nocked a second arrow and aimed at the officer between the carts. She heard the scream of the first officer who had finally reacted. The officer Nilsa was aiming at turned to see what was going on. Nilsa released. The arrow hit him in the right shoulder. The man grunted in pain and started shouting orders while he put his hand to his wound.

Nilsa was not concerned. She knew she was going to be seen in an instant but she still had one more shot to make. She aimed at the last officer at the head of the column who had already located her and was ordering his soldiers to go after her. They would soon catch up with her but that did not worry Nilsa. She had to finish the officer and that was what she was going to do. Her arm did not tremble at all. She released the arrow and the officer got it in the left shoulder. He took two steps backwards from the impact. His face showed a mixture of surprise and relief to see it was not a lethal wound.

Nilsa smiled. She had done her part. She slung her composite bow on her back and took the short one. The first soldiers were already reaching the trees. She would have no time to release. She started backing up into the oak wood, the bow ready to release against whoever came after her. As she was withdrawing her nerves returned and she nearly tripped on a log and fell over. That would have been a disaster because she could already see two Zangrian soldiers approaching through the trees. She raised her bow to aim and as she did her nerves vanished again. She found it curious that the more danger she was in, the closer she was to death, the less nervous she became. Something happened with that strange reaction that she would have to investigate. It might help her find out why it happened and how she could eliminate her nerves in other situations.

She dodged a tree and hid behind it. Carefully, she put her head out and saw half a dozen soldiers chasing after her. It was to be expected. The soldiers were advancing covered by their shields and with their spears ready to pierce her. She started to get nervous again. Those spears were very dangerous and the Zangrians were tough and quarrelsome. She came out from behind the oak and released at the first soldier who was approaching warily. The arrow hit the shield and made him stop. Nilsa seized her chance and rapidly released at the second soldier; she also hit his shield. She had expected as much, being short the soldiers were covered behind their large metal shields, they had been well instructed. Well, it did not matter. Nilsa's function in the assault was as a distraction, she was to lead away a group of soldiers far from the convoy and that was what she was doing.

She lagged back so that the group of soldiers would follow her as she maintained a good enough distance from their spears. If they tired of chasing after her they might try to reach her using their spears as javelins, so this was something she had to watch at all moments. Seeing her lag, the soldiers continued their pursuit. They went on slowly but steadily, determined to capture or kill her. Nilsa's heel hit a tall root and she stopped. She looked down to check the root. Since she had stopped, she released again at her pursuers who were getting closer. They were coming faster than she moved because she was going backwards. She released again and her shots hit a shield and a helmet, the arrows bounced off.

Nilsa hastened to increase the safety distance since the pursuit was becoming dangerous. She knew she could run off like a gazelle at any moment and lose them among the trees. The soldiers could not compete with her in speed and knowledge of the woods. They were wearing armor and shield so they were hampered by the weight they bore. Besides, they took short steps, every step of Nilsa's was like two of theirs. Unfortunately, she could not run and hide, Egil's plan required that Nilsa acted as bait and that part of the soldiers should take it and chase her. So, Nilsa had to go on acting as a tasty river-worm so those ugly perch would keep trying to catch her.

She released again while she was withdrawing, all she had to do was hit the shields. It was simple but what was not so simple was not tripping or missing a step and falling down. She put special attention on avoiding her usual clumsiness or that might be the last thing she did. Suddenly, the soldier running in the third position started to run toward her shouting wildly. He seemed to have tired of this cat-and-mouse game and was running through the trees with his spear ready to launch. Nilsa aimed and released against the soldier. She hit his shield but the man did not stop, he took two more steps and threw his spear with all his might.

Nilsa saw the spear flying parallel to the ground straight to her chest. Almost instinctively she slid to the left and tilted her body as far as she could to get it out of the path of the spear; all in the blink of an eye. The tip of the spear brushed her side and tore a piece of her cloak. Nilsa exhaled, she had avoided the throw by a hair's breadth. She became very nervous all of a sudden. The soldier drew his sword, Nilsa knew she had to defend herself and nocked an arrow. She aimed at the soldier, and as she did her nerves evaporated.

The Zangrian charged at Nilsa with his right hand raised, brandishing the sword, while with the left he held the shield he protected himself with. Nilsa was aware that she only had one shot and that it would have to be a good one or that Zangrian was going to make mincemeat of her. She concentrated and adjusted her shot while the soldier advanced toward her shouting. She ignored the shouts and the run and released. The arrow flew at great speed and hit the soldier in the right wrist, raised carrying the sword he meant to split her in two with. It pierced the protection and found flesh. The Zangrian yelled in pain and lost the sword. He stopped short when he found himself unarmed.

With renewed calm after achieving such a difficult shot, Nilsa nocked another arrow. The soldier raised his shield and hid behind it.

Nilsa did not care about that soldier anymore; the poison would soon deal with him. She released at the next soldier that was approaching and then started to withdraw. She focused on not tripping over any roots and not getting nervous. She went on releasing as she withdrew, leading her pursuers further into the oak wood. She was doing her part and that made her feel surer and less nervous.

Hiding among the oaks, Ingrid had seen the soldiers run after Nilsa. She had had to wait and not rush to help her friend, which had been hard; she always wanted to lunge into the fray, headlong, and more so if one of her comrades needed help. But on this occasion, she could not do it, it was against Egil's plan, and if she had learnt anything these past times, was to completely trust Egil's plans. So, she had had to bite her lip and wait, not following her instincts to help Nilsa.

Ingrid was hiding not far from where Nilsa had been, a little forward, close to the head of the convoy, but she had to deal with the soldiers on that side. She took a quick glance and saw the three officers on the ground and several men trying to reanimate them. They would not be so lucky. The poison they were using would render them unconscious until nightfall. The soldiers guarding the carts were puzzled and even more nervous. Having lost the officers there was no chain of command and each soldier was thinking for himself. This was what Egil had been looking for, since the worst thing that could happen in an army was that the soldiers started thinking. It was not their thing and did not know how to do so, at least not to save the company. So, this was exactly what Egil had wanted to happen and he was getting it. The soldiers were shouting to one another, giving meaningless orders and arguing. Everyone wanted to be in command and voice their opinions in the critical situation they found themselves in.

It was Ingrid's turn to act and create even more confusion and chaos. She aimed at the soldier closest to her position and released. She hit him in the right thigh, catching him by surprise. She nocked again and released at great speed. She hit the soldier beside the first one who was watching his comrade with eyes opened wide. This one she hit in the left leg. The soldier cried out in pain with surprise. He started to point and bark orders to his comrades. Since they did not seem too sure and were shouting at the sight of their wounded comrade, Ingrid released at a third and fourth soldiers while they were arguing among themselves in loud voices. She could not help smiling. Egil was a master of plans, confusion and distraction in order to achieve the purpose.

Suddenly several soldiers came to a decision and seeing that they were being brought down from the distance they ran toward her position to try and eliminate the threat. Very calmly Ingrid released twice more before withdrawing into the forest. Six soldiers chased after her going deeper into the oak wood with their spears ready and the shields protecting their bodies. Ingrid revealed herself and released to draw their attention. She started to move toward the right, using the oak trees to hide. The soldiers advanced after her.

It was just what Egil had guessed would happen. The soldiers went into the forest to kill Ingrid amid war cries. But Ingrid was not fazed. She trusted her training, even before the Higher Training she had received at the Shelter, she had felt confident in herself and her knowledge, now she felt even more so. Inside the forest Ingrid felt ready to face any danger or enemy. She trusted in what she had learnt, in all that she had trained in. She was an Archer of the Wind – Infallible Marksman – Man Hunter and whoever stood up to her had very few chances, if any, of defeating her. And this was not a feeling born of a false superiority, but of one who knew her training gave her a significant advantage in the competition. It was not arrogance. It was confidence in her training.

Truths were proven with actions in every situation. So, she acted. She allowed the soldiers to get closer while she moved from tree to tree. She took out her tiny bow, 'Punisher.' She must keep the soldiers entertained so they would not go back to the convoy and she was going to make sure of that. She came out from behind a tree and released at the nearest soldier. The shot hit the man in the head and his helmet flew off from the force of the impact. Ingrid nocked again without stopping moving. The soldier raised his shield to protect himself and left his ankles and feet exposed. Ingrid's shot did not go to the head but to the right foot. The arrow went through it from top to sole and the soldier was left with his foot nailed to the ground while he grunted in pain.

Ingrid moved fast and a spear brushed her right shoulder

Keeping still would mean receiving a serious wound and so she needed to keep moving, with light swift movements. She hid again while two of the soldiers tried to surround her. She went on moving to the left, the soldier approaching on that side saw her and tried to skewer her with his spear. Ingrid stopped one instant before her body stood right where the soldier expected and was already throwing his spear at. The weapon cleared Ingrid by a hand-span. The soldier had been too hasty, Ingrid aimed at the Zangrian's face. He was just a pace and a half from her. The man instinctively covered his face with the shield. Ingrid saw two exposed legs and instead of releasing she swept him off the ground with a powerful kick. The soldier's legs left the ground and he fell backwards. Before he could recover, Ingrid knocked him out with a tremendous right punch.

The soldier behind her had already passed the tree that separated them and hastened to run Ingrid through from the back. Ingrid threw herself to one side and rolled over her head, the blow missed her completely. Ingrid, on one knee, released at the soldier as he prepared to attack again. She caught him in mid-turn and was unable to cover himself fully with his shield. The arrow plunged into his hip. He grunted in pain, Ingrid knew that the poison would do the rest so she ran off to surround the ones still moving toward her.

It was going to take her a little while but none of those soldiers were going back to the convoy, of that she was sure. She nocked, moved and released. She prepared to deal with the rest fully confident.

Viggo was watching the soldiers defending the carts. There were only about a dozen left, counting those on the carts who were now standing beside them. Lasgol, Nilsa and Ingrid had led the rest off and it was now his turn. He drew his knives and very carefully poured the poison he carried in a wooden container on the edges of the blades, then he put the container back in his belt. He stretched arms and legs to make sure they were not stiff after the long wait. He left his hiding place to the south, at the end of the convoy. He headed to the soldiers who saw him approach with his knives, coming to them as if he did not fear them, as if they could not kill him.

The soldiers started to shout and three ran to meet Viggo who stopped in the middle of the road without reaching the convoy. The three soldiers came toward him shouting questions and telling him to stop, while Viggo waited unfazed. Three other soldiers were watching what was going on without approaching. The fight would start at any moment. Viggo knew that fighting opponents who carried spear and shield was complicated, so he was wary. He had to be. In fact, as much as he boasted how good he was, he really knew that there is always someone better and that even the best fighter can slip and that a misfortune can end the life of the best of all. Because of this he was always wary, and always would be. It was something else to play cocky before his friends and comrades, but that was only an act, not the truth. The truth was this moment, the soldiers coming toward him to skewer him with their spears and he had to face a dangerous situation and be very careful. He might be a swashbuckler and talk too much, but he was no fool, on the contrary he was very clever. The kind of clever who is skillful because he is intelligent and thus, he overcomes all the situations that come his way.

The three soldiers stood in front of Viggo making a small barrier with their shields. Almost at the same time, they lunged their spears at him. With a swift agile leap Viggo took two steps back. The soldiers, thinking their opponent was retreating in fear, charged. Viggo saw them running toward him and with a leap and a pirouette, he passed over the soldiers and landed behind them. He turned at lightning speed and started delivering slashes. The three soldiers tried to turn as fast as possible but between the fact that they were not very quick and they had to maneuver with spear and shield, by the time they had turned, Viggo had already cut them on the back and legs.

"It's been a pleasure," Viggo said and he ran off into the forest. The wounded soldiers went after him and the three that had been watching joined them.

Viggo kept looking back and when he reached the edge of the forest he stopped. He stood in an attacking position and waited for them to reach him. The first soldier to catch up with him tried to stab him in the stomach with his spear. Viggo deflected the spear with his forearm and with tremendous speed he hit the man on the nose with the fist he had his right knife in. The nose broke and the soldier stumbled. Viggo delivered a kick to the chest and threw him backward right when another soldier attacked. He shifted to one side avoiding the spear and then leaping forward he lunged at the shield catching the soldier by surprise and making him stumble to keep his balance. Viggo cut him in the arm and moved back and to one side to face the third soldier. Thrice he tried to reach Viggo who was dodging the spear tip with evasive moves. Before the fourth one arrived, Viggo had cut him on both arms.

Astrid was watching Viggo fighting with the guards. She was also hiding at the end of the convoy, but on the north side. Now it was her turn. There were only six soldiers left defending the carts. She came out in the open with her knives soaked in poison and she lunged to attack the last soldiers, who were watching Viggo fighting with their comrades, unable to decide whether to go and help them or remain watching the carts. They did not see Astrid arrive who took advantage of their distraction, using stealth and her skill to blend in with the shadows.

Before they could see her, she attacked two of the soldiers from the back and cut them on arms and legs with her poisoned knives. Astrid could fight them but that was not the plan. She withdrew at a run toward the place where she had come from. The soldiers went after her, but seeing she was fleeing, they stopped midway unable to decide whether to follow her or retreat.

Astrid turned at the edge and watched them. She had to make sure they did not go back to the carts, so she provoked them by signaling them to come after her. The soldiers could not make their minds up. They wanted to kill her but they had orders to watch what was in the carts.

All of a sudden, the back door of the first cart opened, without any explanation, as if by magic. There was no one there, no soldiers, no one visible. The door closed again after a moment. Astrid went on drawing the soldiers' attention. The three she had wounded were coming at her yelling, claiming revenge. She knew she only had to wait for the poison to have effect, so she dodged them to avoid fighting and keep their attention on her. Astrid noticed that since they had their backs to the carts, they did not see the door of the second cart also opening and closing again.

Suddenly, a part of the cavalry that had run off after Lasgol came

34

back through the trees and headed to the carts. The horses were already level with the carts and the riders reined them in. They were looking around, trying to guess what was going on. Astrid saw Lasgol appear at the edge of the forest, he had come after the cavalry. The soldiers who were trying to finish her dropped to the ground; the poison had had its effect.

There was a shrill shriek, like the call of a royal eagle.

It was the sign.

Astrid withdrew to the forest. Viggo stopped fighting and also went to the forest. Ingrid and Nilsa ran deep into the oak wood, leaving the soldiers way behind.

Lasgol was watching the last soldiers who were still standing. The riders had dismounted and were cursing freely. They had just discovered that the cargo they carried in the two carts had been stolen.

The plan had been a success.

Chapter 4

The Panthers were to gather south of the oak wood, at a more than reasonable distance from the place where they had perpetrated the assault. That was what they had agreed on. Nilsa and Ingrid had arrived first and were waiting with their bows ready on top of a hillock. They were hidden by some blocks of sharp gray rocks that offered decent shelter. They had a good view of their surroundings from the elevated position.

"They'll be here soon, but we should stay alert in case they're being chased," Ingrid told Nilsa as she nocked an arrow.

Nilsa nodded and also nocked and arrow on her bow, watching the forest in front of them and the plains around their location. Everything looked quiet. "They'll have made it, right?" she asked with a little doubt in her tone.

"Egil signaled for us to retreat, so we have to assume they did," Ingrid replied. Squinting to see better, she swept the landscape with an intense gaze, looking for any enemies.

"I want to assume they made it, but Egil might have signaled retreat because they couldn't complete the assault..."

Ingrid sighed. "Maybe, but let's assume he was successful. His plans rarely go awry. They get complicated, yes, but fail? Not likely."

Nilsa nodded as if to convince herself.

"Besides, he didn't give the sign for alarm, only for retreat. So, we should assume he wasn't in danger. If he'd been discovered, he'd have given the distress signal so we'd go to his aid. He was successful, I'm sure of it," Ingrid reasoned.

"I hope so."

A figure came out of the oak wood, running bent. Nilsa got ready to release, aiming at once.

"Stop! Don't shoot!" Ingrid warned.

"Ah, I recognize that light, nimble walk," Nilsa replied, lowering her bow.

"He looks captivating even from here, with his physique and how he moves with such ease..." Ingrid said, watching Viggo approach their position.

"That's because he hasn't opened his mouth yet," Nilsa replied with a giggle.

Ingrid could not help but chuckle. "How right you are, too right…"

Viggo reached them at a run and dropped down between the two.

"How did you do?" he asked, looking at one and then the other.

"Everything according to plan," Ingrid said, nodding.

"Me too. I had some problems in the forest, but nothing serious," Nilsa said.

"By the way, good shots. The officers fell in the blink of an eye," Ingrid told Nilsa.

"Thanks. They were distracted and I got to them before they could react."

"You're getting better every day," Ingrid said.

"I try," Nilsa blushed.

"Yeah, that was good. Pity Egil didn't let me cause a bit more chaos among those Zangrians…" Viggo said regretfully.

"We each had a task to do, and a well thought-out one," Ingrid told him. "We need to follow the plan and orders, or things go awry and get ugly," she said in a warning tone.

Viggo raised his hand as if he were not to blame.

"I always do what I'm told. Well… taking a few small liberties…"

"And those will cost us dearly someday," Ingrid said, wagging her finger at Viggo so he would stop taking those liberties in the future.

"This time I did my part to the letter, Egil won't be able to complain."

"Well, someone's learning," said Nilsa.

Viggo smiled from ear to ear. "I don't want you-know-who to be angry at me," he said, jabbing his thumb at Ingrid.

The blonde archer made a face at him.

"I'm right here. I can see and hear you perfectly well."

"Oops, I hadn't realized," he replied and looked at her, blinking hard.

Nilsa giggled. Then she pointed east.

"Someone's coming," she warned.

Viggo strained his neck to see. Nilsa and Ingrid aimed their bows.

"Don't shoot, it's Astrid," he warned.

"I was finding it difficult to aim," Nilsa admitted.

"That's because she's coming with the sun behind her back and

37

seeking the safest approach. If you'd been distracted, she'd have been here before you could take a clean shot," Viggo said.

"I was also finding it hard to fix the target," Ingrid admitted.

"That's her specialty, and I must admit it's her forte," Viggo said. "I'm not as good at that, can't figure out how she's so good."

"Wow, don't tell me I've just witnessed one of those extremely rare moments when Viggo admits he doesn't do something well?" Astrid said, reaching them.

"One of those rare moments," Nilsa confirmed, and nodded with a look of disbelief.

"Your ears are always alert," Ingrid told Astrid, smiling.

"You can joke about me all you want, but know that I give credit where credit is due," Viggo said defensively.

"Sure, especially regarding yourself," Ingrid said accusingly.

"That's because I deserve credit in so many ways," he retorted, lifting his chin proudly.

Ingrid shook her head. "Yeah, so many." Nilsa and Astrid nodded and laughed.

"Here comes Lasgol," Astrid said, pointing west.

The three friends saw Lasgol approaching them at a light trot with Ona at his side. They reached the hillock and got behind the rocks with the others.

"Everything all right?" Lasgol asked.

"Everything's in order." Astrid winked and smiled at him lovingly.

"I was a bit delayed looking for Ona. Part of the cavalry didn't follow me like we expected," Lasgol said ruefully. "I went after them and Ona stayed behind."

"Yeah, the cavalry showed up at a bad time, but we got rid of them," said Viggo.

"Yes, by a hair's breadth, but in the end, everything worked out," Astrid confirmed.

"Egil?" Lasgol asked, looking around for his friend.

Ingrid made a face. "He hasn't shown up yet—he should already be here."

You think something's happened to him?" Nilsa asked, wringing her hands.

Astrid rose and scanned the edge of the forest.

"Let's hope not. I'm sure he's okay," she said confidently so they would not start worrying.

They waited for their friend. But time went by and he did not come. The lively conversation died out and concern appeared on their faces. Where was Egil? Why was he taking so long? They did not say it out loud, but they were all thinking about it. Another long while went by and nerves began to show.

"I'm going looking for him," Ingrid said, studying the oak forest.

"That's not the plan." Astrid stopped her. "We need to wait here; this is the meeting point."

"But he's not coming," Nilsa replied. "He could be in danger... he might've been captured by the Zangrians," she said, troubled.

"I don't like this. The know-it-all should already be here. He's taking too long," Viggo said, shaking his head. "I also think we should do something. I don't like just standing here with our arms crossed. He might need us."

Lasgol was undecided. On the one hand, he knew Egil wanted them to stay at the meeting point. Going into the oak forest looking for their friend was a bad idea. But something was wrong—he could feel it in his stomach. This delay was not normal. Egil's plans were exact. Delays meant trouble.

"Maybe we should do something..." he started to say.

Suddenly, Ona chirped once.

What is it? Lasgol asked, watching her.

Ona was looking toward the south side of the hillock. She chirped louder this time.

"I think they're coming," Lasgol said.

"And you're right," Egil's voice said—apparently brought by the wind, because there was no one there.

They all turned toward the voice, but they could not see their friend.

"Would you mind revealing yourself?" Viggo said. "It's a little awkward to talk to someone who's not in front of you. Besides, it's a drag."

"Of course," Egil replied. "Camu, you can stop using your Extended Invisibility Camouflage."

I stop using, Camu's message reached them all.

Then Egil became visible and beside him appeared Camu. The creature was wearing some kind of harness on his back and was carrying two large trunks.

"We're late. The load was heavier than we anticipated," Egil apologized, pointing at Camu, who looked exhausted.

Very heavy, he messaged.

"We'll unload the trunks," Lasgol said and hastened to relieve Camu of his load, since he looked as if he could not hold up much longer on his own four legs. Viggo helped Lasgol, and they loosened the trunk on the left side with a harness and pulley Egil had created for the mission. Ingrid and Astrid took care of the trunk on the other side, setting it on the ground.

I rest, Camu messaged and stretched out on the grass. Ona came to him and licked his head.

"Camu was magnificent," Egil told them as he patted the creature's crested back appreciatively.

I very magnificent, Camu messaged. His blue tongue was hanging out one side of his mouth.

"Yeah, sure, you're the spitting image of exuberance," Viggo said, looking at him with his head to one side.

Very heavy, very tired, Camu excused himself.

"I saw the doors of the carts open, but I wasn't sure you had gotten the load," Astrid said, coming over to Camu and stroking his head affectionately.

Egil nodded. "The distraction maneuvers worked perfectly, just as we had planned. Camu and I managed to reach the carts without difficulty. With all the soldiers scattered and busy and Camu using his Extended Invisibility Camouflage skill, no one noticed our approach. Opening and closing the cart doors was no trouble either—I used a powerful acid to corrode the locks and break them. When we really found ourselves in a tight spot was when we tried to load the first trunk. It was larger and heavier than we expected. The mission said to secure the two coffers the Zangrian convoy was transporting, and I had assumed they'd be small ones. The term usually indicates something smaller. I think I'm going to have sore arms, legs, and back for weeks. Luckily, I'd already designed the harness and pulley to load them onto Camu's back. Once we had the first one loaded, we went back for the second one, which turned out to be as heavy as the first. At least that balanced the load on Camu's back. But it was hard to get going. I have to admit that for a moment I thought the cavalry would discover us. They almost crashed into us when we started running away."

Crashing bad. Lose concentration. They see us, Camu messaged.

"Well, then thank goodness they didn't," Nilsa said, shaking her hands.

"It was close," Egil admitted, wiping the perspiration off his forehead. He also looked worn out. "Then we entered the forest, but with all the weight, Camu could barely walk. It was hard work crossing the oak woods. You have no idea how happy I am to finally be here. There were moments when I thought Camu would collapse. It would have been a disaster—I could hear the soldiers behind us, searching for us."

I hold up, I very strong.

"You certainly are," Astrid told him, stroking his side.

"Let's see what we've got," said Viggo, crouching beside one of the trunks.

"Yeah, I wonder what's in them. I thought this was a mission to steal intelligence," Nilsa said, wrinkling her nose and staring at the trunks.

"That's what the mission said. Obtaining valuable military information," Lasgol specified, recalling the orders they had been given.

"Well, it must be a lot of plans and fat books, judging by the size of the trunks and their weight," Ingrid said, sounding distrustful. "A little strange that secrets should weigh so much. Have we been duped and they're filled with rocks?"

"They might be from their weight," Astrid said. "Perhaps we've been taken for a ride. It wouldn't be the first or the last time that counterintelligence prevails over prior information."

"If you'll let me concentrate for a moment, we'll soon find out," Viggo said, producing one of his lock picks and beginning to manipulate the lock.

They all watched, intrigued; all except Egil, who looked as if he had realized what they were going to find. Lasgol looked at him, puzzled. What was going on here? What had Egil discovered?

It was not long before they heard a metallic click and the lock released. Viggo lifted the top of the trunk and stared at the contents with disbelief.

"What have we got?" Astrid asked, looking in.

"What we've got is a load of Zangrian gold!" Viggo cried, picking up two handfuls of gold coins with the Zangrian royal engraving.

"What a prize!" Nilsa cried as she put her hands in the gold too.

Lasgol stared, surprised. "That's a whole lot of gold!" he said, impressed.

"Two whole lots," Viggo specified, opening the second trunk, which was also filled with gold.

"How strange," Ingrid said, puzzled. "This isn't the mission Duke Orten trusted us with. These aren't trunks with enemy intelligence, they're Zangrian gold coffers."

"It looks like Duke Orten had good information he preferred to disguise," Astrid commented, biting a coin to make sure it was real gold.

"Is it good?" Nilsa asked her.

"Good and real," Astrid replied, smiling.

Ingrid was pacing around the two trunks with her hands behind her back.

"The Duke should've informed us of the cargo we were collecting," she said angrily.

"Yeah, except that thieves don't usually go around talking about the loot they plan to steal from their neighbor," Viggo said. "It's bad for business."

"I can't believe the Duke made us steal a load of gold…" Ingrid said, frustrated.

"I can believe it. It's an efficient way to finance his brother," said Viggo, who had lain down on the ground and was tossing handfuls of gold all over himself as if he were bathing in it.

Ingrid shook her head. "I don't think it's right to steal in the territory of a neighboring kingdom… we're not thieves or outlaws," she said, disgusted. "We're King Thoran's Royal Eagles. He should've explained what we were doing here."

"Since when do the noble and powerful give explanations to commoners like us?" Viggo asked rhetorically. He was now pretending to swim as he continued pouring coins over himself from the two trunks.

"This could mean war between Norghana and Zangria," said Ingrid, unable to hide how angry she was.

"That's exactly why he sent us on this mission," Viggo said.

"Viggo's right," Egil intervened. "We were chosen because we could do the job, because we have the skills to accomplish it—to be successful and also to deflect suspicions toward the kingdom of

Erenal, which is precisely what we've done. I left a Royal Erenal Army glove and dagger in one of the carts. Duke Orten couldn't have hidden a forceful robbery from our army or even a group of veteran Rangers—it would've brought on a diplomatic crisis that might have ended in war. But, us being the authors of the coup, with our unique specializations and skills, we made it work. We pulled off this risky and audacious job, a job Duke Orten believed we could do and which could yield him great benefits," he said, pointing at the two trunks.

"Why risk a war for a heist like this?" asked Lasgol, who did not like the current situation one bit.

"The Duke must have received some hint of the gold cargo and was unable to resist," said Viggo.

"He has spies here in Zangria, and also in Erenal," said Nilsa. "He's sent others like us before our group," she said, looking at Astrid and then at Viggo, "Some have never come back. At least that was the rumor among the Royal Rangers at the capital."

"Kings and nobles never play fair; you know that. I don't know why you're so surprised now. This is just another example of it," Viggo commented.

"Thoran's treasury chests are empty. He needs gold," Egil went on musing. "This is a way to fill them, while at the same time weakening the economy of a rival kingdom such as Zangria, who, we shouldn't forget, has its own eyes set on our kingdom. If you think about it, it's a risky hit, but with a twice important reward."

"They shouldn't risk a war for gold," Ingrid snapped. "There are other ways to fill the King's coffers."

"All wars are for gold, or glory, which in the end is again for gold," Egil said. "Filling the treasury isn't that easy. Taxes and trade are the easiest way, and Thoran is squeezing all the nobles. Trade isn't one of our kingdom's strong points. Norghanians are warriors, not traders. He's not getting enough resources, and as you all know, he's not the most patient man."

"What this coup proves is that Thoran and Orten are going all in. They don't care if the price is war with another kingdom. This is troubling…" said Lasgol.

"It proves what we already know…" Nilsa said with a shrug. "They're two dangerous, ambitious brutes."

"It also proves they know we're good. That's why they sent us,"

Viggo said.

"The fact that they didn't tell us what was in the trunks is logical up to a point," said Egil. "Not just because a secret, if told, stops being one, but because Orten didn't want any hesitation or objections to the mission. He ordered us to get the route of the convoy, intercept it, steal the contents of the carts—which was supposed to be military intelligence—and deliver it to him. That was the mission, and whether we like it or not, we need to carry it out."

"We could half carry it out," Viggo said maliciously, raising one eyebrow.

"What are you hinting at?" Ingrid asked him.

"What else could I be hinting at? We keep the gold."

"We can't keep the gold," Ingrid replied, frowning.

"Don't see why not," Viggo replied as he filled his pockets and Ranger's belt with coins.

"Because Orten would know," Astrid said.

"How can you be so sure of that?" Viggo asked.

"What would you do if you gave this mission to a group such as ours? Would you trust us? Being Orten?" Astrid asked him.

"I wouldn't," Ingrid said.

"He will have sent others to watch us," Nilsa reasoned as she began to look around.

"Very likely, yes," Egil agreed. "In my opinion, we have to complete the mission. It's our best choice under the circumstances.

"Are we going to deliver all this gold?" Lasgol asked, surprised. "Wouldn't it be better to take it away and bury it to use later for a just cause, that requires it?"

Egil shook his head. "Orten would know. Through his spies in this kingdom or anyone he might have sent over to spy on us. We need to take advantage of the situation. He tricked us by sending us to carry out a dishonorable robbery. Now that we've done the deed, there's no way back. We have to come up with a way to turn it into an advantage for us."

"Exactly, we take the gold. That's the best advantage," Viggo insisted, nodding hard.

"No, that's not a good course of action. It's better to deliver the gold and earn his trust. Remember that both Thoran and Orten distrust us—well, they distrust me, to be exact. If we fulfill the mission, we'll clear their doubts. The Royal Eagles will have earned their trust. That will benefit us in the long term, more than taking the gold. Trust me; I'm sure. It's the best way to profit from the adverse situation they've pushed us into."

Lasgol took a deep breath. He looked at his friend and saw in his eyes that Egil was planning something. He had that look of already thinking something up that would take place sometime in the future. He trusted Egil—his instincts and plans, his vision.

"If you think that's the best way to gain some advantage from this mess, go ahead. I'm with you," Lasgol said.

"Let's complete our orders, even if they're disdainful. Otherwise, we'll have serious problems," Ingrid agreed.

"Yeah, that's for the best. Duke Orten would cut our throats if we took the gold, I'm sure of it," Nilsa said.

Astrid nodded. "He's a heartless brute but very clever. We should keep our friends close but our enemies even closer. Let's convince him to trust us and then we'll be able to watch him."

"No! I'm not going to deliver the gold! No way!" Viggo cried as he put more coins under his shirt.

"Viggo, you can't take the gold, you heard Egil," Ingrid insisted.

"You're not taking my gold from me!" Viggo shouted, and started dragging the two trunks away, one with each hand.

"He really is impossible…" Ingrid said, rolling her eyes.

"Well, this time he's somewhat right," Nilsa admitted. "It's hard for me to give it up too. The number of things I could buy in the capital with all that gold… dresses, beautiful jewels…"

"I want my castle! I want my duchy!" Viggo was crying as he dragged the trunks with all his strength.

Viggo very funny always, Camu messaged Lasgol.

Honestly, he is. On second thought, it must be terribly traumatic to give up that much gold. After all, he grew up in the sewers of a city…

Poor?

More than poor. He suffered hunger and tragedies, and that marks a person.

Humans complicated,

Very complicated. Lasgol smiled at Camu, who was looking at him without raising his head from the ground.

"Come on, Viggo, give up the gold. After all, it's not even that much. You would only get half a duchy with it," Astrid told him.

"Half a duchy is better than nothing!" Viggo protested and kept pulling the trunks downhill.

"He'll get tired eventually, and when he does, we'll continue with our plan," Ingrid ordered.

They all nodded and watched Viggo, who, tomato-red from the effort, was still dragging the trunks away.

Chapter 5

Under cover of night, just as they had planned, the Royal Eagles were crossing the river that served as a border between Norghana and Zangria. The six riders had chosen a part of the river that was seldom watched. The Zangrian forces deployed along the river had received recent orders to double the watch and stop anyone who tried to cross into the northern kingdom. The Royal Eagles had to assume the Zangrians were already looking for them.

Ingrid led the way. Every now and then she looked back to make sure she did not see Zangrian soldiers pursuing them. The Panthers had carefully chosen where they would cross the river—it was overlooked because the current was strong and it was not used often given the risk it posed, especially at night. Taking these things into consideration, and because it was relatively close to the place where they had perpetrated the attack, the Panthers had chosen this spot.

The current was powerful but the horses were holding up. Egil was having difficulties with his horse, but Lasgol and Astrid were on either side helping him. Nilsa and Viggo brought up the rear. Ona and Camu were not with them; they were crossing the river further up, at a point where the current was less strong. They were using Camu's camouflage skill, so they were not expecting any trouble. However, unfortunately, they were out of range of Lasgol's *Animal Communication* skill, so they could not exchange messages until they had all crossed and reunited.

"The horses are having trouble!" Nilsa warned, raising her voice above the roaring of the river in a worried tone, struggling with her mount to keep from being dragged off by the current.

"That's because they're carrying my gold!" Viggo replied, pointing at Astrid's horse and the saddlebags right in front of him. They had divided the gold among each of their saddlebags and backpacks except Viggo's, because they did not trust him. The gold was having a funny effect on him—he seemed to be losing his mind the more time he spent around it. His gaze became crazed and he lunged to grab the golden treasure. They had almost had to tie him up, hands and feet, so he would leave the gold alone and not try to run off with it.

"When I chose this spot to cross, I hadn't counted on being so weighed down," Egil apologized; he was having a lot of trouble keeping his horse under control.

The river was rushing by powerfully, and the steady, muffled roar of the current warned them that any distraction would drag them downriver.

"Come on, we're almost there!" Ingrid encouraged them as she reached the other shore.

Lasgol looked back and saw torch lights at several points along the river, a little to the south and also to the north. They were searching for them. There was no doubt. The border troops had been warned. If he and his friends were caught, they would be killed—they would not be allowed to reach the other side.

"We have to cross now or they'll catch us! We can't go back!" he said as he tried to lead Trotter where the water was shallower. The brave pony could fight the strength of the current but did not do so well in the deep parts.

"Stay as close together as you can!" Astrid advised them.

They heeded her and continued crossing. With lots of difficulty, they managed to reach the opposite shore. They clambered up onto dry land and stopped behind some reeds to catch their breath.

"Phew… I don't like currents at all. They make me nervous, and you know that's the last thing I need," Nilsa said, shaking her red hair.

"I don't like them much either," Egil admitted as he snorted in relief and stroked his horse's neck.

"The important thing is that we made it. We're already in Norghanian territory. Safe," Ingrid announced. "It's good to be back home."

"Yeah, we almost didn't make it. It seems they didn't see us cross," Lasgol commented as he kept scanning the lights of the border watch on the Zangrian side of the river.

"Well, now that we're home, I think it's a good moment to take the gold and run," Viggo said. "There's a very nice bankrupt duchy to the east of the realm that I think I'll buy for myself."

"Forget about running away with the money and your dreams of nobility and focus on the mission. We're not done yet," Ingrid told him.

"Let me decide. On the one hand the gold… on the other the

mission, duty and all that nonsense..." he replied while he simulated a scale moving his right arm and then the left. "I keep the gold," he announced, and reached for the saddlebag on Astrid's horse. Seeing his move, the brunette slapped his hand away.

"No getting near the gold, you!" she said, wagging her finger at him.

Viggo withdrew his hand, shaking it. "You're such party poopers..."

"We have to keep going to the meeting point," Egil said. "It's not far, and they'll be waiting for us."

"Everybody, be alert. We may be in Norghanian territory, but we're loaded with gold and this is still border land. There might be foreign agents," Ingrid warned.

Lasgol looked around. He did not see anything out of the ordinary but decided to make sure using his *Animal Presence*, *Hawk's Eye*, and *Owl Hearing* skills. Several green flashes issued from his head and body. What he felt seemed to be in order. He did not detect any human presence close by.

They rode at a trot through an open plain until they saw an abandoned, ruined building on a hill. It had been a Norghanian watch post in its day, but now it was half crumbled due to the skirmishes and incursions of the Zangrians over the border at that point.

As they approached, they saw several riders in front of the building. The Panthers slowed down out of prudence.

"Beware," Ingrid said.

Lasgol noticed they were Norghanians.

"Come over, Royal Eagles!" a powerful voice called to them.

They all recognized the voice: it was Duke Orten's. They did as instructed and went up to the riders. There were about fifteen of the Duke's bodyguard with him, all Norghanians, huge and weathered.

They stopped before them.

"Duke Orten," Ingrid greeted him respectfully.

"I see you have all come back," he replied, eyeing all six. "That is good."

"Luckily we haven't suffered any losses, sir," Ingrid said.

"Has the mission been successful?" Orten asked directly.

Ingrid took a deep breath. "It has been, sir," she confirmed.

Orten smiled from ear to ear and leered at her. His smile made him look like a lewd ogre, and Ingrid looked away from the Duke's unpleasant eyes.

"I like my plans to succeed. I already knew you had made it," he said proudly.

"You already knew, sir?" Ingrid asked. Although she could already guess how he knew, she wanted to see if the Duke would reveal his method.

"It's always a good idea to send a backup team, in case the first one is not successful," Orten said. "Isn't that right?" he asked, staring at Egil.

"It's always advisable to be cautious, especially on dangerous missions in enemy territory," Egil ratified.

"You are smart. That's good, as long as your intelligence serves my plans," Orten warned Egil, pointing his finger at him.

Egil nodded with a half bow from his saddle.

"Always at the Crown's service," he assured the Duke.

Orten smiled, satisfied.

"Kyjor and Gurkog, show yourselves," he called.

Two veteran Rangers rode into view from behind the ruined building and came up to them.

"My lord," Gurkog said.

"These are the best Man Hunters of the realm. I like to count on their services. They are like two-legged bloodhounds and loyal to the throne, as they should be," said Orten.

"Always, my lord," said Kyjor.

"I sent them after your trail and they've been watching you, in case the mission went awry…"

Lasgol looked at the two veterans and knew that their mission had only been to make sure the mission succeeded, but that the Panthers returned with the gold. The term "awry" indicated many possibilities.

"That wasn't necessary, sir. The Royal Eagles always fulfill their assigned mission," Ingrid said, in a tone that without being rude sounded slightly offended.

Orten smiled and looked them up and down.

"Where is my gold?" he asked.

"In the saddlebags and backpacks, sir," Ingrid said.

"My men will take possession of the gold now." Orten gave a loud whistle. From behind the building there appeared about twenty more Norghanian soldiers on horseback. They surrounded the group as they exchanged restless looks. "They're only here to make sure there is no foul play. I am not a trusting man," the Duke said, smiling acidly, eyes shining with malice. "Orbazek, take over," he ordered an officer.

A huge soldier dismounted. He signaled to six others, and they came to the group with extended hands, waiting to be given the saddlebags and packs. One by one they delivered the precious load. Viggo was biting his lower lip and clenching his fists in sheer agony as he watched the treasure he had been so close to having depart.

"Is it all there?" Orten asked.

"It is, sir," Ingrid said.

"It wouldn't have occurred to you to lighten the load, would it?" This time Orten was eying Egil with intimidating eyes.

"No, sir. We're loyal and trustworthy. We carried out the mission as it was entrusted to us," he said.

Orten looked at the two veteran Man Hunters, and they nodded. He made another sign to Orbazek, and the officer showed the Duke the contents of one of the saddlebags and one of the backpacks. Orten put his hand in and felt the Zangrian gold. He smiled with pleasure.

"Did you incriminate the kingdom of Erenal as I instructed?"

"Yes, sir. The evidence will point to Erenal," Egil confirmed.

"I will not be unpleasantly surprised when I inform my brother, will I? You have not left any trace that might incriminate us in the robbery?"

"None, sir. You may be at ease," Egil promised.

"This pleases me greatly. It would have been a shame if this mission had ended up with you losing your lives. After all, you do have exceptional abilities that are quite handy to us. Gondabar was not exaggerating when he informed us of the new specialties you had acquired during the higher training with Sigrid. Even if, as I have heard, things did not finish as well as expected. Pity. Anyway, my brother Thoran will be very pleased to know that his Royal Eagles are even more formidable than they were before. This mission has proven as much, since it was not at all easy to fulfill. Besides, it entailed great temptations once achieved, and you have exceeded my expectations."

"Thank you, your lordship," Egil hastened to say, always quick to ensure that Orten was satisfied and trusted them. "Always at the

King's service," he added with a small bow.

"As it should be. You have shown your worth and loyalty. I am sure we will find new opportunities to use your talents," he said, scratching his chin. "Yes, I'm sure we will."

"Does the Duke require further service from us?" Ingrid asked.

"No, the mission is over. Since you have managed to succeed and I do not want to seem ungracious, I am granting you some time off. You have six weeks. You will then return to the capital to receive new orders."

"Thank you, sir, we really appreciate this," Ingrid said.

"Leave now, and not a word about this to anyone. The slightest comment about this mission will be taken as high treason. Do not think I will not hang you if you slip up. I will do so without hesitation."

"Absolutely, sir, we'll keep this a secret," Egil promised.

"Good, leave then." Orten dismissed them with a wave of his hand.

The soldiers around them let the friends through, and the Royal Eagles left the place. They had accomplished the mission successfully and at the same time strengthened Duke Orten's trust in them—and therefore his brother, King Thoran's, too. Something hard to achieve. Viggo, though, rode away cursing all the ice gods.

They rode at a trot, heading west until they lost sight of the Duke and his men. They all felt that the further they were from Orten, the better. They reached the meeting point where they were to join Ona and Camu. To their delight, the two creatures had both managed to cross safely and were perfectly well. The Panthers dismounted and greeted them.

"Everything all right, Camu?" Lasgol asked him as soon as they were together.

Water refreshing. Everything well.

Ona growled twice, unhappily. Lasgol knew the snow panther did not like the river much.

"Where to now?" Astrid asked, letting her mount graze beside her.

"Some rest wouldn't be a bad thing…" said Nilsa, stretching. "I'd certainly enjoy that."

"We're not on duty, so we can rest if we want to," Ingrid said, also letting her horse graze.

"I think we've earned it," Lasgol said with a grin. "The mission was difficult." "Especially the end," Egil joked with a roguish grin.

"The mission has been a disaster and I'm in a very bad mood. I need a Norghanian beer, or better still, a good Nocean wine," said Viggo. "That will help undo the knot in my stomach."

"And it will help you keep dreaming about nobility, titles, castles, and riches," Nilsa said, tilting her head comically.

"You can laugh all you want, but one day you'll see," Viggo replied, wagging his finger at her.

"The village of Olouste isn't far from here, and it's supposed to have a pretty good inn where we could spend the night and rest," said Ingrid.

"A bed, no matter how rustic, is always welcome," said Astrid, stretching her back.

"And they'll have food and drink," Viggo said, sounding a bit more cheerful.

"Good, then, let's go to this inn. With a little luck we might even be able to eat a hot dinner," Lasgol said.

"And we'll get rid of the bitter taste after the meeting back there," Ingrid said.

"Ufff, for that I'm going to need a lot of drink," Viggo said bitterly.

Chapter 6

The inn was quiet that evening. A few locals were drinking their last beers and a couple of travelers were dining late. The Panthers had asked for a table, and the innkeeper, an aging man, thin but with a large belly, had given them one of the two tables in front of the windows of the main façade. Olouste was a decently sized village and the locals were farmers and cattle owners mostly, with a few traders who had their stalls and shops in the main square of the village.

Lasgol had left Camu and Ona at the outskirts. He could not bring them to the inn. Ona would cause too much commotion—it was too late to explain about the panther to the locals. Camu could hide, but his size would not allow him to enter small or crowded spaces easily. So, the pair had stayed in a small forest beside a stream somewhat away from the entrance to the village. Norghanian villages were not good places for either creature. Luckily, they both understood and took it well. They did not even complain. As long as they were together, they did not mind spending the night outdoors. Lasgol was grateful, because it was going to become increasingly difficult to take Ona and Camu with him on his adventures.

The innkeeper came over to their table and brought water, cider, and Nocean wine.

"I hope everything will be to your liking, Rangers," he said respectfully.

"I see you're familiar with our people," Ingrid commented, looking into his eyes.

"I've been managing this inn for a long time. I've seen many of your people pass through over the years. We're close to the border, and it's common to see soldiers and Rangers around."

"And here I was thinking we didn't draw too much attention..." Nilsa commented as she looked around the premises to see whether they were being watched. They were.

"In a village such as this, with your hooded cloaks, armed and with the look of those who know their way around trouble, I won't lie, you stand out," the innkeeper said smiling.

"Yeah, I guess we don't pass for traders," Nilsa shrugged.

"I'll go and get your dinner ready. It's late, but there's always food and rest for Rangers at my inn. My name's Ulregh, at your service."

"We appreciate it," Ingrid said and nodded in respect.

"While you're at it, bring us another bottle. We won't get far with only one," said Viggo, pouring himself a drink.

"Drink will only cloud your mind, not help you," Ingrid told him once the innkeeper had left.

"If I drink enough, it'll surely help me forget this disastrous mission," he replied, pouring himself another drink.

"It wasn't disastrous. We completed it and no one was hurt. It was a success," Astrid said with a wink.

"A pauper's success…" he protested.

"It was only gold, it's not as if you lost something really important," said Nilsa.

"Only gold she says! Only gold!" Viggo cried in disbelief.

"Shhhh, be quiet," Ingrid chided, looking around. "We're not alone. Others can hear us."

"Yeah, better be careful with what we say… remember the Duke's warning. If we even breathe a word about it…" said Nilsa.

"Let's lower our voices and keep our conversation private," Astrid advised, looking askance at the other tables and the counter.

"We'll need to exercise extreme caution around this area," Egil said, lowering his voice. "We're near the border. There might be Zangrian agents spying, and they will have received orders to be on the alert because of what's happened. In fact, they'll be looking for us specifically and what we 'extracted'…"

Lasgol glanced around. The people at the counter were locals for sure. Besides, they had had one pint of beer too many by the tone of their conversations and body language; their balance seemed affected. Those dining at the nearby tables looked like travelers or traders passing through. They were enjoying a late, hot dinner.

"Any of them could be a Zangrian spy," Astrid said, sweeping the room with a glance. "Don't be fooled by their appearances; anyone can pass themselves off as a trader or tavern drunkard."

Lasgol did not think they looked like spies, but he was not good at seeing through deception. On the other hand, a spy would be doing everything in their power to disguise their true intent. Astrid had a lot more experience in this matter. Best to pay attention to her words. What he did notice was that the traveler sitting in the back, a man in his thirties with short brown hair and brown eyes, seemed interested in them. Lasgol watched him out of the corner of his eye—at that moment the stranger was not looking their way. He was having dinner and watching the counter where two locals were talking loudly about cows. Lasgol assumed he was not spying on them. It must have been his imagination playing tricks on him because of his friends' comments. The man could also simply be curious. He and his friends drew attention just by being Rangers, and it was not that odd for people to stare at them. The innkeeper himself had said as much, so he did not think much of it.

Ulregh was not long in bringing their dinner, and it was a pleasant surprise. Old-cow beef stew with red wine and sweet onions, with a side of turnips and carrots.

"It's really delicious," Ingrid said once she had tried it.

"She's right, it's really good," Nilsa told the innkeeper when he brought the second bottle of wine.

"Thank you, miss, everything is a village product—therein lies the secret. No Zangrian spices or those foreign products the salesmen bring around," he replied.

"You grow your own food then?" Astrid asked with interest as she spread sauce on the bread; it was a little hard from sitting out all day but with the sauce it tasted delicious.

"I don't have a garden." He shook his head. "This inn already gives me more work than I can manage, but I know everyone in the village and I know who has the best vegetables," he added with a wink.

"And cows," Egil added with a smile.

"The best in the area: the kind that don't get fat on poor fodder," Ulregh said with anther wink.

"Information is sometimes more valuable than the product itself," Astrid noted, smiling broadly.

"As true as the fact that you eat the pig down to the tail," the innkeeper said and left them to tend to his other customers.

"Speaking of information, great job getting it," Ingrid congratulated Astrid, lowering her voice so she could not be heard.

"Thank you, that's my specialty," Astrid smiled. "I'm the stealthiest and best at being invisible," she said, giving Viggo a challenging look.

Viggo waved the fact aside nonchalantly.

"I'm a better assassin," he replied. He was not going to let anyone mess with him, and he showed her the knife he was cutting bread with as if it were one of his assassin knives.

"You might be better when it comes to fighting, but not at becoming a shadow," Astrid winked at him. She bent to stand right behind Lasgol's back at her side as if she were his shadow.

Viggo watched her and nodded as he put a spoonful of stew into his mouth.

"I'll grant you that."

"I appreciate it. It seems your good mood is coming back," Astrid replied.

"It's the wine, I'm feeling more cheerful," he smiled. "Besides, I recognize the truth and I won't deny you have an amazing skill for everything slippery and somber."

"How flattering," Nilsa giggled.

"I'll take it for what it's worth," Astrid smiled.

"Big guy missed a good adventure and a great stew," Viggo commented, his gaze lost in space.

"It's a pity he couldn't be here with us," Nilsa said, and her face darkened at the thought of their friend.

"He would've loved to be part of the action," Lasgol said. "He would've delivered a few blows."

"And then he would've gulped down the whole dinner with the excuse that his larger body needs more nourishment to function," Viggo said sarcastically.

They all smiled fondly at the memory of Gerd's usual comments.

"Will he be okay? I miss him a lot," said Nilsa.

"We all miss him," Lasgol nodded.

"He's in good hands at the Shelter. Annika will take good care of him until he's fully recovered," Egil said.

"Perhaps we could visit him now that we have a vacation," Viggo suggested. "I feel like seeing how that pie-eating, frustrated farmer is doing."

"I think that's a great idea," Ingrid agreed. "Now's a good time. Later on we'll be assigned another mission and we won't be able to go."

"I was thinking about going by Skad and visiting my home, Martha and Ulf…" Lasgol said. "It's been a while since I've been there…"

"I'd also like to visit my family," said Nilsa. "I haven't seen my sisters in a long time."

Egil was thoughtful for a moment, then he spoke.

"I want to go to the Camp. I need to check some things at the Library and I'd also like to speak to Dolbarar and see how things are going there," he said.

"Is it about the orb?" Ingrid asked.

Egil nodded. "I want to find more information about the orb and its power. It's truly fascinating, something unique and fantastic. I need to find tomes of knowledge that will help me figure it out, help me understand what it is and how we can use it."

"Using it sounds dangerous," Nilsa said as a warning.

"Rather than using it, containing it," Egil explained. "We must consider that it is no mere Object of Power like others in Tremia."

"Isn't it similar to the Turquoise Queen's Star of Sea and Life?" Astrid asked. "It reminds me of that precious object of Uragh's."

"I think not. This orb is an intelligent, sentient object, while the Star was not," Viggo specified. "The Star could generate a great amount of energy, energy which it stored and could then be used in spells. It was powerful, and yet it wasn't like this dragon orb."

"That's significant, don't you think?" Lasgol said.

"Are you hinting that the orb is something else? That apart from having energy inside it, like the Star, it's capable of feeling and thinking?" Ingrid asked, looking un-convinced.

"That's exactly what I think, and that's why I find it fascinating," Egil said excitedly.

"Well, if it feels, it's as though it has a life of its own," Nilsa said.

"Exactly! That's why it's fascinating!" Egil cried eagerly.

"Shhh, you're drawing attention," Viggo scolded him.

"Sorry… I get carried away by all the ramifications and possibilities the orb represents," Egil apologized.

"I still think we'd better throw it to the bottom of the sea, then mystery ended," Viggo said, pouring himself more wine.

"I don't usually agree with Viggo's ideas, but this one seems like a pretty good one to me," Nilsa said.

"Huh, in the end you'll see things like I do, Freckles," Viggo told Nilsa.

"Twisted and dark?" she replied, raising an eyebrow.

"Is that a bad thing?" he said, shrugging.

"I think we all see the danger it represents, but I don't think throwing it in the sea is the best solution," Astrid said. "At least until we know what it is and how dangerous it really is."

"Besides, we have to take into account that Camu believes it's related to him, to his ancestors. He doesn't want us to destroy it," Lasgol said.

"After the mess he got us into, the bug has no vote in this." Viggo shook his head and wagged his finger.

"Hey, pal, we can't make drastic decisions like throwing the orb into the sea without discussing it with him too," Lasgol told Viggo.

"Just because the bug can speak to us now doesn't mean he has a voice in our debates and decisions. I'm adamant about that," Viggo said sharply with his arms folded.

"I haven't said anything about deciding, but we have to at least let him give his opinion. He has feelings and arcane links to this dragon orb we can't understand," Lasgol said.

"I think we should listen to him," said Astrid. "We need to listen to him and get to the bottom of all this. An orb with a dragon inside is no common thing. We've all felt its powerful and that it might even be a sentient being."

"My thoughts exactly," Egil agreed, nodding.

"That's why we need to listen to Camu and see what he can tell us about the orb and its origin," Lasgol said.

"Don't be mistaken, just because the bug's the size of a horse doesn't mean he's not a baby anymore," Viggo said. "We don't listen to the opinion of babies."

"He's not a baby, but it is true he's still a pup…. He's not fully developed—mentally I mean," Ingrid said.

"Youngsters have no say, and that's that," Viggo insisted, trying to end the conversation.

"Wise people listen to all opinions and consider them before making important decisions," Egil remonstrated. "That includes intelligent creatures, big or small, especially when they might have a better understanding about the subject at hand."

Viggo did not reply but made a face showing he did not agree.

"By the way, where's the Orb now?" Ingrid asked Lasgol and Egil.

"I have it." Lasgol opened his cloak and showed them a leather pouch hanging on one side of his Ranger belt.

"You carry it like that? It's dangerous!" Nilsa said, her eyes widening.

"I can't leave the Orb with Camu in case it communicates with him again and makes him do something like last time. I also can't leave it in Trotter's saddlebags—it's too valuable and it might get stolen. It has to be with us so we can protect it and prevent any accidents. At first, I carried it in my bag, but I'd rather have it on my belt, it's more comfortable."

"I think it's too risky to have it so close to your body. What if it gives you a shock?" Nilsa said, upset.

"It's wrapped up in Ranger scarves and inside a leather pouch. I can't touch it even by accident. There's no risk, take it easy."

"Anyway, be careful," Astrid said, worried.

"Don't worry, I am,"

"I can also carry it on me if necessary. It's well protected and I'm not worried about anything happening to me," Egil offered.

"Thanks, friend." Lasgol patted his friend's shoulder.

"If it gives you a shock, you'll get what's coming to you," Viggo warned, shaking both arms vigorously.

"What does Camu have to say about you carrying it? Is he okay with it? I guess he'd rather carry it himself," Ingrid said to Lasgol.

"We've spoken about it at length. He's okay with it. He knows what he did was wrong. He regrets it and feels guilty. If I have the Orb, Camu knows there's less risk of anything bad happening again."

"Besides, the orb hasn't communicated with Camu again," Egil added.

"It hasn't? Not once?" Nilsa asked, raising an eyebrow.

"Not since we left the Shelter," Lasgol said, shaking his head and shrugging, since he did not know why.

"Which is most singular and fascinating," Egil said, again, excited. "There must be a reason. One that explains this sudden silence after it led Camu to it. Why do you think that might be? Why does it remain silent when we know it *can* communicate with Camu?"

"Well, if you don't know, don't ask me," Viggo said.

"It's got me quite intrigued as well," Lasgol admitted.

"I think the silence is good—maybe it won't communicate for another thousand years and we'll be free of any new danger," Nilsa said wistfully.

"It's an Object of Power which, as far as we know, has the

capability of melting huge blocks of ice and of communicating mentally with our dear Camu."

"Communicating and influencing him," Astrid noted.

"True. It persuaded him to use the pearl and open a portal," Egil said thoughtfully as he gazed at the ceiling of the inn.

"Was it Camu or the dragon orb that opened the portal?" Ingrid asked. "I'm not clear on that."

"From what we witnessed, I gather it was Camu who opened the portal on both pearls, the one in the Shelter and the one in the forests of the Usik; with the help of the dragon orb, of course."

"Don't remind me of the Usik. What a bunch of green savages with painted faces, fallen from a tree!" Viggo said.

"We were lucky to get out of there alive," said Ingrid. "The Usik were wild, but they were also skilled warriors."

"With bloodthirsty instincts!" Viggo added.

"It was a very intense experience," said Astrid, going over the incident in her head.

"Remind me never to go near those forests again in my life," Viggo said.

"Let's hope we never have to," said Lasgol.

"Not even a whole regiment of the best soldiers in the realm would come out alive from the forests of the Usik!" Ingrid said.

"Not in this realm or in any other," said Egil.

"So, what's the plan then? Are we visiting the big guy?" Viggo asked.

"Well… I have a personal matter I have to deal with…" Astrid said.

Lasgol looked at her blankly. He knew nothing of any personal matter. They had not talked about it. Astrid signaled that she would tell him later.

"Yes, I also have to make a stop on the way," said Ingrid. "In any case, we have time for both things. Everyone go and get their personal tasks and visits done now while we have time. Then we'll meet up at the Shelter and visit Gerd before we're assigned another royal mission."

"I think that's a good idea," said Nilsa.

"My stop's short," Ingrid added. "Viggo and I'll get there first and wait for you."

"See how you can't go anywhere without me?" Viggo said to

Ingrid, looking at her innocently.

"What I can't do is get rid of you, which is different."

"Maybe it's because deep down you don't want to get rid of me..." Viggo replied with a silly grin from ear to ear.

"Maybe, but very deep down," she said, glaring at him.

They went on eating and chatting for quite a while. At last, after a prolonged conversation, they left the table and went to rest. Lasgol glanced to the back of the room and noticed that the man who had been watching them was still there, which Lasgol found strange. Light hit the man's right arm, and Lasgol thought he saw a silver flash on his forearm. The innkeeper came to show them to their rooms and Lasgol dismissed the incident and followed him. Seeing Zangrian spies at every turn was nothing but a consequence of their exhaustion and all the emotions they had been through.

Chapter 7

Lasgol and Astrid were talking about the situation in a corner of the room they were sharing with Egil. The group was sharing two rooms, since a Ranger's pay was not exactly generous and they always had to watch what they could afford, which was not much. They were used to it, but tonight was different from other nights because of the circumstances—Lasgol wanted to speak to Astrid in private and Viggo wanted to protest.

They could hear Viggo protesting and complaining through the wall—because they had not heeded him and kept the gold, they could not enjoy all kinds of comforts. The complaints could easily be heard from the next room. Ingrid and Nilsa soon got him to shut up so the rest of the inn's guests could rest in peace.

"You hadn't mentioned you had any personal matter to tend to," Lasgol said to Astrid in a low voice. Egil was already in bed reading one of the tomes of knowledge he had gotten at the capital before they had even started their mission. The title was *Deep Magical Power*, a book about magic, spells, and Objects of Power.

"I received a message in Norghania and postponed it until we finished the mission, but I think I should deal with it now that we have a respite. I'll join you at the Shelter as soon as I'm done."

"What kind of personal matter is it?" Lasgol asked, wanting to know more but not wanting to pry; Astrid was reserved about some parts of her life, and he had always respected her privacy. He did not want to press her. He would rather she told him whatever it was when she wanted to and not force her.

"It's a family matter..." she said, lowering her gaze.

"Family? I thought you were alone, that your parents had died. That's what you told me before..." Lasgol said, surprised.

"That's right. My parents died..."

"If you'd rather not talk about something so painful, I understand..."

Astrid shook her head.

"I'll tell you..."

"Are you sure you want to? There's no need, really... unless you're absolutely sure."

"I am, don't worry. I appreciate you being so considerate though."

"I'm here to help you with anything you need," Lasgol said, stroking her hair.

"I know. You see… my father was a Ranger, and he died in action when I was eight years old. My mother had died the year before while he was away on a mission. Unfortunately, she was bitten by a venomous snake. I don't remember much about my parents, only bits and pieces."

"I'm sorry… losing your parents is horrible, but it's even worse when you lose them at such a young age."

"Thank you… the thing is that, since I don't remember them well, the pain and feeling of loss are easier to bear."

Lasgol hugged her and kissed her cheek.

"Your future's going to be much better than your past," he promised.

"With you by my side, always," she replied and kissed him hard.

For a moment they remained in an embrace, kissing, enjoying the great love they both felt for one another.

"Then… who sent you a message?" Lasgol asked her blankly.

"It's my uncle… he's back in Norghana."

"Oh, I didn't know you had an uncle."

"Yes, on my mother's side. His name is Viggen Norling. He raised me after the death of my parents until I joined the Rangers."

"You've never told me anything about him," Lasgol said, surprised that Astrid had never told him about the person who had taken care of her after her parents' death. He wondered why. He did not want to speculate too much, because there could be many different reasons—from not getting along to anything else. He would let Astrid explain.

"Well… there's a reason…. My uncle took care of me, but only partially."

"Oh? Was he not around much? Did he not look after you?"

Astrid made a face. "I'll admit, the first few years he did. Then he started traveling—he began his 'quest,' as he called it—and began vanishing for long periods of time. He spent a lot of time traveling, whole seasons, and from what I found out, away from the realm. He started spending less and less time with me. By the time I turned thirteen, I barely saw him. When I was fourteen, he visited me a couple of times when he came back from his long journeys, which as far as I could guess from what he told me were to the south, to the Nocean Empire."

"Quest? What did your uncle do for a living?" Lasgol asked, interested.

"I don't know exactly. He's some kind of scholar, erudite—an expert in ancient matters. He used to spend a lot of time studying tomes of knowledge. Now that I think about it, he was a little like Egil," she said, pointing at their friend, who was lost in his reading. "Always with a tome under his arm and intent on obtaining new knowledge. As to his 'quest,' he always spoke about it as if he were about to discover the greatest secret of humanity, as if he were going to find something that would change the world, the future of Tremia," Astrid said with a shrug.

"Strange… that does sound a little weird…" Lasgol said.

"It sounded even stranger to me, especially when I was younger and didn't understand how something like that could be more important than being with his family. It was because of this obsessive 'quest' of his that he spent so much time away from home and we became estranged. I think that was also the reason he didn't get along well with my parents. Although he's never said anything, I suspect it."

"Wow. I'm sorry about the relationship with your parents and that he didn't spend more time with you, taking care of you…"

"He did look after me. I never lacked anything from the moment he took me to live with him after my father died. He has money, a large property with a huge, fortified tower. He found me a governess and even a weapons master. They practically raised me, really."

"Pity… but at least you had someone to care for you and instruct you."

"Oh, yes. What I never had was the warmth of a family, the love…. What you enjoyed. At fifteen, when I wrote to him to let him know I was entering the Rangers, he came home by surprise. He tried to persuade me not to enter the corps. He wanted me to accompany him on his 'quest.'"

"So what happened? Because you obviously joined the Rangers. Did he give you his blessing after all?"

Astrid shook her head. "No, he told me that joining the Rangers was a waste of time. That I should come with him. That the quest was what really mattered, that together we'd change the future of the world."

"That doesn't sound too good…"

"You can say it, I don't mind," Astrid said, encouraging him to speak freely.

"Well… he sounds as if his mind…." Lasgol made a circular motion with his finger.

"That's what I thought, and that's why we parted on less than good terms."

"Oh, I'm sorry."

"It's okay. Those things happen. You can't choose your family, only your friends. That's one of the lessons life teaches us."

"That's very true."

"I have my new family in my friends, in the Panthers, and I'm happy with that."

Lasgol smiled in sympathy. "I completely understand. I feel the same about the Panthers."

"Even Camu and Ona," Astrid said, smiling.

"Of course," he nodded repeatedly.

"That's why I hadn't told you anything. And there wasn't much to tell…"

"You can always trust me, you know that," Lasgol said, looking into her green eyes lovingly.

"I know." She smiled back and kissed him.

"And now he's suddenly made contact, after all this time?"

"That's right," she nodded. "He wants to see me, in person. It's something important."

"Curious. Well, it sounds like an opportunity to improve your relationship, don't you think?"

"Perhaps… I don't know. Maybe," Astrid shrugged. She looked uncertain.

"You should seize the opportunity. Family is important. I should know, I learned that the hard way, a way I wouldn't wish even on my worst enemy," Lasgol said with his fist to his heart. "You have to care for your family and, if possible, enjoy them."

Astrid nodded. "It's a bit hard for me. I don't have such strong feelings as you. Or at least they're not the same as yours. Don't get me wrong—I don't wish any harm to my uncle, but I'm not sure I want him back in my life. The time he's been away, chasing after his goal, I've been fine, and I've known happiness," she said, gently stroking Lasgol's face.

"Go, talk to him. It's better to deal with family matters when there's a chance. If he vanishes forever from your life one day, you'll regret it."

Astrid heaved a big sigh.

"Yes… I think I'd better speak with him. I hope it goes well."

"It will. You'll see," Lasgol said, and they hugged each other tightly.

The next morning, feeling well rested and after enjoying a good breakfast at the inn, the group got ready to leave.

"We'll meet at the Shelter," said Ingrid, getting onto her horse.

"I'll come as soon as I see my family and make sure they're all well," said Nilsa, getting on her horse too.

"I'll let you know as soon as I leave the Camp. I'll send Milton to you at the Shelter," said Egil.

"Say hello to Dolbarar for me," Lasgol said.

"And for us," Astrid said, and the rest followed suit.

"I hope he's doing well," said Ingrid.

"I'll let you know," Egil promised as he got onto his horse.

"Say hi to Martha and that grumpy Ulf," Viggo told Lasgol.

"I will," he nodded.

"See you at the Shelter," said Astrid. "I'll see my uncle at his house and then join you."

"Very well," said Lasgol.

"Try not to get into trouble," Viggo said as he leapt onto his mount, and as he did there was a strange jingling.

They all stared at him,

"What was that sound?" Ingrid asked, raising an eyebrow.

"Sound? What sound?" Viggo asked, looking around.

"Don't pretend. You know perfectly well what sound I mean," Ingrid said accusingly.

"No idea," Viggo replied, looking everywhere except at Ingrid.

"It sounded like coins," Nilsa said, pointing her finger at Viggo.

"Snitch," he replied.

"Then you're not denying it. You're carrying coins," Nilsa said accusingly.

"I didn't say that," Viggo denied heartily. "You heard wrong."

"We all heard…" Astrid said.

Ingrid dismounted and went over to Viggo's horse.

"Where are they?" she asked him seriously.

"Ingrid… I wouldn't lie to you, you know that," he said in a conciliatory tone.

"I know you're lying, because you called me by my name and you never do that. Where's the money hidden?"

"Check his saddlebags," Nilsa said.

"It's not there. We checked them before we delivered the load to Orten," said Ingrid, looking around to see whether anyone was listening. She only saw the innkeeper and the stable boy, going about their business.

"That's right… and his rucksack too," Nilsa remembered.

"He's hidden it someplace else," Astrid said accusingly.

"Viggo, don't make me do something I really don't want to," Ingrid said, threatening him with her fist.

"I swear I have no idea what you're talking about," Viggo denied and made a face as if he really did not know what was going on.

"Viggo…" Ingrid stiffened.

"He's carrying it on him, in his trousers," Astrid said, pointing.

"Astrid! You traitor!" Viggo cried, outraged.

"It's for your own good, believe me," she replied, like someone chastising a rebellious child.

"You knew?" Lasgol asked her, surprised.

"Yes, I realized when we arrived at the inn, but I let him go on believing he's smarter than the rest of us."

"I can't believe you took the g…!" Ingrid cut herself off. She did not want to mention the word "gold."

"See? I didn't take anything," he said. "So, we're leaving already?"

Ingrid mounted her horse in a huff.

"The moment we're out of the village and there's no one around, you're going to get what for!" she shouted at Viggo.

"Oh my, don't be like that my beloved blondie, you can't wait to be alone with me," he replied with a roguish grin as he spurred his horse. "I'll be waiting somewhere discreet," Viggo said with a wink, blowing her a kiss.

Ingrid cursed under her breath and rode after him.

Chapter 8

Lasgol stopped before crossing the bridge at the entrance to the village. Trotter snorted as if he recognized the place. He most likely did.

We're home, Trotter, Lasgol transmitted reassuringly.

Trotter shook his head up and down and snorted again.

Lasgol gazed at the houses of Skad in the distance and was overwhelmed at once by a feeling of nostalgia. It happened to him every time he came back. It was strange, since he was already here. It was natural to miss home when you were in a foreign land or in danger, but feeling nostalgic when arriving at your own village seemed less natural—it shocked Lasgol at least. He assumed it might be because of what he had lost and suffered, which all came flooding back the moment he set foot in the area.

He shrugged; he did not know the reason but did not make much of it either. He was not like most Norghanians after all. He smiled. In the end Viggo was right to call him a weirdo. Thinking of Viggo, he wondered what Ingrid might have done to him. He could easily imagine her hanging him upside down from a tree so the gold coins he had hidden in his trousers poured out.

He laughed. It was probably quite close to the actual truth. Yes, knowing them both he was practically sure. Viggo was quite something. Entertainment was always guaranteed with him. Providing you could bear with his acidic ways. Otherwise, he was impossible. Lasgol appreciated him, even if he was like a toothache at times, but Viggo was so genuine and unpredictable that Lasgol could not help loving him with all his virtues and defects—of which he had many!

Happy? You laugh. Camu messaged as he walked beside Lasgol with Ona.

Yes, I'm happy, in a good mood. Coming back home always cheers me up.

I happy too.

Ona chirped once.

I see we're all happy, Lasgol smiled. He noticed that Camu was eying the river, or to be precise, the trout in the river.

Skad pretty.

Yes, it's a pretty village. You leave the trout alone, though. I know what you're thinking.

I do nothing.

No, but you're thinking about it.

You read mind?

No, I don't read minds, but I do know you.

Ah, all right.

Nobody can read minds, Lasgol messaged in an attempt to clear up Camu's concern.

No one?

Well, that's what I think at least. There's no record of anyone reading minds. No one that isn't a crook, I mean.

A crook?

A person who tricks people to take their gold from them or takes advantage of them in some manner.

Stealing?

Yes, with tricks.

Bad person.

That's right. Lasgol was pleased to see that Camu had such a developed ethical sense. The creature wasn't perfect, oh no, but he had the feeling that Camu could distinguish between right and wrong better every day. At least he thought so. He considered how much of a problem it would have been if Camu did not understand or respect good and evil. It would be a catastrophe—Lasgol did not even want to imagine it.

Drokose say Drakonians can read mind.

Lasgol looked at him, surprised.

He said that? Are you sure?

Not sure. But think so.

Maybe you didn't understand him properly. There is magic that's used to create illusions, to trick a person. I think it's called Illusion Magic, and the magi who practice it are called Illusionists. They can make you see things that aren't there. There's also a kind of magic that's used to dominate a person and make them do whatever you want them to. It's called Domination Magic, and the magi who practice this are called Dominators. Maybe he was referring to one of those types of magic, or a similar kind the Drakonians possess.

Maybe.

Lasgol felt a little more at ease; Camu must have misunderstood.

Let's go to the village, Lasgol said, seeing in Camu's face that he was dying to jump into the river.

I camouflage, Camu messaged.

Lasgol was grateful, because entering the village with Camu visible, now that he was so big, would cause a sensation, and not the good kind. The locals would run off, terrified. Seeing a reptile the size of a horse coming into the village would scare the toughest Norghanian warriors. Lasgol's own arrival created enough expectation already; with Ona at his side, the villagers would run and hide in fear. Sometimes Lasgol wished Camu had not grown so big. He could remember when Camu was so small, he fit in his hand.

He sighed. Time passed for everyone, and everyone grew up: humans, snow panthers, and Drakonians. Lasgol wondered how much larger Camu would get. The Creatures of the Ice could live a long time, and their size was colossal. He remembered Misha, who was huge, and some of the other creatures in the Serenity Valley. Yes, Camu would most likely live a lengthy life and grow to a colossal size.

He could also be absolutely wrong and Camu might not live or grow so much. The truth was he and the others had no idea how their friend would develop. All they had were guesses. They would simply have to wait and see which assumption turned out to be right, and it made whatever happened more exciting.

He led Trotter along the main street slowly. Lasgol's hood was down so they could see who he was and recognize him and know Ona would not cause trouble. As he expected, the locals recognized him, and although they moved out of Ona's path, they seemed to trust him because they did not run away—although one or two kids did sprint off when Lasgol and Ona approached.

The villagers he met greeted him courteously and welcomed him, which Lasgol always appreciated. It was mid-morning, a lovely day, and the main street was already pretty busy. By the time they reached the crossing that led to the main square, two figures were there waiting for him: Chief Gondar and his assistant, Limus.

Lasgol stopped Trotter.

"Chief Gondar, Limus," he said, bowing his head respectfully.

"Ranger Lasgol," Gondar greeted him.

"Specialist," Limus added with a smile.

"I'm glad to see both of you," Lasgol said, dismounting and hugging them tightly, to which they both responded equally.

"I see that news of my return has traveled quickly," Lasgol said with a smile.

"Several kids came into the Chief's house, shouting that there was a man with a snow panther in the middle of the village," Limus explained.

"We didn't have to guess too hard," Gondar laughed.

Lasgol smiled. He noticed that the people in the square and surroundings were coming to stare curiously. Lasgol watched Ona out of the corner of his eye, but she was waiting patiently beside Trotter. She did not seem nervous for now, even if she was the center of attention, in particular to the youngest.

"You look well," Lasgol told them.

"Time goes by, but we stand strong," Gondar said.

"Me not so much," Limus smiled. "I have the feeling that any day now I'm going to break like a dry twig."

"Nonsense," Gondar replied. "This one will live to a hundred at least."

"Let's hope we all do," Limus replied.

Lasgol strained his neck, trying to glimpse someone among all the people.

"Looking for Ulf?" the Chief asked.

"Yeah, is he all right?"

Limus chuckled.

"Ulf's as well as you would expect."

"Yes, he's the same as always," Gondar said. "He'll soon hear of your arrival and limp over to your house."

Lasgol smiled. It was reassuring to know that old Ulf was okay.

"Why don't you come by the house when you can and we'll chat about how things are going around here. I'd like that," he invited.

"We will," Gondar said with a nod.

"Very well. See you there then, I'll head there now. I think Ona is beginning to get nervous with so many people around."

"Great. We're happy to see you," Limus said.

Lasgol continued toward his house, an entourage of curious people at his heels. Young people and children mostly. For them the arrival of a Beast Whisperer with his snow panther was an amazing event. Besides, Lasgol was a hero, and a local no less, so the urge to see him was even greater.

He dismounted at the gate of his property. He looked around but saw no one. Opening the gate, he found the garden perfectly tended, the house newly painted, and the roof fixed. He was glad to find it like this. Martha kept the house and the land in a perfect state, better than he could have wished.

"Anyone home?" Lasgol cried as he went through the open gate.

A moment later a woman appeared, coming from the back of the house.

"Lasgol! What a wonderful surprise!" Martha cried, running to welcome him.

"Martha!" He smiled and hugged her tight.

"You didn't tell me you were coming!"

Lasgol smiled. "I didn't have any time. I've been quite busy."

"Ranger stuff?"

"That's right. Top secret mission," he joked, although that was the truth.

"I imagine. The Rangers and their secrets," the housekeeper replied, giving him another big hug.

"I'm so happy to be back, Martha."

"Let me look at you," she said, holding him by the arms and examining him from head to toe. "You're a full-grown man, and quite handsome," she said with a wink.

Lasgol laughed out loud. "No way, but thank you. You look wonderful too," he replied, and it was not a mere compliment. She really looked very well; time did not seem to age her.

"Wonderful? No way, every day I feel the passing of time," she said and waved her hand in denial.

"Well, I think you look great. You must be taking some youth potion," he joked.

"Yes, the kind that peddlers and traveling salesmen sell that turn your teeth black."

Lasgol laughed. "I don't know your secret, but there is one, I'm sure."

"Astrid? Viggo? The others? How come they're not with you? Is everything all right?" she asked, and her expression turned to one of concern.

"Everything's fine," Lasgol assured her with a smile. "They couldn't come this time, they had to deal with personal matters."

"Oh, what a pity, I would've loved to see them."

"Next time," Lasgol smiled.

"I see that Ona and Trotter are with you. I guess the creature, Camu, is too?" Martha asked, looking behind Lasgol curiously.

Camu too, she received Camu's mental message.

Martha started backward. Her eyes opened wide as she looked around her.

"What was that?"

"Don't be frightened, Martha. It's Camu. He's developed the skill of communicating with humans."

Be me, he messaged again.

Martha started again, "I can hear him speaking to me in my head!" she cried, looking flabbergasted.

"Yes. Don't worry, it's his way of communicating," Lasgol told her, holding her by the arms so the good housekeeper would calm down.

"It's so… shocking…" she muttered.

I very shocking, Camu confirmed.

Ona chirped twice.

"Yeah, you're full of surprises. The thing is, they're not all good," Lasgol replied with sarcasm.

"So, I guess he's right here now," Martha said. She did not see Camu but could hear him in her head, so she knew he must be around.

I behind Lasgol, Camu confirmed.

"Good, I was just making sure," said Martha, who, by the look on her face, had not gotten over the surprise.

"We'd better go inside," Lasgol said with a smile and a soothing tone.

"Yes, let's go in. I'll prepare a welcome meal just like the master of the house deserves," Martha announced, happier now.

"You don't need to prepare one of your meals…" Lasgol started to say, but Martha stopped him short with a dismissive wave of her hand.

"The master is back home after a long time away. The least I can do is prepare a worthy welcome meal for him."

"You really don't…"

"Say no more. I'll go to the butcher's right away for a good cut of meat."

Lasgol did not insist, because he knew that regardless of what he said, Martha was going to cook a banquet for him. He resigned himself gratefully.

"I'll settle Trotter in the stable and come right in," he told Martha.

"I can do that."

Lasgol shook his head and smiled kindly.

"A Ranger should always take care of his mount before resting. In my case, my horse and my familiar," he said, indicating Ona. "I'm a Beast Whisperer, and that's how I've been taught."

"Fine, I'll be inside," she replied as she went back into the house. Lasgol knew it would be spotless, but Martha would give it a last inspection before he came in. She insisted on everything being in place, to the last detail.

You'll be fine here, Lasgol transmitted to Trotter after making sure he had hay, straw, water and that he was comfortable.

Trotter snorted and shook his head up and down in recognition.

Trotter happy, Camu messaged.

Yes, he likes being home. And you?

I happy. Like home much.

That makes me happy. And what about you, Ona? You like it?

Ona chirped once and licked the back of Lasgol's hand.

I see you do. Let's go inside and rest.

They reached the house and Lasgol stood at the entrance, considering the door. It was the door of a Norghanian manor—wide, high, and robust—but he had doubts.

Are you going to be able to fit through? he asked Camu.

I fit, the creature confirmed.

You sure?

Try and see.

Well, yes, I guess that's the only way to find out.

Lasgol opened the door and went in, leaving it wide open. Camu went in after him and managed to barely make it through, lowering his head.

Good, for a moment there I had my doubts, Lasgol transmitted to the creature as he shut the door so no one could see Camu from the outside.

Become visible? Camu asked Lasgol.

Yeah, you'd better so Martha won't be startled when you communicate with her. It's always easier when you can see who's speaking to you, even if it's not vocally.

"Come, come…" Martha started to say as she came downstairs. She stopped short, staring at Camu. "Oh my, you're huge!"

I grow, he messaged, along with a feeling of pride.

"I can see that. You're twice as big as the last time I saw you!"

"Yeah, he's grown a little…"

"The color of your scales has changed too, or does it only seem like that?

"Yeah, they're more silver," Lasgol confirmed.

I older, Camu messaged to Martha.

"Oh yes I do believe so, and Ona looks more grown up too, stronger I'd say."

Ona growled once and stood as tall as she could.

"They're both growing. They're no longer pups," Lasgol said with a smile.

"I'll clear some space in the living room so Camu and Ona can be comfortable. I wonder whether Camu will be able to climb the stairs to the bedrooms."

I try, Camu messaged, and he headed to the stairs. A moment later he was going up them.

"He seems to fit," Martha smiled.

"Thank goodness, otherwise he'd burst the handrails," Lasgol replied.

Martha laughed, "Don't let him lie down on any of the beds, he'll surely break them."

Martha and Lasgol moved some chairs and one of the living room tables to leave a wide area free for Camu and Ona to lie down in at will.

"Are you all right here?" she asked them.

Be very well, Camu messaged as he lay down, stretching.

Ona chirped once and lay down beside her brother.

"I'll go to the village to buy food, and when I return, I'll make something delicious for each one of you."

"You're a blessing of the Ice Gods!" Lasgol said gratefully.

"You are the blessing here. How proud Mayra would be if she could see you, all grown up into a fine young man. And so would Dakon."

"Thank you, Martha."

"It's the truth, there's no need to be thankful. I'm off to the market, be right back."

"We'll rest while we wait for you," Lasgol said with a smile. "I'm so happy to be back home."

"As you should be." She returned the smile and left.

Lasgol felt comfortable here in his home, his parents' home, where he had grown up. He left Ona and Camu downstairs resting and went upstairs to his own room. He looked at the big bed and the wardrobe where he could put his clothes in and smiled. Rangers seldom slept in beds and traveled very light. First, he left his weapons on top of the chest in front of the bed. He placed the bows carefully: the composite and the short one, and leaned the quiver full of arrows against the wall beside it. Then he took out his Ranger knife and axe and also left them on the chest; he needed to sharpen them at some point.

He took off his Ranger Specialist's hooded cloak and hung it in the wardrobe. He took out his other set of clothes and cloak and put them in there too. The wardrobe was enormous and looked even larger with the few clothes he owned inside it.

He looked at himself in the full-length mirror on the right of the wardrobe and felt naked without his weapons and cloak. He was tempted to put them all back on but remembered where he was, at home and safe, and that he did not need to. He studied his reflection and thought he looked older than he remembered. He examined himself... yes, he looked more mature. Perhaps it was the exhaustion of the journey and the tension of the last mission. He did not feel any different from the last time he had been home, but Martha had told him he looked older too.

He shrugged. Aging was natural, just like Ona and Camu maturing and growing. He waved it aside. That was life. Time went by, and with each experience you grew up and changed—both in looks and in character, even if it was hard to see and realize. He wondered whether his friends had the same feeling; they probably did. The funny thing was that when he thought of his friends, he saw them unchanged. It was hard to notice how they were changing. Then he thought about how they had first met, at the river on their way to the Camp, and then he had to admit that they had changed, a lot. They had all grown up and matured. And they would go on doing so with every season and every experience they lived through. You could not stop time, no matter how much you might want to. Then he checked himself; surely somewhere in Tremia, some sorcerer, powerful mage, or magical creature must be trying to at that same instant. More so, they might have already succeeded. He shrugged and smiled. Everything was possible in this world, and that was what made it so amazing.

He went on undressing and took off the leather pouch he carried tied to his Ranger belt. He kept the Orb in it, placing it inside the wardrobe without unwrapping it to take a peek at the Object of Power. He only wanted to keep it safe. He would have to tell Martha not to touch it under any circumstance, she would surely want to clean it along with his clothes as she always did when he was home, and he did not want her to accidentally touch the orb and run into disaster. He thought again and went to the working desk on the other end of the room. He remembered it had a large drawer with a lock; he opened it and put the Orb inside. Then he locked it and put the key in his pocket. That way there would be no trouble.

He lay down on the bed, and it was so comfortable that all at once he felt like closing his eyes and sleeping. He allowed himself to drift off and fell soundly asleep. He dreamed of when he was a little boy and lived in the house with his mother and father, about better times, about when they were all happy. The feelings were so pleasant that he slept like a baby and managed to rest deeply, something he had not been able to do in a long time. He was home safe, and he felt wonderful.

Chapter 9

The light of noon came in through the window. It reached Lasgol's eyes and woke him up. He felt restored, as if he had been sleeping for days, but when he looked out the window, he realized he had only been asleep for a short while. He felt well rested though and with a clear head, which he was really grateful for.

All of a sudden, he had a strange feeling, as if some past memory was trying to come to the surface. It puzzled him. Unconsciously he reached for his mother's pendant, the Memory Marker he always wore around his neck. He never took the enchanted jewel off. It had great emotional value for him. He believed it somehow protected him in his path through life. He liked to think that his mother helped him through the pedant. It was a way for him to feel close to her.

Then, as he thought about the jewel, it gave a blue flash. Lasgol was surprised. He had not expected that to happen. He held it in his open hand. He thought of moistening his eye to shed a tear on the jewel as he had used to do when he wanted to call upon some memory, but he remembered what had happened with Izotza, the Lady of the Glaciers, at the Frozen Continent. He recalled her words when she had assured him that, because he shared his mother's blood, he could use the pedant with his own magic.

He decided to follow Izotza's advice. The blue flash that had already occurred, also seemed to indicate he should follow that course. He remembered he had to ask the jewel to show him the memory he wanted and do so with true will. He took a deep breath and as he let the air out, he concentrated and wished with all his heart to see his parents there with him. The nostalgia he was feeling at being back home was so great that it overwhelmed him, and that was what he wished for.

He used his power, his inner magic, to transmit his wish to the pendant, as if he were communicating with the enchanted object. Not knowing exactly how to do it, he turned to a skill he did know: *Animal Communication*. Only, in this case, instead of communicating with the mind of an animal, he would try to do so with the jewel's magic. He was not too sure it would work, since he had already tried to use this skill on people and failed miserably. On the other hand, he had to trust Izotza and what she had taught him. He wished the Lady of the Glaciers were there to help him, but unfortunately, he would have to manage on his own.

He called upon his skill, using his Gift and consuming his inner energy. He focused on the pendant. The skill failed and did not become activated. Lasgol sighed—he had expected as much. He had not even been able to visualize the power of the object to try and interact with it. He was not discouraged but kept trying for a while. Every attempt he made failed. Lasgol knew that to make it work he had to see the pendant's power, and this gave him an idea. He had already developed a skill that allowed him to see auras, including those of power: *Aura Presence*.

He shut his eyes and concentrated. He changed his strategy and called first upon *Aura Presence* to catch the object's aura of power. To his surprise, the skill worked. He found a blue aura made by the object it surrounded. What it radiated was really its power. It shone with double intensity, like two intertwined auras. Lasgol observed the phenomenon, trying to guess what it meant. He thought for a moment, and the only thing that occurred to him was that the object not only had an enchantment but also stored magic. Magic which undoubtedly was his mother's. Lasgol guessed she had imbued magic in the jewel so it would store memories and later allow visualizations of them through the spells she had also put on the object.

He sighed. He did not know if he was right. Maybe the two auras meant something different, but there was no way he could know. Lasgol trusted his hunches and instincts though, so he decided that had to be the explanation. He would tell Egil about it when he saw him again to see what he thought. Since he could already see the pendant's aura, he decided to use his *Animal Communication* skill again to try to somehow transfer his will to the pendant as he did with Ona and Trotter. This was going to be more complicated because it was a magical object, but there was nothing to lose in trying.

He concentrated on the pendant and tried to interact through the skill he had called upon. Surprisingly, since he had failed so far, there was a green flash and he consumed energy from his inner pool. This encouraged him, and he took for granted that he had summoned his *Animal Communication* skill. Still, the flash and the feeling when summoning the skill had felt weird, different from what he was used to when he called upon this skill.

He focused his energy on interacting with the jewel's aura of power, and it reacted emitting a blue flash. Lasgol threw his head back with surprise but did not lose the link he had created between his mind and the object's aura. He had to send it an order, so he thought of something easy that would tell him whether the link had been created and was working. He thought for an instant and made a choice: he wished to witness one of his mother's memories of the same room where he was now.

Wishing hard, he asked the object to show him. He sent more inner energy to strengthen the link and emphasized the wish, making it almost an order. A new blue flash came from the jewel, and to his immense joy an image began to take shape in front of him in the middle of the room. It started on the floor and gathered shape in the middle of what looked like a gray mist which contained the memory.

He could see his mother, kneeling there by the bed, dressing a little boy. He realized the boy was himself; he was seeing himself with his mother. He found it surreal, since the memory was taking place right in front of him and seemed to overlap the real scene. He watched what went on.

"Why do you have to leave?" Lasgol asked his mother.

"I must deal with an urgent matter," she explained, buttoning his shirt.

His father, Dakon, appeared in the image. He was coming into the room.

"Everything's ready," he told Mayra.

"Thank you, Dakon," she replied and looked at him lovingly.

"Can't anyone else go in your place so you can stay?" Lasgol asked his mother.

"Sorry, sweetheart, it has to be me," Mayra said, standing and kissing Lasgol on the top of his head.

"Your mother will soon be back, don't worry," Dakon told him.

"Okay…" Lasgol said resignedly with his head down.

To cheer him up his father said, "While your mother's away, I'll take you hunting and teach you how to get better with the bow."

"I don't know if I'll ever get better with the bow…"

"Of course, you will. If you practice, you'll always get better at whatever it is. So, go practice," his mother said, smiling as she tousled his blond hair with her hand.

Lasgol smiled, and holding his parents' hands, he left the room.

The memory began to fade before his eyes. The mist thinned until the image vanished completely. He did not feel sad when the memory ended, which surprised him. He was happy to have been able to view that scene of his past. To have shared that moment with his father and mother. It was an event that had occurred when he was so little, he had forgotten it. It pleased him to no end to be able to interact with the magical object.

He realized he had developed a new skill, different from the ones he already had. He could now interact with Objects of Power, influence them with his will. At least with some objects, like the pendant. He did not know though whether he would be able to do it with other magical objects. He would have to look into that. Lasgol was not drawn to the idea of interacting with external magic, it was most likely dangerous. Manipulating Objects of Power, runes, and things of a similar nature could quickly end in a fatal accident. He would have to tread carefully with this new skill.

He wondered what to call it. He turned it over in his head and finally decided on *Arcane Communication*. Egil would surely find it fascinating. Lasgol could not help smiling at the thought.

Suddenly, a message reached Lasgol's mind.

People come. Hear footsteps house door, Camu warned him.

I'll be right down, Lasgol transmitted back as he left the room in a hurry and ran downstairs.

I camouflage, Camu messaged.

It's probably Martha coming back from the market, Lasgol transmitted, coming out into the corridor.

More than one person, Camu warned.

Lasgol stood at the door of the house after dodging Camu, who he guessed had stood in a corner. Lasgol used his *Animal Presence* skill and detected two people on the other side of the door.

Good hearing, he congratulated Camu.

The door started to open, and Lasgol took a step back. He realized he did not have his weapons—he had left them upstairs. He shook his head. He did not know why he had thought about them. He did not need to fear anything. He was at home, he had to relax. Being constantly surrounded by danger in his adventures made him act this way subconsciously, out of reflex. Yet there was no need in this situation: nothing bad was going to happen to him in his own home

The door opened and a large figure fell upon him with a frightening roar. Lasgol stepped aside to avoid the person. The next thing he saw was a large man who looked like a roaring bear right by his side. He managed to look at him better once the initial startle was over and noticed the crutch he was leaning on.

"Lasgol! My boy!" the man greeted him, slapping him hard on the back.

"Ulf!" cried Lasgol, recovering from the veteran soldier's assault.

"Of course it's me! Who else would it be?"

"An enraged bear?" Lasgol asked, arching one eyebrow with the ghost of a smile.

"As for manners, absolutely," Martha commented as she came into the house after Ulf. "I met him at the village square. He already knew you were back and came at a speed I could barely keep up with."

Lasgol pictured the scene and a big smile came to his face.

"Give me a proper hug, like a true Norghanian!" the retired soldier demanded.

Lasgol smiled and met Ulf's hug, who squeezed him so hard that for a moment he thought his back was going to break.

"I see… you're still… going strong…" Lasgol stammered.

"Of course I am! Infantry soldiers keep going strong to the grave!"

"And keep shouting as if everyone around were deaf," Martha said as she went into the kitchen to put down her shopping.

"We must speak with energy. Only then do they listen to you in the north," Ulf said, modulating his tone.

"You look well," Lasgol said jovially, seeing that Ulf was unchanged, as rough and like an unleashed hurricane as when he had opened his door to Lasgol when he was a boy.

"So do you, Ranger!" Ulf said, giving him another tight hug that lifted him off the floor. Lasgol could not understand how the one-eyed, crippled soldier managed to keep his balance with his crutch under his arm and him in the air. And with all the alcohol he already had in his system, his breath was like that of a fire dragon.

"If you don't put me down, we won't be able to greet one another in a more civilized manner," Lasgol said to see whether Ulf would put him down, although he did not have much hope.

"This is the civilized greeting of a good Norghanian! Of an infantry man!" he roared without letting go of Lasgol.

Martha poked her head out of the kitchen door and frowned.

"Ulf, will you please put Lasgol down? That's no way to treat the master of the house," she scolded in a stern tone.

"Okay…" Ulf said resignedly as he put Lasgol down. "Don't let it be said that I don't respect the Master of Eklund in his own home," he said and winked at Lasgol as he bowed, leaning on his crutch.

"It makes me happy to see you so well, Ulf," Lasgol said, hugging him fondly once again.

"And why shouldn't I be well?" Ulf asked with a look that said it could not be otherwise.

"Well… time, the hard life… you know…" Lasgol tried to argue.

"What time and what hard life!" Ulf thundered. "That's all nonsense from the proud, square-headed Rogdonians!"

"Come on, you don't really take good care of yourself…" Lasgol replied.

"Of course, I take good care of myself! I take my muscle relaxant every day and it rejuvenates me!" he cried, as if drinking wine were a cure for aging.

"You drink too much, and it's going to bring you trouble!" they heard Martha shout from the kitchen. "Now don't pretend in front of Lasgol!"

"I'm not pretending anything! True Norghanians lead my lifestyle!" he said, entirely pleased with the way he lived life.

Martha's face appeared again at the kitchen door. She examined Ulf from head to toe. "Your lifestyle is the last a Norghanian should lead," she said, pointing the knife she was chopping onions with at him.

Ulf raised both hands without losing his balance.

"What delicious delicacy are you making today?" he asked her with a sweet smile and tone, as if all of a sudden, the wild bear had become a playful puppy.

Martha snorted, shook her head, and vanished into the kitchen.

"Maybe Lasgol will manage to get some reason into that thick, stubborn soldier's head of yours."

Lasgol chuckled.

"She's upset because I spend time at the inn, finding out everything that goes on in the area and its surroundings. That's where you get all the useful information, from the travelers, traders, soldiers, and people passing by.

"And having more than a couple of drinks," Martha added as she appeared and began to set the table.

"Of course. I have to keep my body warm, and also, to have interesting conversations you have to grease the throat—your own and that of others," Ulf smiled. As Lasgol watched him closely he once again had the characteristic feeling that he was before a mountain bear turned into an infantry soldier.

Lasgol tried to help Martha set the table, but she pushed him aside with both hands.

"I'll do it, it's my job."

"Let me help…" Lasgol said.

"The master of the house doesn't set the table. How dishonorable that would be!" she replied, shaking her head adamantly.

"It's no dishonor. The master of the house wants to help."

Martha looked at him for a moment. "Bring the water from the kitchen if you insist, but nothing else."

"Thank you," Lasgol smiled at her.

"Bring me a bottle of wine," Ulf added.

"I see some things don't change," Lasgol said, smiling.

"Why should they change?" Ulf asked blankly, not understanding what was wrong with what he did and why there was any reason for change.

"I'm glad to see that everything's the same," Lasgol whispered into Ulf's ear so that Martha would not hear.

"I'm going to cook the meal now. Make yourselves comfortable," she said as she disappeared into the kitchen again.

Lasgol brought the water and set it on the table.

Ulf saw Ona behind the table. "Well, the kitty has grown," he cried.

The snow panther growled at him.

"She doesn't like it when you call her a kitty. She's a big cat, a powerful one, not a kitten," Lasgol explained.

"Bah, nonsense! She's a kitty to me," he said and made sounds as if he were calling a kitten.

Ona stood with her tail stiff and the fur on her back pricked. She growled at him menacingly.

"You're not going to gain her friendship like that."

"Who says I want to be friends with a wild mountain cat? No way. That's all Ranger nonsense. A Norghanian soldier doesn't befriend snow kitties—he skins them and eats them for dinner."

Lasgol put his hand to his forehead and shook his head.

"That's preposterous, don't pay him any attention," Lasgol told Ona.

"That's life in the army. You Rangers are weaklings," Ulf stated and went to the side table where he knew there was liquor, since Lasgol had not brought him the wine.

"I see you still have the same ideas," Lasgol told him. "I swear, regarding the Rangers you're completely wrong."

"Let me pour myself a drink and you tell me about your latest adventures, see if you persuade me to the contrary," Ulf said while he searched for a bottle to his taste.

"Now that I remember, where's the other creature? That enormous lizard with bulging eyes?"

Camu made himself visible beside Ona and rose so Ulf could see him easily.

"By all the Ice Gods!" Ulf cried, and the bottle of liquor slipped from his hands, startled at Camu's sudden appearance.

Lasgol saw the bottle fly, land on the table, and slide along it. Lasgol slid on the wooden floor, reaching out with his right leg and arm as he moved. He caught the bottle as it fell, two hand-spans from crashing on the floor.

"Got it," he panted, and was left with split legs holding the bottle in his right hand.

"Great reflexes, and even better flexibility. You saved the bottle, thank goodness! It's a very good old liquor," Ulf congratulated him, impressed.

"Thanks," Lasgol replied, putting the bottle on the table.

"The lizard is huge! What are you feeding it? Zangrians?"

"Camu doesn't eat humans, Ulf."

"Well, Zangrians aren't considered humans in quite a few places," he joked as he poured himself a drink.

"You really are something…" Lasgol said, shaking his head.

"They're ugly brawling dwarves; they don't qualify as humans."

Humans they are and ugly too, Camu messaged.

"By the icebergs of the northern sea!" Ulf cried, and he jolted, splashing himself in the face with the liquor he was going to drink.

Funny, Camu messaged.

Ona grunted once in agreement.

"The lizard is speaking to me!"

"Indeed he is," Lasgol confirmed.

"But that's impossible! He's a lizard!"

"He's no lizard, he's a Drakonian, a Creature of the Ice. He has powerful magic."

I more than dragon.

"He's speaking inside my head!" Ulf cried excitedly. His beard and hair shook like crazy.

"It's how he communicates."

"And why in the Snow Trolls name doesn't he speak normally like everyone else?"

"Because he's a special creature," Lasgol explained.

I very special. I powerful, Camu added.

"Get him to stop talking inside my head! This is insane!"

"Don't worry, it's not as if you were very well up there, it won't affect you," said Martha, who had come to fetch some of the good plates.

You not like I speak? Camu messaged to him.

Ulf took half a step back and stared at Camu.

"But if it speaks… that means it can think… right?"

"Of course he thinks, Ulf. He's an intelligent creature," said Lasgol.

I very intelligent.

"This is… very weird… I need a drink," Ulf said, taking the bottle and drinking directly from it without a glass.

Lasgol could not help smiling. For Ulf this was some kind of witchcraft.

"You'll get used to it, don't worry."

"I'm not so sure… I've seen my share of strange things in my years as a soldier, but this is the weirdest thing I've ever witnessed," he said and drank from the bottle again.

"I'd better tell you about our latest adventures. I'm sure you'll enjoy them," said Lasgol.

"I'd also like to hear them," Martha said from the kitchen.

"Of course. I'll tell you both while we eat."

"Wonderful, dinner will be ready soon," she announced.

Ulf managed to calm down with his fourth swig from the bottle and sat at the table. He grew even more relaxed when Lasgol asked him about the latest news regarding the kingdom and the rumors about King Thoran and the court. Ulf cheered up at once and told him all he had heard at the inn. Some of the things were interesting, like the problems the King was having with the nobles because they did not collect what he asked of them, which showed he was short on gold. There were rumors that the King was looking for alliances with the eastern kingdoms since he had not been lucky with Rogdon, the Nocean Empire, Zangria, and Erenal. It appeared that these kingdoms did not want to become Thoran's allies for various reasons, but mostly because they did not trust him. They also thought Norghana was weak at the moment and they could seize the opportunity to try and conquer it. Nothing more appetizing for a powerful kingdom than a weakened one.

"Do you think they'll dare invade Norghana?" Lasgol asked, interested by the rumor.

"This old soldier has seen many wars. Let me tell you that the right question isn't whether they'll dare, but *who* will and when."

"Oh… then you think war is inevitable? That's bad news," Lasgol put his hands to his head.

"Nothing's granted in this life, my boy. Never forget that. What I'm saying is that either our dear King will need to move fast, or any of the other military powers of Tremia will set its paw on his kingdom."

"Then he can still fix the situation?" Lasgol asked hopefully.

"It's possible. Norghana will be difficult to conquer because of its geography and bad weather, but if King Thoran doesn't manage to make the country strong again—economically solvent with a fearsome army—it will be crushed by the other kingdoms. It's happened before, and it'll happen again if nothing's done."

"It seems like a cyclical fight for power that never ends," Lasgol said.

"I don't understand politics or cycles, but I do know that strong kingdoms crush weak ones. So, it has been from the beginning. That isn't going to change in the near future."

"I don't understand that lust for power…."

"That's because you're a good lad," said Ulf, putting a hand on Lasgol's shoulder. "Don't change. Don't let war and evil, or rotten men change you. I swear there are many, in all the kingdoms. Stay away from them. Don't let them contaminate your good heart."

"I'll try…"

"And remember that just as today, Norghana is weakened by the civil war between the east and the west and the conflicts with the Frozen Continent, tomorrow it could be strong again. And then what do you think might happen?"

"Norghana will try to conquer a weaker kingdom…"

Ulf nodded hard. "Just as I was once called Ulf the Ogre! If Thoran manages to build up a strong Norghana again he'll go after Rogdon, or Zangria, even after Erenal. Never doubt it. Such are kings, and so they forge their kingdoms."

Lasgol snorted, "Wow…"

"But let's talk of happier things," said Ulf as he strained his nose to take in the delicious aromas coming from the kitchen where Martha was preparing a banquet. She had already served Camu a huge dish of fresh vegetables from the garden and Ona a nice big ox steak, which she was devouring with gusto. What they were about to enjoy was going to be even more exquisite, and they could not wait to try it.

They were not wrong.

Chapter 10

Lasgol slept till almost noon and woke up feeling refreshed. The truth was that being home suited him wonderfully. He had been chatting with Ulf well into the night and had slept the rest of the night through. He remembered that poor Martha had gone to bed well before they had, looking exhausted and unable to keep her eyes open. Lasgol had told them everything that had happened to the Snow Panthers since the last time he had been home with them.

Now that he thought about it, he realized that he and his friends had undergone many and varied experiences which he found hard to explain in a way they could understand. Martha and Ulf already knew many of their previous adventures, but these last few had been difficult to explain. He did not tell them about Camu and his new skills in detail, simply mentioning them in passing. For now, he would rather be cautious with what he said about the matter.

He got dressed and went downstairs, a little embarrassed about waking up so late. It was not worthy of a Ranger. They always had to get up before sunrise.

"Good morning!" a thundering voice greeted him.

"Ulf! I thought you went home to sleep last night when I went upstairs to bed. You stayed?" Lasgol asked, surprised to see him at the table eating breakfast nonchalantly.

"Well, it was my intention to go home to sleep. I got to the main door and, you see, my balance wasn't too good. I believe there was a storm with high winds last night and that made me lose my balance."

"Last night there was too much alcohol in your body and a storm in your head, you foolish soldier," said Martha, coming out of the back room with a bucket full of water and some rags.

"Well yeah… that might've been it too…" Ulf shrugged.

Martha stopped beside the retired soldier and put her hand on his shoulder.

"The great soldier here, of the renowned Norghanian infantry, had the liquor go up to his head and he couldn't go home. He turned back at the gate and fell asleep beside poor Camu. I found him snoring this morning when I woke up. It was quite a scene, Ulf snoring on top of Camu's stomach and Camu's tail covering him."

Lasgol chuckled at the thought.

"You know what they say, joyful evenings, great mornings," Ulf said, smiling and waving the matter aside.

Ulf snore loud, Camu messaged Lasgol as he lay in front of the table eating fruit.

Yes, I know, it's a deafening sound.

Barely sleep. Ona either.

Ona chirped mournfully.

I'm sorry. He snores as if he were sawing a whole forest with his nose.

Three forests, Camu added.

"Sit and have breakfast with me," Ulf said to Lasgol, pushing the chair beside him, "then we can go to see Chief Gondar and his assistant Limus. They'll be happy to see you. Well, that's if you feel like it and have no other plans."

"That's a good idea. Besides, they'll be able to tell me what's been going on in the County."

"And in the West. Gondar is regularly summoned to Count Malason's castle for meetings where they deal with county matters but also political." Ulf winked his one eye at him. "I've told you everything I hear at the inn, but I'm sure Gondar will have more information."

"Perfect. It'll be good to catch up. We've been at the Shelter training for a long time, and that always makes me lose touch with current affairs."

"One should always be up to date with what goes on in the kingdom," Ulf said, winking again.

"Now that I think of it, I invited Chief Gondar and Limus to come by for a visit. They might do that."

"I wouldn't count on it, with the Chief so busy. Better catch him when he goes home for lunch."

"That's what you do?"

Ulf gave a great guffaw. "That's right. The Chief never misses a meal."

It was noon by the time Ulf and Lasgol arrived at the village square. Lasgol had left Ona and Camu at home so as not to have a crowd following them wherever they went, although Lasgol drew a lot of curiosity himself among the locals.

Just as Ulf had foreseen, they met Gondar as he was arriving at his house. He was dragging a man by one arm. By the way Gondar was pushing him, the man's resistance, and the fact that he was gagged, it appeared the Chief was taking him into custody.

"Howdy, Chief! Want any help?" Ulf offered.

"Oh hello, Ulf, Lasgol," the Chief nodded at them. "No need, I think I can manage," he said and stopped beside them.

"What has this poor wretch done?" Ulf asked, looking the prisoner up and down with his one good eye.

"Public disorder," Gondar said, looking at Ulf, "your favorite misdemeanor."

"Hey! I've done nothing this time," Ulf replied defensively.

"This time. How many times have I taken you into custody for public disorder?"

"More than I care to remember," Ulf grinned.

"Yeah, many more," Gondar said, chiding, although his tone made it obvious he did not really mind Ulf's shenanigans in the village.

"Doesn't look as if this one's up to much public disorder," Ulf commented, jabbing his thumb at the man.

Lasgol looked at the man and had to agree with Ulf. He was an old man, with untidy white hair and a beard, and he was skinny; from his ragged tunic he looked like a beggar. Gondar had him gagged, which was strange. The Chief was carrying a leather bag in his other hand which must belong to the prisoner. The Chief looked like a strongman compared to the pauper.

"You'd be surprised," Gondar replied.

"Is he a beggar?" Lasgol asked, finding an arrest a bit excessive.

"He's a preacher, the kind who preaches about the end of the world. We've been seeing more of those lately. I don't like them at all," Gondar said, shaking his head.

"Preaching about the end of the world?" Lasgol asked blankly.

"Yes. They go from village to village, announcing the end of times is near and similar disasters. They put fear in the hearts of the people. Bad business."

"Oh, I had no idea…" said Lasgol.

"They come and go every now and then. Don't ask me why. It's been a while since they were last seen. They've left us in peace for years, but they're back again. They're a pest. Count Malason warned us; he doesn't want them in the County. We are to arrest them and throw them out of his land."

"But do they belong to any specific religion?" Lasgol asked. He didn't see any symbol or rune that might identify the man as belonging to any religion, local or foreign.

Gondar shrugged. "Wouldn't know. Not of any known religion, that's for sure. They don't mention it openly either."

"Curious…." Lasgol was intrigued. Almost everyone in Norghana believed in the Ice Gods and prayed to them. There were some Ice Temples located throughout Norghana where you could go and pray. They were looked after by Ice Priests who rarely left these temples and spent their days praying to the Gods and asking for their grace. They were easy to spot because they wore long white robes and their hair and beards were also white as snow. They resembled Ice Magi, only that instead of carrying elaborate white staves with jewels of power at their tips, like the magi, the priests carried simple white cedar staves. It was said that the gods listened to the pleas of those who went to the temples and prayed with the Ice Priests. Lasgol had never visited a temple; all of a sudden, he felt the urge to visit one and see what they were like. There was one at each corner of the kingdom plus the one in the center, a massive one in the capital. Lasgol thought he should visit it the next time he was in Norghania. He was not one to blindly believe in the gods, but a little help was always more than welcome.

"They're like birds of ill omen. Better they preach their miseries and catastrophic disasters away from here," Gondar said.

"Let him speak. I want to hear what nonsense he utters," Ulf said to Gondar.

"You sure? He only goes on and on about the end of Tremia," Gondar replied.

"I'd like to hear what he has to say as well," Lasgol said, feeling for some reason that he should hear what the man was claiming.

"Okay. They're your ears," Gondar said with a warning look. He took the gag off so the man could speak.

All at once the man started crying out, as if the fact that he had been gagged to stop him from delivering his message to the masses forced him to do so as fast as he could now.

"And the sky and the earth will burn with the fire of a thousand volcanoes that will obliterate the disloyal, the impure, all those who do not embrace the new order. The end of the era of men is about to come. With every dawn the end is closer. Men will fall and a new era will take over Tremia, over the whole world. Only those of ancient blood will survive and share the new world with the lords of fire!"

"Wow, he does talk," said Ulf.

"The message is somewhat disturbing…" Lasgol said as he watched the man preaching to the heavens as if possessed.

"That's why I made him shut up. He was scaring the children and the old wives of the village," Gondar snapped.

"And you say there are more like him?" Lasgol asked him.

"Yes, that's what the Count told us. Apparently, they come from Rogdon and Zangria."

"Well, this wretch looks Norghanian. At least he speaks our language without a foreign accent," said Ulf.

"No kingdom will be saved. They will all perish under the flames. Rogdon will burn, and with them, the proud lords of the West will burn too. Norghana and all the north will burn—the whole empire will burn. The deserts of the Nocean Empire will burn. The kingdoms of Zangria, Erenal, Irinel, and Tremia will burn. The great State Cities of the East will burn. Everything will burn before the new order settles and the new Masters rule!"

"What a cheerful message this cretin announces," Ulf said. "Can I punch him so he shuts up?"

"No, Ulf. You can't punch my prisoners. Well, you can't punch anyone for that matter, you know that…"

"I forget…. My memory, you know…" Ulf said, smiling, as if that were really true.

"Yeah… you pretend. There's nothing wrong with your memory. The thing is you're a troublemaker."

"Me? No way," Ulf replied, looking offended.

Limus came to them from the chief's house. A group of locals had gathered around them to see what was going on.

"Oh, it's the crier," Limus said, recognizing him.

"And from the embers of the obliterated kingdoms a new world will emerge where those loyal and of ancient blood will live a new life. The disloyal, those who oppose the new dawn of fire, will end up burnt. Reduced to ashes!"

"I'd better gag him again, he's making people nervous," Gondar said, looking around and noticing that the locals were listening to the man, horrified and worried.

"His cell is ready," Limus said.

"Yeah, and my head's beginning to hurt with so much nonsense," Ulf moaned. "So much fire burning and razing everything."

The preacher looked up at the sky and went on speaking, aware that they were going to make him shut up. He addressed his message to the locals who were watching.

"The end of days is near. The great awakening is already happening. The new era is close, and the time of men comes to an end. The great journey will soon take place. The lords of fire will return to rule over all Tremia in their own right!"

Gondar snorted. Tired of hearing him, the Chief put the man's gag back on and dragged him to the house to lock him in the cellar jail. Ulf and Lasgol went with him. Gondar locked the preacher up without taking the gag off. The following day they would escort him out of the Count's lands with a warning never to return.

Lasgol, Ulf, Gondar, and Limus chatted about current affairs for a while, until two men came looking for the Chief. Apparently there had been a fight at the northern mine and they needed Gondar to go and establish peace before things got uglier and they ended up burning the mine. Once Norghanians started a fight they did not know when to stop.

"See you soon, Lasgol, take care," Gondar said.

"You too, take good care of yourself and the village," Lasgol replied.

"I will, don't worry." The Chief ran off to get his shield and axe.

"Don't worry, as long as Gondar is here, the village is well protected and cared for," Limus assured.

Lasgol knew this, and he felt easier.

"I'm also here. I'll make sure everything goes well," Ulf told Lasgol with a slap on his back.

"I'm not sure it's that so good for *us*..." muttered Limus ironically and winked at Lasgol, who laughed out loud.

"Of course it's good! You ought to be happy to have an infantry soldier looking after the village!"

"Retired soldier," Limus noted.

"A veteran with great experience!" Ulf said, puffing out his chest.

"Of course, it's a blessing for the village…. You hardly ever cause fights, conflicts, etcetera…" Limus said, looking comically at Lasgol.

"Trouble looks for me and finds me," Ulf said, making a fist.

"As I said, the village is in the best of hands," Limus said, smiling.

They chatted for a while longer and then left Limus. Ulf had some business at his house and headed there. Lasgol went back to his own. As he walked down the street, he thought about the strange preacher. The message he cried about had left Lasgol with an upset stomach. He was uncomfortable; he did not like the message of destruction at all. He tried to make nothing of it—most likely the poor man was crazy and merely divulging his insanity—but the fact that there were more like him with the same apocalyptic message made Lasgol uneasy and got him thinking.

Back home he played with Camu and Ona behind the house. No one could see them there because the stone wall was high. He also visited good old Trotter resting in the stable. Then he went inside to his room to be alone. He wanted to spend some time working on repairing the fragile bridge Izotza had created to join his mind with his inner pool of energy.

It was a tough task and not comforting, since he did not seem to make much headway. The reward for all his effort was minimal. But he knew he could not give up, because the bridge would break with time and he would lose a great part of his pool of power again. Besides, as the Lady of the Glaciers had told him, he was privileged, one of the few who could keep expanding his power. He had not been born with a limited source of power like most humans who had it. If the bridge broke, his pool of power would not continue to expand. He could not let that happen. He had to take advantage of a Gift of the Ice Gods.

In reality, he had doubts about the matter. He did not feel that his pool of energy was expanding, or that it ever had, which made him doubt that he might be one of those few chosen. On the other hand, he found it hard to believe that someone as powerful and wise as Izotza could be wrong. So, he had mixed feelings. What he could say with complete certainty was that he did not feel his inner pool growing. But it might be because he did not know how to make it grow. Izotza had told him to repair the bridge so the link between his mind and his energy would not break, but she had not told him what to do to make his power grow.

He shrugged. He would have to find out by himself somehow. The idea of having more inner energy and more power appealed to him. He would be able to call upon more skills, which in turn would be more powerful. In fact, he could develop new skills that were even better than the ones he already had. Well, providing he could find the way to develop his power, since so far, he had no idea how.

He had to relax and stop fantasizing, because this led him nowhere and did not help with the task at hand. Standing in front of the mirror, Lasgol looked at his reflection and cheered up. He would do it. Hard work always bore fruit sooner or later, he knew that. He shut his eyes and concentrated. It was difficult to see Izotza's magic in his mind. It was hard, and he despaired since it did not seem as if his efforts were bearing the desired result. He was not improving. He could not manage to locate its origin as he wished to.

To more easily identify Izotza's white magic in his mind, Lasgol used his *Aura Presence* skill on himself. This way he was able to see his three auras: his mind's, his body's, and his power's. Once identified, he focused on his mind's aura. Using his skill helped him and worked, just not as fast as he would want it to. He began to search for a snow-white spot in his mind amid all the green it was made up of.

Seeking out and identifying the spot which he knew was there took him an eternity, even with the help of the summoned skill. This was something Izotza had not warned him of. When he had done it with her the first time it had not been so hard. Now he realized it was likely because she had been helping him with her magic. Afterward, without her help, things had changed. It was not at all easy to find the beginning of the bridge, the end that was linked to his mind.

He braced himself and kept searching. He was going around every corner of his aura looking for the tiny white spot he knew he needed to find. The spot was never in the same place, which made him do an infinitesimal search of his aura. It was a long, tedious process, like looking for a needle in a haystack. It gradually sapped his patience and strength to keep going.

Lasgol was neither very patient nor stubborn, which went against him in this process. Those two qualities came in handy to do the task well. Yet he did not give up and went on analyzing every particle of his aura thoroughly. After a good while he finally found it. He examined the link and saw that the white spot seemed to arch and continue. There it was—there began the icy bridge that linked his mind to his pool of energy. He had no trouble following it from one end to the other once he had found it.

Now he had to repair the frozen link Izotza had created. He remembered her words: 'You must work every day to turn this white bridge into a green one, one that is of your own mind. As you progress, the bridge will change color.' If finding the bridge was hard, repairing it was a thousand times worse.

Magic was difficult and costly. Lasgol was beginning to understand this since he suffered it in his own flesh. In order to repair the bridge, he relied on another skill he had developed: *Ranger Healing*. With this skill he had been able to heal his aura from the influence of external magic and it had worked. It was a skill he still had not mastered completely and which he was still experimenting with. But he had been able to apply it to the frozen link, to the white bridge, and turn it green. It came slowly and exhausted him, all right, but he could change the bridge, which was in itself a victory.

At first Lasgol had not known what to do with the frozen bridge. He had tried to send energy into it directly, but this had not had any effect whatsoever. The only thing that had worked had been the *Ranger Healing* skill. The problem was that this method was painfully slow. To transform a white step of the bridge into a green one had taken him over four weeks of effort. What disheartened him so much was the fact that this bridge had over a thousand steps. He would never finish.

Once again, instead of being discouraged, he set to work. He focused on the next step and, calling upon his skill, sent energy to start transforming it. Concentrated, he worked for hours on the step until he used a great part of his inner energy. He stopped, exhausted, and checked to see if he had gotten somewhere. Part of the step was now green, but most of it was still white.

He snorted, opened his eyes, and looked in the mirror. He was aware that in order to move faster and achieve his purpose he would have to improve his *Ranger Healing* skill so it would allow him to transform more of each step in every session.

"I'll have to work on this skill, develop it," he said to himself.

Discouragement tried to overwhelm him, but he resisted. No one had said it would be easy. "I'll manage to make the link mine. I'll do it. No matter how long it takes."

Chapter 11

At nighttime, Lasgol came down for dinner. He opened his bedroom door to go out and saw that Camu and Ona were waiting right outside, on the landing. Camu was blocking almost the entire width of the corridor and Ona was behind him, both lying on their stomachs, resting peacefully. Camu was staring at the trap door that led to the attic.

Is something wrong? Lasgol asked him when he noticed and followed Camu's gaze.

Attic, go up.

You can't go up to the attic. You won't fit through the trap door. You've outgrown it.

I want go up, he messaged Lasgol with a feeling of melancholy.

You can't, not without making the trapdoor bigger.

Attic fun.

Yeah, because it's filled with things to play with, but you don't fit through the trapdoor. Besides, you're too old to play.

Camu stared at him, blinking hard. Then he tilted his head to the right.

Can't play?

Well, when you grow up, you stop playing.

Why?

Because you're older, and older people don't play.

Play fun.

I'm not saying it isn't, I'm just saying that when we grow up the time to play is over and we have to deal with serious and important things.

Playing important.

Lasgol was thoughtful. Camu was quite right. He scratched his head.

It is, particularly when one's growing up.

Always growing up.

Well yes… that's true. We continue growing up until we die.

Then play until we die, Camu reasoned.

Ona grunted once to show her agreement.

Lasgol looked at them both, and after a moment's thought he had to concede that they were right. Even he would like to continue playing and enjoying himself, forget about problems and obligations for a while. He shrugged.

You're right. We need to have fun and play until we die.

Camu was so cheered that he started doing his happy dance, flexing his four legs and wagging his long tail. He looked comical filling the whole of the corridor with his body, his tail bumping both walls.

Ona started dancing too. At least she was a bit more graceful, although not that much, especially when she wagged her bottom and tail from side to side.

Martha appeared right then coming up the stairs, and when she saw Camu and Ona dancing, she burst out laughing.

"You really have the most amusing friends," she told Lasgol, still laughing.

Dance fun, Camu messaged.

"Let's see how you do it..." Martha said, watching them for a moment and then imitating them.

Lasgol could not believe his eyes as he watched his housekeeper. The good woman was dancing, moving her behind and flexing her legs. If he had not been there looking at her, he would never have imagined it. He smiled and, driven by the joy they were all experiencing, he joined them. He began to imitate Camu and felt ridiculous, but then he heard Martha's laughter and the moment passed. He allowed himself to be carried away by the good mood and happiness of the moment and enjoyed himself like a small kid.

They danced and laughed until someone banged on the door. Judging by the noise, Lasgol knew it was Ulf coming for dinner.

"I'd better open the door before that brute knocks it down," Martha said, and she went downstairs to let him in.

That was good. It's good to play and have fun every now and then, Lasgol admitted to his friends.

Very good, Camu messaged, along with a feeling of happiness.

Ona grunted once, also happy.

Will you let me go down? Lasgol asked them.

Camu and Ona looked at one another, not really understanding what he meant. They were not aware of the space they took up, particularly Camu. Ona turned over and went down nimbly. Camu could not turn and had to retreat backward, moving his long tail, which Lasgol found hilarious. He covered his mouth so Camu would not see him smile; he did not want him to get upset.

"This kitty is vicious," Ulf said to Lasgol while he squeezed his hand.

"You didn't try to touch Ona, did you?" Lasgol asked when he noticed.

Ona was beside the front door with her back pricked and growling.

"She's a kitten, I stroked her."

"Oh, no… you shouldn't have, she doesn't trust you."

"Yeah, I realized that," Ulf said and showed Lasgol his hand with the scratch Ona had given him.

"I'm so sorry, Ulf, but you have to remember she's a great mountain cat."

"Don't worry, it's a simple scratch."

Lasgol went over to Ona and petted her soothingly.

Ona good, he transmitted to her, and with his petting she finally relaxed.

"I'll bring you a washbasin and something to disinfect that scratch. I wouldn't want it to get infected and have to cut off your arm," Martha said, going to the back of the house.

"Hah! That's all I needed. Take off half my arm! I already have half a leg less, and one eye—wow, I'd be a beauty."

Lasgol laughed out loud. "Indeed you would."

After tending to Ulf, they sat down to dinner. At Ulf's request, who wanted to know more about the Rangers, Lasgol told them what had happened during the Higher Training at the Shelter. He trusted both and knew they would not tell anyone. He made sure they understood that what he was telling them they needed to keep secret.

"Oh my, I'm sorry that happened to your friend," Martha said.

"He'll recover, I'm sure," Lasgol replied.

"I've always thought Rangers were strange and slippery. What you've just told us makes them even more twisted."

"They're not twisted, Ulf," Lasgol said defensively.

"Those things don't happen in the army. You train simply and directly, with your axe in one hand and your shield in the other. Blow by blow. Hit and block. Repeating until one of the two fighting can't get back up. As it should be. No craziness, mental scenarios and all that weird stuff."

"There's no craziness…"

"Of course there is!" he cried and put his finger to his temple and turned it, making a madman's face, something he did not have to work hard to do.

"And what about Elder Engla, will she recover too?" Martha asked with concern.

"Yes, we're sure Annika and Sigrid will manage to heal them both and we hope they won't have any serious consequences," Lasgol replied in a hopeful tone. "But it's going to take some time, I think."

Martha nodded.

"Things in the Norghanian infantry are simpler and work a lot better. You see the castle? So go and take the castle. You tear to shreds anyone who tries to stop you and that's it," Ulf said as he munched on a duck leg.

"Yeah, I see that things are done differently in the army…. More intelligently…" Lasgol commented, trying not to put too much sarcasm in his tone.

"What's really impressive is that you've got two additional specializations, even more so when it was so dangerous for your minds," Martha said. "What specialties do you have now?"

"Well, I have…" he put his hand in his shirt and started taking out his Specialist's medallions one by one. "Beast Whisperer, Tireless Tracker, Tireless Explorer, Forest Trapper, and Forest Survivor."

"That's amazing. Your father would be so proud."

"You really think so?" Lasgol had always wanted to make his father proud of his achievements, if he ever managed them. It was a wish that would never come true now.

"I'm positive," Martha said eagerly. "And so would your mother. I'm sure because I knew them so well, and I know you'd fill them with pride, both of them," she said and hugged him fondly.

"Thank you, Martha, that means a lot to me."

"And not only because of the Specializations, but because you're a good person, honest and principled. They'd be even prouder of that."

Lasgol nodded. He knew what Martha meant—it was not only the achievements, it was the person who mattered.

"I know it hurts that they're not here to show you," Ulf said in a paternal tone, something rare in the old soldier, which made Lasgol turn to look at him. "I'd be terribly proud if you were my son," he said and laid his hand on Lasgol shoulder.

"Ulf… thank you…" Lasgol muttered, touched by that rare show of affection in the old bear.

"Well, except for the fact that you enrolled in the Rangers instead of the infantry, and for that I'd probably have thrown you out," he said, all smiles, and downed a glass of wine.

Lasgol laughed and Martha joined him. The evening they enjoyed was so pleasant that Lasgol would remember it for a long time.

When morning came, Lasgol woke up with mixed feelings. He had had such a good time that he wanted to stay and go on enjoying evenings like the last. But unfortunately, he had to get going. Farewells awaited which he knew would be bittersweet. Sweet because of the love he was going to receive; bitter because they were farewells and he had to go away. He got ready, and while he gathered all his equipment, he tried to cheer himself up by thinking that he would soon see the Panthers.

When he was finished packing, he stood before the desk where he had put the orb. He thought of leaving it there under lock and key, or taking it up to the attic and leaving it among the hundreds of things there. He knew that taking it with him meant that sooner or later they would face problems because of the Object of Power. He was also aware that the orb was dangerous and could influence not only Camu, but whoever tried to manipulate it with magic.

He thought about it. He could hide the problem and forget about it. But, life had taught him that not facing up to problems led nowhere good. Problems did not just disappear by themselves. They went on to become bigger and unmanageable and explode in one's face at the worst possible moment. Hiding from trouble, running away from it, was not the solution. He would have to face problems and solve them, one way or another. It was the only way to follow a clear path.

He unlocked the drawer and carefully picked up the leather pouch where the orb was. He fastened it to one side of his Ranger belt, concealed by his cloak. He heaved a deep sigh. He now carried the problem on him, so he would have to deal with it. Luckily, he was not alone—the Panthers would help him solve it. This cheered him and gave him confidence. They would find a way to solve the problem the orb represented, the mystery, since there was still a lot they needed to find out and understand about this Object of Power.

He went downstairs to the living room and found Martha feeding Camu and Ona. He thought it was a touching scene. Both creatures were lying in the middle of the room. Martha had once again moved the dining table to a corner to give them more space. She was serving them a lunch they were both enjoying and was petting them as if they were two Norghanian mastiff puppies she was breeding to look after the property.

"Do you really have to go already?" she asked Lasgol with a sad face.

Lasgol sighed. He did not want to leave; he felt so well at home that leaving was the last thing he wanted. But he needed to see Gerd, make sure everything was going well. It did not seem right to remain at home any longer knowing that everything here was going well when he did not know how his friend was faring. Besides, he wanted to see Gerd and give him a big hug and cheer him up and try to help him in any way he could.

"Yeah... it's not that I want to leave, I feel happy and content at home, but I have to go and see a friend and deal with an important matter."

Can't all of it wait? Can't you stay a little longer?"

"I'd love to, but I have to go on my way," Lasgol said, spreading his hands in apology.

"Your visits are always so short..." Martha said regretfully, eyeing him fondly.

"A Ranger's life is busy and urgent," he smiled shyly.

"And yours especially," she replied, raising her eyebrows.

Lasgol shrugged. "Things happen to me... but they also happen to other comrades," Lasgol said, making light of it.

"I'm not sure it happens to all of them..." Martha said. "Be very careful out there. The world is a dangerous, ruthless place."

"Don't worry, Martha, I'll be careful."

"I know it's not my place... that I'm simply the housekeeper looking after the property when the Master's away. Maybe I shouldn't tell you, but as a friend of your mother's I feel it's my duty to say it..."

"Of course, you may say it, Martha. You're not just the

housekeeper, you're family to me. You may always speak freely to me. I truly appreciate and esteem your concern and affection for me."

"Thank you, Lasgol, you're a dear," she said and hugged him tenderly.

The front door opened and Ulf came in like a hurricane.

"Already hugging and kissing? The lad's going to soften that way," he scolded Martha.

"He won't soften because we show him some love, don't be daft," Martha retorted, upset.

"A true Norghanian only needs the stick, no petting, in order to become a good man," Ulf stated.

"That's utter nonsense, Ulf. Lasgol, don't you go paying any attention to him, he's living in another era."

"In an era when all true men made their way with axe blows, not like now when they're all weaklings," he said, waving his hand to indicate they were all good for nothing.

Lasgol found himself in the middle of their exchange, and he watched, amused. He knew that Ulf's mentality was that of a Norghanian who had spent over a hundred years frozen in ice and just woken up. For him everything was solved with blows and axes, and whoever did not use these methods was half a man. Lasgol smiled. Ulf's vision of life was as simple as it was wrong, but he was who he was and would never change no matter how many times others made him see he was wrong.

"You couldn't be more wrong," Martha told Ulf. "There's nothing worse than a brute who deals with everything by force."

"Hah! Tell me that when the Zangrians invade us or when the Wild Ones of the Ice are destroying our village."

"That's not going to happen, don't be a bird of ill omen," she said, wagging her finger at him.

Ulf brute but fun, Camu messaged Lasgol.

Yeah, he has a wild, somewhat mistaken, idea of life.

Ona not like Ulf.

Don't blame her. Not everyone likes Ulf.

I like.

I'm glad, because I love him dearly, even if he has such a peculiar personality.

"It could easily happen, or else it'll be us who attack the Masig, or Rogdon or whoever. After all, we're Norghanians!"

106

"You're a loud brute. Stop making all that noise and behave yourself," Martha scolded.

"Me, a loud brute? Oh, stop it!"

"Don't deny it, everyone knows you are, even poor Ona. Look how she's watching you with her ears back for all the noise you make."

"Of course I don't deny it, of course I am. Like a true Norghanian should be!"

Ona growled at him for shouting.

"Look here, see?" Martha said, pointing at Ona.

"Oh, the kitty will learn to love me, she's just not used to my character yet," Ulf said smiling and reached out to touch Ona.

"Don't…" Lasgol tried to warn him. He had no time. Ona lashed out at Ulf, who with unusual reflexes for a veteran such as he was, withdrew his hand just in time to avoid the panther's claws.

"Almost, but not quite… I was expecting it, kitty," Ulf said to Ona with a naughty smile and wagged his finger at her.

Ona growled at him again.

"You're not going to earn her trust like that," Lasgol told him.

"By your next visit I'll have her eating from my hand," he assured them, looking at Ona with his good eye.

"By their next visit she'll bite off your hand," Martha said. "And she'll be justified, seeing how rough you are and how badly you behave."

Lasgol sighed. There was no way to solve that. But the scene seemed to him very homey, with Ulf, Ona, and Martha arguing, Camu smiling, and himself in the middle. He felt comforted and smiled. He would miss all this. The good thing was he knew he would be able to return soon, on his next leave, and everything would be the same and he would be able to enjoy scenes like this one that would make him feel good. He thought of Astrid and of bringing her with him so she could be a part of all this and enjoy it with him. He wondered how she was faring with her uncle. Surely not as well as he was.

Chapter 12

Ingrid knelt before the grave on the deserted hill; she could see a wide valley with a relatively small town in the distance. The grave had a simple headstone with no markings or identification.

Tears ran down her cheeks while she searched for words of love, respect, admiration, and gratitude in her heart.

"Is this her grave?" Viggo asked. He was holding the reins of their horses a few steps behind, looking at the anonymous, plain grave.

"It is," Ingrid confirmed without turning around.

"But her body isn't buried here, is it? If I remember correctly from what you told us about your aunt, the Invincible of the Ice left her to die when they found out she was a woman."

"No, her body isn't buried here," Ingrid said. "During a campaign with the Invincibles, my aunt had the misfortune of being hit in the chest by an enemy arrow. When the camp surgeon examined the wound, her secret was discovered... they found out Brenda was a woman."

"They shouldn't have killed her for that...whether she was a woman or man made no difference, what mattered was how good she was with a sword," Viggo said.

"She was quite skilled, as good as any of her comrades. She was an Invincible in her own right. Since her youth she trained day and night and became an exceptional soldier. To avoid men giving her grief about being a woman, she cut off her hair and hid the fact."

"It's a pity she had to do that," Viggo said ruefully.

"It is. The world, life, isn't fair," she replied.

"How did she join the Invincibles?" Viggo asked her, trying to remember what Ingrid had told them about the matter.

"My aunt became a great infantry soldier. After a battle in which only a few of her regiment survived, the Invincible of the Ice came to the rescue. An officer who had seen her fight was impressed with her skill with the sword and he invited her to join them."

"And she accepted."

"She did. She wanted to prove she was as good as an Invincible

108

and that she was no less than them for being a woman."

"Did she prove it?"

"She did. She went with them on several campaigns as one of them until she was wounded."

"And that was the end of her journey."

Ingrid nodded. "They tried her for lying, although they really did so because she was a woman in a company that only accepted men in their ranks."

"They shouldn't have done it."

"Life is tough and unfair, more so if you're a woman in a world of men," Ingrid said bitterly. "They sentenced her to the 'traitor's fate' for lying and tricking the Invincibles."

"I understand she didn't survive. Did you ever find out more about what happened?"

Ingrid heaved a deep sigh. "They abandoned her, without curing her, in enemy territory during a winter campaign. She never came back, nor did I ever hear from her. She died."

"Sorry. That's a sad end for a strong woman."

"She left me her teachings."

"And she proved she was as good or better than the best soldiers: the Invincible of the Ice," said Viggo.

"She did. Her words are always with me. *Don't let anyone ever tell you that you can't do something because you're a woman. We can do anything, everything, even things they can't do. Always remember this.*"

"Is that why you're always outdoing yourself in the Rangers?" Viggo said. "To be the best, like your aunt was?"

"I follow her teachings. If she got to be an Invincible, I'll become the best among the Rangers. I'll be First Ranger. There's never been a woman First Ranger—I'll be the first. Everyone in the kingdom will know. I'll lead the way for other young women to follow my footsteps."

"I see… that'll be your way of honoring your aunt…"

"Yes, because of what they did to her. And not only for all the women who will come after; I want to see a Norghanian woman as a First Ranger, or as General of the Invincible of the Ice. I want to see a queen reign in Norghana without the need of a man."

"You won't find it easy to reach those goals. I doubt Thoran will accept any of them. I don't think he's exactly a progressive-thinking king. He's rather reluctant to change and further the advancement of women."

"I know. But my aunt always said that the brave are forged through difficulties. So, that's what I'll do. Nothing's going to stop me."

"I don't know, Ingrid… that's a very lofty goal…"

"Doesn't matter. I'll make it or fall in the attempt."

"You won't fall as long as I'm beside you. I'll hold you up and help you keep going."

Ingrid turned to look at him. "You will? Really?"

Viggo nodded hard. "I will. You can always count on my support."

"Thank you…" Ingrid said. She had not been expecting that from Viggo. "I'm surprised and pleased."

"I share your principles, what I don't fully see is how to achieve them. I don't want you to end up being a forgotten martyr, like your aunt, who gave her life for noble causes and didn't make it."

"She managed to plant the seed in me, and I'll follow her example and fight to achieve what she could not. I'll plant my seed in others like me, like my aunt did."

Viggo nodded. "I'll be at your side. It's going to be a tough journey."

"I won't be able to get rid of you, will I?" Ingrid asked with a certain rare vulnerability in her tone.

"Never," Viggo smiled. "You're doomed to bear with me until the end of times."

"Lucky me," she smiled, pleased.

"One thing… if Brenda isn't buried here, then why have we come all the way here?" Viggo asked, bowing his head.

"This is the place where she wanted to rest for all eternity, that was her wish. I had to respect it."

"Oh, I see…"

"I like to think she's here in spirit. That's why I've come here to this place to honor her."

"You'd better not say anything about spirits, because knowing us, surely her ghost will come out of her grave and we'll find ourselves in some new trouble," Viggo said, trying to cheer Ingrid with the joke.

"Do you mind letting me offer my respects to her alone? I need to do it in my own way."

"Yeah, of course. If you need me, I'll be right here with the horses."

"Thank you. This is important to me."

"If it's important to you, then it is to me too," Viggo said seriously.

Ingrid looked at him to make sure Viggo was not being ironic. But he was dead serious. He was stroking the horses to keep them quiet and looking at the valley below with the town in the middle. She turned back toward the grave and began her tribute.

"Thank you for your teachings, my dear aunt. Not only the military lessons, but those of life as well. You taught me to fight, to wield a sword, but you mostly taught me to be a strong, proud woman. You taught me what honor is, love for family and country, and because of all this I'll never be able to thank you enough. You're my hero."

While Ingrid was offering her respectful gratitude, Viggo listened carefully, discreetly, pretending not to, but he was interested—everything about Ingrid interested him. Her relationship with her aunt, which had marked her life, which had made her who she was, or at least had put her on the path of being who she was, interested him.

When Ingrid finished her tribute, she rose and walked back to Viggo. He had withdrawn a little, not too much, in order to give her space and privacy.

"Are you all right?" he asked her, noticing her eyes were moist.

"Yeah… it's been good for me to come. I needed to unload my soul and thank her for everything she did for me, and to let her know how much she meant to me."

Viggo nodded. "I would've liked to have someone like that in my life. A father figure, a role model to follow."

"You don't have anyone like that in your life?"

"No, no one. I never did."

"Sorry. It's important to have someone to guide you and teach you about life."

"We aren't all so lucky," Viggo said, bowing his head.

"You'll really be with me? Helping me along the way?" Ingrid asked him, and her tone was serious,

"I will. Always," Viggo said without hesitation.

"Why? My path and yours are so different."

"Because I love you," Viggo said seriously, staring into her eyes.

Ingrid did not know how to react. She had not been expecting that answer. Something so deep and personal. She had thought Viggo would give her one of his sarcastic jokes.

"Are you... are you sure?" she asked him, giving him the chance to correct his statement or say something that would break the deep importance of the moment.

"I am," Viggo replied.

"I..."

"Don't say anything." Viggo stepped forward and kissed her with passion. Ingrid let herself be carried away, and they melted into a kiss as deep as it was transcendent.

At mid-morning they continued their way toward the town below the hill. It was the town of Tonsberg where Ingrid had grown up and where she had shared so much with her aunt. It was little more than a village dedicated mostly to cattle raising. The locals had farms with cows and sheep, some with large numbers.

"I like the idea of seeing where you grew up," Viggo commented as they looked at the town's entrance in the distance.

"There's not much to see, it's a small village. There's more cattle than people in this area."

"Are you serious?"

"Yes. The farms have quite a number of animals, about ten per family member. That's the usual around here."

"I can't imagine so many animals together."

"That's because you grew up in a city."

"In the slums of a city," Viggo specified.

"Well, here things are different. There are cows and sheep all over the fields," said Ingrid and pointed at a distant farm where they could see cattle grazing.

Viggo shook his head. "Frankly, I can't picture you among cattle. It seems weird."

"My family had no cattle. My father was a Ranger, so I grew up in a small farm where my mother tilled the land."

"Oh... I see."

"My aunt's family had no cattle either, and you know that she became a soldier."

"Was your aunt your mother's or your father's sister?"

"My mother's."

"Do you have any other family?"

Ingrid shook her head.

"No one. My mother died years ago. One day she went to sleep and never woke up," Ingrid said in a dull tone with a shrug.

"Wow, I'm sorry."

"Thanks. It was a long time ago. My uncle died too. He had episodes from what happened to him and my aunt... they were assaulted when they were young..."

"I remember you told us."

"So I have no one left. I haven't been back here in a while. When I left to join the Rangers, I didn't think I'd ever come back."

"Can we see your home?"

"Why do you want to see it? It's small and plain. I don't even know whether it will still be in one piece."

"Just to see where you grew up. I'd like to see it to understand you better," Viggo said, smiling.

"I'd prefer it if you paid attention to what I say and stop trying to understand me."

"That's the character and leadership that drives me crazy," he replied, blinking hard.

"Shut up and look at the cows," Ingrid said.

They continued following the path that led to the small town. They could see cattle grazing on both sides but did not come across any farmers.

"I wonder how much a dozen cows would cost," Viggo said.

"Why would you want to know? Are you planning on becoming a farmer all of a sudden?

"I don't know, they look so nice, grazing there so peacefully. They ease the spirit."

Ingrid looked at him, puzzled. "If you say so..."

"But of course, in order to buy cattle, you need money..."

"Oh, I know where this is going," Ingrid said, spurring her horse to move away from Viggo. "I don't want to hear it."

Viggo spurred his horse too and caught up with Ingrid.

"I think we should keep the gold. After all, it's only a little and Count Orten hasn't missed it, so there's no need to return it."

"The answer is no," Ingrid said, snorting hard. "You were

behaving so well I almost didn't recognize you. I was starting to worry."

"You've got to admit that we did all the work and risked our lives. We should have a small compensation," Viggo insisted. "I'm the same Viggo, charming and irresistible as usual," he said, beaming.

"Doing the job and risking our lives is our duty as Rangers. We already have a reward, it's call 'pay.'"

"You must be kidding right? The pay we're given isn't enough to even feed the horses. It's not worthy of someone with my talent. They ought to pay me a bag of gold for every mission I'm charged with."

"You can negotiate that with Gondabar, see how it goes."

"I think I will. I'm sure he appreciates my worth."

"I'm joking. You're not going to talk about that with the leader of the Rangers. Have you no sense of duty and honor?"

"Hmmm... duty... honor.... I'll keep the gold, it's a lot more attractive."

"You'd better be joking, because you're making me angry."

"My beautiful blondie, don't get all riled up. You know my morality, my sense of good and evil, is somewhat blurred... it comes and goes. Honor and duty are well and good, but the gold... it beckons to me," Viggo smiled, all charm.

"How can you say that and remain so calm? A true person is firm about the lines between good and evil, honesty and duty, and never crosses them."

"I'm working on that," said Viggo, putting his hand over his heart. "Truly, I swear. Every day I spend with you, the lines become clearer."

"Yeah, sure..." Ingrid frowned. "I don't believe you. Everything that comes out of your mouth is pure nonsense."

"Truly and honestly, you are my guiding light leading my drifting ship in the night," Viggo said sweetly as if reciting a poem.

Ingrid raised her arms in despair. "That's all I need, you getting poetic! By the Ice Gods, why's this punishment forced on me? What have I done to deserve this?"

"Perhaps you severely offended the Gods in a previous life and now in this one you're being punished. Although, if you think about it, you probably did the Gods a favor and they're now rewarding you in this life with my wonderful company and fervent love and devotion."

"Only you could look at things that way."

Viggo shrugged and smiled.

"It's one of my best qualities—that, and my unequaled charisma."

"Your best quality is uttering the biggest crap about yourself without flinching. You should blush with shame from all the nonsense your tongue runs off with."

"My mind's quick and my tongue's sharp," he replied, sticking his tongue out at her.

Ingrid rolled her eyes.

"And my fist's hard. We'll see how fast you put your tongue away when my fist pays a visit to your pretty mouth."

Viggo put his tongue in at once.

"What's with the aggressiveness! You've got to learn to control that fierce temper of yours."

"Yeah, and you should control that tongue of yours."

"So you're going to return that gold to Orten? What a waste."

"We can't return it, because if we did, we'd be admitting that we betrayed him. That *you* betrayed him, to be exact, but he could hang us all because of you."

"You think so? It's just a little gold, Orten took most of it."

"How much you took doesn't matter. What matters is that you took it, and that's treason. Don't you understand?"

"Not really, to be honest."

"Ugh!" Ingrid snorted. "I swear, sometimes it feels like I'm dealing with a small child."

"That's because, deep down, I'm a naughty little kid."

"A toothache! That's you, a bad toothache. You can't steal, ever! And least of all from the King or his brother, no matter how little it is. They'll hang you for it."

"What a pair of brutes. It's not that bad…"

"Yes it is! It's a matter of honor! You can't steal from them, or disobey or betray!"

"Yeah, yea … they'll take it the wrong way, I understand."

"So, get it into that thick melon head of yours!"

"But the gold, it was so shiny…"

"Forget shiny and use the little brain you've got."

"I'll try, but I can't promise anything. I sometimes get these urges," Viggo said, looking innocent.

"You'd better not get any 'urges' at my side, or I'll strip you naked and leave you tied to a tree."

"Oh dear, when you get all romantic and sexy… you really do it for me," he replied and winked at her mischievously.

"Not romantic or sexy! It's so that the forest animals can attack you, see if you learn something!"

"Oh…"

"Although I'm sure you wouldn't learn the lesson."

"Most likely not," he grinned.

"You'd better mark those lines between right and wrong and drop the subject, you numbskull!"

"Would you mind not calling me numbskull? I know you're fond of the term, but it doesn't exactly go well with my 'best Assassin of the realm' status."

"Oh, it doesn't?" Ingrid turned to Viggo with a look of incredulity.

"Ingrid…"

"Yes…'" she replied, staring at him, feigning boredom.

"Don't you think it's wonderful how well we get along?"

"Well? What do you mean we get along well? We're like a cat and a dog!"

"Yeah, but we're like a cat and dog that love one another after all."

Chapter 13

They soon arrived in the town, and as they rode nonchalantly along the main street, they noticed something strange: there were no people in the streets. They looked around but could see no one, not in the main street or the ones they crossed and left behind.

"You told me your town was quiet, but this is a tad too much," Viggo joked as he gazed at the houses on both sides of the main street. Doors were shut and curtains drawn.

"This is weird. Where's everyone?" Ingrid asked, looking both ways, puzzled.

"That's a good question; maybe they've all gone to a festival outside of town," Viggo said with a shrug.

Ingrid rose in her saddle and strained her neck, turning her head around to better catch any sound. "I don't hear any music or festive noises. Everything's too quiet."

"Maybe they're building a barn or fixing a bridge. Many people would go to help with something like that."

"Many people, yes, but not everyone," Ingrid commented, still looking around everywhere, puzzled. "Where are the children and older people?"

"Maybe they're just shy? Although knowing you and you being a local, that would surprise me."

"Don't be silly. I don't like this at all."

Viggo wrinkled his nose. "It does seem quite weird. Bad weird."

"Yeah, I think so too…" Ingrid said. "I've never seen the town like this. Not even during the purple fever when everyone stayed inside."

They arrived at the town's square and nothing had changed. It was deserted. Not a soul anywhere. It was as if all the people had left town at once. All the houses' doors were closed. Not just that, but the curtains and shutters were also shut.

"Are you sure people live here?" Viggo asked as he scanned the square. "Have they all gone and left town?"

"I doubt it. A town doesn't just empty like that. This is strange, there has to be some reason," said Ingrid, looking around, also wrinkling her nose.

All of a sudden, the door to one of the houses opened. It was the biggest house, made of stone.

"Watch out," Viggo warned Ingrid, pointing at the house. "That's the Chief's house."

"Noted," Ingrid replied as she swiftly nocked an arrow and aimed.

"Has Jurgensen sent you?" a strong voice asked from inside the house.

Ingrid and Viggo exchanged glances.

"No, Jurgensen hasn't sent us." Ingrid said.

"Are you sure?" the voice insisted.

"I'm sure," Ingrid replied firmly.

"Who are you then? Mercenaries?"

"We're the King's Rangers," said Ingrid.

There was no answer. A moment later, a head appeared around the door. Blue eyes watched them.

"Rangers? Who sent you?"

"No one, we're just passing through," Ingrid said.

The man came out. He was tall and strong and was armed with a shield and war axe. His head was bandaged and he was dragging one foot.

"He's wounded," Viggo whispered to Ingrid.

She nodded.

"Don't shoot!" the man said, taking a couple of steps out the door and then stopping. "I'm the town Chief, my name's Alkateson."

Ingrid lowered her bow.

"Don't trust him, it could be a trap," Viggo whispered again.

"Are you wounded? What happened?" Ingrid asked as she lowered her bow.

"We were attacked," Alkateson said.

"Yeah, that's obvious, and obviously you weren't very lucky," said Viggo.

Slowly, heads began to peep out of windows and doors.

"Look, there are people in the houses after all," Viggo told Ingrid with a nod.

"They were hiding. They must be terrified to all be hiding," Ingrid said quietly for Viggo's ears only.

"Something bad has happened, that's for sure," Viggo guessed.

"Can we be of any service?" Ingrid offered.

"We'd appreciate the Rangers' help. I asked Count Sterval for help, but he hasn't sent any…"

"And why's that? The lord of this county has the obligation to defend his people."

"He does… if it's in his own interest. That's not the case, I'm afraid," Alkateson explained.

"Wow, think of that, a noble acting on his own interests, that's odd," Viggo said with great irony.

"If you come inside, I'll explain better," Alkateson invited.

"I don't trust him," Viggo said to Ingrid.

"If you try anything funny, you'll pay with your life," Ingrid warned the Chief.

"I swear I have no intention of trying anything. I find myself in a desperate situation. The town is in trouble. The last thing I want is to antagonize two Rangers who might be able help us."

"I can assure you it wouldn't be in your best interest to antagonize us," Viggo said as he passed his own thumb along his throat in warning.

Alkateson raised his arms above his head with the shield and axe, leaving his torso unprotected so Ingrid could shoot if she wanted.

"I swear I won't try anything."

Ingrid made a sign to Viggo to dismount. Now they could clearly see more people behind windows, and their faces showed the fear they felt.

Ingrid and Viggo stepped toward Alkateson, who waited with his arms raised.

"You first," Viggo said, indicating the door with one of his knives while he put the tip of the other at the Chief's back as a warning.

They walked into the house and met a sorry scene. At one end of the hall a man who looked like an aged Healer was tending two wounded men. The wounds looked serious and the floor was all bloodied. At the other end three men lay dead on the floor, covered with blankets.

"That's Sendagil, the town's Healer, and these are my assistants. As you can see, they're badly wounded or dead," Alkateson said sadly, shaking his head as if that would erase the scene, only it was impossible.

"What's going on here? Explain yourself," Ingrid demanded.

"The town's been attacked. By about twenty men. We stood up to them, and well, we managed to reject them, but they killed a dozen people who had volunteered to help repel the attack."

"Then you knew they were coming? That they were going to attack you?" Ingrid asked him, trying to understand what was going on here.

"Yes, it was only a matter of time…"

"But why would they attack you? Who were those men?" Ingrid asked.

"Come with me to the dungeon and you'll understand."

Ingrid and Viggo looked at one another.

"No tricks," Viggo threatened.

"I have no strength left," the town Chief said, leaving his axe and shield on a table.

They went down to the dungeon and saw a large man of about forty years of age. His face and part of his tunic were stained with blood.

"Come to set me loose, you idiot?" he asked the chief rudely.

"No, Jurgensen, I'm not letting you go. I told you that."

"Then it's your death and that of the two with you if they interfere." The prisoner pointed his finger at Ingrid and Viggo.

"Put that finger away," Ingrid said, her tone serious.

The man looked at Ingrid and lowered his finger.

"We'll see who ends up in pieces," he laughed.

"This is Victor Jurgensen. He's the cause of the attack. He got drunk and killed a man at the tavern."

"He started it. Served him right," Victor barked.

"He was unarmed, and you slit his throat with your knife."

"He insulted me."

"I'm sure you don't even remember what you argued about, you were so drunk. Everyone in the tavern saw how you pushed him and then killed him in cold blood."

"He was a dirty peasant. Who cares whether he lived or died," Jurgensen mocked.

"The King's law and me," the Chief said.

"You're going to die, you and anyone else who resists when my brother comes to get me out. And he won't be long. I advise you to run and not look back. If you stay, you'll be cut to pieces."

"Who's his brother?" Viggo asked.

"The second richest man in the county. He has land and many heads of cattle."

"Don't forget to tell them that we're the Count's cousins too," Jurgensen said in a cocky tone.

"That explains why the Count didn't want to help you, Alkateson," Viggo said.

"Unfortunately, yes."

"Your actions and the actions of your people do you credit," Ingrid said to Alkateson as she began to understand what had happened.

"No matter what you do, my brother will get me out of here. He'll come with his men and burn the whole town down to the foundations for arresting me. Didn't those who came to rescue me yesterday tell you?"

"Yes, they told me, and I told them what I told you—I'm not letting you go."

"So they'll raze this house, the square and its surroundings. My brother's going to enjoy himself."

"The King's law will have you hang," Ingrid told him.

"The Count wouldn't hang me, even if you took me in chains to his castle," Victor said, laughing loudly.

Ingrid looked at Alkateson.

The Chief bowed his head.

"I'm afraid the Count would let him go. They're family, cousins."

"I'll kill him now. Problem solved," Viggo said as he brought out his knives in a swift movement.

Victor started back in fear.

"You can't kill me in cold blood!" he roared.

"Why not? I'm a Ranger, and you're guilty of murder. I can pass the King's justice here and now," Viggo said and tapped his knives against the metal railing of the cell.

Victor flattened himself against the back wall, backing up as far as he could from Viggo.

"He must be tried," Ingrid said.

"But the Chief already said that the Count won't do it, so I'll judge and execute him myself," Viggo offered.

"Remember we were talking about some lines we're not supposed to cross…" Ingrid warned.

"Yeah… is this one of them?" Viggo asked her, a lock pick

already in his hand to open the cell.

"Yup, one of them..."

"Well... I felt like acting as judge and executioner," Viggo said, pointing one of his knives at Victor.

"Maybe later," Ingrid said.

Victor was white as snow now. He was trying to melt into the back wall—anything to get away from Viggo.

"Let's get out of here. I've seen enough, and it stinks in here," Ingrid said, staring fixedly at the prisoner.

They went back upstairs where the Healer was still trying to save the lives of the Chief's two assistants.

"Will they live, Sendagil?" Alkateson asked him, looking hurt and worried.

"It's too soon to know. The wounds are ugly, but I'll do everything in my power."

"I appreciate it, they're good men."

Sendagil nodded and glanced at Ingrid and Viggo.

"I know you," he said, addressing Ingrid.

"Yeah, I know you too. But I'm not sure you'll remember me..." Ingrid said.

"You're Stenberg's daughter, aren't you?"

Ingrid nodded. "Yes, I am."

The Healer smiled, recognizing her.

"You have your father's eyes and your mother's face."

"I've always been told that," Ingrid nodded.

"And I see you have your aunt Brenda's warrior character," he said with a nod at the weapons Ingrid was carrying.

"I hope so," she replied. "I'm a Ranger."

"A worthy daughter of your father's and clearly following in your aunt's footsteps," Sendagil smiled, nodding. "I couldn't imagine it otherwise."

"I wouldn't want it otherwise," Ingrid said.

"I didn't know you were a local," Alkateson said, regarding her with fresh eyes.

"I am. I was born and raised in this town. I'm Ingrid Stenberg."

"Pleased to meet you," Alkateson said. "I grew up two towns north of here, in Valhigen. About five years ago I came to live here. I became Chief after old Ulgresen died from the attack of a bear. He was trying to chase the creature away from one of the farms. I got his post after he passed."

"I remember Ulgresen, he was hard as stone but a good chief," said Ingrid.

"He was," Alkateson nodded. "It was hard to earn the people's respect. I had to prove my worth."

"Wow, I can't decide whether to congratulate you or not," Viggo said. "According to our friend downstairs, you're not going to see tomorrow."

"The situation is complicated indeed…"

"You can hand over that pig and save your skin. Why don't you?" Viggo asked.

"Two reasons. One, because I have honor and I won't let a murderer free because of fear. And two, because even if I let him go, that doesn't guarantee the good people of this town will be saved or spared. Victor's older brother, Wolfgang, lord of the Jurgensen family, is a sadistic brute from what I've been told. I've only met him once, but I saw him beat a man almost to death because he had crossed Wolfgang's path entering the tavern. The group Wolfgang sent made it clear that if I didn't hand over Victor, he would raze the town and kill us all."

"That's why they're hiding; they're scared stiff," Ingrid guessed.

"He has about thirty thugs with him. He's the most important rancher in the county. They have land and a great deal of livestock. He's well connected and has gold from his cattle business."

"Wolfgang is a dangerous man and a sadist," Sendagil warned them as he came over after tending to the wounded. "He's killed before, and he'll do it again. He believes it's his right due to his station—he thinks he's untouchable. Justice won't come near him in this county."

"Perhaps the Count's justice won't, but the King's will," Ingrid said, indicating Viggo and herself.

"I see you have your father's and aunt's character and passion," Sendagil said. "But I must warn you, in this case you'd better seek help. You'll need more Rangers. You won't be able to stand up to Wolfgang, his foremen, and his men."

"There's not much we can do," Alkateson said. "The town's brave men and women who joined me in the defense are dead or wounded in their homes. I'm afraid you're on your own."

"When do you expect the attack?" Ingrid asked.

"They'll arrive this evening, from what one of Wolfgang's men said when we faced them yesterday."

"We won't have time to warn the Rangers and receive reinforcements," Ingrid said, frowning.

"What if we take the prisoner with us?" Viggo suggested.

"I'm afraid that wouldn't improve our fate," said Alkateson. "Wolfgang will destroy half the town and kill whoever he finds if his brother is gone when he comes to free him."

"Yeah... we can't risk that," said Ingrid.

"Maybe it's best that I hand him over. I don't want any more town innocents to die," Alkateson said downheartedly.

"Or we could handle it ourselves," Viggo suggested as he toyed with his throwing knife.

"Killing Victor would be even worse," Alkateson warned. "Wolfgang's revenge will be terrible if we execute his brother. He'll kill half the town, I'm sure of it."

"I think my partner has something else in mind," Ingrid said, looking at Viggo, who grinned mischievously.

"What does he mean?" the Chief asked blankly.

Sendagil turned to listen to what they were going to say.

"Viggo and I will deal with the situation."

Chapter 14

Night was falling by the time several men took away the Chief's two assistants. Sendagil was going with them, and he raised his hand in farewell.

"Good luck!" he wished them.

Ingrid nodded in reply.

"Luck is overrated," Viggo said with a mischievous smile while he poured several poisons on the three pairs of knives he had lined up on the table.

Alkateson came into the house.

"Everything's ready. I've organized the evacuation of the town as you requested. They're going to the yellow cedar woods in the northern hills. They'll be able to hide and escape to the caves higher up if they're pursued."

Ingrid nodded. "I want you to go with them too."

"No," he shook his head hard. "I'm staying to fight with you two. What you're planning is madness, I swear, but even so, I'm staying. It's my duty to defend the town. I'm staying and fighting beside you."

"We're both used to madness and impossible situations; it's our specialty," Viggo said, beaming confidently, completely sure they would get out of this successfully. "But our methods aren't recommended for others. You'll get hurt," he warned the Chief.

"You're in no condition to fight," Ingrid told him, indicating Alkateson's wounded leg.

"I can't go up a mountain either with this leg. I'm staying. I'll fight and die here, it's my duty."

Ingrid looked at Viggo.

"It's his life, he has a right to decide how to live it and end it," Viggo said with a shrug.

"As you wish. It's your decision," said Ingrid as she started preparing her arrows on the other side of the table from Viggo.

They both worked fast but carefully to prepare their weapons and ammunition.

Viggo was finishing applying poison to his knives and Ingrid was separating her arrows into three groups. On one side she placed the

Elemental arrows. Their tips were marked with different colors to identify them easily: red for Fire Arrows, blue for Water Arrows, white for Air, and brown for Earth. On the other side she had prepared the special arrows for her tiny bow, Punisher. Then the regular arrows for her short bow, Swift, the fastest bow she could nock and release with. And finally, the arrows for her Spot-On composite bow, the one she never failed with.

Alkateson watched them, intrigued, while he tried to emulate them, sharpening his axe and strengthening the round wooden shield which already had a crack from a heavy axe blow.

"When things get ugly, we won't be able to protect you," Ingrid told the Chief.

"I understand. Don't worry about me."

"I like the Chief, he doesn't fear death," Viggo said as he tucked his knives in his belt.

"You're a good honorable man. There should be more people like you," Ingrid said, and her tone sounded like a farewell.

"Thank you," Alkateson said with a deep sigh. "I'm doing what I think is right. If I have to die for it, I will."

"Let's get into position," said Ingrid.

"Yeah, let's go," said Viggo.

Night fell on the town square. The silence of an abandoned town reigned—a silence that was broken by the noise of about thirty galloping horses approaching.

Amid shouts, howls, and loud voices, Wolfgang and his men arrived at the town square at full gallop on Norghanian farm horses. They were carrying torches and were armed with short bows, axes, truncheons, and the kind of poles used to manage cattle as spears.

"Chief, hand over my brother Victor!" Wolfgang cried from the middle of his group of men who were restlessly shining their lights on the houses in the square while trying to control their horses.

The Chief's door opened, and Alkateson appeared in the threshold covered by his shield, his war axe in hand.

"Your brother has been arrested for murder. I can't hand him over," he said in a calm tone.

"Hand him over now or I'll burn the town to the ground!"

Wolfgang yelled.

"He's being delivered to the Rangers to be tried and sentenced," Alkateson replied.

"No one's going to try my brother! Give him to me!"

"The law is the same for everyone. The fact that you and your brother are the richest farmers in the county and the Count's cousins doesn't put you above the law."

"You stupid fool! Of course it does!"

"I don't think so."

Wolfgang cursed, enraged.

"Last chance! You hand over my brother, or I'll kill you and burn down the town. Your choice!"

Alkateson watched Wolfgang's men gathering in the square, waiting for a signal to kill whoever they found and burn down the houses. He took a deep breath.

"I won't hand over your brother. Justice will deal with him, and you too if you don't leave the way you came with all your men."

"You've signed your death sentence and the fate of this town. Kill him! Burn everything!" Wolfgang ordered his men.

Two of Wolfgang's men dismounted and ran to attack Alkateson. The chief prepared himself. Even wounded, he could still fight and was a strong, seasoned warrior.

Several men went to throw their torches inside the houses close to the Chief's and those surrounding the square, intending to set them on fire.

An arrow flew from the roof of the Chief's house and hit one of the men as he was about to throw his torch through one of the windows he had broken with his pole. Upon contact with his arm the Water arrow burst into ice, and the man's arm and torch were suddenly covered by frost. He could not throw the torch in, and it fell to the ground, frozen.

A second arrow followed the first one and hit another of the men. This one was an Air arrow, which on impact gave the man a shock that ran through his torso and arms. He fell off his horse, and the torch fell with him.

"Archer!" Wolfgang cried and pointed at Ingrid on the Chief's roof.

Several of his henchmen aimed their bows to shoot at Ingrid. But before they could release, she shot again, hitting one of the men carrying torches with an Earth arrow. It unsaddled him just before he could throw the torch into a shop. The explosion of earth and smoke stunned and blinded the man beside him who was also carrying a torch; it fell out of his hand. The horse, frightened by the fire under its feet, reared and threw its rider off.

Five arrows were released from the whirl of riders toward Ingrid. With a swift movement, she flattened herself on her back on the roof. The arrows flew over her body without even brushing her. She got on one knee, and with her Spot-On bow she hit another of the henchmen as he was about to throw a torch into a building. This time it was a Fire arrow, which upon bursting enveloped the rider's torso in flames. He fell off his horse trying to put out the fire and scared the mounts of three other riders.

"Kill that archer!" Wolfgang shouted.

Arrows were released, seeking Ingrid's body as she lunged to one side to dodge them.

While the attention was focused on Ingrid, a figure came out of one of the far end houses of the square, moving with absolute stealth and speed. He approached two of the riders from behind and brought them down from their mounts with two precise knife strikes. Before anyone could notice what had happened, Viggo went into another house and vanished.

Alkateson had brought down the two men who had attacked him and shut the door of his house, pushing with all his might, since three other men were trying to reach him. He managed to shut the door and locked it from the inside.

"Knock that door down! Get in and kill the chief!" Wolfgang yelled, furious.

The Chief's house had barred windows and the door was made of oak and very thick. It was not going to be easy to get in. A dozen henchmen tried to bring the door down or pull the bars out of the windows but could not do it.

"Tie ropes to those bars and pull them out with the horses!" Wolfgang yelled.

While several men followed these instructions, others managed to set fire to a couple of houses on the sides of the square. But the fire did not spread, and curiously, the men who had gone into the houses to light the fire never came back out.

"Go up the adjoining houses to the roof! Kill the archer!"

Wolfgang ordered his men.

Following his orders, several of his men went into the two houses adjoining the Chief's. Three men appeared on the roof on the right and two more on the roof left of Alkateson's house, but before they could set foot on the Chief's roof, one of the men received an arrow in the stomach and another in the torso. They had not even seen the archer. They fell off the roof onto the pavement below.

"Hellfire! Kill that archer at once!" Wolfgang shouted in frustration.

"He's behind the chimney!" one of the henchmen on the roof said.

"Let's attack in unison! He won't be able to shoot us all!" said another.

The three men climbed onto the roof to the chimney as fast as they could with their weapons in their hands. Then suddenly, Ingrid emerged from behind the chimney, and as she moved, she released from Punisher, hitting the only man carrying a bow. The other two, armed with pole, axe and shield, tried to reach her. Ingrid moved backward, putting distance between herself and her enemies, and released again. She hit the one with the pole in the middle of his forehead. His head was thrown back from the impact, and he fell backward from the roof.

As Ingrid was fighting on the roof, Viggo was passing from one house to the next through the balconies and roofs, like the lethal assassin he was, without being seen. He finished four other henchmen he found in the houses trying to set them on fire. They died, stabbed without knowing what or who had killed them.

Wolfgang's men were trying to pull the bars out of the windows with ropes tied to their horses. They did not look as if they were succeeding, but with three horses pulling at the bars of the left window, they managed to make the bars yield.

"Pull on that window and we'll have it!" shouted Wolfgang.

The bars gave way and the horses carried them away.

"Come on! Get in!" Wolfgang yelled at his men.

One of them went in through the window a moment before the last attacker on the roof fell off with an arrow in his heart.

Wolfgang dismounted and went in through the window after his men. The last three who tried to follow their boss did not manage to. Viggo appeared behind them as they were bending to go inside and dispatched them with amazing speed and precision.

Inside the house, Alkateson was struggling to fight off the blows of the two men who had come in with Wolfgang, while the leader and the other two were checking the hall.

"Where is my brother?"

"Downstairs… in a cell…" Alkateson replied from the floor where he was being held by the two men.

"The keys. Give them to me."

Alkateson threw them at him.

Wolfgang caught them in the air and gave them to one of his men.

"Bring my brother."

The man ran downstairs.

"Do we kill him?" one of the men holding the Chief asked.

"No. My brother will. I'm sure Victor will enjoy killing this idiot who believed himself bigger than the Jurgensens. No one's bigger than the Jurgensens in this county! This county belongs to my family! We're the law here!"

"The law… is the King's law…" Alkateson muttered. He was bleeding from his head, leg, and another wound in his torso.

"My cousin the Count makes the law here! And my cousin is supported by our livestock!"

"I… know that…"

"And you thought you were going to try my brother? Do you really believe you can try me, you fool?"

"No… I don't…"

"Of course not!"

Victor appeared with the other man.

"Brother!" he cried and hugged Wolfgang. "I knew you'd come for me!"

"And here I am. I have a gift for you," he said, pointing his finger at Alkateson on the floor.

"Give me a knife, I'm going to take his bowels out!"

"Here you are. Cut him open like a pig," Wolfgang said, handing him a long knife.

Victor stepped over to Alkateson.

"Now there'll be justice for the Jurgensens," he said, about to stab him in the stomach. He drew his arm back for the thrust. There was a whistle, and Victor's head snapped backward. The body fell back like a felled tree.

"What...?" Wolfgang stared at his brother on the floor. He was dead. A small arrow had sunk in the middle of his forehead.

"Sir!" cried one of the men beside him, pointing at the stairs that led to the upper floor.

At the top Ingrid was nocking another arrow on Punisher.

"Victor! No!" Wolfgang cried, seeing he had been killed.

"It's the archer!" the man who had brought Victor up from the dungeons said, and he ran upstairs after Ingrid. Wolfgang's other companion ran to help.

Ingrid released at the first one and caught him in the heart. He fell dead a step below her. She delivered a tremendous kick in the face to the second man coming up, and he fell down the stairs, coming to a rest at Wolfgang's feet.

"Kill that woman!" He yelled at his two remaining men holding Alkateson down. They both turned to face Ingrid, who was already nocking another arrow on Punisher.

A shadow came in through the window. Without being seen, moving with lightning speed and without any sound, Viggo passed by Wolfgang at a run and slid on the floor with momentum behind the two men as they started up the stairs.

"Look out!" Wolfgang cried.

"Too late," Viggo said in a whisper, and he stabbed the two men in the legs.

Both henchmen fell on the stairs, grasping their limbs amid cries of pain.

"I'm going to kill you!" Wolfgang howled. And he moved toward Viggo with his axe in one hand and his knife in the other.

Viggo turned around.

"I doubt it," he said with a lethal smile.

Wolfgang moved forward and raised his axe to strike Viggo.

"Careful!" Alkateson said from the floor.

Viggo waited for the blow to fall, dodged it at the last instant, and finished Wolfgang in the counterattack.

But the blow did not come.

Ingrid's arrow hit Wolfgang in the heart and pierced him through. He fell on his knees.

Alkateson got to his feet with difficulty.

"I'm not going to judge you. They've done it already."

"You are declared guilty. The sentence is death," Viggo told Wolfgang.

Wolfgang fell forward, dead.

Chapter 15

Rays of radiant dawn lit up a new day in the town of Tonsberg. It was a lively, clear day, come to wash away the darkness, fear, and despair the town had been immersed in previously.

Inside the Chief's house, Ingrid was treating Alkateson's wounds so they would not get infected. Several stitches had re-opened during the fight and she had to suture them again. He was lying on the long table on one side of the hall. The floor was bloodied—from those who had tried to attack the house and died in the attempt, but also with the Chief's blood.

The outside light cheered up Alkateson, although he was exhausted from the fight and the loss of blood.

"I didn't think I'd see another dawn," he said with a deep sigh.

"Man of little faith. You should never lose hope. Least of all when you're doing the right thing," Ingrid told him as she finished stitching his head wound.

"You're going to look quite handsome," Viggo joked while he dragged Victor's body out of the house. He had already dragged Wolfgang's body out, as well as one of their men who had died inside.

Not much to lose. I was never attractive," Alkateson said, smiling, his face covered in dried blood from his head wound.

"Oh, you're not so bad," Ingrid replied. It was the first time she had seen the Chief smile. "Besides, what matters is what's in here," she added, jabbing his chest with her finger.

"I guess so," Alkateson said, staying as still as he could.

"A pretty face and charismatic personality will always be more convincing," Viggo said, pointing his thumb at himself.

"I see he's not exactly humble," Alkateson said to Ingrid.

"Humility is overrated. What matters is one's worth, and you've proven yours well enough," Ingrid said.

"It was my duty… I had to do it."

"You've gone beyond duty, I can assure you. You're a hero. The people will remember this. We'll remember."

Alkateson snorted. "I would've died, and many of the

townspeople with me, if it hadn't been for you two. You're the real heroes."

"Isn't that right? I always say so to Ingrid," Viggo said from the door. "She refuses to accept it, but I know we're Norghanian heroes. One day ballads will be sung about our feats all through the north. There won't be a troubadour or poet who doesn't know our amazing achievements and epic missions."

"Finish getting the bodies out and stop the nonsense," Ingrid chided.

"It's not nonsense, you'll see that I'm right. I'm always right in the end. And these corpses weigh a ton. What do they eat around here?" Viggo protested as he finished taking out the last dead body.

"I'm telling you, I can't believe what you've accomplished. I thought I was as good as dead. I thought we were all dead," Alkateson admitted, blinking quickly as if to make sure he was there, and it was not all a dream. "Because I'm alive, aren't I? This is real."

"Yes, you're alive," said Ingrid, touching Alkateson's head wound, which made him flinch.

"See? Awake, alive, and kicking, like a pig in a sty."

Alkateson smiled painfully.

"I'd been told that Rangers were tough and excellent fighters, but this is beyond anything I might've imagined."

"You should never lose hope," said Ingrid. "Every now and then things we couldn't imagine happen."

"Oh, indeed. Thank you for saving me and saving the town. Thank you from the bottom of my heart."

"There's no need for you to keep thanking us for helping. We did what we had to do. We're Rangers, and it's our duty to intervene and assist you. We'll never allow an injustice to occur in our presence."

"I'm not so sure other Rangers would've done what you two have. I don't mean only the fact that you stayed to defend the town, but also how you finished all of them. It was unbelievable."

"Awesome. It was awesome," Viggo said from outside.

"Can't you stop spying for one moment?"

"I'm an Assassin, I've been taught to always be alert and listen to everything around me."

"Even if the conversation is none of your business?" Ingrid said as she cleaned the suture needle to put it away in her belt.

"Oh, even more in that case," Viggo's face appeared behind the door with a big smile.

"Don't be a melon head, and check whether any of them are still breathing."

"Okay. If I find any of them still breathing, I'll finish them."

"Did I tell you to do that?"

"Not in so many words, but if not, why do you want me to see if anyone's still alive?"

"To save them!" Ingrid raised her arms in the air in despair.

"Well, that's a waste of time and energy…. They attacked us and tried to kill us. Why would I want to save them?"

"Because it's the honorable thing to do with those defeated in battle."

"Oh, fine, I see. Here we go again with the subject of lines… and whether to cross them or not…"

"Look and see whether any of them are alive, and if they are don't kill them!"

"Fine, but let it be noted that I still think it's a waste of time. In any case, they'll be tried and hanged for what they've done besides attacking Rangers. So, it's a waste of time," Viggo protested, raising his voice in the last sentence so Ingrid would clearly hear him.

"I see you two get along well," Alkateson commented with a light smile.

"Like a cat and a dog," Ingrid replied as she finished bandaging his head. "I've applied a pomade against infections but watch that wound."

"I will, thank you. Sendagil will do the cures for me, he's a good healer."

"Very well. It'd be a shame if an infection were to take you away to the realm of the Ice Gods after surviving all this."

"Yeah, it would be a tad sad."

"As for what we've done, it's not that important. Victor and Wolfgang were a pair of bullies who yelled better than they fought. As for their men, they weren't well-trained soldiers, they were farm hands, ranch foremen. Yes, they could use weapons, but their skill with them was far from efficient. All they had were numbers, and they didn't even know how to use that to their advantage. When the enemy has numbers, you don't confront them directly in the open. You hide and prepare and take down the enemy little by little until you get to the leaders. Or if the shot is clear, you take down the leaders, problem solved."

"I didn't know that. But even so... you tell it as if it were a lot easier than what it really was. Maybe those brutes weren't good with weapons, but they could kill and you two finished them all. That's amazing. I was there and I saw it."

"And part of the credit's yours," Ingrid said.

"Thank you. It's been an honor to fight beside you, even if I couldn't do much."

"I hope you can learn something from this that might serve you in the future."

"I have. Everything I've been through these past hours and what you've told me is engraved in my head and heart with fire."

"That's very good." Ingrid looked outside. A deadly silence reigned in the square. "When do you expect the townspeople to return?"

"I told them to remain hidden. I doubt they'll come down before sunset. They'll be thinking Wolfgang and his men killed all three of us and they won't want to take any risks."

"Considering there haven't been any significant fires, they'll see the town hasn't been damaged. That should make it clear they can come back. We need Sendagil, and we still have to bury all those bodies. It's not good to leave corpses in the open, least of all in the town square."

"Yes... they'll attract scavengers and spreads diseases..."

"Exactly."

"Let's hope they come soon then."

"Curiosity is usually a strong motivator," Ingrid said with a wink, and she was not mistaken.

Viggo walked into the house.

"Done. Six living who were playing dead. I've tied them up and taken them to the smith's shop nearby."

Wounded?" Ingrid asked him.

"Yeah, the six, and I didn't kill them."

"Good. Let's hope Sendagil comes down from the hills soon."

By late evening, as Alkateson had predicted, they glimpsed a couple townsmen between some buildings. They had come as scouts

136

to see what had happened. What they were least expecting was what they found: Victor and Wolfgang lying in the middle of the square, with almost all their men, dead. Sitting nonchalantly in front of the smith shop was Viggo, as if he had just finished his farm chores.

"You can come closer, there's no danger," he said.

Both locals approached cautiously, maintaining a prudent distance. The scene was horrible, all those dead men. Chief Alkateson came out of the house to greet them.

"Welcome. I want you to go back and tell the people there's no danger. I don't want everyone to see this scene, so pass along the word that only strong adults should come to help us move and bury these wretches. I don't want the children, women, and elders to see this. It's not pleasant."

The two men nodded.

One of them said, "I'm glad you survived, although I can't figure out how you managed to get rid of all of them."

"Because these Rangers are exceptional and they dealt with Victor's men," Alkateson said.

"We're also magnificent," Viggo said, beaming.

"Go now," said Alkateson.

The two men nodded and ran off, barely believing what they had just seen. Before getting out of range of the square they turned to look one more time, to make sure they had not imagined it.

It was already midnight when the group that had come back finished carrying the bodies away to bury outside the town. They told the rest of the townspeople to return to their homes. The people found everything empty, as if nothing had happened. Some blood spatters on the ground that had been missed during clean up was all that remained of the attack on the Chief's house.

Sendagil took care of Alkateson's wounds.

"I'm glad to see you alive," he said.

"We're glad to see you," Ingrid replied.

"I had guessed you had a lot of your father and aunt in you. This confirms it."

"Thank you, it's an honor to hear that," Ingrid said with her hand to her heart.

"When you finish with him, there are six prisoners who need your care," Ingrid told Sendagil, who nodded.

"I'll help you, in case any of them are rabid," Viggo said with a wink.

"Thank you, I'll check on them."

They both headed to the smith shop, which was being watched by two young, strong townsmen armed with spears.

One of the older women came over, staring at Ingrid.

"You're Brenda's niece, aren't you?"

"Yes I am."

"You might not remember me. I'm Aurora, the miller's wife," she said as she fixed her hair, which had gotten tussled up in the hasty flight.

Ingrid looked at her for a long moment.

"Yes, I remember you. You used to give us rye bread with pork sausage."

"Yes, that's me. You and your aunt loved it," she said, smiling.

"Who wouldn't!" Ingrid said, as if it were an outrage not to like such a delicious delicacy.

"I'm so glad to see you in town. Thank you so much for what you've done, I have no words to express what we all feel."

"Yes, you've rid us of those rotten-hearted villains," said another woman who was listening nearby.

"I also knew your father and your aunt," another of the older women said. "Your aunt was a good friend and had a spirit I've never seen in anyone else. You're worthy to be called her niece."

"Thank you so much," Ingrid said. The fact that they remembered her aunt and father touched her deeply.

"We must thank you somehow for all you've done," one of the elder men said.

"We'll roast an ox," said another one.

"That's an excellent idea," Alkateson commented, his mouth watering. So much effort had drained him of energy, but a good roast was a cure for anything.

"Say no more—we'll roast a pair of oxen and have a celebration feast."

"Make sure the oxen come from Wolfgang's herd," said Alkateson.

"Oh, for sure!" cried several voices at once.

It was not long before there were two good fires roaring in the middle of the square ready to roast two good oxen. A dozen men took charge of each animal. While they roasted the meat, the locals brought beer and wine to celebrate the Chief's and the Rangers' victory, one that would be remembered forever in town and in the whole county.

The feast went on well into the night amid singing and dancing around the fires. No one felt like going to sleep. They were alive and the town was intact. They wanted to celebrate. Gradually the younger people retired and then the elders. Ingrid and Viggo spent the night at Alkateson's house. The chief had fallen asleep exhausted and been carried off to rest.

It was an evening the town would never forget.

At midmorning, Ingrid and Viggo took their leave of the Chief and the locals who had all come out to see them off and wish them luck.

"I'll send a letter to our leader, Gondabar, in the capital, explaining what happened so you won't have any trouble with Count Sterval," Ingrid told Alkateson.

"Thank you, although I doubt we will. He's not a very determined man; his cousins did what they pleased with him because of that. Besides, he wouldn't go against Rangers' actions, it might get him in trouble with the King," Alkateson said, shaking his head.

"Even so. I'll ask Gondabar to remind the Count of his duties to his subjects. I'll also ask him to send some Rangers on visits to this county every now and then so the Count and his men know they're being watched."

"Thank you, that would be helpful."

"In any case, if you need us, send a message to the Rangers at the capital. They'll make sure we get it," Ingrid promised.

"That won't be necessary," Alkateson smiled.

"I'll also ask Gondabar to send Rangers to take away the prisoners. They'll be tried at the capital. They'll pay for what they did here."

"Thank you. We've put them in the dungeons for now. Wounded as they are, they won't be a problem."

"Take care, Chief," Ingrid said.

"You too."

"We have a tendency to get into trouble, so taking care is

relative," Viggo said with a wink.

They mounted their horses.

Alkateson wished them good luck and thanked them again.

"Good luck, and thank you for everything!"

"I'll come back for a visit as soon as I have a break," Ingrid said.

"You'll always be welcome here," The miller's wife replied.

They set off, following the road that left the town amid grateful shouts and applause.

"Isn't it nice to be leaving like this, with the applause of a grateful town almost carrying us onto the next adventure."

"Don't go all poetic on me..."

"You have to admit that all this warms your heart a little. Don't deny it," Viggo said, looking back and waving at the townspeople as they were leaving.

"Stop waving and strutting and behave like a true Ranger."

"We've earned their admiration and respect. I'm not strutting. We've done an excellent job and you know it. Admit that at least."

"If you promise you'll stop waving like royalty and getting all poetic, I'll admit it."

"Fine," Viggo offered her his hand; Ingrid took it and they shook. "Deal?"

"Deal, "Viggo smiled.

"Okay, I admit we did a good job."

"Wonderful," Viggo insisted.

"Fine, a wonderful job,"

Viggo beamed.

"Thanks, that's a real compliment."

"And now we'll ride in peace. The way to the Shelter is long."

"Of course, my blonde heroine of the glaciers."

Ingrid rolled her eyes.

"My ears will bleed internally with all the nonsense you pour into them."

"Then I'll die of love holding your hand."

"Shut up and ride, my sweet numbskull."

They both vanished from the sight of the townspeople once they passed the last hill.

Chapter 16

Egil rode into the Camp, and as soon as he left the camouflaged palisade behind, he felt as if he were coming home. He experienced a pleasant inner feeling that told him this place was his home. He took a deep breath, and the characteristic smells of the Camp filled his lungs. He looked at the stables and the workshops, the Rangers on duty at the entrance and the lookouts, and smiled. It was all so familiar and comfortable that it made him feel good.

He rode through the center of the Camp, and several veteran Rangers who were busy with different tasks stopped to watch him and greeted him with respect when they recognized him. Egil had pushed back his hood as was customary upon arrival, his Ranger and Specialist medallions hanging around his neck. He had already shown them to the watch at the entrance, but he had left them out so the inside watch could see them too. With all that had gone on with the Dark Rangers, vigilance was absolute at the place, and anyone arriving was closely scrutinized. There would be no more murder attempts or treachery at the Camp. Surveillance had been doubled, as well as safety measures; as far as Egil could see they had not lowered their guard, since watchful eyes followed him as he rode by and he was sure they were prepared to release several arrows if necessary. This pleased him. They should not let their guard down. They had to protect the Camp and its leaders.

He saw a first-year contender asking a veteran Ranger about him as he rode by. The veteran told him he was Specialist Egil Olafstone. This caused looks and whispers among the first- and second-years who were nearby. They seemed to know who Egil was, which he found somewhat odd since he had not been to the Camp in a long time. Besides, those contenders were first-years, so they had never crossed paths with him. He rode on and heard his name and surname mentioned by a couple of other contenders. This was followed by more whispering from another group further on. They knew who Egil was. He thought it curious that they knew or were interested in him.

He arrived at the Library and stopped at the door. He looked in through the window and recognized the two librarians who ran the place and helped the contenders with whatever they needed. The picture of first- and second-years studying at the long tables touched him. He was home. He had the urge to go in and say hello but decided to postpone it until later. First, he had to see Dolbarar and tell him the reason for his visit.

He reached the first bridge that led to the House of Command and looked at it. Countless memories of past times overwhelmed him. He smiled. He had gone through many experiences there while he was training to become a Ranger and many more when he was helping Dolbarar with his tasks. Egil greeted the two Rangers guarding the door and showed them his Specialist Medallion so they would let him through.

The two Rangers nodded and let him in.

Egil thanked them, opened the door, and went into the House of Command. He looked around the well-known hall and saw two Master Rangers he recognized at once.

"Egil! What a surprise! Welcome," Esben greeted him as he got up from the table where he was preparing what looked like fishing hooks. The man strode over to shake his hand.

"Thank you, Master Ranger," Egil replied, taking his hand and feeling the strength of the shake.

"We weren't expecting to see you here…" Haakon said by way of greeting, raising an eyebrow and looking askance at him. He did not move from the armchair he was sitting in, reading a book in front of the fireplace.

"I hadn't planned on coming to the Camp either, sir, but something came up and I had to come."

"Has Dolbarar summoned you?" Esben asked, inviting him into the hall with a wave.

"No, sir, I've come for personal matters," Egil said succinctly.

"It must be something important then. As a rule, Specialist Rangers don't usually visit unless summoned. Least of all one so distinguished," Haakon said, sounding like someone trying to discover the reason for such visit.

"It's probably nothing, but it's always good to make sure you have all the information needed in order to come to the right conclusion," Egil replied.

"Are we to understand that you have come to do some kind of

study?" Haakon insisted.

"That is correct, Master Ranger," Egil said without elaborating, which made Haakon eye him intensely. He was dying to know Egil's interest, something Egil was not going to reveal.

The door opened and Ivana came into the House. She was followed by another woman of about sixty years of age, with long white hair which she wore in several braids. Egil did not know her. She was tall and thin, her face was pleasant, and she had big, round, blue eyes.

"Well, Egil, we weren't expecting you," Ivana said in greeting as she placed her bow on a hook above the fireplace.

"Master Ranger of Archery," Egil nodded respectfully.

"He's come to do one of his studies," Haakon informed her.

Ivana turned around. "Shouldn't you be on a mission? You're part of King Thoran's Royal Eagles, and I understand he keeps you busy."

Egil nodded. "His Majesty keeps us pretty busy, that's true. I'm on leave. We've just finished a mission and been granted some time off."

"Is everyone all right?" Esben asked in a concerned tone.

"Yes, everyone's fine. We had no casualties. Some bruises, but nothing serious," Egil said nonchalantly.

"You've obviously been well trained," Ivana said.

"Indeed we have, Master Ranger," Egil said, watching the woman he did not know, intrigued.

Ivana noticed. "Forgive us, you haven't been introduced. This is Sylvia Vivekasen, the new Master Ranger of Nature. She's taken over Eyra's position," Ivana said. "And this is Egil Olafstone, I'm sure you've heard of him," she told Sylvia.

The woman looked at Egil and nodded.

"Of course I've heard of Egil Olafstone and the Panthers, or Royal Eagles," she said and smiled. When she did, her face lit up and she seemed to grow younger. Egil thought she must have been beautiful when young.

"It's a pleasure to meet the new Master Ranger of Nature," Egil said with a deep bow.

"The pleasure's all mine," she replied, also with a formal bow.

"Sylvia is doing a great job leading the School of Nature," Esben commented.

"Thank you very much, Esben. It's a position of high responsibility and I'm trying to live up to it," she said gratefully with a small bow.

"Oh, you are, don't worry about that," Esben said. "You're doing well. Your knowledge and experience are vast."

"Well, I do have years of experience," she smiled.

"And knowledge, otherwise our leaders wouldn't have supported your taking over," Ivana said, sitting in another armchair in front of Haakon.

"Gondabar and Dolbarar had several candidates for the position as far as I heard," commented Haakon, "and ultimately, they chose you, so you must be worthy. Now you simply need to prove it by training the youngsters we're sent. Let me warn you that they're less outstanding every year and come with greater aspirations."

"The new batches are hungry. They want to go far. They all want to be Royal Eagles," Esben said as he continued making hooks from a box of components he had on the table.

"They come with great aspirations, that's true," Ivana agreed. "They think they're going to conquer the world. And they are disappointed when they find out they're not as wonderful as they thought they were."

"Yes, they're a real nuisance. I've taken my contenders down a notch or two," Haakon said. "If anyone mentions they want to be like the Royal Eagles, I make them suffer triply. Unfortunately, they know there are two Assassins in the Royal Eagles and that's why they want to join my school."

"They also know there are two Archers I trained," Ivana added. "I also quell their burning aspirations in the first lesson. They think that because a few have achieved so much and made a name for themselves that everyone can do the same. They're quite mistaken."

"Dolbarar and Gondabar are happy. It's been years since we've had so many first- and second-year contenders," Esben said. "All of a sudden, becoming a Ranger is once again something honorable and appreciated in Norghana."

"Wasn't that the case before?" Egil asked as he listened to the news. He was interested, and more so if they had anything to do with him and his friends. They had been out of touch with what went on in Norghana, and he wanted to catch up as soon as possible.

"Not quite. Unfortunately, a few Rangers have lost their lives the last few years. That and the lack of riches make it a less sought out profession among our young," Esben said with a gesture of disapproval.

"Something that is changing thanks to our heroes and the feats they've been performing," Haakon said ironically, pointing one of the knives he was sharpening at Egil.

"And all the rumors going around about them," Ivana added.

"Rumors? What rumors?" Egil asked, surprised. He had not been aware there were rumors about them.

"How you saved the King and his brother, and how he's named you his Royal Eagles for secret missions of great importance. People let their imaginations wander... they invent all sort of stories," said Ivana disapprovingly.

"They've also heard that you're so good that you've even obtained more than one specialization. That rumor is going around now like wildfire," Haakon said.

"The Royal Eagles are becoming a legend among the Rangers," Esben said with a smile. "All the first-year contenders want to be like them and ask a thousand questions we can't answer," he added as he sat down at the table again.

"We have to get their heads out of the clouds," said Haakon. "No one should think this is a stroll in the forest where you come out a Ranger."

"It's only natural that they're interested in Egil and his comrades, since they form a wonderful group that has achieved amazing things," Esben commented.

"I wasn't aware that we'd awoken such interest..." Egil said, quite surprised. He was beginning to understand the looks and whispers among the first- and second-year contenders as he had entered the Camp.

"Well, now you know," Esben said, smiling. "You're famous."

"How are things at the Shelter?" Sylvia asked him, looking interested. "I'm a friend of Sigrid's. She was my teacher and mentor. I hope she's all right. It's been a while since I've seen her and I miss her."

"We heard some rumors about things going awry with the new training system her brother was developing..." Haakon said, waiting for Egil to elaborate.

"Some Rangers who were training as traditional Specialists in their last year have been through the Camp and mentioned something along those lines. They didn't specify beyond the fact that there had been problems," Ivana added.

"Most likely they didn't know what happened," Esben ventured. "Am I wrong, Egil?"

Egil was thoughtful. It surprised him that they did not seem to know what had happened. How could he explain? There was a lot to cover and the story was complicated. Best not to go into detail right then, not without explicit permission from the leaders. They would get the information from Sigrid, Gondabar, or Dolbarar. He decided to summarize without revealing too much.

"The Elders are all well, but yes, there have been problems.... Engla..."

There was silence, and they stared at Egil.

"What happened to Engla?" Haakon asked in a serious tone.

"She had an accident during the Higher Training. She was... hurt..." Egil said.

"Is it serious? What kind of accident?" Sylvia asked.

"She's recovering. Annika is looking after her. Gerd was also hurt. She's treating them both."

"Gerd was hurt too?" Esben got to his feet with a look of concern on his face.

"Perhaps it would be better if the Ranger leaders explain what happened when they deem it right," Egil said, seeing that the Master Rangers had not been informed yet of all that had happened.

"You can do it," Haakon demanded.

"I don't feel comfortable talking about it... not without permission...." Egil apologized and said nothing more.

"He's right. Dolbarar will tell us when he deems it right," Esben said. "If he hasn't yet, he must have his reasons."

"I hope they both recover," said Sylvia. "If they need my help they need only ask, it would be an honor to be able to assist in such a delicate situation."

"Dolbarar will tell us what's been decided," said Ivana. "He knows we're all at his disposal and ready to help the Rangers and the realm."

"If there have been problems, does that mean you did not obtain the additional specializations you went to train for?" Haakon asked, raising an eyebrow.

Egil had the impression that the question was malicious, as if Haakon hoped they had not succeeded. Was he jealous of all they had achieved in different areas? He could not fathom Haakon's reasons, but the Master Ranger did not appear to be on the Panthers' side. It could also be because of his aspirations within the Rangers' ranks. Perhaps the fact that Sigrid had failed might have an effect on their promotional ladder which Egil was unaware of. Maybe Haakon's hostility was related to his own desire to reach higher positions of leadership. It could also be plain jealousy eating at him. Or both. The Panthers would have to keep an eye on Haakon until they understood his motivations. Also Ivana's, since her attitude toward them was also not too friendly. Although, on the other hand, she was not friendly to anyone, like Haakon. They were both surly with everyone, without exception. They belonged to the old school of thought represented by the proverb: *spare the rod and spoil the child.*

"Egil?" Ivana asked.

"Oh, sorry, I was lost in my own thoughts."

"Very typical of you," Haakon replied with a sarcastic half-smile.

"That's because he has a well-furnished head and is always thinking," Esben defended him.

Egil smiled. "Answering your question, we did manage to complete the training and obtain new specializations," he said, unable to hide a certain pride in his voice.

"Really? And how's that? What specializations have you obtained?" Haakon asked him, and he stopped sharpening his knives to look at Egil pointedly.

Egil wondered whether to tell them or not. Since the granting of specializations had been official and they were wearing the medallions around their necks, he guessed there would be no problem in telling the Master Rangers. Sigrid had already told Gondabar, and their new specializations would be noted as official in the Rangers' files.

"Have Ingrid and Nilsa obtained new specializations?" Ivana asked, interested, with a keen look at Egil.

"Ingrid obtained the Specialties of Infallible Marksman and Man Hunter to add to the Specialty of Archer of the Wind she already had. Nilsa obtained the Specialty of Mage Hunter."

"I knew my girls would make it!" Ivana cried in triumph, lifting her chin proudly.

"Astrid and Viggo?" Haakon demanded.

"Astrid achieved Stealthy Spy and Forest Sniper to add to her Specialty of Assassin of Nature. And Viggo became a Stealthy Poisoner and Forest Assassin besides his Natural Assassin Specialty."

"Impressive! Two additional specializations each!" Haakon cried in astonishment. "I would have imagined it of Astrid, but not of Viggo," he commented with a look of satisfaction. Egil watched him. He looked surprised but proud, and his chin was lifted too, defiantly.

"Did Gerd get a specialization, or did the accident prevent him from it?" Esben asked fearfully.

"He did," Egil nodded. "Beast Master."

"Oh, it suits him like a glove! It's perfect for him!" Esben said, pleased. "And Lasgol? Surely, he got some other specialization, knowing his potential and all his efforts to reach his goals."

"Indeed. Lasgol obtained the Specialties of Forest Survivor, Forest Trapper and Tireless Explorer to add to Forest Tracker and Beast Whisperer he already had."

"Five specializations! That's prodigious!" Esben cried, raising both arms to the sky.

Ivana and Haakon exchanged a look of surprise and nodded.

"He always showed uncommon potential," Ivana said. "Since the Schools Tests."

"Yes, a very unique potential, a strange one I would say," said Haakon, thinking out loud.

"And what about you, Egil? As I understand, you belong to the School of Nature," Sylvia said.

Egil looked at her and nodded. "That's correct. My school is that of Nature. My Specialties are Expert Herbalist and Healer Guard."

"That's honestly impressive!" said Sylvia, nodding, pleasantly surprised.

"A great achievement, Egil!" Esben cried.

"Two specializations?" Haakon raised his eyebrows and looked at Egil up and down, as if he could not believe it.

"The truth is I wasn't expecting it, so I'm very proud of it," Egil admitted.

"Well, if you drew admiration before, when the contenders of all four years at the Camp find out that you've obtained several specializations, you're going to be the envy of all and the example to follow," Ivana said.

"You'll also awake jealousy among the veterans, not only the young ones," Haakon said, making a face.

"You'll be an example for all Rangers to follow," Esben said.

"Thank you, but we aren't aware of any of this. We only do our duty," Egil said with a shrug.

Suddenly, a figure came down the stairs. It was Dolbarar.

"What's all this to-do?" he asked, but when he saw Egil he understood. "Well, it seems the north winds have brought us a surprise visitor to the Camp," he said with a pleasant smile.

"Sir, it's an honor to be back in the Camp," Egil replied with a respectful bow.

"Come upstairs with me. We have a lot to talk about and a lot to catch up on. Besides, I have something important to tell you," Dolbarar invited him.

"Of course, sir," Egil replied. He took his leave of the Master Rangers and went up with Dolbarar to his rooms. What would the leader of the Camp want to tell him?

He would soon find out.

Chapter 17

Egil followed the Camp's Leader to his study.

"Come in and make yourself comfortable," Dolbarar said to Egil, who sat down in a chair before the desk of the Camp's leader.

"I'm happy to be back here and to see you," Egil said.

"I'm glad you've returned as well. You look well, a full-fledged Specialist," Dolbarar replied, sitting behind his desk.

"Thank you, sir," Egil smiled. He was delighted to see Dolbarar. He felt great respect and affection for this man who did everything to form new Rangers and ensured the corps was honest and honorable. Egil respected very few men, and none did he respect as much as Dolbarar.

"You are missed here. Your help in the library, and dealing with my correspondence and various matters was priceless."

"Thank you, I liked being able to help and I enjoyed my Library tasks very much," Egil admitted.

"I wish you could return to the Camp and stay here to continue helping. I'm sure things would run a lot better here with that good head of yours."

"I'd love to… but I can't. I'm a Royal Eagle now, and I have other duties which prevent me from returning here unless I'm on leave."

"Yes, the King and his brother keep you busy, Gondabar has told me. He hasn't said much about the missions, but I guess they're of a delicate nature."

"Indeed, sir, very delicate."

Dolbarar nodded and smiled.

"I understand. We'll see what the future brings. We never know where we'll be in the future or what problems we may need to deal with."

"Very true, sir. I was wondering how your health is?"

"Oh, I'm well. Thank you for asking. I feel absolutely rejuvenated. Sylvia is giving me a special treatment to keep my body revitalized. It seems to be having a good effect on my aging system," Dolbarar said, chuckling.

"I'm glad to hear that, sir. We need strong and healthy leaders."

"Both Gondabar and I are well looked after. Besides, after what happened to me with the poisoning, we've taken extreme precautions and care."

"Caution is always the best strategy," Egil agreed, glad to know they were taking measures so that it would never happen again. The Rangers could not allow themselves to lose leaders like Dolbarar and Gondabar; they were necessary for the future of the corps.

"I believe you've met Sylvia, the new Master Ranger of Nature, haven't you? She's the one treating me."

"Yes, sir, I just met her downstairs."

"I'm delighted she accepted to take over the position of Master Ranger of the School of Nature. We had several candidates, but she was without a doubt the best prepared and most apt for the post. Her knowledge and experience are vast. She's been a Ranger in a variety of positions for over fifty years."

"I didn't know her. I'd never seen her around Camp or at the capital," said Egil, inviting Dolbarar to tell him more about her.

"She has been to the east of the kingdom, looking after Count Orlesson and his second cousin Count Ulwarson. They're noblemen of delicate health because of their advanced age. The King needs them alive because they're part of his support at Court. Sylvia has been treating them and has kept them alive beyond all expectations. She is a skilled healer and an expert herbalist. She was my main candidate for the post. I've known her for many years—so has Sigrid, Sylvia studied under her. It was hard to persuade the King to let her take over the vacant post after what happened with Eyra…. It still pains me. My heart hurts just remembering."

"It was an unthinkable betrayal," Egil said, nodding, feeling sorry for Dolbarar, whose most faithful collaborator and good friend had betrayed and tried to kill him.

"It was," Dolbarar nodded heavily. "But let us leave the past behind, there's nothing we can do now."

"We can only learn from the past and keep going."

Dolbarar smiled at Egil. "You're growing wiser by the day. Never stop learning."

"I won't, sir," Egil promised.

"Getting back to Sylvia. We had to send another good healer, Elvira Gustafson, a Healer Guard, to look after the two noblemen.

Sylvia was her teacher."

"In that case, she'll be a great teacher here and will help keep you healthy," said Egil, hoping she would take good care of Dolbarar so he would live for a few more years.

"I think so too," Dolbarar said with a smile. "She says I still have to take several restoratives because the poisoning has left my body very weak. She's right, you know. I get tired much quicker. It could be age, I am growing old…"

"I think you're looking great," Egil said with a smile.

"Thank you, the truth is I feel very well. I just wish I was ten years younger," Dolbarar smiled back.

"Oh, anyone over thirty wishes that. I'm glad that you feel so well," Egil said.

"Speaking about news and replacements, I don't know whether you've been told that we have a new First Ranger," Dolbarar commented.

"No, no one's told me," Egil replied, wondering who it might be. The Panthers had talked about it, and Nilsa had told them that the names more often cited were of two Royal Guards who had been with Gatik for a long time and knew the position and responsibilities well. Besides, they were talented fighters and Rangers.

"Yes, after what happened with Gatik, which was a tragic surprise, we've been deliberating the choice of a new First Ranger."

"Anyone I know?"

"I doubt it. He's been doing missions for the King. He's an accomplished Specialist, a Natural Assassin. They say he's the best in the kingdom."

Egil immediately thought of Viggo, but dismissed the idea almost at once. Viggo could not be First Ranger, no matter how much he proclaimed himself to be the best Assassin in the realm. His friend might be a great Natural Assassin, but he was certainly far from being the best among all the Rangers. Even among the Panthers there were a couple better than him, at least in Egil's opinion.

"A Natural Assassin? Isn't it a little strange for someone with that specialization to be chosen as First Ranger?"

"It was by specific request from Thoran. According to our King, no one is better than an assassin to catch another. He's worried about his life."

"He fears a murder attempt?"

Dolbarar nodded repeatedly.

"Thoran is always afraid of being murdered. Well, him and the majority of monarchs."

"I see," Egil said. "The intrigues for the throne, internal and external, are always present."

"Indeed. Make sure not to find yourself entangled in them," Dolbarar warned in a firm tone.

"Don't worry, I won't get involved."

Dolbarar nodded. "I'll take your word for it. The new First Ranger's name is Raner Olsen. He is an exceptional Ranger and Assassin. He also has good leadership qualities and he follows the Path."

"Let's hope he doesn't deviate from it as Gatik did."

"Let us hope. Of the five candidates we selected among all the Rangers, I must say he's one I liked best. Since the decision was between the Rangers' leaders, Raner got the most support, including the King's."

"Then His Majesty, Thoran, must be pleased."

"Satisfied rather. He's rarely pleased."

Egil nodded. "When I return to the capital, I'll have the chance to see Raner."

"Introduce yourself to him if the occasion arises, I'm sure he'll want to meet you. You and the rest of the Panthers."

"I will. It's always good to get to know our leaders, and he's one of them now."

"Yes, he is. I believe the choice is good. He will do his duty both to the King and the Rangers."

Dolbarar was thoughtful, and his expression changed from kind to troubled.

"Changing the subject… if you don't mind, I'd like you to tell me about what happened during the Higher Training. I would like to hear it from you, because it will help me understand it better. What Gondabar has informed me of and what I have asked Sigrid directly bring up many doubts and questions."

Absolutely, sir. I'll tell you what happened with as much detail as I remember."

"Very well, go ahead."

Egil told Dolbarar everything that had happened during the Higher Training. He tried to be as objective as possible and stick to the facts. While Egil was telling him, Dolbarar put two cups on his desk and served a tisane he had brewing already. Egil took a sip, taking a brief break, and then went on explaining while Dolbarar listened and drank. When Egil finished his story, Dolbarar looked at him thoughtfully.

"I'm so sorry to hear about Engla and Gerd. I do hope they recover fully. Thank goodness this was not an irreparable tragedy…"

"It came close…"

"Yes, that is what worries me most about this whole matter. The risk is too great."

"Sigrid is aware of that—that's why she shut down the program after the incidents."

"A wise decision, which I share. We can't take such risks with the lives of contenders and teachers."

"I think so too, although the program offered great potential."

"I would like to maintain a certain discretion until Sigrid has the whole study of what happened and the conclusions well documented," Dolbarar said. "Once we have those conclusions, we'll be able to make better decisions."

Egil nodded in agreement.

"The worst thing we can do now is talk about it openly without understanding it fully. It would lead to each person reaching their own wrong conclusions about the events. That would be bad not only for Sigrid, but for the whole effort to create Specialists. And I think it might even call into question the whole Rangers' training."

"People tend to make their own hasty conclusions, and it wouldn't be good for the Ranger corps, I completely agree. It's a pity it went so wrong…"

"What are you concerned about, Egil? I know you, and I can tell by your look."

"I wouldn't want this incident, what happened with the Higher Training, to remain hidden or ignored. It's important, in my humble opinion, that all the events and reasons are analyzed properly. We must find out what went wrong."

Dolbarar nodded repeatedly; he knew what Egil meant.

"I understand your concern. Let me assure you that what happened will not be buried and will be cleared. Both Gondabar and I, even Sigrid, want to know exactly why it went wrong. We want to get to the bottom of this matter and find out why it went awry."

"In order to revisit the Higher Training again if the causes are found and solved?"

"There will be a long debate about that. It's a complex decision. I'm sure Sigrid will want to continue the program if the issues are found and there's a way to solve them. I am not as certain that Gondabar will give his approval even so, seeing what has taken place and the implicit risk."

"I understand."

"But, in spite of everything that went on, I believe some congratulations are in order."

"Congratulations, sir?"

"Yes, for the Snow Panthers."

"Or for the Royal Eagles, sir?" Egil said, wondering whether he was referring to the last missions they had carried out.

"You will always be the Snow Panthers to me," Dolbarar said with a wink and a smile.

Egil smiled back.

"What congratulations do you mean, sir?"

"For what you have achieved at the Shelter during the Higher Training. Gondabar sent me word of the specializations you have all achieved despite all the problems you encountered. This is really outstanding. I'm proud of all of you."

"Oh, thank you, sir," Egil said, feeling honored.

"I have always known the Panthers are a special group. Its members are all extraordinary, and together you are a true force of nature—now that you have obtained your specializations, more than ever. I am sure you will obtain formidable achievements others can only dream of."

"You really believe that? You think so?" Egil was surprised Dolbarar had such high expectations from them.

"I'm certain of it. You've already proven how impressive you are on several occasions. You have saved the Rangers and the realm, which is an incredible feat. But, now that you have completed your training and have some experience, I believe there are no limits to what the Snow Panthers can do. You will overcome any obstacle before you, no matter how difficult it seems. You will reach whatever goal you set for yourselves. You are ready and you have extraordinary talent, each one of you, and in different areas. The talents and skills each of you has, combine well and make you a formidable group."

"Thank you, sir..." Egil said, moved by Dolbarar's words of praise.

"You will be feared by Norghana's enemies and admired by the kingdom's friends," the leader of the Camp assured him. "You are destined to do great things, and now that you're prepared, together you will achieve them. I am positive. You are an exceptional group... quite extraordinary..." Dolbarar repeated and was thoughtful. "I can definitely foresee great things in your future."

"Thank you, sir, your faith and support mean a lot to us."

"You can share what I have just told you with the others and give them a big hug from me when you see them again."

"I will, sir. It will mean a lot to them."

"I am sure that our leader Gondabar has congratulated you as well for obtaining the specializations."

"He has. He congratulated us on our return to the capital, before we set out on the mission we just carried out. But he was also troubled with the Higher Training incident. We spent most of the time talking about it and trying to explain what happened at the Shelter."

"That's only natural, it is his responsibility and it was a serious incident," Dolbarar said. "I am sure Gondabar is proud of what you've achieved, even if his duties would not let him express it as you deserved."

"A leader's responsibilities are a heavy burden."

"That is a great truth. So tell me, Egil, to what do we owe your visit? I'm sure you haven't come all this way only to see this old master," Dolbarar said, smiling.

"Seeing you is one of the reasons. The other is a study I'm conducting which I need some help with."

"A study, I knew there was something. What is the study and how can I help you?"

"You see... I'm studying Objects of Power. One in particular: Orbs of Power. I thought that perhaps here, in the Library, in the restricted area, there might be something about the subject."

"Orbs of Power...." Dolbarar was thoughtful.

"Are you familiar with the matter?"

"Not much, I'll admit, but I do know a couple of things. Magi and Sorcerers use orbs to store energy, power as they call it. I have read that. I've also spoken to Magi and I can confirm it."

156

"The magi imbue the orb with their power?"

"Yes, but not necessarily. The power may come from another place or object and the mage simply redirects it and stores it in the orb."

"Interesting. Then the power in an orb may come from a different source, an unknown origin, maybe not even human."

"Correct. The magic or power stored in an orb might be of any origin of power."

"Could that magic be sentient?"

Dolbarar scratched his chin. "I don't think so. From what I know, it's only energy—power, magic in a pure state, but not alive in itself. That's as far as I know, which doesn't mean I'm right. The arcane paths are inscrutable and not one of my strong points. Everything I know about magic I've learned out of curiosity; it's a subject that has always interested me. Well, and out of need as well. Many times magic crosses the path of a Ranger and they need to fight it or go around it and, if lucky, use it to their advantage. That's why we study it and have tomes of knowledge about magic matters."

"I see…"

"But as I said, this is a concrete and specialized subject. It's certainly a matter for Magi, not Rangers. It's out of our range of knowledge."

"Is there a tome in the Library I might consult about this in particular? I'd appreciate it."

"Maybe…. I'm not sure whether on orbs exactly, but there are some tomes about Objects of Power."

"Will I be allowed to consult them?" Egil asked in a pleading tone.

"Of course, Egil. You are trustworthy," Dolbarar said, looking straight into his eyes with absolute trust.

"Thank you very much, sir."

"Go and consult. If you have any more doubts, I am here to help you if I can. Here is the key, you'll need it to gain access," Dolbarar said. He opened one of the drawers in his desk, and handed Egil the key.

"Thank you, sir. I'll go right away."

"I guessed as much. You'll be staying at least a couple of days, so I'll make sure you have your old cabin."

"There's no need, I can sleep in the general barracks with the other Rangers."

"Because it's you, I want you to have your old cabin. There you will not only be more comfortable, but you'll be able to work in peace."

Egil thought about Ginger and Fred which he always carried in his saddlebags, albeit safely packed in a new transporting box he had prepared.

"The truth is I could do with some quiet and solitude, sir."

"I thought so." Dolbarar smiled.

"Thank you very much, I really appreciate it."

"You've earned it. Tell me, where will you go once you leave here?"

"I'm going to the Shelter to visit Gerd and Engla."

"In that case, before you leave, come see me."

"Absolutely, sir."

"Go. I hope you find the answers you're looking for."

"Thank you, sir." Egil left Dolbarar's rooms. He went downstairs and only found Esben in the hall - the other Master Rangers had left to pursue their daily tasks.

"Everything all right?" Esben asked.

"Everything's okay," Egil said and waved goodbye to him.

"Sylvia asked me to tell you that she would like to see you when you have a moment. You will find her in the house of the School of Nature."

"Thank you, I'll visit her as soon as I can," Egil replied. He left the House of Command and headed to the Library. As he was leaving, he realized Dolbarar had not told him why he wanted to see him. He also thought it odd that Sylvia should want to speak to him. He had just met her. He shrugged and went on walking. He would find out what they wanted from him in due time.

Chapter 18

Word had gone around the Camp about Egil's arrival. If the contenders had looked at him with interest and whispered about him upon his arrival, now they were doing so openly and were even pointing their fingers at him. He heard awed murmurs and the occasional word of admiration. Egil was not used to this and found it shocking; in fact, he was used to the opposite, being insulted and underestimated for who he was and belonging to his family.

It was a nice change, and Egil smiled at several third-years who were staring at him openly in front of the library, as if the new First Ranger had come to visit. Now that he thought about it, Egil would like to meet the new First Ranger and see what he was like after what Dolbarar had told him. Not to see what he was physically like, or how skilled he was— Egil was sure he must be an exceptional Ranger, or he would not have been chosen— Egil just wanted to see what he was like as a person.

He went into the Library, and simply smelling the scent of old books, mixed with that of the contenders brought back so many memories he could not help smiling. He had spent so many hours there, he missed his studies and all the plans he had thought out in that place— many and varied.

The three head librarians came to greet him the moment they saw and recognized him. They welcomed him with tight hugs— well, as tight as old librarians who spent all day in a library could hug. Egil was glad to see them in good health, although they looked even older than when he had last seen them, and even back then they had already seemed to be about a hundred years old each. He talked with them for quite a while, explaining the details of his busy life. For the librarians, who never left the Camp, it was wonderful to hear the tales of Egil's busy life.

The various contenders who were at the Library stopped studying to listen to the greetings and conversation Egil and the librarians exchanged. While they chatted, Egil remembered the good times when he himself was working at the Camp and had spent his time in the Library. Good times he remembered with longing. His life now was full of mysteries, action, and adventures, and he loved it, but he felt a bit sad that he could not be there at the Library, helping the contenders and reading and learning, which was something he really loved. He had spent many good hours there, day and night. He specially loved the nights. Being able to read by the light of an oil lamp in absolute peace without a soul around was priceless.

Suddenly, Gerd's image and that of the rest of his friends' came to his mind and his nostalgia vanished at once. He would rather be with them and go through fascinating adventures, not knowing what waited around the next corner than be alone in that Library. Yes, he preferred the life of the Panthers to that of a librarian, no matter how much he loved reading and learning. He took his leave of the librarians and went down to the lower floor, to the restricted chamber where he hoped to have some luck and find important information that could help him.

He unlocked the door and went into the deserted chamber. He was not surprised it was empty; it was not uncommon for the Master Rangers to use it unless they found themselves with some quandary that required special consultation. The books there were rare and precious, the subjects they dealt with not common at all.

Egil wasted no time and started searching. He knew the hall well, since he had spent a lot of time there and knew where the books were that he needed to consult. He did not know whether he would find answers in them, but he had hopes they would shed some light on the orb.

He hoped to have more luck than at the capital. He had already been to the Royal Library with Gondabar's permission granted by the King. The Royal Library was magnificent and contained hundreds of tomes of great value considering that it was a Norghanian library, which in general were rather poor and uncommon places in the kingdom. The Norghanians were not exactly a cultivated people. They preferred fists and war axes to books. It was a shame that his fellow countrymen were such brutes and so little inclined to study and learning. In this matter he was rather envious of the educated kingdom of Erenal where arts and books of knowledge were well appreciated. King Leonidas boosted arts and sciences and invested in libraries and knowledge, quite the opposite of his Norghanian counterpart. Thoran was in trouble, and the gold he managed to obtain was used to strengthen his army, not invested in culture and helping his people— there was no doubt about that.

Egil thought it would be an unthinkable feat to change the King and his people's culture, even just a little. He would have to think about how to do it and bring Norghana out of the age of steel into that of knowledge. It seemed a difficult dream to make true. But everything began with a plan, a simple plan on which to build other, more complex ones. He smiled. He just had to work determinedly until he reached his goal.

Unfortunately, he had not found the information he sought after at the Royal Library. Most of the tomes were historical and told of the great feats of the Norghanian leaders, their battles, conquests, marriages, deaths, and similar information. There were also books containing the history of Tremia's main kingdoms. No matter how hard he searched, he did not find advanced tomes of magic and arcane subjects that he did not already know from his own prior studies and investigations. Not that there was no study material— there was plenty, with whole books devoted to the nature of magic and its possibilities, including the Talent or Gift and its appearance and development. It was only that Egil already knew what they told. He remembered that Dakon, Lasgol's father, had taken those same tomes home with him to help Lasgol with his Gift when he was a little boy.

Some tomes were devoted to the Ice Magi: their history, origins, power, and similar aspects he found interesting and added knowledge he did not have about that kind of magi and their magic. He found this informative and specific of Norghana. Outside the kingdom there were no Ice Magi, so it was a unique and very Norghanian area of study. He found other tomes about different types of magic, but whose contents were general and did not delve deep enough into the concepts as Egil would have liked. They mentioned the differences between magi, sorcerers, shamans, warlocks, and other types of people who practiced magic, but without any depth into characteristics— or more importantly their secrets. Egil wanted to know the types of magic, their peculiarities and arcane entities. Unfortunately, the tomes he found were superficial on the subject. Most likely each school of magic would keep its secrets under lock and key somewhere hidden and well protected. On second thought, probably in more than one place and watched by more than a single mage.

He had found several tomes about the magic of center and north Tremia but could not find anything interesting to help him with the investigation about the orb. It was true that, as he learned a little more about magic, it was becoming more difficult to acquire new knowledge of it. This was mostly because of all the Panthers' experiences and the magi and Objects of Power they had been in contact with. Egil wrote down everything he found out in his travel journals, and most of what he read in the tomes he had already gathered in his journals. He had quickly realized that the Royal Library's selection was not going to be especially revealing. The most precious tomes would not be found in a library.

After looking and looking, he had been forced to stop, since he did not find anything about orbs in any of the volumes he consulted in the Royal Library. Still, he was not discouraged. Obtaining this kind of important knowledge was never easy, this he knew well.

Thinking back to his experience searching the Royal Library, Egil had an idea. The fact that there were no revealing tomes about magic in the Norghanian library did not mean there were not books on the subject somewhere else in the Royal Castle. They had to be in the tower of the Ice Magi. With this idea in his head, he went to see Gondabar to get the necessary permission to access the tower and consult the tomes kept there. The reply was not long in coming. The Ice Magi refused outright. No one who was not an Ice Mage could enter the tower and consult their tomes. And least of all a Ranger. Egil was not surprised, since he had been expecting this answer, but he had to at least try. Gondabar insisted, but he did not manage to get their permission.

The leader of the Rangers was quite put off by the refusal. He believed all the King's corps should collaborate and help one another whenever necessary, but there was not much he could do. If it were a matter of importance for the kingdom, he could go to the King, since Gondabar had no authority over the Ice Magi, but since it was not a matter of relevance to the kingdom, but rather a personal one— a study Egil wanted to peruse— he decided it was not convenient to bother the King.

Egil knew that if he did not find the information there, there was still the prominent Library of Bintantium located in Erenalia, the capital of the kingdom of Erenal. The problem was finding the time to go there to consult their tomes. And he was not so sure he would find the desired information if he went to the Great Library of Erenal, so the journey might be in vain. But, he did know that the Master Archivist of Arcane Knowledge was there and that he and his librarians studied the magic arts. Without a doubt he would have some information on the matter of Egil's investigations.

He snorted. The problem was, he did not have time to go there and come back before they had to report at the capital to embark on a new Royal Eagle mission. He was also not sure the Master Archivist would share his knowledge about the matter with a foreigner. He hoped so, but he had no assurance that the man would. He could ask for the information by letter or messenger, but that would take too long. He had experienced as much when he was searching for information on the strange illness that had afflicted Dolbarar. It had been a hard task to make the librarians pay attention to him, and then the Master Archivist had denied him the information.

He shook his head. He would leave the option of the Library of Bintantium in Erenal for last. He did not have that much time. Now that he was here in the forbidden chamber of the Camp's Library, he had the chance to find what he was looking for, and he was going to take advantage of it. He lit a couple of oil lamps to better study the tomes.

He searched among the tomes of magic and arcane matters on the shelves against the walls. He recognized several tomes that were already familiar to him and started with those—*The Gift and its Manifestations, Ice Magi, Blood Magic, The Development of the Talent, Analysis of Curse Magic, Magic of the Four Elements, Enchantment of Objects, Theories About Magic and its Origin, Dark Magic,* and *Ranger Magic.* He put them on the large study table in the middle of the room and began to read, deeply concentrated. It was not long before he realized it was going to take him quite a long time to read all the tomes, since none of them specified orbs either in the title or the index. He was not daunted. If there was something he loved, it was losing himself in tomes full of knowledge. He was going to enjoy the search.

He spent all day reading and searching and forgot to eat. He plunged into the tomes well into the night. When he was already dropping off from exhaustion he still went on a little longer. He finally fell asleep on one of the books. He woke up startled and half asleep and went to his cabin to rest. He had had enough for one day.

The following morning, he continued with his search. He worked on the tomes until noon. He went to the dining hall for lunch, but he had to leave quickly because he drew too much attention among the contenders. As he was leaving the dining hall, he crossed paths with Master Instructor Oden, who was coming in.

"Sir," Egil greeted him, standing to attention out of habit.

"Ranger Specialist Egil, Royal Eagle," the instructor replied with the same intense gaze as usual.

"I'm glad to see you, sir," Egil said.

"You don't need to address me as 'sir' anymore, you outrank me now," Oden said with a light smile.

"Oh, all right, sir."

How are the Panthers? I've heard rumors that you're still getting into all kinds of trouble, just like you did when you were here at the Camp."

"We're fine, sir, and yes, it does seem that we have a tendency to find ourselves involved in complex situations," Egil admitted.

"You were always different, the amount of trouble you got me into," he said with his gaze lost, remembering.

"I'm sorry, sir..." Egil tried to apologize.

"Don't you have any regrets? I always knew you were special. I have a good nose for that kind of thing," he said, putting his finger to the side of said appendix. "If you could see the pretty boys I get sent now, weaklings with no courage or honor and certainly zero future as Rangers," he said this loud enough— and his voice was already powerful—so it would be heard throughout the dining hall. At several nearby tables, conversation stopped and heads bowed.

"You are unique and an example to follow. Give my regards to everyone and tell them to take good care of themselves. The kingdom needs you," Oden said with a wink.

"Thank you, sir."

"And you all, go back to your duties!" he shouted at those who were listening to their conversation.

Several groups of contenders of different years left the dining hall quickly.

Egil could not help smiling.

"I see that things don't change around here."

"And they won't as long as I'm Master Instructor," Oden said as he moved away to harangue the contenders at two tables at the far end.

Holding back his laughter, Egil left the dining hall and decided to go and see Sylvia before heading to the Library to continue his search. He was intrigued by whatever the new Master Ranger might want from him. He arrived at the house of the School of Nature, entered, and found Sylvia at work. She was preparing some kind of potion over the fire.

"Good day, Master Ranger," Egil greeted her with respect.

"Oh hello, Egil, come in," she said and waved him closer.

Egil went over to the worktable, and all at once the memories of the years he had spent studying with Eyra rushed back. He had learned so much there and he had enjoyed doing so. He loved to learn anything related to the School of Nature.

"By the look on your face I guess this place brings back good memories," Sylvia noted, as with hands protected by heavy, treated leather gloves, she poured a green liquid from a crystal container into a larger one which already had a blue liquid. Upon contact there was a reaction, a blue-green gas that went up to the ceiling. The remaining resultant liquid turned orange.

"Yes… it does bring back good memories."

"I guessed as much. The same thing happened to me when I came back to give my first lesson here."

"Esben said you wanted to see me."

"Indeed," she replied, putting the container to cool in ice water. "From what you mentioned, you're a Specialist Healer Guard."

"Yes, it's one of the two specializations I obtained."

"The other one is Expert Herbalist, right?"

Egil nodded. "I feel very fortunate."

"I doubt fortune had anything to do with your getting those specializations. I'm sure it was the result of a lot of study, dedication, and intelligence," she said, smiling.

Egil bowed his head, slightly embarrassed.

"Those are two specializations that combine well. In truth, Expert Herbalist combines well with all the Nature Specialties and even others of Expertise and Wildlife. The knowledge of plants and components is essential and helps in all the Specialties."

"That's my belief too. It's a unique Specialty that provides expert knowledge that can be used to complement others."

"What I find more interesting still is that you are also a Healer Guard."

"Oh…"

"It's my favorite specialization," Sylvia admitted.

"And the one you have," Egil added, looking straight into her eyes.

"I see that Dolbarar has told you about me," she said, tilting her head and smiling.

"Just a little. He mentioned that, before accepting the post of Master Ranger of the School of Nature, you were an experienced Healer Guard."

"I also have much knowledge of Expert Herbalist and Forest Alchemist, even if I don't possess those Specialties. The truth is, I've been too busy performing my work as a Healer Guard," she said with a smile.

"From what Dolbarar told me, you're a skilled Healer Guard. I'm sure you also have a lot of knowledge of the other specializations."

Sylvia smiled, "I enjoy my profession and study every day. Experimenting and learning from practice is another of my pastimes."

"Mine too," Egil said.

"I've heard about you, and the Snow Panthers," Sylvia suddenly said.

"I hope that what you've heard is good," said Egil, raising an eyebrow.

"Excellent, and I have good references from people I highly trust who are quite respectable. I am also aware of everything that happened with Eyra, and I know it was you who uncovered her treachery and eventually stopped her before it was too late for Dolbarar and the kingdom. And that's why I want to help you."

"Help me? How?" Egil asked blankly.

"With knowledge," she replied, staring into his eyes.

"The greatest of treasures," said Egil.

"That is what they say. Do you believe it?"

"I believe it," Egil nodded emphatically.

"Then you're like me," Sylvia replied with a smile. She took off her gloves, turned around, and went over to a locked closet and opened it. From inside she took out a leather bag and came back to where Egil was standing.

"I want to help a young Healer Guard to become a skilled Healer Guard."

"I still have a lot to learn and improve," said Egil, who was fully aware he was far from his goal.

"And that's where I come in with my offer to help," she said, pointing at herself with her finger. "When I was your age and was beginning my path as Healer Guard, you know what it was I always missed having when I faced difficult situations?"

"No, Ma'am, I don't."

Sylvia smiled. "Having a mentor with me to help me with the problems, illnesses, and difficulties I encountered on my way and which I had to face and defeat on my own."

"Yes, that would be good. It's a feeling I share. The same thing happens to me now that I'm a Healer Guard, and it will happen even more…"

"I'm glad you share my view, because that's why I asked you to see me," she said, putting her hand into the leather bag. She took out a thick tome with tanned leather covers. It had the symbol of the Healer Guards engraved on the front cover.

"What's this tome?" Egil asked, unabashedly intrigued.

"My treasure," Sylvia replied.

Egil threw his head back. "Treasure of knowledge?"

"That's right. This tome is a collection of good remedies. The most effective according to my own experience, gathered along the years. I have used almost all of them in real situations and they have worked well. Those I have never needed to use and are in the tome I have collected from good, reliable sources. This will help you face almost every illness and complication you will ever find."

"Is it a compendium summary?" Egil asked, he was beginning to see why she called it her treasure and its worth. The Rangers had huge tomes of knowledge, but they were at the Shelter, the Camp, or in the Tower of the Rangers in the Royal Castle. They were too large and heavy to carry on missions.

"Yes, something like that. Only of very effective cures and remedies. Whenever you encounter an illness or a wound, you'll simply need to consult the book and look for the indicated solution." Sylvia handed Egil the volume.

"Wow… this is fantastic…" said Egil, opening the tome and starting to read.

"It's focused on Norghanian illnesses and remedies. Outside our kingdom it will be less useful, but I'm sure you'll still be able to use it.

Ice Fever is the same in Norghana as it is in Irinel, no matter how far one kingdom is from the other. The potion to prepare is listed by Norghanian components and plants, so if you find yourself in Irinel you'll have to look for complementary plants and substitute them."

"I... thank you!" Egil was already leafing through the book, looking at illnesses and remedies.

"I'm sure it will help you and, from what I've been told, with your prodigious head you'll soon know it all by heart."

"Not so prodigious," Egil said, reading the text written in small, spidery handwriting. "I might need a magnifying glass."

"It's possible, yes. I tried to use as much of each page as possible, so I'm afraid I used a really tiny handwriting," she said apologetically.

"But it's clear and the sentences are precise. I won't have any trouble. Besides, I do have a magnifying glass."

"A well prepared young man is worth at least three."

Egil smiled. Then he was thoughtful.

"Why give the book to me?"

"I know everything there is to know in it and don't need it anymore. Besides, I had a copy made in the capital, which I will keep here in the Camp."

"Yes... but why me?" Egil wanted to understand the reason for the gift, which was priceless and would definitely come in handy. Sylvia had just met him, and it was strange that she wanted to give it to him. Or did she want something in return?

"Because you had a bad experience with Eyra, and I want you to know and see that we are not all like that."

"Oh... there's no need..."

"There might not be, but I'd like to do it. Eyra tricked and betrayed you, but I'll help you, and the Panthers whenever I can. I know it won't repair the broken link of trust with the Master Rangers, but it will strengthen it a little. I don't want there to be distrust between us."

"Thank you, Ma'am, I appreciate it. It's not necessary, but I do appreciate it."

"It's the best I can do after what happened. I want to make sure you know that you can trust me, and this gesture," she said, nodding at the tome in Egil's hands, "is to establish friendship and trust. This is what I would like."

"I'm grateful for this gesture. I'll take good care of this treasure."

"Good. It will be the first step in our friendship," Sylvia said, offering Egil her hand.

"Good," Egil replied and shook Sylvia's hand with conviction.

A new friendship was formed between them at that moment.

Chapter 19

Egil went back to his study of the orb. For two whole days, with barely a break, even to sleep, he was locked up reading every tome that might be remotely related to the subject of magic, in search of some mention of the orbs. Despite all his efforts, he was not having much luck. He could not go through all the volumes stored there either; there were too many, even if he only focused on the ones related to any kind of magic. He would need several weeks to do a thorough search, and he did not have the time right then.

He focused on the most likely books, leaving the rest aside. He continued searching, reading as fast as he could, skipping some chapters, reading through others, looking for references to orbs or similar Objects of Power. At last, his efforts were rewarded. He found two different references that might be significant. The finding, if not definitive, was a start, and he was pleased, because he had been about to lose hope of finding anything there.

In the tome *Creation and Treatment of Objects of Power*, Mage Alrich Torsen explained in complete detail how to create objects that could later be made into ones of power. The book was quite technical, and Egil did not know many of the terms used. As well as the elaborate process it mentioned. It was not something they would have studied in the Rangers or anything he had ever heard of. One of the processes drew his attention. It was based on the use of glass, but not just any glass. Alrich wrote about using a special glass of unique characteristics: Dragon Glass. Egil immediately found this interesting, since the orb was made of a material similar to glass. The fact that the term 'Dragon' was mentioned seemed quite revealing. Unfortunately, it made no mention of an orb or sphere as such, referring only to the material used in the making of powerful magic objects.

He read intently, trying to memorize every word. He decided it would be more efficient to write the most important parts in one of his notebooks. So, he did. Alrich explained the existence of a special glass believed to have been tempered by the magic of the ancient dragons. Because of this, it had such special, superior properties to any other material. The mage mentioned an almost unbreakable hardness and ability to emanate energy or magic. Alrich also mentioned that several fragments of glass of different sizes had been found in several places in Tremia, some of them without any specific shape, bits of base material to work with. Alrich had been trying to forge them without much luck. It was not possible to give them any shape, at least not by traditional methods. He had also tried using human magic, with the same result. But Alrich was continuing his experiments on the material since its potential was immense.

Other fragments of Dragon Glass had been also found in their finished form, shaped like a weapon. A spear tip, a shield, and the tip of an arrow. Egil found all this fascinating. Weapons of Dragon Glass, indestructible and conductors of magical energy? The fact that they were rumored to have been created by dragons made the matter even more fascinating. Perhaps the orb was built from a similar material, or even Dragon Glass itself. Perhaps in the same way.

"This is fantastic!" Egil cried. No one heard him, since it was late at night and he was alone in the hall.

In the tome *Imbuing Power and its Derivations* by Enchanter Jasen Xertos, Egil found another distant reference to what he was searching for. It did not mention orbs specifically either, but it could very well be applicable. Jasen explained that it was possible to imbue power to objects with certain characteristics that allowed them to retain and store that power. It mentioned that Jasen used mainly silver and glass and that he was able to imbue power into these materials. In his experiments he had found that they stored the magic for a variable period of time according to the type of material, the enchantment used, and the power of the mage doing the enchantment.

What caught Egil's attention most was that it mentioned that some magi masters in this art were capable of imbuing power so that it kept a living being alive. The enchanter gave the example of a silver cage imbued with magic, to maintain a canary that belonged to the king alive. The bird lived over a hundred and fifty years. Jasen also mentioned putting a similar enchantment on a glass vase to hold a butterfly, and said butterfly lived over two hundred years inside the enchanted object.

"Fascinating! Objects imbued with power to keep creatures alive," Egil muttered excitedly.

He went on reading the two tomes and writing down in his

notebook everything he found of interest. At last, exhausted, he closed the two volumes and put them back on their shelves before going to his cabin.

He had not exactly found what he was looking for, but all this new information helped him continue investigating and conjecturing about the orb. Besides, these were interesting discoveries. Unfortunately, he had no choice but to get going on his way. He had to see Gerd and reunite with his friends at the Shelter. The study had to be put on hold. He would continue later on when he had another chance.

The next morning, on a quite dismal day, he gathered his things and got ready to leave. Before doing so, he went to say goodbye to Dolbarar as the leader had requested. The guards let him through the door the moment they saw it was him. The Master Rangers were all teaching their lessons, so Egil found the ground floor of the House of Command empty. He went upstairs to say hello to Dolbarar.

"Hello, Egil, come in," the leader of the Camp said. He was working at his desk, writing letters and messages to send to the capital.

"Good morning, sir."

"I guess you're here to say goodbye," Dolbarar said.

"Yes, I hate to admit it, but I must go on my way," Egil said, spreading his arms in a gesture of apology.

"Did you find the information you were looking for?"

"Not exactly, but I gathered new information and I've learned some fascinating things."

"I call that success," Dolbarar said, smiling.

"Indeed, sir. Acquiring new knowledge must always be seen as something positive," Egil smiled back.

"I understand you're leaving for the Shelter to see Gerd and Engla," Dolbarar said, almost as a question.

"That's right, sir. I want to make sure they're all right and if they need help, do as much as I can for them."

"That does you credit. You have a kind heart," said Dolbarar.

"It's the least I can do."

"I said I wanted to talk to you about something important,"

Dolbarar said, twining his fingers.

"Yes, sir, I remember."

"You see, I want you to escort someone to the Shelter."

Egil's eyes opened wide. He had not been expecting that.

"Of course, sir," he said.

"I need this person to get there safely."

"Who do I have to escort, sir?" Egil asked, raising an eyebrow. The request was strange.

"You'll know soon enough. Go to the stables and wait for their arrival."

Egil nodded.

"Good luck."

"Thank you, sir."

Egil left Dolbarar's studio and went downstairs. He was surprised that Dolbarar had not told him who he had to escort, but he knew the leader had his reasons.

The door of the Command House opened and Esben walked in.

"Egil, I've barely seen you. Where have you been?"

"I've been looking for information for some research I'm conducting."

"Buried in books, I guess," Esben said, raising an eyebrow.

"I'm afraid so. Now I must leave."

"Already? But you just arrived."

"I'm going to the Shelter. I'm meeting the other Panthers there. We want to see how Gerd and Engla are doing."

"Of course. Do me a favor and give a good hug to every one of them. Give Lasgol and Gerd a double one" he said. "You know I love my Wildlife guys a little more than the rest," he said with a mischievous smile.

Egil smiled too.

"Absolutely, one's own School comes first," said Haakon, appearing behind Esben as if he had materialized out of the blue. Egil started from the surprise.

"But we can't admit it openly," Esben said, putting a finger to his lips.

"Nonsense. I admit it openly all the time. Those of the School of Expertise are way better than the rest of the Rangers."

"No they're not," countered Esben.

"They are, and by far. You only need to see who the new First

173

Ranger is now."

"You mean Raner Olsen?"

"In the flesh. A disciple of mine, I might add."

"I'm not saying he's not a great Ranger… but those of Wildlife are too."

"He's First Ranger. The best among all the Rangers, of course," Haakon said, oozing pride.

"That I can't deny," said Esben.

"If you're going to the Shelter, I want you to take something to Engla from me," Haakon told Egil.

"Yes… of course." Egil had no idea when Haakon had heard he was going to the Shelter, but the Master Ranger had clearly found out.

"It's a gift, so don't lose it on the way."

"Of course I won't lose it, sir," Egil replied, frowning.

"Engla was my teacher and taught me everything I know. I hold her in great esteem," Haakon said.

Esben nodded. "I know for a fact it's mutual."

"We of the same School are fond of one another. Also, congratulate Astrid and Viggo. They are an example of what you can achieve as part of the School of Expertise."

"I will…" Egil said blankly. Haakon was not one to praise anyone, least of all the Panthers. He wondered what might be behind the change of heart. Gifts and congratulations to Expertise Rangers, and a First Ranger also from Expertise? Egil found it all a bit suspicious.

Haakon took a black box out from under his cloak and handed it to Egil.

"Have a good journey," he wished Egil and then left. After a moment there was no trace of him.

"Tell the Panthers to come by when they have a break. I'd love to see them," said Esben.

"I will, Master Ranger."

"Very well then. Take care of yourselves, and try not to get into too much trouble," Esben said with a big smile that implied he already knew they would.

Egil left the House of Command and headed to the stables. He had a strange journey ahead of him. Who would his companion be?

Chapter 20

Nilsa rode into the city of Prejurice. It was a small city in eastern Norghana which had never become a great urban center, although the locals had always entertained that dream. The city's traders and merchants were always trying to boost the growth of the city, but without access to mines or the sea, they could not make the city grow enough to become important. The small wall surrounding it was a perfect example: high and pretentious at the main gate and low and weak around the back of the city.

She studied the locals as she passed them. The population was made up of farmers, wood cutters, craft artisans, and traders. The artisans included tailors and weavers the city was known for, and this was why it had always had the hopes of becoming a well-known and important city. It *was* notable to a certain point, since many nobles ordered their clothes from Prejurice tailors. Nilsa had always been interested in fashion—that was a given, seeing she was from this city.

She headed up one of the streets parallel to the main avenue and went to the area where the weavers, tailors, and cloth markets were located. It was Nilsa's favorite part of the city and where she had spent most of her childhood. She used to run away to see how the cloth was dyed, and how they made or wove the clothes for the noble women of the court. It fascinated her. If it had not been for her father's unfortunate end, Nilsa would have probably ended up a seamstress. She loved to imagine and design dresses.

As she went by the weavers, the characteristic smell of the dyeing mixtures and other strong scents they used filled her lungs. She remembered the countless times she had snuck into the workshops to study the process. She smiled—they were good memories, although many times she had ended up punished for wandering around without permission. A little further up, following the cobbled street, she arrived at the tailors' shops and stopped in front of the most famous in the city: Sondersen Brothers, Tailors. Without getting off her horse, she looked inside the shop, which now covered the two adjacent buildings. Things must be going well for the Sondersen brothers.

Nilsa remembered with a mischievous smile that they had both given her what-for on several occasions when she had been caught sneaking in the shop. They were very good with needle and thread but also wielded a clipboard with ease. Just thinking about it made her shiver. They had left her bottom smarting more than once, although that was not the worst; the worst was when they told her mother and she, ashamed, had beaten Nilsa again with her 'iron shoe' what Nilsa and her sisters called the shoe their mother used to teach them 'life lessons' with, when they misbehaved. In Nilsa's case, this had been often.

She continued up the street until she arrived at the shops that sold complements for the dresses and clothes of the court nobles. There were jewels for the ladies, daggers with jeweled handles, and luxury armor. She stopped her mount in front of the most luxurious shop, that of Trader Ifalmerson. Looking at the dress infantry armor on display at the door, she was awed. A real beauty. It must cost a fortune. A nobleman came out of the shop with old Ifalmerson, the two of them talking about the armor.

Nilsa bowed her head and watched. She recognized the nobleman. It was Count Ogner, a local noble of modest lineage whose lands were to the east of the city. Most likely he was seeing how he might acquire that luxury piece to show off at banquets and other formal occasions. For a moment Nilsa imagined Viggo buying the suit of armor with the gold he had wanted to keep and going to another nobleman's house, all elegant and proud. Just thinking about it made her giggle. She decided to continue riding through the city— it brought back memories she had forgotten. Life with the Rangers was complicated, and even more so if you were a member of the Royal Eagles and the Snow Panthers. She had not had much free time to think about the past, her early youth and hometown. Being back in the same streets she had run through as a child getting into trouble made her tingle, and she could not help chuckling.

She was riding with her hood up to go unnoticed, as was the Ranger custom. This way no one would recognize her and she could enjoy her ride through the city, seeing it and its citizens again in peace. Because of her red hair and freckled face, Nilsa drew attention as it was. Away from her city, where she was well known, to other parts of the kingdom, she was usually taken for a visitor from the distant kingdom of Irinel in the east. The people of Irinel were mostly redheads with freckles like her. It was curious, since they were features Nilsa had been born with. Ingrid clearly looked Norghanian with her blonde hair; Astrid not so much with her dark hair, and Nilsa's red hair also did not look Norghanian. When Nilsa had asked her mother, Ulsa, she had sworn the whole family was of Norghanian descent.

Nilsa personally did not think twice about the whole matter. It was true there were some people in Norghana with fair skin, red hair, and freckles like her, but they were rare. There were not many like Astrid either with jet-black hair. Nilsa was used to others assuming she was from Irinel, and it did not bother her. She sometimes liked to imagine she was a descendant of some noble of that kingdom, perhaps a princess, and did not even know. She giggled at the thought. No—she was no princess, nor did she want to be one. She was a Ranger Specialist, and she was happy with her lot in life. It had cost her dearly, and every drop of sweat and suffering had been worthwhile. That was how she felt, and she was especially proud to have achieved the specialization of Mage Hunter.

As she was turning onto the main street, she saw two soldiers of the local guard at a crossroads. They were on duty, watching the people go by and looking bored. She recognized one of the two; it was Isvan, a brute as large as he was short of wit. He was larger and uglier than the last time she had seen him; he looked like an albino troll. She remembered how that brute and his friends had tortured her for being herself. The beasts had treated her cruelly because Nilsa was different from the others and a girl at that. It had been rough. That was why she detested people who bullied those who were different. The bullying she had suffered had helped her become strong. As she often said, her skin was tough— disdain and insults did not go through.

As she rode past the two guards, she reined in her horse.

"Are you with the city guard?" she asked.

Isvan lifted his head to stare at her, but he saw nothing but a foreigner in a hooded cloak.

"We are, yes. And what's it to you, stranger?" he replied rudely with a grunt.

"You should be more respectful," Nilsa chided.

"And why should I respect you?" said Isvan as he reached to his belt for his axe.

Nilsa put her hand to her neck and showed them her Ranger and Specialist medallions.

"She's a Ranger," said the other guard, who was more weathered than Isvan, elbowing him.

"Oh... I hadn't realized..." Isvan muttered, scratching his head.

"I am," Nilsa said, uncovering her head and letting her red hair and freckles shine in the reflection of the noonday sun.

The two soldiers stared at her with eyes half-closed, blinded by the red flash.

"Does the Ranger need directions?" the older guard asked.

"You don't remember me, Isvan?" Nilsa asked, staring at him.

"I... don't...." He shook his large head.

"I'm Nilsa, Etor Blom's daughter."

Isvan's troll face lit up as he recognized her.

"Nilsa... yes. I didn't know..."

"That I was a Ranger Specialist?"

"No, I wasn't aware..."

"Is she the local Ranger?" asked the other guard, whom Nilsa had decided was from out of town.

"I am. Isvan and I have known one another since we were little children. Isn't that so?" Nilsa glared at the brute.

"Yeah... since we were kids." The bully nodded and lowered his gaze, ashamed.

"I just wanted to stop and say hi."

"Oh... okay," Isvan said, looking at her blankly.

"I hope you're taking good care of these streets and the families who live here," Nilsa said in warning.

"I do."

"We do," the other guard joined in.

"That's good. I want my family to be well-protected. They will be, right, Isvan? For old times' sake."

"Yes, yes... of course... your family will be well looked after," the brute promised, understanding the message she was implying.

"I wouldn't want to come back from some mission for the King and find out no one had taken good care of my sisters and mother," Nilsa said, and this time her tone took on a veiled threat.

"They'll be fine, I swear," Isvan promised.

"I can promise the Ranger that we'll keep the streets safe," the other guard chimed in.

178

"That's good, I'd appreciate it," Nilsa said, nodding. "See you," she said, and putting up her hood, she went on along the main street.

As she went into the heart of the city, pleased with her words to the brute and the small lesson she had taught him, she remembered more of her childhood there. Not everything had been bad, now that she thought about it. She had always had her sisters, and the three had defended, supported, and loved one another. They had overcome every obstacle and kept going. She went by several shops and remembered how her sisters always wanted to buy pretty things from them but they had not been able to because they never had money. Every corner of every street brought back some conversation, mischief, or game with her two sisters.

Her family's house was in the higher part of the city; at the beginning of the higher part to be precise. Her father, who had been a Ranger like her grandfather before him, had enjoyed a modest pay, and they had not been able to buy a better house in the higher section of Prejurice. Nilsa lifted her gaze and looked at the top of the hill. She stroked her horse's neck. Up there was where the richest traders and merchants lived. And at the very top of the city were the small palaces where some lords of lineage and relatives of nobles at Court lived.

She sighed at the thought of her mother. For Nilsa, social position, gold, and having pretty things like jewels and dresses had never been important. Perhaps because she came from a humble family and had never had them. Besides, she was not jealous, not that way. She envied Ingrid's fortitude and Viggo's skill with his knives— although she would never admit it to him—but not riches or position and power. Those things had never interested her. It was not so with her mother, however. Maybe that was why they had never really gotten along well. Her mother had always preferred her two younger sisters: Mirial and Sondra. The fact that Nilsa had always preferred a bow to dolls and dresses and had chosen to join the Rangers had not helped their relationship either.

She stopped and gazed down at the lower part of the city where the less fortunate and the workers lived. Both areas were clearly distinguishable by the quality of the buildings and the cleanliness of the streets and houses—how well cared for one part was and how abandoned the other was. Even the mud and filth seemed to respect gold and did not climb to the higher section of the city.

Soon she arrived at her home. It was a little two-story house with a small garden out front and another in the back where there was also space to keep the horses. She took hers to the back. She did not see her sisters or mother; they must be having dessert, given the hour of the day. She looked after her mount, and when she finished, she went back to the front as if she had just arrived.

She put on her hood and knocked on the door, bowing her head.

The door opened, and a girl slightly younger than herself, but who looked very much like her, appeared on the threshold.

"Yes, what do you want?" the girl asked, distrustful.

"You don't recognize your own sister?" Nilsa asked without raising her head or removing her hood.

"Nilsa! It can't be! What a surprise!"

"Hello, Sondra. You've grown," Nilsa said with a big smile, taking off her hood so her middle sister could see her.

"You've grown more! I'm so happy to see you!"

Both sisters hugged tightly, filled with joy.

"You look wonderful," Nilsa said, studying her sister from head to toe.

"And you look like a real Ranger!"

Nilsa laughed. "I hope so, what would be the point otherwise?"

"Come in, Mirial and Mother are going to be so happy!" Sondra said, dragging her inside.

As soon as she stepped into the house she had grown up in, a thousand feelings and memories burst in Nilsa's heart and head: the entrance hall, the walls, the stairs that went up to the second floor. The living room that could be glimpsed from the doorway, the furniture, the characteristic smell of the house—everything reminded her of the home she had left to join the Rangers.

Ulsa and Mirial were sitting in the old living room.

"Nilsa! Sister!" Mirial jumped up and ran to hug Nilsa, whose eyes moistened seeing her baby sister had become a young woman.

"It's been so long since we've seen you. Why haven't you come before?" her sister asked, her eyes also moist.

"The Rangers keep me busy," Nilsa smiled.

"You look too pale and thin," said her mother, rising to her feet.

"Hello, Mother. You look good," Nilsa replied, and she meant it.

"You can take care of yourself in the city better, even though times are messy with the wars."

"Yes, I know," Nilsa nodded.

"Come give me a hug," her mother said, opening her arms.

Nilsa stepped into her mother's embrace lovingly. The fact that they did not get along that well did not mean Nilsa did not love her mother; she loved her very much.

"You're all skin and bones. Don't the Rangers feed you? Even your father was fuller, and he never stopped traveling from here to there."

"I think I'm just built like that, Mother," Nilsa shrugged and smiled.

"I'm glad to see you home, my child," her mother said, and it sounded genuine.

"I'm also happy to be here."

"This has always been your home and always will be," Ulsa said.

"Thank you, Mother, that means a lot to me," Nilsa said, wiping a tear that ran down her cheek.

"Tell us everything!" Sondra said.

"Yes, in full detail." Mirial joined in dragging her to sit the old family sofa.

Nilsa sat down and looked at her two sisters, filled with love. They were very different, both physically and emotionally. Physically, Sondra, the middle sister, was the most like Nilsa but they had different personalities. Mirial, the youngest, did not look much like Nilsa but they were similar in character. They both took after their father, while Sondra took after their mother's personality.

"Prepare a strong tisane to honor your sister's return," Ulsa told her daughters.

Nilsa told them about the kingdom's capital, how big and impressive it was, and the amount of things they could find that would amaze them there. While they listened, they drank herbal tea and ate cookies, Nilsa entertaining them with her capital city stories.

"We have to go some day!" Sondra begged her mother with pleading eyes.

"Yes, I want to see it too and visit every corner," Mirial added, joining in her sister's plea.

"Journeys to the capital are expensive, and it's a dangerous place. Nilsa is only telling you about the good things, but it's also filled with outlaws, mercenaries, thieves, and other lowlifes," Ulsa said, looking disgusted at the idea.

Nilsa did not want to contradict her mother and went on telling them several adventures she knew would amuse them without needing to give gory details.

"What adventures!" Mirial cried, her eyes like saucers. It was obvious she also wanted to enjoy those adventures.

"You have to be brave and well-trained to go on such adventures," Sondra told her with a face that showed mixed fear and fascination.

Ulsa heaved a deep sigh. "You were always different from the other girls. When they were all playing with dolls, dressing their hair and getting pretty, you only wanted to shoot with a bow and learn to ride," her mother said in a critical tone.

"Not always. There was a time when I enjoyed playing with clothes. More making them than wearing them, but well, dresses nonetheless."

"That phase didn't last long. You soon started to learn to fight with your fists, not ladylike at all," her mother said in open criticism.

"Life dictates our needs, Mother. We're not all born to be perfect young ladies," Nilsa replied.

"Seeing how clumsy you were, you were never going to be one anyway. Your clumsiness cost me three sets of cups and saucers no less, and expensive ones at that."

Nilsa shrugged. "As I said, I wasn't born to be a lady. That's why I'm a Ranger."

Ulsa looked sad. "I asked you not to, I begged you not to join the Rangers. Did you heed me? No, of course you didn't."

"I always wanted to be a Ranger..." Nilsa said defensively.

"Yes, to emulate your father, and look what happened to him... how he ended..."

"He died defending the kingdom with honor. He's a Norghanian hero."

"He died at the hands of a sorcerer who pulled his heart out. Is that a way to die? What good is being a hero if you end up like that?"

"Better to die serving the kingdom like a hero than hiding in a hole like a coward," Nilsa replied, unable to disguise her anger. She could not let Ulsa disparage her father's sacrifice

"Don't be so sure. Your father won't have entered the realm of the Ice Gods without a soul. He'll be wandering the Frozen Continent for all eternity, frozen like a specter."

"Those are baseless beliefs. I don't believe it," Nilsa said, seeing the fear in her younger sister's faces.

"Well, you should. And you should leave the Rangers before you end up like him."

Nilsa raised her arms. "Let's not argue, Mother. I've come to visit you and see how you are. Let's have a loving reunion, I beg you."

"Fine, you're right," Ulsa snorted, letting out her frustration. "Besides, we have good news to celebrate," her mother said, and her face lit up.

"Oh yes? What news is that?" Nilsa asked, looking at all three.

Mirial and Sondra looked at one another and said nothing.

"Your sister Mirial is engaged! She's soon to be married!"

"Well, that is amazing news," Nilsa said, looking at Mirial.

"Yes... it is..." she replied shyly, and Nilsa noticed she did not look as happy as a bride should be.

"She's marrying the Pelesen's son, Josh," Sondra said.

The surname rang a bell, and Nilsa tried to remember.

"Wow! That's one of the most important families in the city!" she cried.

"The third most important. They have several weaver workshops and a tailor workshop that's popular among the local nobles," her mother confirmed. "Your sister will have everything she wants. She'll live surrounded by luxury," she added, beaming.

"Very impressive," Nilsa commented, looking at Mirial and noticing she was not saying anything, which puzzled her.

"And of course, since we'll be family, we'll be invited to parties and receptions in the higher part of town," Sondra said with a delighted face.

"My most sincere congratulations, little sister," said Nilsa.

"Thank you," Mirial said, serving some more tisane in the four cups, one of which had been repaired even though the crack was still visible.

"I was sure Mirial would marry well," her mother said. "After all, she's easily the prettiest of my three girls."

"Mother... I'm not, don't say that," Mirial protested.

"You are, and you know it well. You've always had the boys after you."

"That's true. Boys vie for Mirial's attention," Sondra said.

"I hope you've made them suffer," Nilsa said with a giggle.

"Quite a bit," Mirial confirmed, giggling too.

They enjoyed the conversation and the tisane. Nilsa felt happy there with her sisters and her mother. She had missed them a lot. She cast several inquisitive glances at Mirial but she looked away. She had the odd feeling there was something wrong with her sister's wedding and wanted to find out what it was. She would have to wait for Mirial to open up to her about it. Nilsa decided not to press her and wait. She knew her baby sister well— sooner or later she would confide in her.

Chapter 21

Nilsa woke up with a smile on her face. The three sisters had slept in the same room like they used to when they were little. Nilsa had shared a bed with Mirial and Sondra had slept in the other, not wanting to part with the other two under any circumstance. Nilsa was delighted to have shared the room with her beloved sisters one more time. Used to sleeping anywhere they could find with the Panthers, sleeping in her own bed at home with her sisters was a priceless luxury; she felt such a good feeling could not be bought, even with all the gold they had stolen from the Zangrians.

The sisters had talked well into the night. Nilsa had been obliged to tell them an infinity of things in all kinds of detail and also answer thousands of questions. All of it amid cries of surprise and admiration at what she had to tell. Before she had finished telling them something they already had questions to ask her. Her sisters' curiosity was insatiable. But Nilsa was not surprised. They had never left their hometown; all they knew was what they had seen and heard in Prejurice and the rumors running around. They had never experienced the 'outside world' and were dying to. Hence their interest in knowing more and more of what Nilsa had lived and experienced . The adventure with the Turquoise Queen totally blew their minds; they could not even begin to imagine it. Or everything Nilsa told them about the Frozen Continent, with the Wild People of the Ice, Semi-giants, Arcanes of the Glaciers, and Tundra Dwellers. Nilsa's adventures seemed like unreal, epic fables their sister was telling them, only she had really lived through them and come out victorious.

They shared breakfast in the morning amid laughter and giggles, and Nilsa was able to be herself and not worry about being nervous or clumsy. She was home, and no one judged the way she was—well, perhaps her mother did, but not her sisters. After breakfast, Nilsa, Mirial, and Sondra went to check the shops on the main street as they had in the past whenever they had free time.

Walking the streets with her sisters filled Nilsa with joy. They chatted about everything and nothing, laughing and giggling. They stopped at the market and Nilsa bought them some sweets since she had coin from her Ranger's pay. She knew her sisters barely had any money of their own and felt good providing for them. Being a Ranger was an honorable profession, and it also provided one with enough coin to live, Nilsa was realizing for the first time. As a rule, the Panthers did not have time to even *think* about spending their pay, least of all actually spending it. She was happy to treat her sisters and commented she would like to buy something for their mother.

"I know what she'd like," Sondra said and led them to one of the shops with women's clothes.

While Sondra explained to the shop owner the jacket her mother had mentioned liking, Mirial and Nilsa looked at the dresses on display inside the shop.

"How are you, Mirial?" Nilsa asked, giving her an opening to talk if she wanted to.

"Well..." she replied shyly, bowing her head. She took a couple steps and then stopped. She looked at Nilsa. "To be honest, not great," she admitted.

"I thought I noticed something," Nilsa said, putting her hand on her sister's shoulder.

"It's the wedding..."

"Tell me, you know you can trust me."

Mirial looked around. A couple of town ladies were shopping, but they did not seem to be paying attention to them, busy checking out the clothes.

"I don't want to get married," Mirial told Nilsa, lowering her voice and staring into her eyes.

Nilsa threw her head back, surprised. That was not what she had expected.

"What do you mean you don't want to get married?" Nilsa asked in disbelief.

Nilsa began to understand what was going on.

"I don't love him," her sister said firmly.

"You love another and that's why you don't want to marry Pelesen?"

Mirial shook her head vigorously.

"It's not that."

Nilsa was puzzled. She put her hands on her hips and whispered: "Then what is it? Tell me, please."

"I just don't love him. I don't want to marry him. There's no one else," Mirial said, shaking her hands in denial.

"Oh, wow... since you have so many suitors, I just assumed..." Nilsa apologized.

"He's been courting me. Being who he is—and I won't deny he's handsome and elegant—and everyone's expecting me to get married... I was sort of obliged to accept his courting. Mother insisted a lot. Well, everyone did, really. I was supposed to be so happy that he'd noticed me, you know, since we have no means.... The courting went well. I wanted to take it slowly. I was debating whether to go on or not, but before I came to a decision, I found out he wanted to marry me with an early proposal I didn't dare refuse."

"You bewitch the men," Nilsa joked to soothe her sister's anguish.

"It's not that I'm not flattered by the fact that one of the most handsome and influential young men in the city wants to marry me, I am. But I don't want to marry, I want to live my life. Leave this city and see the world, like you have."

Nilsa smiled. "In that case, do it. Don't marry and seek your fortune away from here. The fact that we have no means or position doesn't mean we don't have options. They are smaller, but if we look for opportunities we can find them. Besides, you're smart, pretty, and educated. You'll make it without trouble. I did it, and so will you, I have no doubt."

"Your words are a balm of peace for my soul, sister. But it's not so simple..."

"Because of Mother?"

"Because of Mother, and the situation."

"What situation?"

"The fact that the wedding has already been arranged and announced. The whole city knows. Mother arranged everything with Jorgen Pelesen, Josh's father."

"They've planned a massive wedding," said Sondra, who was coming out of the shop with the gift for their mother under her arm. "All the influential families of the city and even some nobles will attend."

"So? Let them rot. Cancel it and that's that," said Nilsa, frowning. She had spoken with a raised voice, and the ladies inside the shop turned to look at her.

"We'd better go outside," Sondra said.

They moved away from the shop.

"If the wedding is canceled, the Pelesens will be ridiculed," Mirial explained.

"It would be a great embarrassment," Sondra added.

Nilsa shrugged. "They're rich. Don't worry, they'll survive."

"But Mother and Sondra... they'll suffer," Mirial said, concerned. "The Pelesens, and because of their influence the other important families, wouldn't forgive them."

"They'd make our life impossible. We'd have to leave," Sondra said determinedly.

Nilsa took a deep breath.

"I see... I hadn't considered the implications for you two." Nilsa started to feel restless, her nerves overcoming her. Under no circumstance did she want her family to suffer. She had to help them, but the situation was complex, with ramifications that could alter her mother's and sisters' lives, and not exactly for good.

"The wedding is in four weeks..." Mirial said with bowed head. "If I were a good daughter and sister, I'd accept the marriage without a second thought. It's the most convenient course of action—we'd all benefit and be happier."

"Except you," Nilsa said, unable to hold back her anger.

"The more I think about it, the more I see I have to accept my fate."

"You'll have everything you could ever want, I'm sure you'll be happy. Besides, you're marrying a handsome lad," Sondra said. "Mother always says so."

"That doesn't mean Mirial will be happy," Nilsa said.

"It doesn't?" asked Sondra blankly. "What else could we want than to marry well?"

"Look at me, little sister. Do you really think I'd be happy marrying well?" Nilsa asked Sondra, spreading her arms.

"You're different. You've always been different,"

"Mirial is too. She has to find her own happiness. She's not responsible for Mother's or yours, nor is she for mine."

Sondra bowed her head. "You're right, sister."

"If you don't want to get married, don't. I'll support you against anyone," Nilsa said to Mirial.

"So will I," Sondra joined her.

Nilsa hugged both her sisters. She found it hard to not start quaking with nerves and excitement, but she was sure of one thing— she knew what she was telling Mirial was the right thing. She felt it in her gut.

"I'm so happy you came," Mirial said, giving her another hug.

"It seems like I came just in time," Nilsa said, laughing.

Her sisters joined in her laughter.

"What are you planning on doing?" Sondra asked, looking at Mirial and Nilsa.

"Are you absolutely sure you don't want to marry Josh?" Nilsa asked Mirial to be sure. "It's not pre-wedding cold feet?"

Mirial sighed deeply. "I'm sure. I'm not in love. I don't want to get married. It would be a mistake."

"Then there's nothing more to talk about. You're not getting married. If one day you do, let it be because you really want to and are deeply in love. That's what I want for myself as well."

"This is going to be big... Mother's going to have a stroke," Sondra warned.

"Most likely, yes. But if there's something I've learned in the Rangers, it's that if we stick together, we'll make it through," Nilsa said and held their hands. "We'll get by together," she promised, clasping her sisters' hands.

"We'd better go home and explain to Mother," said Mirial.

"Let's go, we'll be at your side," said Nilsa as she tried to control her nerves with all her might. She knew it was going to be a tremendous disappointment for their mother and that it would bring about a terrible argument. Nilsa also knew their mother would blame her. That made her more uneasy than anything else. Her mother might never forgive her for instigating the breakup.

They headed home to break the news to their mother. The closer they got, the more nervous Nilsa became. She was walking hand in hand with Mirial to give her courage while Sondra walked behind them. They arrived at the house and realized they had a visitor. A well-dressed man was waiting with three well-groomed horses in front of the house.

Mirial looked at Nilsa, horrified.

"It's Josh. He must have come to visit."

"Well, take courage. It might be the right moment to tell him. We're with you," Nilsa said, glancing at Sondra.

"We are," she nodded.

Mirial snorted. She greeted the man outside, Josh's manservant, and went inside. They found their mother chatting amiably with two young men in the living room. Both men were tall, handsome, and well dressed.

"Mirial, look who's come to visit," their mother announced.

"Josh, this is a surprise," Mirial said, looking at Josh.

"The number of guests keeps growing, and my father has sent me to see how we can sit them all at the great banquet."

"Still more guests?" Mirial asked, looking daunted.

"On my family's side, I'm afraid. You know my parents want to please all their relatives," Josh said, eyeing Nilsa.

"I see," Mirial replied. "Josh, this is my sister Nilsa. She's come to visit," she said.

Josh studied Nilsa from head to toe.

"A pleasure to meet you. We'll soon be family," he said with a charming smile which revealed white, perfect teeth. Josh was tall, blond, thin, and had blue eyes. Nilsa found him quite handsome.

"Pleased to meet you," Nilsa replied with a pleasant smile.

"This is my cousin Albes," Josh said, introducing him to Nilsa. She nodded.

"Are you the Ranger?" Albes asked her. "Mirial told us she had a sister in the Ranger Corps, serving the King."

"I am," Nilsa confirmed.

"Well, what do you know, I've always wanted to meet a Ranger," Albes said, and by his defiant tone and the inquisitive look he gave her, Nilsa guessed he was a troublemaker and was measuring her up.

"In fact, I wanted to talk to you about the wedding…" Mirial said to Josh as she threw a glance at Nilsa out of the corner of her eye.

"Absolutely, go ahead. What's worrying you?"

"We'd better talk privately."

"Fine, as you wish."

"Shall we go out to the back garden? There's a little privacy there," said Mirial.

Josh nodded, and they went out the back door of the house into the garden.

"Some cookies?" Ulsa offered Albes.

"Thank you, ma'am," the young man said, taking a couple. Like Josh, he was tall and thin and had blond hair and blue eyes but was not as handsome. There was a devilish gleam in his eyes.

They could not hear the conversation from inside the house. Sondra made worried glances at Nilsa, and she made unobtrusive signs for her to be calm while Albes and Ulsa chatted.

"The ceremony will take place, and that's all that needs to be said!" they heard Josh shout suddenly at the top of his lungs.

They all looked at the back door.

Josh came back in, enraged.

"Josh… you have to understand…" Mirial was saying as she came in after him.

"You're the one who needs to understand, Mirial! I'm not going to be left looking ridiculous before my parents, my family, my friends, the whole city!"

"What's the matter?" Ulsa asked, upset by the shouting.

"You'll marry me, or you'll rue the day you met me until the day you die! I swear by the name of the Pelesens, I'll ruin your family!" Josh shouted in a fury and stopped in the middle of the living room.

"Josh… no…" Mirial followed him to the center of the room.

"I will not allow this outrage. Under no circumstance," he told her in a resounding, serious tone. "I'll make sure, personally, that your mother is shunned throughout the city. Everyone will mock her, mock you. I'll make sure you're the laughingstock in town. No one will talk to you. No one will sell you anything. Everyone will turn their back on you as if you had the White Fever. I'll make sure you lose all the miserable things you have, like this house," he said, gesturing at the walls. "Your sister Sondra won't have any suitors; she won't be able to marry or have a family. I'll make you leave here with nothing but the clothes on your back, and wherever you go I'll use my influence to make a torment of your lives. You'll live the rest of your lives in the most absolute misery. Have I made myself clear?" he threatened her, glaring into Mirial's eyes with hatred and rage.

"Let's all calm down," Nilsa warned Josh while she herself struggled to not explode. Josh glared at her furiously.

"I'll calm down whenever it pleases me!" he said haughtily.

"Now is the right time," Nilsa said calmly but firmly.

"No one leaves a Pelesen in the lurch," Albes threatened all of them with his finger, fury in his voice.

"Put that finger down before it suffers an accident," Nilsa growled—she would not let them threaten her mother and sisters in their own house.

"Josh... I swear it wasn't my intention..." Mirial tried to explain, but the young man was done listening and interrupted her.

"I want your definite answer tomorrow morning. I'm going hunting with Albes in the southern forests. Afterward I'll come here for your answer. You'd better, all of you, say yes, as we planned," Josh said, looking at all four of them one by one.

"You'd better leave now," Nilsa said sternly and showed them to the door.

The two cousins left in a huff.

Ulsa, who was white as snow from the shock, looked at Nilsa.

"What... what have you done? You've... brought ruin upon us!" she mumbled and dropped to the old sofa like a dead weight.

Chapter 22

That afternoon was a long one Nilsa would remember for a long time. Her mother was mortified. They could not get her to recover from the shock. For a moment the three sisters thought Ulsa was literally going to die. She had experienced some kind of attack—she could not breathe and clutched at her chest while she mumbled that this was their ruin, the end for them. They had to make her lie down and watch after her because she looked as if she were about to have a heart attack.

"Should we call the healer?" Sondra asked, a little scared.

"I doubt he can help her, but it's not a bad idea," Nilsa replied as she watched their mother lying on the bed looking at the doors of death. "He should have some compound that can help her somewhat."

"It's all my fault," Mirial said, sobbing, covering her eyes with her hands. "I'll never forgive myself."

"It's not your fault. It's that cretin of a fiancé of yours and his cousin. If he had behaved like a gentleman and accepted your refusal like any decent person with honor, this wouldn't have happened at all."

"He took it badly," Mirial said, weeping.

"Worse than bad," said Sondra.

"That's because he's a spoiled brat, vain, pampered, and without an ounce of kindness. He's no doubt had everything in life given to him since birth and has never been denied anything. That type of person ends up being absolutely selfish. Insufferable egomaniacs," said Nilsa.

"Ego… maniacs?" Sondra asked.

"People who only love themselves," Nilsa explained.

"Ah…"

"I have friends who read a lot and use words like that," Nilsa smiled.

"I knew he wouldn't take it well, but I wasn't expecting something like that. I didn't do anything to lead him on intentionally, you know that. I had no intention of hurting his feelings. Honestly,"

Mirial sighed, depressed.

"We know that, don't worry, little sister. It's not your fault. It's entirely Josh's. He's so vain, it's high time someone told him a few home truths," Nilsa said, wrinkling her nose in disgust.

"It was horrible," Mirial said amid halting sobs. "Mother will never forgive me, ever. I've brought ruin to the family."

Sondra bowed her head. "We'll have to leave the city and go far, far away..."

"Right now, you go get the healer and see what he can do for Mother," Nilsa told her.

Sondra nodded and ran off.

"I can still change my mind and say yes..." Mirial said mournfully.

Nilsa turned to her sister, put both hands on her shoulders, and, looking straight into her eyes, said, "You're not going to change your mind. You're not going to yield to threats. You've made the right decision. The way he reacted proves it."

"But... the disgrace and the misery we'll have to endure because of me..."

"It would be more disgraceful and miserable to have that cretin for a husband. Can you imagine what your life would be like with that selfish prick?"

"He's never acted that way before... he's always been kind and charming. In all the time he spent courting me, he constantly gave me little presents and treated me like a princess."

"But you had to have seen something in him that made you reject him. You have good instincts, better than mine. I had to learn the hard way," Nilsa said, remembering what had happened with Isgord. "Be grateful for it—if you were a little more like me, you'd have ended up married and regretting it every day."

"I doubt it. You're my role model," Mirial said.

"That makes me proud, little sister," Nilsa smiled. "But I swear I'm not the brightest in the kingdom. Particularly in matters of cute boys and love. I have a weakness for the handsome and bad," Nilsa admitted with a giggle.

Mirial smiled at her older sister's confession.

"Thank you for telling me that, it makes me feel better."

"You're welcome. It's the simple truth. Lucky for me, I can never decide between all the boys I like. I get nervous and confused. So I

194

try to stay away from that kind of trouble. I send them off, problem solved." She winked at Mirial and smiled.

"You're the best," Mirial smiled back and hugged her lovingly.

"Besides, why would you want to marry when you're so young? Live your life and enjoy it," Nilsa said with a wink.

"It's because of the situation—Mother... the family..."

"Don't worry about the situation or Mother. You have to live your own life. It does you credit to want to help your mother and the family if they need it, but you can't burden yourself with all the responsibility and chain yourself down. I'm telling you out of experience."

"But Mother, and Sondra?"

"They'll be fine. Find a way to make a living. Being so smart and pretty, you shouldn't have any trouble making a way for yourself, then send some money home to help them. It's what I do."

"Yes, Mother told us you send her part of your pay to help us out. Thank you."

"Of course, I do. I owe it to Mother for raising me, and to you because I'm the oldest and it's my duty to look after the family. It'll always be my responsibility, and I'll never stop doing it. You can count on me now and in the future. I'll always help. We're sisters. And Mother and Sondra also. Otherwise, I'd have no honor. Father wouldn't approve."

"You're the strongest woman I know," Mirial said, eyes shining with admiration.

Nilsa laughed out loud. "I've been growing up. I'll have to introduce you to Ingrid and Astrid, two of my comrades and good friends of mine. When you meet them, they'll change the way you look at the world."

"I think I'd like that."

"One day we'll have to make it happen then."

Ulsa shifted in bed. She was having nightmares and mumbled muffled words and cries of horror.

"Poor Mother, it breaks my heart to see her like this," Mirial said.

"I know. Her dreams and aspirations have been shattered. But you can't live life through your daughters... it makes me sad she does it."

The entrance door opened and Sondra came in followed by Rudolf, the healer. He was in charge of looking after the sick in this part of Prejurice. There were other healers and surgeons of more renown in the higher section of the city, but they could not afford them. That kind of healer would not have attended them since they only called on the residences of the important families. Rudolf was an older man, in his sixties, gaunt and bald, and his prices were fair.

The good healer examined Ulsa, and it did not take him long to determine what was wrong. Sondra had already told him their mother had received an emotional blow—without specifying what it was, of course. Rudolf prepared a strong tonic and some salts to help her recover and told the sisters to have some hot food ready to restore her. So she would sleep more peacefully that night, he prepared another tonic, this one made with plants that would induce sleep.

"Is it a sedative?" Nilsa asked.

"That's right. To help her sleep tonight. Pour a thimble of this in a hot tisane and have her drink it."

"We'll do that, thank you," Mirial said.

"Your mother is a strong woman, she'll pull through. She only needs to rest in order to recover from the shock she received."

"She took it so badly…" Sondra commented, worried.

"Some people take things too much to heart. Others less so. Such is human nature. Take care of her and love her. That will restore her."

"Thank you, we'll do that," Sondra promised.

"If she gets worse, which I doubt unless she receives another shock, call me and I'll come at once."

The three sisters thanked the healer for his diligence, paid him, and watched him leave. The good healer was busy with several patients he had to visit in that part of town.

They watched over their mother, who woke up at dusk and sat up in bed.

"Mirial, you have to fix this. Tomorrow morning you'll talk to Josh when he comes and tell him it's all been a mistake, that the wedding is on," Ulsa said beseechingly and haltingly, breathing with difficulty.

"Mother… I…" Mirial bowed her head.

"Mirial's already made her decision, and it's the one she'll stick to tomorrow," Nilsa intervened.

"If we don't fix this, it'll be our ruin," her mother said, sobbing. "We'll end up in misery."

"Maybe, but even so, Mirial shouldn't marry against her will, and least of all for nothing more than money and social status," Nilsa said firmly, crossing her arms.

"You're foolish," her mother scolded. "You went to the Rangers against my will and now you're driving your sister to ruin. You're destroying her future."

"That's not how I see it, Mother. I think Mirial's doing the right thing and saving her future," Nilsa replied.

"You're a bad daughter and an even worse sister. You always have been," Ulsa said accusingly. "What kind of example is this for Sondra?"

"An example she'd do well to learn from, and which I strongly recommend she follows, if that's what she wants," Nilsa said, looking at her sister.

Sondra was looking at her mother and sister in awe, her gaze going from one to the other.

"This is our ruin," said Ulsa and started sobbing and shivering as if she were going to have another seizure.

Mirial drew Nilsa to one side so their mother would not hear them and get even worse.

"Nilsa... perhaps I should..." Mirial said.

"No. You stay firm." Nilsa shook her head.

"What's going to happen to us?" Sondra asked as she came over to listen.

"Nothing we won't be able to deal with," Nilsa said with a deep breath. "I'll see to it."

"Are you sure?" Mirial asked her.

"I am. Just let me handle it," Nilsa said, nodding.

"What are you going to do, sister?" Sondra asked. "Can we help?"

Nilsa smiled and shook her head.

"You'd better let me handle it. Look after Mother."

Mirial and Sondra exchanged concerned glances as they considered what Nilsa might do.

"If you say so," Sondra agreed.

Mirial nodded. "You're the oldest and have more experience, you should know what's best."

"Thank you, sisters," Nilsa said.

None of the four women slept at all that night. They were all worried about what had happened and kept going over it in their heads, plagued about what would happen to them. Their future seemed terribly uncertain.

Chapter 23

The morning was crisp. Josh and his cousin Albes, with three of their servants, were hunting the forests south of the city. They rode good Norghanian horses. Both young men, from prestigious families, carried expensive hunting bows. The servants carried spears to attack the quarry and protect their masters. They were following the trail of a family of wild boar.

"We have them, sir," one of the servants said to Josh as he pointed at a sow that had stopped to face them. She was protecting five piglets not older than two months.

"Surround them so they can't escape," Josh said as he nocked an arrow.

"We'll have a feast today," Albes said, licking his lips as he eyed the piglets with bright eyes.

"As soon as Mirial takes her words back and does as I say," said Josh.

"Absolutely. That woman doesn't know her place. How embarrassing," Albes replied.

"I'll teach her. With the whip if necessary. It'll give me great satisfaction. Some women think because they have a nice face and figure they can do with us what they please. Not me. Oh no sirree!"

"Well said, cousin."

"She'll pay for the effrontery. How she'd even dare consider it! She'll pay with blood!"

"That way she'll learn what her place is," said Albes.

"Serving her husband, that's her place!" Josh cried furiously.

"And without a word!" Albes added.

They got ready to charge at the sow mother. Josh made a sign to Albes to attack at the same time so they could kill her from the saddle. The animal had no chance if they attacked her from both directions; she would get confused and not know who to defend herself from.

They were about to attack when there was a whistle. Something was cutting through the wind at great speed. An arrow appeared from within the trees and hit the bow Josh had in his hand.

"What's going on?" he cried. Caught by surprise, he lost his bow.

Albes turned his head toward his cousin when he heard his cry. A second arrow hit the bow he was aiming with and disarmed him.

"We're under attack!" Josh cried, looking around.

"By who? I don't see anyone!" Albes looked all around them wildly. "I only see trees and bushes."

A third arrow hit Albes full in the chest and burst with a cloud of dust. He fell off his horse and dropped to the ground, stunned.

"Defend me!" Josh yelled to his servants, who were looking around unable to see who was attacking them.

A second Earth Arrow hit Josh full in the forehead. It burst with dirt and smoke and knocked him down with the impact. He fell off his horse and hit the ground hard.

"Help us!" Albes called to the servants.

An arrow flew by, grazing the ear of the nearest servant.

He cried out and spurred his mount. He galloped away at full tilt. The other two servants did not need an arrow to persuade them—they galloped away after their comrade.

"Cowards!" Albes shouted from the ground.

Both rich young men remained lying there, stunned and half-blinded. Josh's face was swollen and marked. A large lump had appeared in the middle of his forehead the size of a goose egg.

Slowly, from behind some bushes about two hundred paces away, the attacker revealed herself. She switched her bow, slinging the composite on her back and grasping the short one before walking calmly to where the two pampered brats were lying.

"Well, it seems your servants aren't very loyal. I bet you don't treat them too well," Nilsa said mockingly.

"Who... are you...?" Josh asked, trying to glimpse their attacker's features with difficulty. "Oh, allow me to take my hood off," Nilsa said and pushed it back so they could see her face and curly red hair.

"You! Mirial's sister! How dare you!" Josh started to say, totally outraged.

"You're going to regret this!" Albes shouted at her.

"It looks like I need to teach you a lesson or two, because it seems you're wrong and maintain an archaic outlook on life."

"You'll pay for this outrage, woman! No one attacks a Pelesen," cried Josh.

"First of all, I am a Ranger and I have the King's permission to attack whoever I deem convenient. In fact, I have permission to kill whoever I deem convenient for the good of the kingdom."

"You wouldn't dare…" Josh said, looking scared.

Nilsa released at the vain prick with her short bow, this time to the right of Josh's head, who put his hands to his head and flattened himself down on his face.

"Don't hurt him," Albes begged her.

Nilsa turned and released at Albes, who was sitting on the ground trying to recover. The arrow plunged deep into the ground between his legs close to his privates. Albes, terrified, put his hands to his crotch to make sure everything was still there.

"Now that I have your attention, let's get to the lesson. A woman's place, you vain, male-chauvinistic cretins, is what she decides and wants. Not the one you decide for her. Is that clear? Or do I have to use another arrow for the message to sink in?"

"Yes, yes," Josh said, nodding without looking at Nilsa.

"Let's continue the lesson then. A woman's place is the highest position. Ruling, leading, teaching. Your place, on the other hand, is the lowest, not because you're men, but because you're scruple-less morons and pampered, good-for-nothing brats. Do you understand?"

"We understand," Albes nodded, eying Nilsa's bow, terrified.

"You respect a woman, you love her and honor her. Every moment of every day. Do you understand?"

"Yes, yes, we understand," Josh said, nodding with a horrified look on his face. Nilsa was aiming at him with her bow.

"I hope this lesson has been engraved in your minds. I won't mind coming back to remind you, and the next time I'll engrave it with fire on your foreheads," she said and released between the two with a Fire arrow which burst into flame when it hit the ground.

Both men skittered along the ground, trying to escape the flame.

"There's no need… for you to come back…" Albes said, moving his hands with tears in his eyes.

"Please, let us be," Josh pleaded with misty, terrified eyes.

"Now that I think about it, I have an Archer of the Wind and an Assassin of Nature I'd like you to meet. I'm sure they'd be delighted to teach you what a woman's place is."

"That won't be necessary…" Josh said, raising a hand. He was holding back tears of terror.

"Very well. Now listen to me carefully, Josh. Mirial isn't going to marry you. You're going to call the wedding off. I'll let you have the privilege of announcing it. You can say you've changed your mind and save your worthless honor. One thing though—you'll treat my sister and family with the utmost respect, now and forever. Nothing but good words will ever come out of your mouth regarding them. You'll ensure their life in the city is comfortable and peaceful. That goes for your cousin too. Am I clear?"

"Yes, crystal," Josh replied as he wiped the tears from his eyes.

"If anyone asks about your face, say you suffered an accident while hunting. There's no need for further explanation."

"Yes, yes, an accident," Josh nodded.

"If I find out that you don't fulfill your part of the deal, I'll come back and shoot to maim. Don't make me come after you, because you can be sure you won't see the arrow that ends with your future offspring."

"No need, I swear!" Josh cried, terrified.

"I swear too," Albes joined him.

Nilsa nodded.

"See you never, you cretins," she said and left.

Nilsa went back to her house. Her sisters and their mother were waiting for her, sitting in the kitchen where they were trying to have breakfast. Unfortunately, they were not in the mood and could not eat.

"Where did you go so early?" Mirial asked her, worried. "You left before sunrise."

"What happened?" Sondra asked before her sister could finish her question.

Nilsa smiled and raised her hands.

"Take it easy, everything's fixed."

"What do you mean?" their mother asked, still looking quite wan. Her face had traces of tears.

"I mean the situation that's been worrying you. I decided to take matters into my own hands and solved it. There's nothing to worry about now."

"What? How?" Ulsa asked with a horrified look on her face. "What have you done? I know your outbursts."

"I went to see the gallant suitor," she replied ironically.

"Oh no!" their mother cried. "Our only chance was that Mirial would say yes this morning and make her peace with Josh when he came by."

"He's not going to come," Nilsa said, making a face and shrugging.

"Why isn't he going to come? He said he would," her mother asked, getting more upset, fearing the worst. "What have you done?"

"I've had a friendly chat with him and his cousin while they were hunting. He won't come, today or ever. And he won't give you any trouble either."

"He won't?" Mirial asked, her eyes widening.

"The wedding is off."

"By the heavens! This is our ruin! What have you done?" Ulsa cried, putting her head in her hands.

"There won't be any repercussions for calling off the wedding," Nilsa told them as she grabbed an apple from the fruit bowl. It slipped out of her hand, but she moved swiftly and caught it before it touched the floor.

"How's that possible?" Sondra asked, raising an eyebrow. "I find it strange after what happened yesterday and knowing how the rich react…"

"Having money is all well and good, but it doesn't make you untouchable. No one is untouchable. Not even the King himself. That's something I've learned with my comrades."

"What did you do? Tell us," Mirial begged with a look of hope on her face.

"What I've done is make sure that little rich boy and his family never bother you again, not now and not in the future. You'll never hear from them again."

"If the wedding is off, the Pelesens will seek our ruin," said Ulsa, "you can't change that."

"I've handled it, Mother. Trust me. You can go on with your lives as if nothing had happened."

"Really? I don't have to get married?" Mirial asked with hope-filled eyes.

Nilsa smiled. "You don't have to get married. You can choose your own future here or away from this city. Whatever you wish."

"Nilsa this is wonderful!" Mirial said, hugging her tightly with tears of joy.

"I knew you'd fix it!" Sondra said, and she joined her sister in an embrace with lots of joyful kisses.

"Are you sure, Nilsa? We won't suffer the rage of the Pelesens?" their mother, who had stopped weeping, said.

"I'm sure, Mother. You can rest in peace. Believe it or not, I'm now capable of dealing with many things. I'm no longer the clumsy, nervous, restless child you remember. Well, that's not all true—deep down I still am—but I've grown up. I have much more confidence in myself now. I can deal with complicated situations. Life's experiences and the friendships you make along the way forge character."

Ulsa's face softened. She seemed to understand what Nilsa was saying.

"I guess your joining the Rangers wasn't such a bad thing after all..." she admitted and smiled a little.

"It was the best decision of my life. I've managed to become not only a Ranger, but a Specialist, a Mage Hunter, which is what I always wanted."

"Your father would be very proud of you. I'm sure," Ulsa said.

"Thank you, Mother. That means a lot to me."

"I know you and I don't always see eye to eye... I'm more traditional, more of a conformist, but I want you to know I love you very much. You're my daughter, and I love you."

This touched Nilsa's heart. She went over to her mother and hugged her tightly.

"I love you too, Mother."

They both joined in a tight embrace, and tears ran down both their cheeks.

For a moment the four women did not speak. They let the tender moment sink in. This did not happen very often, and they all wanted to enjoy it.

Nilsa looked at her two sisters and wagged her finger up and down at them.

"You two, my dear sisters, let me give you a piece of advice."

"Sure, go ahead," Mirial said, and Sondra nodded.

"My advice is that you follow your own path and aim for the stars. Don't let anything stop you, least of all the pretty or bad boys at hand. Stay away from their kind and continue on your path in life until you reach your goals. Whoever puts in the effort and never

204

gives up achieves their dreams."

"We will," both girls said almost in unison.

"And stay away from boys," she warned with a mischievous grin.

"What are you going to do now?" Ulsa asked Nilsa.

"I'll stay another couple of days more to enjoy my time with all of you. Then I have to go on my way. I'm going to visit a friend who's recovering from a serious accident. I want to see how he's doing."

"I hope he'll be fine," Mirial said.

"So do I," Nilsa said, and the concern showed in her voice.

"And afterward?" Sondra asked her. "What will you do next?"

"Afterward, duty calls. I'll have to go on some special mission for King Thoran."

"Be careful," her mother said with a look of concern on her face. "Remember what happened to your father…"

"I will. Don't worry. What happened to Father isn't going to happen to me. I'm a Mage Hunter, and besides, I have a group of friends who look out for me, and I them. An amazing group."

"We'll miss you so much when you leave," Mirial said, hugging her again.

"Very much," Sondra agreed, hugging her too.

"So, let's enjoy these couple days. We can all miss one another later."

"That's true," Mirial laughed.

"Ah, and if you come across Josh by accident, you might not recognize him. I busted his face, literally," Nilsa said, beaming. She raised both eyebrows, gave one of her little hops, and went up to her room.

Her mother crossed herself while she begged the Ice Gods for mercy. Her sisters were left with their mouths open wide, unable to utter a word.

A while later, Nilsa was still reflecting on what had happened. She smiled and giggled. She was still the same Nilsa—restless, clumsy, and nervous—but when the situation demanded it, she became Nilsa the Mage Hunter, deeply influenced by Ingrid and Astrid with whom she had shared so many adventures. She gazed at the ceiling and smiled from ear to ear. She liked who she was gradually becoming. She had not lost her identity, and now she could handle difficult situations on her own. Yes, she definitely liked this mature Nilsa. She would keep working on her insecurities and clumsiness, since these would always be part of her, but she would learn to control them. In fact, she realized that when things got tough, she was less clumsy and became less nervous. The day would come when she would not even notice.

In the midst of these thoughts, she fell asleep, with a great smile on her face.

Chapter 24

Astrid rode to the large, fortified keep in the middle of her uncle's sprawling property. She had not told her comrades, or anyone for that matter, that her family was wealthy. 'The rich kind,' as Viggo would say. She had not mentioned it precisely to avoid Viggo's mocking and jokes, and because she did not want her friends to treat her any different because she came from wealth and land. Unlike Egil's family, hers was not noble; she had no title granted by the King, and her family was not responsible for a whole county or duchy and their people. Yet her family had quite a few properties and gold. Hers was a well-to-do family whose assets came from the trade her uncle's family had started over a hundred years before. Astrid had always refused to be a 'rich girl' and had fought to be a rebel instead.

She had not been on her uncle's land in a long time, and she felt strange. On the one hand, good memories of when she was a little girl and had lived there under her uncle's protection came flooding back; it was natural to remember the nice parts of one's past. She felt nostalgic and even a certain well-being as she faced the entrance, riding along the path lined by elm trees. On the other hand, bitter and even painful memories came to mind as she approached her old home. Moments when she had felt lonely, forsaken, abandoned by her family.

She remembered her tutors gratefully. They had been good to her, but still, they had not been able to replace her family's love. They had not tried either. That had not been their role. Her uncle paid them to instruct her and that was what they had done. She did remember old Alvis with fondness and gratitude though. He was her uncle's valet and looked after the property and the house. He had also looked after her, caring for her and teaching her much of what she had learned there. She hoped he was still going strong; he must be in his seventies already, so Astrid was not sure he would still be around. The last letter she had received from Alvis had been two... no, three years ago, concerned about her well-being. Astrid had written back, telling him how happy she was with the Rangers and that he did not need to worry about her. Now she felt bad for not having kept in touch with good old Alvis. He was surely all right—he had to be. If not, Astrid would be distraught.

She arrived at the entrance of the great keep and contemplated it. It was well-kept and the roof looked like it had recently been partly re-done, as did the windows. This meant it had been prepared to accommodate the master's return home. The renovations must have been done with his blessing. She found it strange that her uncle liked this enormous fortress-house so much. It was not as pretty or as comfortable as other properties he had on the coast. As a child, Astrid had traveled with her father and uncle to those properties, and she remembered them being beautiful mansions, more than worthy of a rich trader. This huge keep would hold off a siege without any trouble and it was safe and defendable, but it was not exactly pleasant, to the eye or the body. Many passersby thought it was a Norghanian military stronghold. It had been, but her uncle had bought it, together with the land that surrounded it. Astrid had never found out why.

A middle-aged man came out to welcome her. He was tall and broad, completely bald, and looked at her with lively, light-blue eyes. She was surprised by his attire. He was wearing a long gray robe with two silver circles, one inside the other, embroidered in the middle of his chest. Astrid did not know the meaning of that symbol, but she had a hazy, distant memory of having seen it before. She could not remember when or where, but she knew that symbol. He was carrying a broad short sword and a long dagger at his waist. If the clothing was uncommon, the way he was armed was even more so. Those were not Norghanian weapons—from the handles and style they looked like they were from the kingdom of Erenal.

"Welcome, Miss Astrid, it's an honor to have you back," the man greeted her.

Astrid looked at the man. She could not remember him, but he seemed vaguely familiar.

"Thank you, it's good to be back."

"Coming home brings comfort to the soul," he said, and in so doing he seemed more familiar still.

"Do we know each other?" Astrid asked, looking at the man's white, round face.

"We met many years ago, when milady was a little girl, but you wouldn't remember me."

"You look so familiar…"

"At the time I was thinner and had long blond hair," he smiled.

"What's your name?" Astrid asked, trying unsuccessfully to remember him.

"Albon Iresone, at milady's service."

"Albon… Iresone…" Astrid was trying to remember him but could not, although she could not get rid of the feeling that she knew him.

"Has milady had a good journey?" he asked.

"Yes, it's been a while since I came to this county. I enjoyed riding through this area again."

"If you allow it, we'll look after your horse," Albon said, making a sign to another man dressed like him who was drawing water from a well.

Astrid nodded and dismounted. She took her weapons and gear from the saddle. "Bestand will take care of your mount," Albon said as the other man approached.

Astrid nodded.

"I wonder whether Alvis is okay…" Astrid said, concerned because Albon had come out to greet her instead of the old valet who used to welcome all visitors.

"I'm pleased to say Alvis is in good health, he's inside."

"Oh, since he didn't come out to greet me, I was worried."

"It's only natural. Although his health is good, age forgives no one, and Alvis is now only in charge of the inside of the keep. I handle the outside and the surrounding land," he said, waving his hand. "It was too much for him to continue handling it all. Your uncle decided this was best."

"I understand." Astrid was glad to hear her old caretaker was still well.

"Come with me, please. Your uncle is waiting for you. He's looking forward to seeing you again."

Astrid took these words as Albon being kind, since she seriously doubted her uncle would actually be looking forward to seeing her. In fact, she wondered why he had called her home. The letter she had received was succinct. He just said she should come see him urgently, that they had urgent business to discuss. After not hearing from him for years, the letter sounded strange. She even thought he might be dying and that was why he was calling her to his side. Was she here to say goodbye?

"Is my uncle in good health?" she asked Albon to clear her doubts.

"My lord enjoys an enviable health," he replied with a smile as he waved her toward the entrance.

"I'm glad he's all right." Astrid said.

"If you allow me, I'll take your personal belongings," Albon offered, reaching out with his large, weathered hands.

Astrid shook her head.

"Rangers handle their own gear personally."

"Of course, forgive my ignorance, it's the first time I've dealt with a Ranger."

"There's nothing to forgive," Astrid said.

Albon pushed the door open forcibly. It was an enormous, reinforced door, of the style used by Norghanian lords in their keeps, built and secured to withstand a siege. It weighed a ton.

In the hallway she met two men on watch duty, one by the heavy entrance door and the other by the door that opened onto the living quarters. They were tall and thin, in their thirties, and had short dark hair and darker skin than usual in the north. They were also wearing the same singular gray robes with the strange symbol in the middle of the chest. Astrid's eyes went to the weapons they carried; both had the same Erenal style—broad short swords and long daggers. Although Albon and Bestand were clearly Norghanian, these two guards were not; their features were more southern. They were not Zangrian because of their height, so she guessed they were from Erenal.

They went inside, and Albon led Astrid to the great central hall. It was like the throne hall of the Royal Castle, only much humbler and smaller in accordance with the keep, which although grand and lordly, could not compare to a castle, least of all the Royal Castle.

"If you'll be kind enough to wait here, I'll let Alvis and milord know you've arrived."

"Of course," Astrid said with a nod.

"If you need anything, please, you only have to ask," Albon said as a man walked into the hall carrying a tray with water and some fruit.

Astrid nodded again and smiled.

Albon left and the new arrival offered her the water and fruit.

Astrid declined the offer and noticed the great fireplace that presided over the hall. She remembered it well: the heat it gave off when lit and how pleasant it was to sit there on the bearskin rug in the cold winters. She looked at the two armchairs on one side of the barred window and the large table in the middle of the hall. She had spent countless hours there studying, eating, living. Contrary to many Norghanian halls, this one had two of its walls lined with tomes and scrolls; her uncle had ordered two immense bookshelves built to cover the high walls, and they were filled with books.

She left her bow, quiver, and traveling rucksack on the table before walking over and picking one of the books. *Secrets of the Desert Dunes* was the title; it was not exactly the kind of reading one would expect to find in the house of a northern lord. Astrid paced the floor in front of the bookshelf from one end to the other, checking its height and the hundreds of tomes her uncle kept in it. Memories flooded back, of her instructor teaching her there and of the books she had read and tried to understand.

She walked over to the bookshelf on the other wall and ran her gaze along its books. She had spent countless hours between those two bookshelves, choosing and reading book after book. There was not much else she could do in the keep. The nearest village was half a league away, and when she had been little, she did not remember there being more than a handful of guards and a gaffer to run the place. She noticed that the man who had brought her the water and fruit had stayed by the door, standing at attention. She certainly did not remember men wearing strange tunics and armed like these around her when she was little.

She remembered her hours of reading there and how she had once sneaked into her uncle's private library on the third floor. It was immense. He had joined several rooms together and created a library with countless volumes. Astrid had been punished when she was discovered, because she had been forbidden to go there. Her uncle's most precious possessions were in that library, or so he had told her, and no one was allowed in without his permission. The tomes and scrolls stored in there were treasures of incalculable value.

It was funny, how all these forgotten memories were coming to the surface now that she was here. She was also overcome by a powerful feeling of loneliness, a muffled sadness. She remembered why she had left the keep and gone to join the Rangers. She had not regretted it for a moment. Her loneliness had ended the day she set foot in the Camp. She had put everything she had learned here from her uncle's books and instructors to good use in her training and after graduating.

The door opened, and a man in his seventies wearing a simple gray tunic came into the room.

"Alvis!" Astrid cried and ran to hug him.

"Young miss, I'm so happy to see you!" Alvis said, beaming, and spread his arms open to welcome her.

Astrid hugged him tightly, overjoyed to find him alive and well, although she noticed the man was mostly bones.

"Alvis, aren't you eating?'" Astrid felt his arms, which were like two dry sticks.

The old man smiled. He had kind green eyes, his white hair was cropped short, and his face and nose were sharp. From a distance he looked stern, but the moment he smiled his face changed into that of a charming man.

"At my age you don't get so hungry," he said apologetically with a shrug.

"Are you sick?" Astrid said, concerned, looking into his eyes in search of an honest answer.

"No, no, not at all. I'm great," Alvis replied, waving his hands in a reassuring gesture.

"Well, I think you're too thin," she chided. "You need to eat more and take care of yourself."

"On the other hand, young milady looks very grown up, strong and vigorous," Alvis noted, redirecting the conversation at Astrid as he looked her up and down, smiling and nodding.

"I've trained long and hard these last years with the Rangers. Now I'm all muscle," she smiled, flexing her arms.

"Milady has always had a lot of muscle," Alvis said, pointing at her head.

Astrid laughed. "Yes, I've also had to use that one a lot too."

"What a joy to have you here again, miss. I've missed you sorely," the old man said with a face that betrayed his affection for her.

"I've missed you too," Astrid said and hugged him again.

Old Alvis' eyes moistened with the show of affection.

"Milady has come to stay, or is it a visit?" he asked her.

"Only visiting. Now that I'm a Ranger, I owe myself to the

kingdom. I can't stay long. I have to see to other obligations,"

"Of course, I understand. It saddens me, but I understand. I would've liked you to stay for a while. Having you back home brings back so many and such good memories…"

"Not all good," Astrid said, indicating two decorative vases against the wall which her uncle had brought from one of his journeys. "Remember when I broke them with one of my summersault jumps?"

Alvis laughed. "Of course I remember, miss. Hard to forget the time it took me to put all the pieces together so your uncle wouldn't notice."

"If it's any consolation, you should know that all the races through the house, jumps, and summersaults and other antics I spent my time engaging in, served me well in the Rangers."

"It's no consolation because of the countless pranks I had to put up with, but I'm glad," he replied, joking and smiling.

Astrid felt like a little girl talking to her grandfather in the presence of old Alvis. The good man had done so much for her when she was little. He had always been at her side. Since the day her uncle had brought her to live there, Alvis had always looked after Astrid and worried about her as if she had been his own daughter. Her heart softened with the memories of the good times spent with him playing, making mischief, learning, and receiving good advice and wisdom.

Astrid kissed the old man's cheek.

"Thank you for looking after me as if I had been your own flesh and blood, for all the love you gave me and all you taught me. I have it all stored in my heart." She put her hand over her chest for emphasis.

"Milady… you're going to make me weep. Looking after you and seeing you grow into a woman has been the greatest satisfaction of my life."

Astrid looked at him lovingly.

"I'm glad to have made this visit, even if it was only to see you and hug and kiss you."

"This old caretaker is beyond grateful," Alvis replied with a look of deep love on his face.

"Let's sit down, tell me everything that's happened during my absence," Astrid told him and headed to the large sofa where they had spent so many hours.

"Very well," he agreed. They sat down. "So many memories... the countless good times we've spent here, reading, talking.... It seems like only yesterday, even though it's been quite a few years now."

"Yes... it does, doesn't it?" Astrid said, feeling the same.

"During the time milady has been away with the Rangers things have been quiet here in the house of my lord Viggen Norling. Too quiet, if I'm honest. Most of the time I've been alone, looking after the house and the lands, with the sole company of the hands and other workers of the property. It's been quiet, but solitary and quite boring. A little more activity would've been good."

"Oh...." Astrid felt bad for the good old man. She had been so busy with the adventures of the Rangers while Alvis had been here all alone in the large keep. "I'm sorry you felt lonely..."

"Don't you worry, miss, I've been all right and my health is still good, and that in itself is a great fortune. I can't complain."

"Hasn't my uncle been at home much? I assumed he would have come back from his last journey."

Alvis shook his head.

"He came back shortly after milady left to join the Rangers. He spent several weeks dealing with some local business and then left again. He's been away for most of this time. He only came back a couple of times, and for short periods. You know him, his work keeps him away for long periods of time."

"Yes, practically all the time," Astrid remarked with a touch of bitterness, since it had been the same when she was living there. She felt as if she had grown up without a family. Her parents had both died and her uncle had always been away. Alvis was the closest thing she had to family.

"And Albon, and all those armed men? Has my uncle brought them with him?" Astrid asked.

Alvis nodded. "They're his personal guard. Things have become dangerous and milord needs protection, here and particularly when he travels abroad. Trading with foreign kingdoms is a dangerous lifestyle. You need armed protection when you travel."

"Yes, I can imagine. He's always had guards with him, but these look, I don't know, somewhat different.... The clothes they wear are strange, don't you think?"

"I wouldn't know what to say, miss. I'm not a man of the world. I can assure you they're kind to me and help with all the chores, besides doing watch duty and defending milord and the property. I'm personally quite pleased with them. They aren't very chatty though," Alvis said with a smile. Then he became serious. "They're milord's guard, and it's not my place to discuss them. I'm sure they do their duty to milord's desires."

"I understand my uncle's need to have guards. It's not important, it just struck me as a little peculiar."

"Luckily you're both home, and old Alvis is thrilled to have you both with him."

"And I'm happy to be here."

"Your uncle will be glad to see you."

"He's called for me. Do you know why?"

"I'm afraid your uncle doesn't share his plans or intentions. He never has. I'm nothing but his valet. Family or important matters aren't entrusted to me. It wouldn't be proper for a servant to have knowledge of his lord's important matters."

"You're much more than a servant. You practically raised me on your own."

"Thank you very much, miss," Alvis said, quite moved. "I had a lot of help from the many instructors your uncle hired. And thank goodness," he smiled, "I've never been good with weapons."

"I remember the fighting instructor, Grondag," Astrid said thoughtfully, thinking back. "Strong and agile. He had a good hand with the bow and knife. His teachings have served me well."

"I'm glad to hear it. Your uncle brought him from Norghania; he had been instructing several Court nobles. Your uncle had trouble persuading him—I believe there was a good bit of gold involved," Alvis said with a wink. "Grondag had a solid reputation and made a good living in the capital."

"I didn't know that…. To me he was just another instructor."

"All the instructors, milady, were of great renown. Your uncle made sure only the best were in charge of your education."

"Wow, that can't have been cheap. I'd never thought of that."

"Milady was young. It's natural that these things didn't cross your mind. Luckily, your uncle has a great fortune and could hire the best tutors no matter the cost. I can swear to that."

"I'll have to thank him for that…." Astrid felt bad for not

realizing her uncle's careful selection of tutors and thanking him. She vaguely remembered several different tutors and instructors who had passed through her life and taught her different subjects, from fighting, to literature, to geography, to the History of Norghana and Tremia.

"I don't know why your uncle has asked you here, but I'm sure it will be something important."

At that moment Albon came into the room and walked over to them.

"Your uncle wishes to see you," he told Astrid.

"Very well." Astrid rose and looked at Alvis. "I guess I'm about to find out why I'm here." She smiled at him and followed Albon out of the room.

Chapter 25

Astrid followed Albon to the second floor where her uncle had his study. As she went up the wide staircase and faced the corridor, she had the odd feeling that the place was smaller than she remembered. She had always thought the great keep was immense, a city in itself. Now it did not seem that big. It was curious how, to a child's mind, her world had seemed massive and full of so much to discover; but now that she was a grown woman and had experienced other places and worlds, her big home did not seem so large.

They went by the great library, which still seemed immense. It was so large it had two doors, one at each end. They were open, and Astrid took a quick glance inside. There were hundreds and hundreds of books, placed on large shelves that ran along the walls from floor to ceiling. In the middle of the room was a large round table for studying. Several chairs and some small tables were placed in the corners of the library. She thought of Egil. He would find the place fantastic. Her friend would surely stay there for days if allowed.

Astrid admired books for the vast knowledge they housed that a person could obtain from. But she did not find them as fascinating as her friend Egil. She was more prone to action than study, even if she had been brought up reading a lot, something uncommon in Norghanian society, especially for a girl. She had her uncle to thank for her exposure to books. He had made sure she was well educated, and the fact that she was a girl had not been an issue at all, as it should be. She was taught and trained with weapons and books. She was grateful for this, because unfortunately, this was not the rule for all girls and women in Norghana. That needed to change. Women ought to have the same opportunities, treatment, and rights as men, and one day it would be so. Women like Ingrid, Nilsa, and herself would work to achieve that future and, like them, there were many others changing the kingdom's future at that same moment. The Rangers made no differentiation between genders either. For them the fact that you were a woman had no positive or negative implications. Astrid had liked that from the first day she joined the corps.

217

They continued down the corridor until they reached her uncle's study. There was a man guarding the wrought-oak door. He was dressed like the others in that odd attire and carried the same weapons. Astrid was surprised there were guards posted outside the door of her uncle's study inside the keep. No one would be able to sneak in there, least of all with so many guards. Why did her uncle feel the need to keep guards posted outside his door? She thought it was curious. She did not remember her uncle having guards at the door of his office while she was growing up; she remembered dropping in to see him without any trouble. She had needed to knock first and wait until her uncle gave her permission to come in, that was the respectful thing to do.

Albon knocked and went in.

"Your niece, milord," he said with a slight nod.

"Come in, dear niece," came a honeyed, deep voice.

Astrid went in and saw her uncle coming toward her from behind his working desk with open arms and a smile on his face.

"Dear uncle," she returned the greeting, went toward him, and they hugged.

Albon left the room and closed the door behind him.

"Let me look at you. You're so grown-up and such a warrior… if you allow me to say so, with that look and clothes."

"I'll take it as a compliment, Uncle," she smiled.

"Forgive me, you surprised me with that forest warrior look."

"I'm a Ranger. This is how we look." She smiled as she watched her uncle. He was just as she remembered him, his hair whiter but otherwise well preserved. He was in his mid-forties although he looked older from a life of traveling and exposure to the weather. He was tall and thin, pure muscle, with dark hair and green eyes like her mother, and like herself. Astrid looked a lot like her mother; others used to say they were like two raindrops. Seeing her uncle again, she realized he resembled them a lot as well. He had an undeniable air of similarity.

"And here I was thinking you'd follow in my footsteps and become a scholar. You always loved my books," he said, indicating two bookshelves he had in his study filled with volumes that looked priceless. Astrid also noticed a bigger showcase where her uncle kept relics from different kingdoms. There were gold masks, ceremonial daggers, tribal necklaces with precious stones, royal seals, strange runes engraved on rocks, and other objects she did not even recognize. What caught her eye was that they were exotic, foreign, and some of the objects even looked arcane.

"Life takes unexpected turns, Uncle."

"That's very true. Come, sit and let's talk. We need to catch up. It's been a long time," he said and waved her to a comfortable, elegant, big chair in front of his working desk. He sat behind the desk.

Astrid sat down as she watched her uncle. He looked good, and the energy in his motions and voice indicated he had not lost his edge with the passing years. At least, it did not seem so.

"Tell me, dear niece, how are the Rangers treating you? Are you happy? Do you regret joining them? What have you been doing? Are you allowed to tell me, or is it all a royal secret?"

Astrid smiled. "That's a lot of questions."

"Forgive me, it's the excitement of seeing you again. It awakes so many feelings in me. I want to know everything about your life, especially these years we haven't seen one another. I'm intrigued. I want to know how you've changed, who you've become now that you're a woman and not the child who still lives in my memories."

Astrid nodded. "I feel very well—fulfilled, to be honest. The Rangers are my family now. I feel honored and happy to be a Ranger. I can't tell you much about what we do; I'm not at liberty, but you know that," she said, knowing her uncle had knowledge of all kinds of cultures and their history and peculiarities, among them Norghana, which he had mastered perfectly.

"I'm glad to hear it. It's a pity you have to serve the present monarch. Norghana has had better ones, although it's true that, over the years, there have been much worse ones too," he said, raising an eyebrow.

"The Rangers serve the kingdom. Whoever sits on the throne is beside the point," she replied with a shrug. "There's not much we can do about it. I'm sure there have been better and worse kings."

"Yes, that's usually the case in most aspects of life. That's a good policy to follow— better to stay away from the fights for power and the throne. There'll always be some king or another, and they'll always come to the throne covered in the blood of their rivals."

"Yes, I believe so," Astrid nodded.

"Speaking of politics and our King, I believe he has serious financial problems. This attracts more added trouble," Viggen commented with a wave of his hand that indicated more problems were about to come for the monarch.

"I see that you closely follow what goes on in Norghana. That didn't use to be the case.… Your interests used to take you to foreign lands."

"Let's say that my interests in the past led me to foreign lands. It doesn't mean I wasn't interested in what went on in Norghana, just that I was more interested in what happened in other places. I owe myself to my 'quest.' That has always been my main focus, and is still my greatest priority. The future of all Tremia depends on it."

Astrid sighed. She had expected to find her uncle changed, that he would have left behind his compulsive search. Unfortunately, it did not seem to be the case. He was still the same, which saddened her a lot. She began to realize that the journey to see him, to try to reconnect and strengthen family ties, would be in vain.

"I thought you'd have finished your search by now and that was why you had come back," she said, unable to hide the disappointment in her voice.

"I came back because the search has brought me back here, to the origin, to where I started," Viggen explained, pointing his finger at the floor under his feet.

"I see." Astrid lowered her gaze. She pitied her uncle. All his life pursuing a crazy dream, and now when it seemed they could be a family again, it turned out that nothing had changed, that everything was still the same. The only thing that mattered to him was his search, not her. She was angry at herself for thinking her uncle would have changed after all this time and that this reunion was to unite a family. It clearly was not. He had come to continue with his life's mission, not to reconnect with her. He did not care about her. Viggen cared about nothing but the search. She remembered again the feelings she had felt so often and experienced again the pain and loneliness that came with them.

"Life takes unexpected turns and leads us to places we hadn't expected to see again. Or places we left that we must return to," Viggen explained.

"Then if the search has brought you here, why have you made me come?" Astrid asked, not without certain anxiety in her tone which she tried to hide, since she did not want to upset her uncle. He was in charge of his life, and it was not her job to judge how he lived it and what he devoted his time to. Yet, it hurt that she was not among his priorities.

"You see… we're living in historical moments, uncertain, but of a transcendence like we have never experienced in all the history of our great continent," her uncle said.

"Do you mean the rivalries within the kingdom? The fact that there may be a war with Zangria, or the Frozen Continent? Or do you have information about the conquest plans of the Nocean Empire or Rogdon? Or is it the Alliance of the State Cities of the East seeking to expand their power?"

Viggen shook his head, "It's not that. I'm not saying that all that couldn't happen, because it could, my dear niece. The kingdoms and their monarchs are always plotting to take over neighboring kingdoms, or those they see as weaker: to become more powerful and fight other kingdoms trying to do exactly the same. Rivalry and strife between kingdoms in order to be the most powerful on the continent is very common. No, I'm referring to something a lot more transcendental. The wars between the kingdoms of Tremia are something secondary—there have always been and will always be, as long as men rule over the continent. Such is politics, and such are kings and their ambitions."

"What are you referring to?" Astrid asked, frowning. She did not understand, although the message seemed to her a little upsetting.

"What is to come will change Tremia completely. The kingdoms you now know will find themselves forced to decide to join the change or perish if they confront it. I fear that, knowing the present monarchs, they'll perish before accepting the new order."

"New order? What do you mean, Uncle?"

"The era you know, the one we live in at present, is reaching its end. A new era is about to begin, one that will change everything forever."

Astrid stared at her uncle, trying to understand what he meant. "I assume you mean the political landscape of Tremia will change…" she tried to clarify.

Viggen nodded. "Not just the political, but also the natural order. Man will cease to rule over Tremia. Their time is coming to an end."

Astrid was puzzled. "Man? Us?" she asked, indicating her uncle and herself. "You mean to say that we'll no longer be the rulers of

Tremia?"

"That's right. Man won't be the dominant being anymore," her uncle confirmed, and he said it in a tone of total conviction.

"So… if it's not man, and I'm assuming it won't be animals, then who will rule over Tremia?"

"The All-Powerful Supreme Lords," he said, and the statement had the strength of a hammer hitting an anvil.

Astrid threw her head back. What did all this mean? What was her uncle saying? She looked at him with an expression that betrayed the immense confusion she felt.

"All-Powerful Supreme Lords? You mean some kind of… gods? Are you saying new gods will arrive in Tremia?" Astrid was staring at her uncle with wary eyes, trying to understand the implications of what he was saying.

Viggen thought about it and nodded. "To man they will be like gods, yes. Humanity will have no choice but to serve them. We'll all have to serve the supreme lords."

"If we have to serve them, that implies they'll be the new monarchs of Tremia…"

"That's right. They'll be the lords of all the known world. Nothing and no one will be able to stand up to their power, since they'll be able to do anything."

"We won't be able to defeat them? None of the kingdoms will?"

"None. Not even if they united against the new lords at their arrival, something they won't do. The kings and queens of Tremia refuse to work together—they won't join their forces in a single block, in a great army. They're too arrogant and distrustful. They will all fall, they and their great and powerful armies, because they're no rival for the new lords," Viggen prophesized as if he were an oracle reading the future of the continent.

"It doesn't surprise me they don't unite and are distrustful of one another. The little I know of monarchs, and what I've heard tell of them, points in that direction."

"Even if they did, they would still perish, since the supreme lords are all-powerful."

"If they're so powerful and we have no choice but to serve them, that's not good for us. Are you foretelling a new era of horror?"

"I'm stating that a new era is coming and that the Supreme Lords will be our lords and masters. So I see it, and so it shall happen,"

Viggen said, raising his arms to the ceiling.

"And where are these lords, these gods you're talking about?"

"They haven't arrived yet, but they're close to doing so," Viggen said firmly.

"Close to arriving?" Astrid asked, wanting to understand what he meant. This sounded terrible, and she wanted to make sure she understood what her uncle was referring to. She had a sick feeling in her stomach that was getting stronger.

"The signs say it must be so. The 'Arrival' is close," he assured her, nodding repeatedly. "I've studied it for a long time, and I can assure you the signs are appearing."

"When will this 'Arrival' you think is coming occur?"

Viggen looked up at the ceiling and thought for a moment.

"The 'Sleeper' has awakened at last. This much we know. We've felt it and confirmed it. Once it starts its journey, it'll begin to prepare the 'Arrival.'"

Astrid put her hands to her head.

"Uncle, what you're telling me doesn't make any sense," she said, annoyed. "You speak of a sleeper, an arrival, a new natural order in Tremia, of all-powerful, supreme lords. It all sounds crazy.... Are you sure this is all true? Have you verified this?"

Viggen leaned forward in his chair and put his elbows on the desk so his head would be closer to his niece's.

"I know everything I'm telling you sounds strange, since you've never had any knowledge of it. Your parents wanted it that way, and I respected their wishes."

"My parents? What did my parents know about what you're telling me?"

"Quite a bit. I shared my studies and knowledge with them. Even then I knew of the Arrival of the Supreme Lords. Unfortunately, I didn't know the how or when, which is what's been more difficult to ascertain. It's been many arduous and fruitless years of countless failure. But there have been a few successes, and these have allowed us to move forward, deciphering a mystery as important as it is complex."

Astrid shook her head, and her dark hair swayed from one side to the other.

"If they knew of the arrival, of these powerful gods, why didn't they want you to tell me? Did they not believe you?"

"Your mother, my sister, did. Your father—well, let's say he had his reservations about my studies and conclusions."

"And why didn't they want you to tell me?" Astrid asked distrustfully.

"They wanted you to follow your own destiny and didn't want my ideas and theories to influence you."

"So that I wouldn't follow you on your journeys and expeditions?"

Viggen nodded. "They knew you'd be tempted—traveling to exotic kingdoms, pursuing complex mysteries and arcane secrets is difficult to resist when you're young."

"Oh... I see."

"They wanted the best for you, and I respected their will."

"And I'm deeply thankful, Uncle. I want you to know how much I appreciate and how grateful I am for everything you've done for me."

"It was my duty. I'm your uncle by blood. There's nothing to be thankful for. We're family," Viggen said, shaking his hands in denial.

"Yes, there is. I realize now that I'm back here. You took care of me when I was left alone. You gave me a home, looked after me, educated me, trained me, and helped me become the person I am today."

"Oh, you've done all that by yourself. I simply put a grain of sand that was the means. I would've liked to be here with you more, but the search called me," Viggen said apologetically.

"Even so, you did a lot for me, and I want you to know I'll always be grateful for it."

"I'm pleased," Viggen nodded. "But now, my dear niece, you must listen to me. I swear that everything I'm telling you is the truth. It might sound somewhat eccentric, crazy even, I know. But I can assure you that my lifetime of studies, travels, and investigation have been to reach this transcendental moment, the beginning of the change."

Astrid sighed deeply. Her uncle's words sounded delirious indeed.

"Then a new time is coming. A new era and some all-powerful, supreme lords are going to rule Tremia," Astrid said, and the words sounded strange coming from her own mouth.

"I want you at my side when the day comes. You're family," Viggen told her.

"What for, Uncle? Tell me…"

"I can't tell you more. It's best you don't know more. Trust me, your uncle, your family," he said, spreading his arms and looking at her intensely

"It's not that I don't trust you… but my place is with the Rangers."

"I understand," Viggen nodded. "It saddens me, but I understand your reasons."

"It's not that I don't want to be by your side…. What you're telling me sounds really outlandish though…"

"I can't explain more now. One day you'll understand. When it begins, you'll realize. When that day comes, I want you to come for me and stay with me. You'll be safe with me. You'll be able to help me, be a part of the new future. Those who help the supreme lords will be rewarded in their new realm."

"And if I don't?"

"Then you'll end up either enslaved or dead, like the majority," he stated as if it were an inexorable truth.

"Uncle, those are very strong prophecies… horrible prophecies…"

"They are, but they'll come true. A new time has been born, and with it, a change the likes of which haven't been seen in thousands of years. You must be with me. I can protect you. You are my blood, and I want to protect you."

"Thank you, Uncle… I'll keep it in mind…" Astrid said. She did not know what to think of all of it. It sounded to her like the folly of a grandiloquent mind. For a moment she thought her uncle had lost his mind. But no, he was sane, very sane. He was coherent. The problem was he actually believed in the apocalyptic prophesy.

"Do so and remember my words. Come for me when the Supreme Lords arrive."

Astrid felt a sickness in her stomach that was multiplying by the moment.

"I'll remember them, Uncle."

"Go and rest. We'll talk more tomorrow. I'm sure you'll want to enjoy your old room. I think you'll find it just as you left it when you went to join the Rangers."

"I'd like that, yes," she replied, trying to find logic in the strange conversation of catastrophic omens without understanding it.

Confused and intrigued, she headed to her bedroom. The conversation with her uncle had not gone as she had expected, not at all.

Chapter 26

Astrid walked into her bedroom, and the moment she set foot in it she felt like the child she had once been. Time seemed to go back a few years, to when she lived there and it was her bedroom. As her uncle had told her already, the room was the same as she had left it. Alvis had kept it intact. This touched her. For a moment, as she passed her hand along the wardrobe, dresser, bed, and other personal objects of hers—a silver hairbrush, a jewel box her mother had given her, a dagger from her father that was still there, all lined up, waiting—she was ten years old again, when this room had been her own enchanted realm.

While she was flooded with memories from each object in the room, she realized how much her life had changed. From being a little, dreamy-eyed girl who spent most of her time alone, she had become a Stealthy Spy/Assassin of Nature/Forest Sniper. She was proud of how much she had accomplished, of who she had become. What impressed her most was that she had done it all by herself, without anyone's help. Her parents had not been able to help her unfortunately, and she would not have wanted her uncle's help anyway. She had done it alone and knew she deserved the credit for her success.

She also thought of the Snow Panthers and Ona and Camu, of the strong link that united them all, a stronger link than blood. You could not choose your family, but you could choose your friends. Her uncle was her family, and she appreciated everything he had done for her. She would always feel grateful to him and would respect and honor him for it. But the link she had with the Panthers was a lot stronger and deeper than the one she had with her uncle. And that was without counting Lasgol, the person she loved with all her heart. Ingrid, Nilsa, Egil, Gerd, Viggo, Ona, and Camu were her family now, and she was happy it was so. She would not want it any other way.

She found a couple of dolls she used to play with that brought back yet more childhood memories. She also found her training sword and bow in a great trunk at the far end of the room. She took them out and left them on the floor, looking at them while memories of training sessions with her instructors came back to her. She had never been very good with the sword, now that she thought back. But she had been good with the bow, knives, and a dagger. Her instructors had rewarded her when she did her exercises well, and she remembered times when they had congratulated her, as well as others when she had been reprimanded for not living up to what was expected of her, mainly in the art and mastery of the sword.

Luckily for Astrid, instructors and tutors came and went without leaving too much of a mark on her life. The only person in the keep who had had a profound effect on Astrid was good Alvis, who had always been home and helped her with everything. She wished her uncle had been as attentive and affectionate as Alvis. Unfortunately, he had always been away. And the worst thing was that, when he came back, he would rob her of Alvis for several days. He took the valet to his study or the library so Alvis could help him with his investigation and needs, and Astrid did not see Alvis again until her uncle let him go, usually after several days. Now that she thought about it, there had been times when, after one of her uncle's journeys, she had not seen Alvis for weeks. It was already bad enough that her uncle was barely at home, but that on top of it he would deprive her of the only person she could count on as company had been terrible.

She did not know why she was remembering all these things about her past; most likely because she was back in her bedroom and it was just as she had left it, her whole childhood seemed to come back to life in her mind. Most of the memories that came to her were not very happy, which left her feeling a bit depressed. But feeling sorry for herself, her past and her bad luck, would not change anything, so she focused on how good her life was now with Lasgol and the Panthers. She felt better at once.

There was a knock on her bedroom door, and Astrid opened it. It was one of her uncle's assistants bringing her a tray with some dinner. She thanked him and sat down to eat on the large pink-and-white bed. She lifted the dish cover and saw that her nose had not misled her: reindeer stew with potatoes, peas, and basil. One of her favorite dishes. The bread with it was fresh, baked that day. For dessert there were candied fruits, some of them foreign. She guessed her uncle's cook had also come back to the keep. This was going to be a nicer stay than she had anticipated. Well, not counting her uncle's extravagances—his blasted search and the supreme lords and their new era. Just thinking about it made her stomach turn.

Astrid took a deep breath. She did not know what her uncle was searching for with such yearning, but whatever it was, she hoped he would find it someday, for no other reason than to end the folly that had consumed him for more than half his life. He could still enjoy the good years left to him. He was rich and educated, with contacts and influential friends at the Court, the kind of friends you made by doing business with them and letting them earn a good pinch. Her uncle was intelligent, worldly, and clever, with business and connections. Astrid had never understood how he of all people, with all those qualities, was so consumed by a mission, a goal that seemed unreachable and which she could not understand.

She enjoyed the exquisite dishes, trying not to think of her uncle and his oddities. She had come to his call, as was her duty. She could not turn her back on him—he was her uncle, her relative after all— but if the visit turned out to be fruitless, it would not be her fault and she would leave the way she had come, having done her duty. She went to bed with these thoughts. On her bedside table was an old volume she must have been reading before she left. She picked it up and saw it was *Legends of the Far East* by Archibald Esposito. She remembered she had begun to read it and had been enjoying it, so she started to re-read it. It was not long before she fell asleep.

It was midnight when Astrid heard horses outside. She opened her eyes and sat up in bed. She was used to sleeping outdoors and being alert to the forest's sounds. Besides, her training to become an Assassin had made her a light sleeper. She had learned to wake up at the smallest sound. Lasgol joked that she woke up to the walk of a field mouse on the grass. Considering that Lasgol was also quite a light sleeper himself, Astrid took this as a compliment. She was already prone to waking up to the least sound though, and if you added the fact that she had been trained to not be surprised while asleep, it was natural that many nights she was awakened by one sound or another.

She went over to the window and looked outside. Her bedroom, one of the best in the keep, was located on the third floor and looked out of the front of the structure. From her window she could see the entrance and a large part of the property. Six riders were arriving.

Without turning on her light, she watched them. The torches burning at the front door allowed her to see them quite clearly. They wore silver-gray hooded cloaks, and she did not recognize anyone. What she did find strange was the hour of their arrival and the fact that they were allowed inside the keep. This should not be happening. No one coming at such an uncouth hour should have access inside— unless her uncle was waiting for them.

Intrigued, Astrid decided to investigate who the riders were. She got dressed and retrieved her knives. Careful not to make any noise, she opened her door and checked whether there was anyone in the corridor. It was clear, so she left her room and headed to the stairs. When she reached them, she flattened herself against the rock wall and listened. The sound of footsteps and voices reached her from the floor below, so she started going down, treading carefully and silently, pressed against the wall. She had to go around quite a way, since the keep was large and her bedroom was right in the middle.

She went down the eastern stairs to the second floor and stopped when she reached the stone landing. She would run into the corridor at the turn. She poked her head out quickly to take a look down the long passage. She did it so fast that no one noticed. She saw three guards posted in the corridor—one at the study door and the other two at the doors of the great library. The fact that the doors to the library were closed and guarded was odd. She remembered passing them earlier, and they had been open. But the fact that they were closed at night did not seem strange; it was a good measure to protect the books, particularly if one of the torches that lit the corridor fell off its hook and caused a small fire. Besides, the books had to be protected from rodents, one of their worst enemies.

Yet it made no sense to have guards posted at the door. She strained her ear, wanting to make sure her guess was correct. The corridor was long and the library was huge. She could not manage to hear anyone inside, no matter how hard she tried trying to catch any sound. But she strongly suspected the riders were inside with her uncle. Otherwise, the guards would not be there. A guard was there to protect something, and it would not be books, no matter how valuable they might be to her uncle—least of all three guards.

Yes, they had to be inside. Astrid wanted to know what they were up to, especially after the weird things her uncle had told her, so she decided to take a look. If Viggen caught her spying he would not take it too well. If they were behind closed and guarded doors it was because he wanted to keep whatever they were doing secret. But that was why she had to take a look and find out what was going on. In all certainty it would have to do with his search, since otherwise it would not be so urgent and her uncle would not be meeting with anyone at that hour of the night.

The first thing that came to her mind was to get rid of the guards. Her training was already telling her what to do and how to execute it in this situation. The problem was that she could not knock out the guards, because it would be difficult to persuade her uncle it had not been her doing. Especially being the only guest and having the skills necessary to do so. Nope, she quickly discarded that option. No fighting, no using her Assassin of Nature's skills. She would have to use Stealthy Spy techniques, which were a lot cleaner and would ensure she did not have to explain anything to her uncle. Well, that was if everything went smoothly, which was impossible to guarantee. Luckily, she knew the place well, and that was an advantage.

She went back up to the third floor quickly and without any noise. Then she faced a corridor and followed it until she reached the middle. There the corridor crossed with another. The keep was divided into four areas. Two large corridors divided them from north to south and east to west. It was a robust and simple construction model, the kind that lasted a thousand years. Basically, the keep was made of four smaller towers inside it. Astrid remembered studying the plans with her uncle. He had explained that structures built like that were capable of resisting attacks even from catapults and were easy to defend. That was because on every floor, the rooms had barred windows which allowed defenders to shoot at whoever might be attacking.

Astrid smiled. She had a better memory than she thought, and this would come in handy now. She went along the corridor to the room directly above the library. It was a huge bedroom for troops with almost fifty camp beds with trunks in front. There were two large rectangular windows, and as she had expected, they were barred.

There were armories and two large wardrobes against the walls; she opened one of them and found what she was looking for. Among a cloud of dust that almost made her sneeze, she found a knotted rope. It was used to fix the damage on the outer walls. She took it and left the room. She went up to the last floor of the tower. She had to be careful here—there was always a guard here since it was under the roof and you could see the whole land around the keep for leagues and leagues. There would be at least one guard, perhaps two, posted behind the battlement under the roof.

She was not wrong. As she moved along the floor, she found one guard to the east and another to the west. None were moving. They did not seem to be doing the rounds. They were simply guarding each side of the keep. She listened carefully and heard snoring. One was asleep like a log. She noticed how he was leaning against the wall but still standing. That guard had talent—to fall sleep standing like that was not easy. She needed him to stay like that for a good while. Sill crouching, she put her hand in her Assassin of Nature's belt and picked a container, then she took out a special assassin's needle and poured the container's liquid on it. With extreme care, crouching and in total silence, she crept up to the sleeping guard from behind, as if his shadow were coming back to him. With a swift move, she stuck the needle in him and withdrew it at once.

The guard felt the prick. It took him a moment to react; he jolted awake and put his hand to his neck, slapping it, thinking it had been a mosquito that had just stung him. He did not even turn, although even if he had he would not have seen Astrid, who in the blink of an eye had already stepped back to the corner to wait for the result. The poison took effect quickly. It was 'Sudden Sleep' a potent narcotic made of three plants that were difficult to find. This time the guard fell to the floor. Astrid had already foreseen this, and she caught him as he fell. She left him sitting against the wall, sleeping without snoring this time. The narcotic would make him sleep till dawn, and when he woke up, he would not know what had happened to him. He would have a headache and a mosquito bite on his neck. He would not say anything, since falling asleep on watch duty was the worst thing a guard could do; the punishment was severe.

Astrid looked down from the battlement. She moved until she was in the right position and tied one end of the rope to one of the roof beams. She let the other end drop along the rocky façade. A moment later she let herself down the rope. She went down two-and-a-half floors and then the rope came to an end. She still had to go down a floor and a half more, but she would have to do so without the rope. She spent a moment testing the strength of the wind. When you climbed stone walls, wind was an essential factor to consider. That, and how smooth the façade was. She measured it and noticed it was not too strong, so she made her decision and started climbing down the wall, seeking holds for her feet and hands.

She managed to climb down half a floor. She could see the windows of the library below and the light coming out of them. She was close. Astrid flattened herself against the wall and looked for handholds and footholds as she descended. She remembered that another of the things she had liked to do as a child was climb up the walls of the keep. Blurry memories of climbing up the façade to the cries and shouts of instructors and tutors demanding she come down came unbidden to her mind. She had forgotten about that. Yes, she had done it often, now that she thought about it. She seemed to have been quite the mischievous child. She smiled and kept going down carefully; she was beginning to see why she was so good at getting into fortresses.

She reached the left library widow at last. She held onto the bars and placed herself in such a way that she could hold on and also see into the room. The inner curtains were drawn but the thick outer curtains were not, so she could see what was going on inside. The oil lamps in the library lit up the room.

Seven men were standing around the large round table in the middle.

Her uncle was one of the seven.

He had a strange ceremonial object in his hand.

Chapter 27

Astrid watched the scene, eyes like saucers. She did not know what was going on in there, but she had the feeling it was important. The meeting she was witnessing was not something normal that happened often. The six men who had arrived during the night were dressed and armed the same as her uncle's guards, so Astrid assumed they were working for him. They were all middle-aged, and from what she could glimpse, they were all weathered men. They must have been working with her uncle for a long time; by their looks it seemed they had seen conflict. She had the feeling they knew how to fight—these were no simple guards. It was only a feeling, but she was almost never wrong with these kinds of things.

The fact that they were all dressed alike was not strange in itself, since lords and nobles required it once you entered their service. As a rule, they wore the colors of the house with its coat of arms. But these men wore the long gray robe which had the two silver circles—one inside of the other—embroidered on the chest. That was not the color of her uncle's house or his coat of arms. They looked like clerics, or some kind of religious group, and not Norghanian but foreign. Perhaps Erenal? They had religious orders there, as well as in Rogdon and east in the Kingdom of Irinel. In any case, they were armed and looked rather like mercenaries. Religious orders did not carry weapons as a rule…. Strange. Perhaps her uncle belonged to some armed religious order? She found it hard to believe. She could not remember hearing him talk about any religion, not even the Norghanian faith. He had left that to the tutors and instructors.

Her line of thinking surprised her. But it made some sense. In particular if you added it to her uncle's esoteric message. A new era was going to begin, a new order that was going to be imposed on Tremia. All-Powerful Supreme Lords she would have to serve. If she linked the message with the appearance of the group, it did give the feeling that it was some kind of brotherhood or guild with religious motives. To what god or gods they gave their efforts to, Astrid had no idea, but she wanted to understand.

"Where did you find it?" she heard her uncle asking one of the six riders while he observed the object in his hands with great interest. He was holding it at its spherical base.

Astrid squinted to focus on the strange artifact her uncle was holding in his hands. It was a silver sphere the size of a cantaloupe. About thirty long rods came out of it, also silver colored. No matter how much she stared at it, she had no clue what it might be or what it might be used for. She had never seen anything like it. It was obviously not a decoration. Her uncle and those other men would not be interested if that was the case. It had to be related to the famous search somehow. She decided not to jump to conclusions and keep watching to see what she could find out.

"In Silanda, in the south of Rogdon at the border with the Nocean Empire," the man replied. He looked the oldest.

The voices reached her quite muffled, so Astrid had to put her ear closer to hear better. She could understand what they were saying, but she feared that if they lowered their voices, she would lose them.

"Well, well, I have never thought of it being there. I've visited Silanda several times, led by the search, but I didn't manage to find anything there," Viggen said.

"It was hidden by one of the local ethnicities," another of the men said.

"Desert peoples or Rogdonians?"

"The desert, milord," the oldest one said.

"Milord, is it what we think it is? What we've been searching for so long?" another of the men asked. He looked Nocean.

"The description we have of the holy object, based on the studies I've done, it's quite similar to this one," Viggen said, looking at the object closely in the light of one of the lamps.

"Then you can confirm, milord, that these are The Quills of the True Blood?"

"We'll know soon. If they really are, the discovery will be of great importance," Viggen said as he kept examining the object from different angles.

"That's what we hope, milord."

"Have you manipulated it in any way?" Viggen asked.

"No, milord. We found it hidden inside an amphora, and we brought it without touching it or even evaluating it," the veteran of the group assured.

"You've done well," Viggen said as he placed the object on the table and took his hands off it.

Astrid watched how the sphere, with all the quills on its surface, stayed perfectly balanced on the table. She blinked hard, thinking her eyes were tricking her. The sphere should fall to one of the sides, dragged down by the weight of the long quills which looked metallic. But there it was, in perfect repose and equilibrium. One that would be impossible for any normal object.

"And the quills will always point to the pure of blood," one of the riders recited like a prayer.

Viggen turned around and went over to a huge bookshelf filled with volumes. He passed his finger along them, reading their titles until he reached the one he was looking for. He took it out. It was a thick book and must have weighed a considerable amount. He took it to the table and set it on the other end of where he had left the odd object with quills. His men backed up to give him room. Viggen opened the tome by the middle.

Astrid was expecting her uncle to consult some data about the object in the tome. She was wrong. The tome was not a book, but a fake. Inside was a silver-colored box, which her uncle took out. With the book closed you could not tell what was hidden inside it because the book looked completely normal on the outside. A wonderful hiding place for something of value, Astrid had to admit. Among the hundreds of books in that library, who would imagine that one of them hid anything. Astrid was left thinking that perhaps her uncle had more books like this one in which to hide his secrets. Probably— and in other places in the huge keep too.

Viggen opened the square metal box and took out what looked like a huge broken fang. He left it on the table. At once the quills sticking out of the sphere began to vibrate. First the movement was silent; they swayed rhythmically, as if touched by a breath of air which certainly was not blowing inside the room. Then they started to emit a sound like a long, shrill whistle. The vibration of all the quills increased until, driven by them, the sphere rose above the surface of the table up to two hand-spans while all the quills vibrated with the shrill whistle.

Viggen raised his arms.

"We've found it—these are The Quills of the True Blood!" he confirmed, eyes bright with excitement.

The six men knelt and bowed their heads.

"The day is near, the quest will soon be completed," Viggen announced.

"The All-Powerful Supreme Lords are coming," one of the men said.

"To guide us to a new dawn," another man said as if in prayer.

Astrid had to get a better grip on the window bars to keep from falling from shock when the strange object levitated above the table. She did not know what that thing was that her uncle had taken out of the box or why the sphere with quills had reacted that way, but it was clear something strange was going on there.

The more she watched the scene, the greater her impression that her uncle and his companions belonged to some kind of order. Could it be that his famous 'quest' was the search for some god, one of those supreme beings? In that case, all of it would make some sense. Could that be it? Could it make sense, armed men pursuing something, dressing like a religious brotherhood? Astrid was beginning to realize that something important was indeed going on here. What she was witnessing, the strange prayers they were reciting, were significant.

Viggen put the fang back in the silver box. When he did, the quills stopped vibrating and the whistle slowly quieted. After a moment, the object settled down on the table in perfect balance. Astrid knew that object had power—what she had just witnessed was magic, not religion, even if her uncle and those men seemed to be mixing both.

"Rise, my brothers," Viggen said with an accompanying gesture.

The six men rose.

"What does milord wish us to do?" the most veteran asked.

"Now that we have The Quills of the True Blood, we must find the Sleeper. He's already here, and will need our help."

"So it will be done, milord," they all said in unison.

"Go and prepare the Arrival. We must finish the quest—it's our sacred duty."

"We will, milord," they replied as one.

Astrid could barely believe what she had discovered. She would never have thought her uncle might belong to something like this. A trade consortium? Absolutely. A guild of international merchants too, since he had spent his whole life traveling and trading. But not this bizarre group. It was true he had been pursuing some quest his whole life, and Astrid was beginning to glimpse what he was looking for, even if she did not fully understand it. What concerned her most was how what she had witnessed fit in with everything her uncle had told her about the supreme beings and a new era. Everything was secret and apocalyptic.

"Come closer, brothers."

The six men stepped up to their master. Viggen picked a quill out of the object and handed it to the first man, who took it and got down on his knees. He touched his forehead with the quill and then stood and stepped aside, keeping the quill in his gloved hand. One by one they each received a quill and repeated the salute.

Once they had finished, Viggen bowed his head to them.

"Go, find it. We must complete our sacred mission," he said and waved them to the door.

The six men nodded and left.

Astrid stayed a bit longer, watching as her uncle put away the tome on the bookshelf and then covered the quilled object with a scarf. He picked it up carefully and took it with him when he left the library. Astrid knew it was time to move and started up the wall toward the rope to reach the roof. It was easier than coming down, and when she arrived at the top, she found the guard as she had left him, knocked out. She retraced her steps, left the rope where she had found it, and went back to her room as if she had never left it. But she had, and everything she had witnessed had made her uneasy and left her with a feeling that something terrible was hanging over all of them.

The next morning Astrid came down from her bedroom at sunrise. The riders who had arrived during the night had already left to fulfill her uncle's strange mission. Astrid waited in the great hall for her uncle to come down; she had a thousand questions she needed him to answer. She took a book from a shelf and started leafing through it.

"Miss Astrid," a voice greeted her.

She turned to see Alvis bringing a tray with breakfast.

"Good morning, Alvis," she greeted him back with a smile.

"Here's your breakfast," her uncle's valet said, leaving it on the table. "I hope it pleases you."

"Thank you, Alvis, I'm sure it will."

"I'll leave you alone to enjoy it in peace."

"Wait, Alvis. Where's my uncle? Is he up already? I need to talk to him."

"Your uncle is making preparations to leave, something pressing."

"He's leaving?"

Alvis nodded. "Some important matter requires his presence and he's getting ready to leave."

"I have to see him," she said urgently.

"They're waiting for him outside. They're about to bring the horses," Alvis said.

"I'll go outside then." Astrid hurried to the entrance.

"As you wish, milady," she heard Alvis say as she left the room.

Astrid passed between the two guards at the open entrance door and went outside. Four of her uncle's men were bringing five horses. Astrid did not see her uncle, so she waited for him to come out.

Viggen appeared a moment later. His men were waiting in front of the keep and Astrid was between them and the door.

"Good morning, Uncle."

"Good morning, my dear niece," he replied kindly, but his eyes betrayed concern; Astrid noticed he was wearing similar attire to that of his men, a little more elaborate and with silver bordering. He was armed with a long sword and a dagger at his waist. He stopped in front of Astrid.

"Are you leaving, Uncle?" She wanted to know what was going on and why he was leaving so suddenly.

"I must see to a matter of extreme urgency," he said.

"But I've just arrived… I thought you wanted me to stay." Astrid needed answers.

"And I do. I'm sorry I have to leave like this. Stay. It will only be a few days."

"Can't I come with you?"

"I'd like you to, but not this time. It's still not the time. Later on, when you understand what's at stake."

"Then your departure is related to the search…"

Viggen nodded. "It is. That's why it's so important. Otherwise, I wouldn't leave."

"Where are you going? What are you looking for?" she asked with a little despair in her voice seeing her uncle leaving again, leaving her, as he had done so often. After what she had witnessed, she needed answers.

"I know you want me to explain what's going on. I will. But not now—it's not the right moment, and I must leave at once."

"Uncle..."

"Stay. I stand by what I said. I want you to be with me in this new beginning, in this new era that'll soon be here."

"I need answers, Uncle."

"I know. I can't give them to you right now," he replied and sighed deeply. "I'll be back soon. Stay here," he said and got on his horse.

"I can't wait here without answers," Astrid warned him.

Viggen nodded. "I understand. We'll talk again soon. Take care, dear niece," he said in goodbye. He signaled his men and they left.

Astrid saw them ride off and felt once again like the little girl her uncle had left behind with her heart broken. Only she was no longer a child and she was not being left behind. She was not going to wait for his return. She would go on her way. She was going back to the Panthers. The situation her uncle was involved in did not concern her. More so when he had not wanted to explain clearly what it was about. What Astrid had got out of her visit was that her uncle was the same. He had not changed, and what was worse, he was involved in something that made her stomach turn. He would have to fend for himself. She was going to the Shelter, back to her real family, the Panthers.

Chapter 28

Lasgol stopped beside a stream on one side of the road. They were already close to the Shelter, less than a day away. The weather was good, and he decided to stop for a rest and enjoy the surroundings.

Rest? Camu messaged.

Yes, it's a good place for a brief stop. I need to refill the water skin, and Trotter will want to drink and cool off a bit.

Trotter snorted and shook his head up and down.

Ona chirped once.

I thirsty too.

Well, I see you all want to rest. Go and cool off in the water. Lasgol knew that what Camu really wanted was to play in the water and that Ona would join him. Poor Trotter would step aside to drink and graze a little fresh grass. Before Lasgol had finished his thought, he heard a loud splash and a neigh. He turned to look and saw Camu in the middle of the river, splashing and jumping, and poor Trotter moving away all wet. Ona was running along the riverbank.

Lasgol smiled as he set his bows, quiver, and traveling rucksack against a tree and sat down between its roots. That scene, so typical of them, gladdened his soul. There was nothing like being able to enjoy a little peace, the road, and the beautiful Norghanian land. In the forests and lands of his country he felt content.

With the sun on his legs and arms, Lasgol relaxed, enjoying the mild temperature. He heard more splashing and a growl from Ona. He strained his neck and saw them playing again in the middle of the stream; Camu was trying to catch his sister, who was a lot more agile and quick than he was. He was happy to see them having fun. They had spent a complicated time at the Shelter. Both Camu and Ona had suffered during their escape through the White Pearl.

For the moment Camu was behaving well, which surprised Lasgol and left him wondering. The creature had not asked to keep learning to fly and had not asked about the Pearl or opening portals. It was weird. Why did Camu not want to know anything about it? After all, they were new skills he had developed—well, that he was developing, since he could not control them yet. It would have been natural for him to want to develop them to their utmost capacity, and of course master them completely. Yet that was not the case. Camu had not even mentioned them. This left Lasgol at a loss and wondering whether the strong scolding he had delivered and the Panthers' criticism had anything to do with it. He assumed it had—Camu was very sensitive. He felt guilty about what had happened; perhaps he had scolded them too much? Now it was Lasgol who felt guilty.

He shook his head. No, he had scolded appropriately. What Camu and Ona had done had been wrong, and they had to understand, Camu as much as Ona. But the fact that Camu did not want to move forward with his new skills was significant. The skill of opening portals in Pearls was one thing, but why had he not asked to keep learning how to fly? That was a fantastic skill, and Lasgol knew Camu was delighted with it. In fact, the creature was very proud to have the skill. So, given this was the case, why had Camu not said anything else about training flights? Because of the accident he had suffered in his last attempt? Because he had broken a leg? Had the trauma paralyzed him? Was that why he did not want to fly again? Maybe—some traumas prevented people from continuing their normal lives; at least, that was what Egil had told him. Lasgol did not know much about the behavior of people or animals: the psychological realm was a mystery to him.

Camu had not said anything else about the orb either. Lasgol had asked him whether the orb had tried to communicate with him. So far it had not. The fact that Camu never mentioned the orb puzzled Lasgol. Perhaps the experience in the forests of the Usik had taught him a lesson, but Lasgol seriously doubted it. The creature was impossibly hardheaded. He was not one to learn lessons the hard way. It was odd that Camu was not interested in the orb. After all, it was family, as Camu himself had told them. The unfortunate thing was, when Lasgol had a bad feeling about something not adding up, he was usually right.

Lying there with all these matters going around in his mind, he started thinking about the orb he carried with him under his cloak, tied to his special Ranger's belt. Egil had begun to refer to the object as the 'dragon's orb' because of the faint image of a dragon inside it. Now the whole group called it that. Lasgol wondered how it was possible that such an object even existed—more so when Egil was

242

convinced the orb somehow felt and was intelligent. Just the thought that a magical object with power could think made Lasgol shiver and his skin prickle all over.

Many questions began to fill Lasgol's head. How had it managed to project the image of the dragon on the inside of the great block of ice it had been trapped in for over a thousand years? And how had it managed to melt the ice? With its power? Did it have so much of it? The orb must have done it by radiating a powerful energy, which made it dangerous. Had it been an accident? Lasgol shook his head. He had not had the impression there had been any accident; it looked quite deliberate. But, how had it managed to get rid of the ice? Because it had gotten rid of it. Was that what it was after?

He found it hard to imagine that something like that could happen. He had not really contemplated the idea that the dragon's orb had in fact done exactly that until this moment. And if that was what had really happened? The idea made more sense the more he thought about it. It had not been an accident, and it had probably not been by chance. It had broken free, and it had done so at the moment they were there. If this was the case, as he suspected, there had to be a reason for it.

He looked out of the corner of his eye to see where Ona and Camu were and did not see them. They must have continued their games along the river and were out of sight. He tried to continue resting. He shut his eyes. But all those questions about the orb kept turning around in his mind and would not let him rest. He forced himself to relax, to empty his mind and not think about anything. He could not. Questions about the orb assaulted him again. Since he had no answers to the questions bombarding his mind, he decided to examine the orb and see whether it gave him any new feeling that might help him answer some of those questions.

He opened his cloak. There it was, well wrapped up inside the leather pouch to prevent it from giving him a shock that might end his life. Careful not to touch it accidentally with his bare hands, he took it out of the pouch and put it on the ground between his legs. He knew it was not a good idea to investigate on his own: it was always safer to have Egil beside him to help with the study. But looking at it from another angle, if he was alone, no one would end up hurt if there was an accident. No one other than him.

With the help of a knife, so as not to touch the crystal object, he unwrapped it and left it uncovered on the ground. When the tip of the knife touched it, it gave off a tiny silver flash. It looked like a warning; something like "Beware, I have power," or so it seemed to Lasgol. Inside the orb he could glimpse the miniature frozen dragon. It was the frozen dragon without a doubt. It was identical, although it was faint and incorporeal, floating inside the orb.

Lasgol watched the dragon floating in some arcane substance, and it looked alive indeed. It was not some carving or statuette inside a crystal orb. It was moving. Not much and slowly, but it appeared to be moving with the undulations of the substance it was suspended in. That was something else that caught his attention. The dragon was suspended in that power, which is how Camu had referred to the gas or substance inside the orb. It was almost transparent, but every now and then it showed wavy, silver traces.

The more he observed it, the stranger it seemed to him, both the foggy silver substance and the perfectly detailed, albeit minute dragon. It looked like the work of a master craftsman. Maybe it was. Maybe it had been created by a magical craftsman. Some mage of great power. That was Egil's working theory and the reason why he had gone back to the Camp to do some research. He might be wrong, but Egil was rarely wrong. What was clear was that this exquisite object was magical and powerful. Its creator, therefore, following logic, must be even more powerful.

Lasgol tried to communicate with the object. There was a risk, but if he went about it carefully, nothing bad should happen. At least as long as he did not touch it, something he was not intending to do, even with leather gloves on. He needed answers, and the more he analyzed the orb, the more questions he had. He did not have a single answer, and that was driving him crazy. He took a deep breath to relax; he needed to be calm and in control of his emotions.

He concentrated by shutting his eyes. At once, instead of studying the orb, he felt less worried with fewer questions in his head. He thought this was funny, he would have to tell Egil. He called upon his *Aura Presence* skill to see whether the orb had an aura he could discern. He figured it would not have one, or if it did, that he would not be able to perceive it, since dealing with arcane objects was not one of his fortes. He thought about Enduald, the Mage Enchanter, Sigrid's brother. He would probably know how to interact with the object. He would also want to keep it. Magi were not prone to letting an Object of Power pass them by without claiming it, least of all one as powerful and strange as this one.

The skill activated, and Lasgol glimpsed a circular aura around the orb which emitted a strong, silver glow. What was curious and frightening was that he noticed it with his eyes shut. He opened them a little, and the glow was so strong, it blinded him at once. He had to shut his eyes again tight to protect them. He was forced to turn his head away to recover. It reminded him of Camu's aura-of-power glow, which was also blinding. Lasgol was feeling the magic's presence and its power.

Now that he had detected the aura, Lasgol decided to use his *Arcane Communication* skill. It had worked with his mother's pendant, which was an Object of Power, so it might work here too, although this object was much more powerful. Best to be careful. He felt like a child playing with fire. He focused on the orb and tried to interact using his skill, seeking to create a link which would allow him to communicate—or if not communication, at least some form of interaction. Lasgol did not know whether he could manage something and was uneasy, but he was determined to go ahead, even though his stomach told him it would be best to give up this idea.

He opened his eyes and saw the dragon inside the orb moving. Suddenly the substance of power it was floating in, began to change color. It started getting darker. Lasgol tried to establish communication by sending more of his own energy into the skill so it would interact. The color changed yet again and took on a silvery-black tone. Then a bright glow hit Lasgol's mind. He tried to bear it but could not; it was too intense for him to control the light. He had the clear feeling that if he did not yield, he would not only lose his sight, but his mind as well.

He shut his eyes tight; this had not been a good idea. The orb's aura of power would consume him if he kept trying to interact with the object, best to stop. Only a great mage who could protect their body and mind from the orb's power should try to manipulate it. This had definitely not been a good idea. They were going to need outside help to study the orb, help from a powerful mage. That would probably end in a conflict of interest, since the more powerful the mage was, the greater his desire to keep the orb.

All of a sudden, Lasgol felt the urge to touch the orb, to stroke it. He thought it odd and shook the idea off. He knew he should not touch it, that if he did he would get a shock that might kill him. Even so, he felt the need to stroke it, to have the orb in his hands. He shook his head, trying to resist the urge. It felt imposed, like it did not come from him. The orb was trying to persuade him to touch its crystal surface with his hands. For a moment he was unable to resist, and he stretched both arms to reach the object. Lasgol's mind seemed incapable of controlling them. His hands got closer to the orb, as if guided by the object. The tips of his fingers were about to touch the orb.

Somewhere deep in his subconscious, a feeling of great danger assaulted him. He knew that if he touched the orb he was going to die. At the same time, he could not avoid touching it. His hands stopped, brushing the translucent surface. He could feel it but not see it since his eyes were still shut. Two forces were struggling in his mind—one attracted his hands to the orb, and the other pushed in the opposite direction. The struggle intensified, and Lasgol used all his willpower to move his hands away from the crystal sphere, because he was about to die—he knew it, but he was trapped. His hands would not move away. The force attracting them was as great as that with which he was trying to pull back.

He had to stop the orb or it was going to kill him. Why was he doing this? Why did it want to kill him? How was it doing so? How was it influencing him? As he tried to reason through this, in the midst of great mental effort, he realized the orb was influencing him because he had tried to interact with the object. He knew he had to stop the contact he had established. He interrupted the *Arcane Communication* skill he still had activated.

At once the urge to touch the orb vanished from his mind. He moved his hands away and opened his eyes. The glow had vanished too. The orb was back to looking like a normal object, at least as normal as a dragon orb could be. It did not emit any kind of glow of power, or if it did, Lasgol could not see it anymore since he had stopped his own skill.

He took a deep breath and moved away. He had been on the brink of dying. The dragon orb had tried to kill him. He did not know whether it was some defensive mechanism because he had tried to interact with the object or whether the object simply wanted to kill him or anyone who tried to manipulate it. Yet it had interacted with Camu and had not harmed him in any way. Was it because they were in some way related? He thought it might be that. Camu was a creature of the dragon family, a Drakonian, and although they still did not know what that meant or its ramifications, he could see more and more clearly that Camu, dragons, and the orb were related.

He snorted. He did not like the situation or the implications of it. The orb wanted something, something it had influenced Camu for, and it had been left very clear that if a human tried to manipulate it, the orb would try to kill the person. Nilsa's and Viggo's idea of getting rid of the magical object did not sound so outrageous in view of this. It was dangerous, and they could have a deadly accident simply by keeping it. Luckily, it could not attack them as long as they did not touch it. Lasgol wondered why this was the case. Was it a limitation of the object's magic itself, or was there something preventing it?

He watched it for a while, his eyes focused on the dragon floating inside the crystal sphere. The silver dragon gave him the willies. Not only because of what had just happened and the fact it was a dragon, albeit a miniature one locked up in an orb, but a dragon none the less—there was a reason. He had a sinking feeling thinking about it. A shiver ran down his back and his stomach turned.

He covered the orb again and put it back in the pouch, which he tied to his belt under his cloak. Hidden there, it seemed less dangerous. But the feeling stayed for only a moment. He knew it was an illusion; the dragon orb was definitely going to bring them trouble, serious trouble.

The sound of splashing in the river came back, and Lasgol turned to look at the water. Camu was running after Ona, who was soaking, poor thing. They reached him and Ona shook herself off. Since she was a good and smart panther, she did it far enough not to splatter Lasgol. Camu did the same, only he had no fur and so did not shake off much water since he did not get soaked. Water slid off his scales.

I see you've been having fun.

River fun, Camu messaged.

Have you been frightening Trotter?

A little…

Aw, poor Trotter. Lasgol looked around the tree and saw the pony grazing a little further away.

Keep going? Camu asked.

Yes, we'll soon see Gerd.

Ona chirped once.

Gerd good, we want see Gerd.

Me too. I hope he's feeling better.

Gerd well, I sure.

Let's hope so… Lasgol was also hoping Gerd was okay, but he had his doubts. He did not want to worry Camu and Ona and said no more. They would soon see him, and then they would find out.

Let's get on our way, Lasgol transmitted.

Good.

Trotter, come, Lasgol transmitted. He was not sure his mental message would reach the pony from that distance.

Trotter snorted and cantered toward them.

This surprised Lasgol; his power was growing. Before he would not have been able to communicate with Trotter at such a distance, and the improvement encouraged him.

Let's go see the big guy, he transmitted to his friends, and they set off.

Chapter 29

Gerd was sweating profusely. His shirt and doublet were soaked. He flexed his knees and squatted down with his back straight and his arms stretched out front, keeping his balance throughout.

"Thirty…" he counted out loud.

"Keep going, you're doing well," Loke said as he watched Gerd's back, in case he lost his balance and fell backwards.

The giant rose slowly. Loke reached out behind him to support him in case he toppled over. They had been doing the same exercise for weeks, and until now he had not managed to do so many squats without collapsing, whether from exhaustion or losing his balance. It was the first time he had completed the exercise. Loke said nothing so Gerd would not lose his concentration.

"Thirty-one…" he said, and as he rose, he took a deep breath.

"You are going to outstrip me," Engla commented as she, also soaked in sweat, sat in front of Gerd, watching him.

"How many did the Elder manage today?" Gerd asked her before attempting the next squat.

"Thirty-five," Engla replied. "The last five were torture, so you had better be prepared."

"I am. I'll try to outdo you," Gerd said, frowning.

Annika appeared, coming from the Lair.

"This is not a competition," The Elder Specialist of Nature gently scolded them. "I love the forest you have chosen for practice," she told Loke.

To avoid the rumors and whispers of the already-training specialist contenders, they did the workout sessions in the middle of the Ringed Forest. It was a beech forest with a circle of stones in the center which looked like a stone ring. It was a perfect place to work out without being bothered, since from outside the forest, once they entered the circle of rocks they could not be seen.

"It's a good, discreet place. I keep telling them it's not a competition, but they don't pay too much attention," Loke replied.

"Well, a bit of healthy competition is not only fun but good for you. It pushes you to reach further, and with that we'll improve sooner," Engla explained.

"These are recovery sessions—they must be understood and taken as such," Annika said, wagging her finger at them.

"No one is saying they're not. We simply try to make the most of it with a little healthy competition," Engla said with a mischievous grin.

"Let me remind you that when we started rehabilitation you could barely walk ten paces. Don't take the effort too far, or it will have negative repercussions on your bodies," Annika told them.

"Thirty-two …" said Gerd, puffing from exertion.

"Loke, make sure they don't overdo it," Annika pleaded.

"I try, but as I said, they tend to ignore me," the Masig Specialist replied with a shrug.

"Well, if they don't pay attention, when they fall down don't help them. Let them hit the ground hard. Perhaps then they'll learn to listen," Annika said with a wink.

"We'll do as you say," Engla said to Annika. "The thing is, it's very frustrating to not be able to do the simplest and easiest of exercises."

"I understand, but no matter how frustrating and despairing it is, you have to go slowly. You can't force recovery. Least of all when there's a mental breakdown involved and an imbalance of mind and body," Annika said.

"It's… very… frustrating…" muttered Gerd as he continued the exercise. He was going slowly, out of prudence and because his body would not obey him as he wanted. No matter how much he wanted it to go down or up, his body followed another rhythm, as if the order arrived with great delay. And not only that, but it also cost him dearly to do anything, as if his muscles and nerves were iron and could not bend.

"Extremely. I feel as if we were learning to walk again. As if we were three years old," Engla said.

"It is something like that," Annika told them. "For you, Elder Specialist of Expertise, it must be the worst of tortures, after spending a life exercising and training body and mind, precisely so they would be a perfectly deadly weapon."

"I have no words to express what I feel," said Engla. "It's as if I'd lost everything I've worked for my entire life. As if the Ice Gods had stolen it from me for having offended them."

"It's a bitter punishment... that's for sure..." Gerd grunted as he tried for another squat.

"I can only imagine it. I know I'll never get to fully feel what you're going through. A young man with all his life ahead of him, robbed of his strength, of his energy. A Master with a whole life of learning behind her. You've both lost a lot. One in his future and the other in her past. Yet, you are making progress, you are improving; we'll help you recuperate what's been taken from you."

"The Elder will help you recover," Loke told Engla.

Annika nodded. "We'll keep working until you do. I've brought you the revitalizing potions. Take them as soon as you finish today's exercises."

"We will," Engla assured her, and she reached out for Annika to hand them to her.

Gerd went on with the exercise while Engla, Annika, and Loke watched him. Upon reaching the thirties, he had begun to have real trouble.

"Keep going, you have to catch up to me," Engla told him.

"Thirty-three..." Gerd grunted.

"Take it slowly or you'll lose your balance," said Loke with his arms stretched behind Gerd in case he fell.

"Be careful..." Annika warned.

The big guy did not want to give up. He knew he could do it, he only needed to concentrate and draw strength from his stomach. He continued the exercise before the alert eyes of the three.

"Thirty... four..." he snorted and almost toppled over. Loke held him.

"I think you've had enough," Annika said in a concerned tone.

"Let me... try one more..." Gerd said, although he was exhausted.

"Are you sure?" Loke asked him.

"Yes... I know I can..."

"We can leave it as it is. I don't mind winning," Engla grinned ironically.

"No... one more... I want to try..."

"You can barely stand," Annika said, worried.

"I can. One more..." Gerd pleaded.

"Fine. You're both very stubborn," Annika groaned, giving up.

Gerd took a deep breath. He had no more strength and was dead tired, but he had to try and tie with Engla. He was not doing it to avoid losing, but so the competition would stay alive. He also believed that constantly competing was helping them recover faster. At first, they had been doing the rehabilitation exercises separately, out of respect for Engla's rank. But she herself had suggested they do the rehabilitation together precisely to compete against one another, since she believed they would advance faster that way. She had not been wrong. Compared to how they had started, they were doing much, much better.

With a proud grunt, Gerd began his last squat. He managed to lower his body without losing his balance, which was a feat in itself.

"Come on, you can do it!" Engla cheered him.

"Don't worry, if you fall, I'll catch you," Loke said at his back.

Annika was biting her lips.

Gerd clenched his jaw, drew strength from his core, and started to rise. Halfway up, he stopped. It seemed he was going to go to one side. He managed to keep his balance by sheer rage, not wanting to collapse.

"You've got it!" Engla cried.

Annika snorted, and her face looked anxious.

"Careful, don't fall," she warned.

Gerd wrinkled his nose and kept lifting his huge body. He felt as if he weighed five times more. But he did not collapse, and he pulled with all the strength he had left. He managed to straighten up.

"Thirty... five..." he muttered and snorted in relief.

Loke withdrew his stretched arms.

"Great job," he congratulated Gerd.

"Thank... you..."

"Great achievement," Annika said proudly.

"Tomorrow we'll try to break the record," Engla told Gerd defiantly.

"And... we'll... do it," he replied with a tired smile.

"Drink your potions, or else you won't even be able to get back to the Lair."

They waited a while for Gerd to slightly recover. Then they both drank their potions, and it was obvious by the look on their faces that the taste was not exactly pleasant.

"Let's go back to the Lair, you need to rest," Annika said.

They started back, Engla and Gerd walking slowly. They could not run. Every couple paces they were forced to stop from the mere effort of walking or because they had stumbled.

"It's really sad that this short journey we used to do with our eyes closed and without any effort is now so hard to tackle," Engla said, in a tone between frustrated and disheartened as they were leaving the forest.

"Very true. I used to have prodigious strength, and now simple exercises and squats are tremendously hard for me to do," Gerd commented, also dispirited.

"You're progressing, and that's what counts. Let's not let evil thoughts dishearten you," Annika said.

"It's not that, it's just that progress is so slow," Engla said. "It's going to take us years to recover at this pace."

"Your bodies and minds need time to heal," Annika replied. "We must be patient and celebrate the advances you're achieving."

"We know they're achievements, but so tiny that it's as Elder Engla says, it's going to take us an eternity to recover," Gerd said, worried and sad.

"You'll keep recovering," Annika said with a smile. "We'll make it happen, trust me and trust yourselves."

They continued to the entrance of the Lair. It was noon, and Gerd was feeling low-spirited. But what he saw at the entrance to the cave made him happy right away.

Ingrid, Viggo, Lasgol, and Ona were waiting there with smiling faces.

"My friends!" Gerd called out when he recognized them, waving at them joyfully. He began to walk faster to reach them and lost his balance. Loke was watching him though, and he grabbed Gerd's arm and straightened him with a pull before he could fall to the ground.

"Come here, let me give you a bear hug!" he said to Viggo. Gerd tried to lift him off the ground, but he lost balance and started falling backwards with Viggo locked in his arms. Watchful Loke stopped them from falling. Lasgol and Ingrid pulled Viggo back, helping Loke.

"Could you be more clumsy, you mountain of muscle!" Viggo protested.

"My balance isn't very good," Gerd apologized, embarrassed.

"I see the Panthers have come to visit," Annika said, smiling. "How are you all?"

"We're all well, Ma'am," Ingrid replied with a respectful bow.

"I'm glad to hear it. You look good indeed," Annika said, looking them up and down with a gleam of affection in her gaze.

"We've just finished our morning rehabilitation exercises," Engla explained, pointing at their sweaty clothes. "It's been a good session—Gerd almost outstripped me today."

"That's wonderful, Gerd!" Lasgol said, delighted, slapping him on the back.

"Elder Engla, this means the rehabilitation is going well then," Viggo said in a questioning tone.

"It's going, but very slowly," Engla replied in a frustrated tone.

"They're both doing wonderfully. They have an iron will. They're improving, rest assured," Annika said in a calming tone.

"That's great news," Lasgol said, pleased. "We've come to see how things were going. The rest of the Panthers must already be on their way. They'll soon be here."

"We'll be happy to have them here," said Annika. "Now we'll leave you so you can have a proper reunion. I'll warn Sigrid of your visit and we'll prepare your accommodations," she added.

The Panthers nodded gratefully.

"There will be an afternoon rehabilitation session," Loke told Gerd.

"I'll be there," Gerd promised.

"Very well, we must keep competing," Engla said.

Gerd nodded.

Annika, Engla, and Loke disappeared into the Lair.

"How happy I am to see you!" Gerd cried.

"And we're so happy to see you too!" Lasgol said.

"Did you come together, or did you meet on the way?" Gerd asked.

"We met on the way, a day ago," Ingrid replied.

We happy to see you, Camu messaged.

"And I'm thrilled to see you, Camu—well, or not see you," Gerd said to Camu with a guffaw as he looked around, unable to see him.

Ona chirped and rubbed herself against his leg.

"Ona, beautiful," Gerd said, stroking her head. In order to pet her, he bent over slightly, lost his balance, and started to fall.

Lasgol and Viggo hastened to catch him before he hit the ground.

"You're more like Nilsa every day," Viggo said with a mocking grin.

"Don't be so mean to him," Ingrid said reproachfully.

"It's okay. I know I'm clumsy," Gerd admitted. "By the way, where is Nilsa?" he asked.

"She must be on her way," Lasgol said, waving at the entrance to the valley in the distance.

"And Egil? Have you seen him?"

Ingrid and Viggo shook their heads.

"Have you seen him, Lasgol?" Gerd asked him.

"No, I haven't. He went to the Camp to find information in the Library, that's all I know."

"We're also missing Astrid," said Ingrid.

"Yeah, I hope she comes soon," Lasgol said, and he could not help but sigh.

"Let's see what they have to share, family visits are usually complicated," Gerd said, as if they could be a nightmare.

"Not mine. They're not," Viggo said with a malicious smile.

"That's because you haven't got a family," Ingrid snapped.

"Correct. And if I had one, I'd stay away from it. They'd surely want to benefit from my achievements and fame."

"What achievements and fame?" Ingrid replied, looking at him as if he were out of his mind.

"Those I'm collecting with my service to the King," Viggo said, puffing up his chest.

"Oh yes, your feats are legendary," Ingrid snapped sarcastically.

"You don't want to believe me, but rumors of our feats are all around, particularly mine. I'm soon going to be famous throughout the kingdom."

"Won't that be counterproductive? Considering you're an Assassin and you have to move around incognito and all that assassin stuff," Gerd said with a smile.

Viggo thought about it and made a face.

"Weren't you soft in the head?" Viggo said, touching Gerd's temple with his finger.

"Soft my foot! I have some trouble with coordination, balance, and mobility. My head's working very well, thank you," Gerd replied.

"Well, as far as I know, those functions are ruled by the head. So, your noggin's not as good as you think."

"I can still hit at a short distance," Gerd threatened him with his fist.

"I bet you'd miss my face by a hand-span," Viggo teased.

Viggo always trouble, Camu messaged to Lasgol, along with a feeling of amusement.

"I'll hold him, let's try," Ingrid said, standing behind Viggo's back, holding his head with both hands and looking at Gerd.

The giant smiled from ear to ear.

Gerd try, see if hit.

Camu says to try and see how much you're improving," Lasgol said with a wink at Gerd.

"No way!" Viggo cried, as with the nimbleness of a snake he freed himself from Ingrid's grip and slid away from danger.

Gerd laughed, and Ingrid, Lasgol, and Camu joined in. Ona dropped on the ground and rolled over. Lasgol interpreted it as her way of laughing too, although he was not sure how much she really understood of what was going on.

They chatted a while outside the Lair, telling Gerd what had happened with their last mission.

"Oh, I would've loved to be there!" he cried enviously.

"You would've come in handy, big guy, the trunks with the gold weighed tons! Your muscles would've been put to the test," said Viggo.

"Don't worry, we always have the next mission," Lasgol told Gerd to cheer him.

"I'm afraid I'm still not ready to go on the next one."

"You keep working hard and you'll get there," Ingrid said in a cheerful tone.

"And until you come back, we'll have to make do, but don't take too long, or we'll have to replace you with some oaf with muscles and no brain who are so common in Norghana," said Viggo.

"Don't you dare replace me!"

"You take too long and you'll see," Viggo threatened him.

"Ignore him, he's just messing with you. Of course, we're not going to replace you," Ingrid said reassuringly.

"Really, I don't see why not. We're missing muscle in the group, and I bet we could find someone who snored less," Viggo insisted.

"No one's going to replace you," Lasgol said reassuringly too.

Viggo was smiling. He had managed to plant the seed of doubt in the good giant.

"When I recover completely, the first thing I'm going to do is give you a good blow to the head," Gerd said to Viggo.

"Well, make it this year, huh," Viggo made a face.

They continued talking, and of course Viggo went on messing with Gerd. In the end they all ended up laughing at the jokes, in a good mood and happy with their reunion.

Chapter 30

As they arrived at the Cavern of Spring they found that their bunk beds had been prepared and the screen had been placed so they would have some privacy, just like their accommodation during the Higher Training. They chose the same bunks, laughing, leaving their gear in the trunks.

Lasgol first, then Ingrid and Viggo after him, recounted their adventures to the others. Lasgol had enjoyed a relaxed stay in Skad, but Ingrid's and Viggo's visit had been the opposite. What had happened to them and the way they had solved it, left the rest very impressed. Gerd and Lasgol congratulated them warmly for the courage and honor they had shown, as well as the skill they had shown in combat. Ingrid waved it aside, saying they had only done their duty. Viggo stated it was nothing but another of his feats that would be commented about throughout Norghana.

At noon Sigrid appeared in the cavern, looking for them.

"Welcome back to the Shelter," she greeted them with a pleasant smile.

"Thank you, we're happy to be back," Ingrid said with a respectful bow.

"I understand you have come to visit. Are you on leave?" Sigrid asked.

"That is correct, Mother Specialist," Ingrid confirmed. "We still have a few days off before we have to go back to the capital for our next mission."

"I am glad you have come. It will be good for Gerd to see you. Rehabilitation is a tough process, and he needs cheering up," she said, looking at Gerd with eyes loaded with guilt.

"We'll make sure he does," Lasgol promised, stroking Gerd's back.

"We have prepared the same accommodation you had during the Training. You will be well taken care of and will have some privacy. I guess Camu is with you."

"Indeed he is," Lasgol said.

I here, Camu messaged.

"I am glad you are here, Camu. Gisli will be pleased too."

"We'll try not to let him frighten the specialist contenders," Lasgol said.

"I am afraid the rumors that the Royal Eagles have a Creature of the Ice with them is already flying among the Rangers. The Specialists who were training at the same time as you glimpsed Camu, and now the rumors are quickly spreading."

"Those screens couldn't hide him completely," Viggo said. "It was inevitable."

He can't stay in his camouflaged state all the time," Lasgol explained to Sigrid. "He's tried and has managed to make his skill last longer, but he still has a long way to go before he can camouflage all the time."

Only a while, not all day, Camu explained.

"It is natural. I do not see any problem in the rumor that you have a Creature of the Ice with you. Others would find out sooner or later. It would be worse if the rumor was about you having a dragon."

Viggo opened his mouth to say something, but Ingrid elbowed him to keep him quiet.

"We'll try to be discreet regarding Camu," Lasgol said. "Rumors are usually unavoidable, but there's no reason to feed them."

"I must warn you that if before there was a lot of talk about you, now there is a lot more," Sigrid said. "Your fame is growing, because of your achievements in missions, for saving the kingdom, for having more than one specialization, and now we have Camu added to it all. You are becoming true celebrities among the Rangers. I hope it does not go to your heads. It might be lethal."

"It won't, Mother Specialist. I'll personally make sure it doesn't," Ingrid said confidently.

"Very well. I do not want you to be overconfident or let the fame and glory blind you or blur your senses. That could be deadly."

"We understand, Mother Specialist," Lasgol said. "We're never over-trusting or confident, and we're not going to start now."

"I hope so. For your own good," Sigrid said in a tone of advice or admonition.

"Thank you for the warning, Mother Specialist," Ingrid said.

"I want the best for you and for the Rangers. It is my duty to make sure of it," Sigrid said. "Especially in your case, with what happened during your Higher Training. I am indebted to you and I will do everything I can to help and protect you."

"There's no need..." Lasgol began.

"We knew there were risks," Ingrid said. "The decision was ours, and we took part in the training knowing that."

"Even so.... What happened is my responsibility, and because of that my door is always open to you. This extends to the Shelter. You will always be welcome here. I will not ask you why you have come or what for, you are free to come and go. You can also come to me whenever you want. I will help you in any way I can. You only have to ask."

"We appreciate it, Mother Specialist," Lasgol replied. He was aware of the great honor of being able to come to the Shelter without needing to ask for permission or give explanations to anyone.

"I will leave you now so you can get settled. I am sure your visit will cheer Gerd a lot," she said and looked at the giant fondly, who went all red. "I will not have much free time—unfortunately Enduald and Galdason are away so I am short-handed—but I will try to make time for you if you need me."

"Has anything serious caused them to leave?" Ingrid asked, raising an eyebrow.

"Yes and no. The problem is the melting that occurred in the cavern of the frozen dragon. They are investigating it. They have not found an explanation for the event. What they did find were traces of a singular energy, power. They have gone to consult with a mage expert in matters of arcane energy in the Kingdom of Rogdon. They will come back once they have spoken to him. I hope they return with some plausible explanation for what happened, which is a real mystery."

"Let's hope they find answers," Lasgol said, looking at his comrades out of the corner of his eye, and he could not help but reach under his cloak where the pouch with the orb was hanging. No one said anything.

"Very well. Consider yourselves at home. Stay away from the contenders so they do not get lost in dreams of grandeur and exalted aspirations," Sigrid said with a mischievous smile.

"Don't worry, Mother Specialist, we'll stay clear of them," Ingrid promised.

Two days later Nilsa and Astrid arrived. They had met on the road to the Shelter. There were more hugs and greetings, and happiness reigned over the reunion. Lasgol was overjoyed at having Astrid in his arms again and seeing that she was perfectly all right. They went outside so Gerd could take a stroll, and while they peacefully walked, Nilsa told them everything that had happened during her visit to her family.

"As you can see, my visit wasn't that bad," Nilsa commented while they were walking toward the Pearl, one of the walks Gerd had to do. The ramp to the Pearl was excruciating for the giant.

"What a visit..." Gerd stammered from the effort. Ona was walking beside Gerd and moaned. The panther seemed to have noticed something was wrong with the giant and it appeared she wanted to go with him to help. As usual, Camu walked behind the group in his camouflaged state.

"What a situation you had to deal with," Lasgol said.

"I'm sorry your mother took things that way," Astrid added.

"Well, in the end we made our peace. It wasn't that bad," Nilsa admitted. "Other times we've had more painful separations. Besides, I was able to help my sisters and spend time with them, and I value that a lot. It's filled my soul with joy, I mean it. Just that made it worth it, regardless of the difference of opinion between my mother and me."

"What you did was superb!" Ingrid congratulated her. "I'm certainly proud of you," she told her friend with a big hug.

"Honestly, I felt great afterwards."

"You showed courage and honor and you defended your family. You did very well. More than that, you were sensational!" Lasgol said.

"And you showed character and fortitude," Astrid said, patting her on the back. "You can certainly feel proud of yourself."

"Thank you... I don't know where it came from..."

"From your heart," Ingrid said, making a strong fist. "Always act like that."

Nilsa nodded repeatedly.

"Look at that... it turns out you're gutsy after all," Viggo said, not ironically, but with a surprised look on his face, even impressed. "Congratulations, clodhopper."

"I'll take that as a compliment, coming from you," Nilsa said.

"It is a compliment," Viggo assure her, smiling at her fondly.

"Wow, congratulations from you was the last thing I was expecting." Nilsa threw her head back, eyes wide open from the surprise.

"I might be a little sarcastic and like to make a scene messing with my friends, but I give credit where credit is due. You were great, and I'm impressed. Very well done," he repeated and made a deep bow.

Nilsa was speechless.

"Thank you…"

"You surprise me every day," Ingrid told Viggo and gave him an unexpected kiss.

"Well, if I had known that was coming, I'd surprise you more often," Viggo said when Ingrid stopped kissing him.

"But make it good surprises, I've already had enough of the other kind," Ingrid said, wagging her finger at him.

Viggo gave her his mischievous smile.

Halfway up they had to stop. Poor Gerd could not go on. He was huffing and puffing, trying to fill his lungs with air. Every step was torture for him, and the hill made it ten times worse. Yet they all knew Gerd would not give up. He was a Snow Panther—he would go on and reach the Pearl.

While Gerd recovered, Astrid told them about her strange visit to her uncle's home and what she had witnessed. As she was explaining it, her friends' faces showed great puzzlement. When she finished telling them, they all looked at one another blankly.

"Your uncle's a most eccentric character…" Ingrid said with a raised eyebrow. "I wonder if they really are some kind of armed religious brotherhood or something similar. There aren't any in Norghana, as far as I know, but I do believe they exist outside the kingdom."

"What you've told us sounds to me like some kind of sect that worships dark lords and divulges the end of times," Viggo commented.

"Yeah, the message… the new era… it does sound like the end of the world or something…" Gerd said as he tried to recover in order to face the end of the climb.

"What's even funnier is that I've also heard a similar message," Lasgol told them.

"From one of my uncle's men?" Astrid asked, looking lost.

"No, this was a poor wretch, a preacher. He was in Skad. The message was even more alarmist than your uncle's, but similar in essence."

"That can't be good... two apocalyptic messages which two of us have heard in different places and from different people—this is beginning to smell rotten..." Viggo said, wrinkling his nose and shaking his head. "Trouble's in sight."

"It could be a coincidence. They don't have to be related," Ingrid said. "Lasgol, it isn't the same message, is it?"

"No, not exactly. The preacher said the sky and the earth would burn, that a thousand volcanoes would destroy everything and that those disloyal and impure and whoever didn't embrace the new order would perish. That the end of the era of men was coming."

"The part about the end of the era of men fits in. My uncle also said that. Nothing about fire though," said Astrid.

"Well, I foresee that this is a new problem coming at us," Viggo said with his sarcastic grin. "The weirdo has gotten us into new trouble."

"Me? What have I done?" Lasgol asked, raising his hands.

"You attract the worst trouble. It's as if you were jinxed or a sorcerer had cursed you at birth. Thank goodness I'm here to get you all out of these messes," Viggo replied, all smiles.

"Yes, thank goodness you fix all the messes we find ourselves in," Ingrid said in an acid tone.

"The preacher, and others like him, are spreading that apocalyptic message throughout Tremia, not just Norghana. I have nothing to do with it."

"It is curious that the preacher and Astrid's uncle should talk about a new era and the end of the era of men," Nilsa mused. "The truth is, it gives one the chills."

"Let's not jump to conclusions. We don't know whether they're related or if they even have any merit. They could just be the crazy ideas of people not in their right mind," said Ingrid. "And I'm sorry, Astrid."

"Don't worry, the idea crossed my mind too," she replied. "The thing is, I've spoken with my uncle and he didn't seem crazy at all. Did he have some weird ideas? Most certainly."

"Let's not attach more importance to the matter. Let's wait and see what Egil thinks of all this. I'm sure he'll have some brilliant idea. These subjects fascinate him," said Ingrid.

"Yeah, the other trouble-finder. You'll see the mess these two get us in…" Viggo said. "I'm going to start sharpening my knives, preparing poisons, and looking for cream for burns—we're going to need it. I can see myself all tan with my hair singed," he said, beaming from ear to ear.

"Yes, we should calm down. They don't have to be related or be something as terrible as it sounds," said Nilsa, who was breathing hard to let her nerves out.

"We hope…" said Ingrid, who did not look sure at all.

"In the end, I'm going to be happy for not having a family. What strange family visits you've had," Viggo said, laughing.

Astrid and Nilsa looked at one another and laughed out loud.

"You know? You're right," Ingrid told Viggo.

Two days later, Egil arrived. As he approached the entrance to the Lair, he was remembering the conversation he had had with Dolbarar and the person who was with him at the stables before he left.

"Ready to leave?" Dolbarar asked him, coming into the stables along with a Ranger-cloaked figure beside him.

"Ready," Egil nodded, looking at the figure, but since their hood was on and their head was down, he could not tell what Ranger it was.

"This is the person I want you to accompany to the Shelter," Dolbarar said with a wave at the figure beside him.

The Ranger pulled their hood back, revealing a well-known face.

Egil was surprised. It was not a Ranger, although she was dressed like one.

"Healer Edwina…." He greeted her with a small bow, quite puzzled.

"Specialist Egil," she greeted him also with a small bow.

"I'm sending Edwina to the Shelter so she can help with Engla's and Gerd's healing. She needs an escort and you're the perfect candidate, apart from the fact that you're already going there."

"Of course. It'll be an honor to escort the Healer."

"Thank you, Egil. I'm afraid I'm no Ranger and I'm not used to traveling. I'll delay you and probably be a nuisance," she apologized.

"On the contrary. You'll make the journey a lot more pleasant," Egil replied with a smile. The good healer was right. She was not used to the harsh outdoor life or long journeys. It had been years since she had left the Camp, and even there she spent most of her time at the Infirmary.

"You're a dear," Edwina said with a big smile.

"Please make sure Edwina has a good journey and arrives safe and sound to the Shelter," Dolbarar told Egil. "I don't like sending her, but given the situation it's the right thing to do."

"Sir..." Egil began to say, having a bad feeling.

"Yes, Egil?"

"The fact that you're sending Edwina to the Shelter means things aren't going so well with Engla's and Gerd's recovery, doesn't it?"

Dolbarar heaved a sigh. "It's not that they're not going well, don't worry. But the recovery is not going as fast as we would like it to. That's why Sigrid has asked me for Edwina's help. Traditional healing is working, but it's going very slowly, far too slowly. Edwina might be able to accelerate the recovery with her Healing Power."

"Let's hope it can help," Edwina said. "I'm not always able to. There are limitations for everything, including magic. I will do everything I can to help them, but I can't promise I will be able to. If Annika and Sigrid are having difficulties, with all their knowledge and experience, let's not assume I can work miracles. I hope that with my healing power and their healing combined, we'll be able to go forward with their recovery."

"I see. I'll get you there safe and sound."

"Thank you, Egil."

"Besides, I'll be able to learn from the Healer's knowledge. I'm afraid I'll question you the whole way to gain as much knowledge as I can," Egil said.

Edwina laughed out loud.

"I'll do my best to bear the questioning and the travel. It's going to be a long journey," she said, clearly teasing him.

Dolbarar smiled. "Knowing you two, you'll get there without realizing it, immersed in deep conversations about magic and healing."

"That's likely." Egil smiled too.

"Very well. Egil is ready to leave," Dolbarar said.

"So am I. You said it would take two or three days, and you were right," Edwina replied.

"In that case, you had better get going before I bore you with one of my stories," Dolbarar joked.

"We'll leave at once, sir," Egil said.

"I wish you both good luck," Dolbarar said. "Keep me informed, and tell Sigrid I want good news with each step forward."

"I'll do that," Edwina said.

Egil thanked Dolbarar.

"May everything go well and may you be able to come back soon," he said, then he hugged them both goodbye.

"I will miss you. Go."

Edwina and Egil set out. The healer's horse had already been waiting. Egil was pleased. It was going to be a pleasant journey, and they were bringing help to Engla and Gerd. He was feeling optimistic.

And he was not mistaken. The journey had been a delight for Egil, since he had been able to chat with Edwina about many subjects, mostly about healing magic. He had taken many notes in one of his notebooks. In a selfish way, he was sorry they were already arriving at the Shelter, since he would not be able to continue his conversations with Edwina. On the other hand, he could already glimpse Gerd and his friends at the entrance of the cavern, and his heart filled with joy.

Chapter 31

Egil ran to hug his friends while Edwina watched with a smile on her face.

"Wise guy!" cried Viggo, giving him a tight hug and laughing.

"It took you forever to arrive!" cried Nilsa, who also lunged to hug him and did so with such enthusiasm she almost knocked him down.

Astrid hugged him more gently and kissed his cheek.

"We've been waiting for you. I have lots of things to tell you, the kind of things you're interested in."

"Fantastic, I hope they're fascinating things," Egil replied eagerly.

"We've missed you, pal," Lasgol said, also hugging him tight.

"And I've missed you too," Egil said, laughing.

"I've really missed you!" Gerd said, hugging him, unable to stop a few tears from running down his cheeks.

"Yeah, I'd also weep if I couldn't get rid of the nerd even by hiding here," Viggo said, seeing Gerd's tears.

"Don't be such a numbskull," Ingrid said to Viggo as she hugged Egil.

"I see we're all here," Egil said, looking at his comrades for a moment. "So how are you, big guy?" he asked Gerd.

"I've been better, but I'm managing," he replied, wiping his tears.

"Dolbarar sent help which I think will be very good," Egil said with a wave at Edwina.

"Healer Edwina, what a joy to see you again," Lasgol greeted her.

"I'm also happy to see you all," she said.

The rest of the Panthers also greeted the Healer. While they chatted and welcomed her, Egil went over to stroke Ona, who was waiting to be petted.

"Good Ona. Beautiful Ona," Egil said, scratching her head.

And me? Camu messaged him, along with a feeling of complaint.

"You too, Camu. Where are you?"

Behind Ona.

Egil stretched his arm until his hand met Camu's body.

"How are you, Camu?"

I very well. Poor Gerd problems.

"Yes, but don't worry, the Healer will help him."

Heal Gerd?

"I'm not sure she can heal him completely, but I do hope she can help."

With magic?

"Yes, with her healing magic."

Happy. I can't help. I not have healing magic.

Don't worry, that's what Edwina's here for. She'll help Gerd."

Several people came out of the lair to see what the commotion was.

"Edwina, how good of you to come!" Sigrid greeted her, spreading her arms open and hurrying to meet the healer.

Edwina also opened her arms and the two women hugged affectionately.

"You needed me and I've come to help you," the healer said.

"Thank you so much for coming and for the help you bring," the Mother Specialist said gratefully.

"Well, we'll see whether I can really do something," Edwina said as she looked at Gerd talking to Egil out of the corner of her eye.

"Whatever help you can offer will be appreciated."

"You're looking good," the Healer said to the Mother Specialist.

"You look great. Time doesn't seem to affect you."

"It's a trick," the healer said with a wink.

Sigrid nodded. "Your healing magic."

Edwina smiled. "That's right."

"Edwina, long time no see!" another voice cried. It was Gisli with Annika and Ivar, all coming to greet the Healer.

The Elder Rangers covered Edwina with hugs and compliments. There were few occasions when they could get together, since Edwina rarely left the Camp and the Elders, the Shelter.

"Let us go inside, we have a thousand things to talk about and catch up on," Sigrid said to Edwina as she waved them toward the Lair.

"Absolutely. Besides, I want to examine all of you," Edwina said, looking at each one from head to toe.

"Oh, we're great," Gisli assured her. "Annika keeps us youthful with her potions."

"I don't doubt it, but I insist. I want to give you a check-up with

268

my magic. It can find illnesses and problems that remain hidden in the body. A timely detection can save a life."

"You're so right," Annika said. "Let's go inside, and then you can examine us all with your Gift. I can only see what my eyes and experience allow me to see, and it's far from what your magic can find."

"I'm sure it's not necessary, we haven't been sick in years..." Ivar said, not too happy.

"Do not pay any attention to him," Sigrid said. "What happened to Engla has affected him a lot and he does not want to even hear about magic."

"My magic is of the healing kind. It doesn't harm an organism—on the contrary, it tries to heal it, repair any anomaly it finds."

"I know. Nothing was going to happen either with the Higher Training in our minds, and look how that turned out..."

"It's not the same," Annika assured him.

"If you don't want me to examine you, I won't," Edwina said in a conciliatory tone.

"I would rather stay away from magic for the time being," Ivar said, and he crossed his arms protectively over his torso.

Edwina nodded. "Will I be able to examine Engla? Dolbarar has sent me for that..." she asked Sigrid.

"I don't think so," Ivar replied, shaking his head. "She's not going to allow it, not after what happened. She's against any use of magic on her body or mind."

"I asked Dolbarar for help and I hope Engla will give in to reason. It is better that we talk about this inside," Sigrid said, looking at the Panthers, who were still chatting joyously, happy to be together again.

Edwina and the Elder Rangers withdrew to their cave and left Egil and his friends to enjoy their reunion.

In the evening they went with Gerd to his rehabilitation session with Loke, and they witnessed how the poor giant suffered doing simple exercises. They were really shocked to see how almost nonexistent Gerd's coordination was. Loke had devised a simple exercise where he threw apples at Gerd so he would catch them, first with his right hand and then his left. He threw them gently and from a short distance, so it would be easy for the giant. Even a child could have done it, but Gerd did not catch any of the apples. It was shocking and terribly sad. Loke threw an apple and Gerd started reaching with his hand after the apple had practically passed him by. It was as if his body and mind were un-synchronized. It seemed like the orders his mind sent reached the body only after great delay.

Gerd felt embarrassed and was holding back tears of frustration. His comrades cheered him and tried to help him with different pieces of advice, but unfortunately nothing worked.

It was as if Gerd's reaction time had decreased by a hundred. There was no doubt that something had broken inside the good old giant. By the end of the exercise, he managed to brush an apple with his right fingertips, and Loke took it as a tremendous achievement. They all congratulated Gerd and encouraged him to keep trying.

Nilsa had covered her face with her hands and was standing way behind Gerd because she felt so sad for the giant that she was crying. To see Gerd, who was a force of nature, in this state broke her heart. If anyone did not deserve this, it was him. Nilsa would give anything to be able to help him. The big guy said nothing, but he was suffering greatly. To find himself so crippled must be destroying him inside. They all felt like Nilsa and were trying to hide it so their friend would not notice. It would not be good if he saw how sorry they were, and they were all sure Gerd would not want their pity. Ever.

After the exercises they went back to the Lair, They had eaten something and were now resting in their bunks in the Cave of Spring. They were alone; the contenders had gone out to practice, so they seized the opportunity to talk about the latest news with Egil, who was listening attentively to everything that had happened to his friends. He was extremely interested by what Astrid and Lasgol had to say.

"Interesting and fascinating," Egil said afterward, "particularly about your uncle, Astrid."

"Do you think there's any truth in these prophecies about the end of the world?" Ingrid asked him.

Egil was thoughtful for a moment. "I don't think we should worry too much. So far, we have two non-related instances with a similar message, although not identical. Therefore, it's premature to conclude they're related. It could very well be two different messages that had nothing in common. There have always been premonitions about the end of humankind or the end of the world, and there always will be. It's in the nature of man to foretell when everything's going to end. Particularly in certain men. But why they do so, escapes my understanding."

"I guess it's because their lives are so horrible they're looking for a way out," Nilsa speculated.

"Or because they've been brainwashed," said Viggo.

"Or they're simply afraid of the future and this is their way of dealing with it," Egil reasoned. "What I know is that it's quite common. There have always been this type of catastrophic premonitions and those who encourage them. I also know they've never come to pass. I don't think they'll come true now either, so we shouldn't give it too much importance."

"Thank goodness, because it sounded awful," Nilsa snorted, relieved.

I also less worried, Camu messaged from where he was lying between the bunk beds. Ona was sniffing at the screen that enclosed their area to give them a semblance of privacy.

"Well, I'm not very convinced," Viggo said to Egil, looking at him with his head to one side.

"If Egil thinks we don't need to worry for now, then let's not worry," Gerd said from his bunk where he was resting from the day's efforts.

"Well, for me, what happened in my uncle's study seems quite strange," Astrid said. "It gave me a bad feeling. He spoke of a 'Sleeper,' an 'Arrival,' a new natural order in Tremia, and of 'All-Powerful Supreme Lords.'"

"Putting it that way, it makes my skin prickle," said Nilsa. "Especially the 'all- powerful, supreme lords' bit."

"It makes my hair stand on end," Gerd added. "I don't know who the sleeper might be, but I'm going to have nightmares after hearing about it all."

"It does sound like a catastrophic prophecy, the kind that talks about the end of the world," Viggo said, making a face. "Especially that part about the new natural order. That sounds awful. I think I'm going to start sharpening my knives and preparing my poisons right away."

"I think your uncle has lost it, no offense intended," Ingrid told

Astrid.

"Don't think I haven't thought of that too," she replied heavily. "But he looked so sane."

Egil nodded. "It's all singular and very intriguing. But we don't know what your uncle's searching for or the goal of the great search he's devoted his whole life to, like you told us. We also don't know what he wanted the quills for or what he's going to do with them. The message he gave you is troubling: a new era, the sleeper awakening, the arrival of the supreme beings with such great power. All of it could be a premonition or a big fat lie…. The problem is, we don't know whether there's any truth to all of this. As Ingrid has insinuated, we also don't know whether your uncle is right in the head or not. He could be suffering from delirium. I'm not saying he's crazy, but he might be a little off track."

"No need to skirt around the point, Egil, go ahead and speak clearly. It's my uncle, but I won't be offended," Astrid assured him.

"Very well," Egil nodded. "We might be before an order or brotherhood that's seeking a secret goal. Perhaps they're seeking to bring these supreme lords, their gods, to our world. Brotherhoods, particularly religious ones, place the worship of gods as their ultimate reason. Everything your uncle and his order are pursuing, if it is indeed an order, may not even have the least effect on us or the kingdom. There have been and there will continue to be these kinds of organizations, religious or not, which pursue their own secret goals. They don't need to have any relationship with us or be dangerous."

"Hmmmm…." Astrid made a similar face to Viggo's, not convinced.

"As for the preacher you met in Skad, Lasgol," Egil said, looking at his friend. "There have always been and always will be fools who announce to the four winds that the end of the world is near and similar things."

"Then you're telling us we don't need to worry, isn't that right, Egil?" Ingrid asked him.

Egil smiled and shook his head.

"What I'm telling you is that right now we don't have enough information to come to a conclusion that will lead us to think we ought to worry. We're talking about the end of the era of men, of a possible cataclysm or apocalyptic event. It's too big and important to consider with such little information, information we don't even know is really true. Imagine if we tried to explain it to our leaders…"

"Well, they'd look at us as if *we* were the crazy ones," said Ingrid. "It's one thing for them to trust us and a very different thing to come to them bringing this catastrophic news without any proof."

"King Thoran would kick us out of the castle," Nilsa said.

"No one's going to believe us without a shred of evidence. Well, I don't believe it either, to be honest," said Gerd.

"You don't want to believe it because you don't want it to happen, which is different," Viggo told him.

"I need to know more to take it seriously," Ingrid said. "For now, it's only rumor without any evidence, coming from unreliable sources. Your uncle sounds a bit… you know…" she said, moving her finger in circles to the side of her head.

"It sounds crazy, I know. But it troubled me, and that's why I had to tell you," said Astrid.

"And you did well," Egil said, "since together with Lasgol's story, it makes it into something singular. What we should do is remain alert, and if new information comes to the surface that might be related to these two strange instances, we'll have to reevaluate whether we ought to worry or not."

"So, to sum up, we wait to see whether anything else comes up before we really worry," said Viggo.

"That's right, in a nutshell," Egil said, smiling.

"I agree," said Ingrid. "We have no real reason to worry right now. Besides, so far it doesn't concern us."

They all nodded in agreement. Astrid and Lasgol looked at one another. They had more doubts than the others but, as Egil said, they needed something more concrete and serious to start worrying. On the other hand, they already had enough concerns as it was.

They finished telling Egil all their new adventures and he did the same. He told them what he had found out in the library at the Camp and about Sylvia's gift.

"Don't trust the person who gives you a present without a reason," Viggo said with a suspicious look on his face. "She must want something."

"I'm not at all trusting," Egil replied with half a smile.

"You're so suspicious of everything," Nilsa chided. "I think it's a nice gesture."

"And the reason for the gift seems adequate," Astrid joined in.

"I'll remain neutral on the subject," Lasgol said, raising both hands.

"It will be good to have that book, at least until Egil knows everything by heart," said Ingrid.

"I doubt I can memorize everything…" Egil said.

"I bet it won't take you that long," Gerd assured him.

"I guess we'll see," Egil shrugged.

"I'm rather intrigued by the new First Ranger," Nilsa said suddenly. "I wonder what he's like."

"He certainly can't be better than I am, no matter what Dolbarar says," Viggo proclaimed. "I'm the best Assassin in the kingdom, not him."

"The fact that you believe something doesn't make it true," Ingrid said.

"Sure, go ahead and keep teasing me, but he's only a Natural Assassin, whereas I have three specialties: Natural Assassin, Forest Assassin, and Stealthy Poisoner," Viggo said, puffing up like a peacock.

"Sure, but I bet he has a lot more common sense," Ingrid snapped.

"I doubt it, and by the way, isn't that the post you covet? Well, let me tell you they've robbed you of it," Viggo said, opening his eyes very wide.

"I haven't been robbed, I'm still not ready. Contrary to others, I know my limitations. I'm not good enough or have enough experience to become First Ranger. But don't be mistaken, because I will be First Ranger. I'll be the first woman to be appointed to that position, I swear it."

"I love it when you get all fiery," Viggo said with a lovesick look on his face.

"I don't know why I always fall for your taunting," Ingrid said, putting her hands to her head.

"Do you think the orb is made of this Dragon Glass?" Lasgol asked Egil suddenly, changing the subject.

"It's a plausible theory," he replied.

"Camu, do you know anything about this Dragon Glass?" Lasgol asked him.

Not know, was the negative message.

"You don't know what the orb is made of either, do you?" Egil asked him.

The message was once again negative.

"And what is inside it? Because this story about the butterfly that lived for five hundred years has upset me greatly," said Viggo. "What if that dragon is alive inside the orb?" he said, shaking off a shiver.

"That couldn't be, could it?" Gerd asked.

"It'd better not be, because if it is, that's a lot of potentially dangerous magic we're talking about here," Nilsa said.

"Camu, did you feel it was the dragon inside the orb that was communicating with you?" Lasgol asked.

No... not know... be more like presence...

"Then it wasn't the dragon?" Egil asked.

No... not dragon in orb... not sure...

"It's better that way," said Nilsa.

"Remember, we shouldn't jump to conclusions," Egil told them. "We're investigating, and I'm sharing shreds of information I found which I consider significant and are related, or might be related, to the orb. But I can't guarantee there's a link. There might not be any and we'd be jumping to the wrong conclusions."

"I'm more interested in the fact that you can make weapons with this Dragon Glass, indestructible weapons and magic energy conductors," Ingrid said. "Especially the indestructible part."

"That's what the tome said. I can't say whether it's true or not, how they were built, or what for," Egil said apologetically.

"We can guess they were created as weapons of great power. For some powerful king," said Astrid.

"Or some warrior sorcerer," Lasgol said.

"That guess fits the idea better," said Egil. "Being magic conductors, they could be easily bewitched and even store power."

"So, whoever has one of those weapons could become very powerful," said Ingrid.

"Better to not even touch them. In case they react like the orb," Nilsa said.

"Yes, that might be the case too. That only certain people could wield them," Egil said.

"People with the Gift?" Astrid asked.

"I guess so, yes," Egil confirmed.

"It might be that the wielder must have some specific kind of

Gift," said Lasgol.

"That's also possible..." Egil said and was thoughtful. "It's fantastic to speculate with the discoveries we're making," he said when he came back to reality.

"Yeah, sensational entertainment," Viggo replied. "I'm about to hit my head on the wall, that would be more fun."

"Oh, don't mind us, go ahead. We think it's a great idea," Nilsa said mischievously.

"Very funny," Viggo replied.

"Better he doesn't hurt his head, he's already damaged enough," Ingrid added.

"More than I!" Gerd joined in.

They all laughed at the joke, even Viggo, who tried to look offended and broke down in a sigh before laughing with them all.

To finish catching everyone up, Lasgol told them what had happened to him with the orb when he had tried to interact with the object using his own magic.

"You shouldn't have done it alone. The orb is dangerous," Astrid said, looking worried.

"Nothing happened," Lasgol said soothingly.

"Nothing happened by very little," she corrected him and took his hand. "Promise me you won't try these things if we're not with you. I'd die if anything happened to you."

Seeing how anxious Astrid was, Lasgol had no choice but to yield.

"I promise, I won't try again on my own."

"It must be a defense mechanism of the orb," said Egil.

"A very twisted mechanism," said Viggo.

"Well, at least it didn't shock him like it did you," Gerd said.

"That's probably what it intended. That's why it tried to bend Lasgol's mind to touch the surface of the object," said Egil.

"That's twisted—it's like tricking you to stab yourself in the heart with your own dagger," Viggo said.

"Something similar, yes," Egil had to admit.

"Camu, do you know why it did that?" Lasgol asked.

Not know.

"I'd say it doesn't want magic used on it," said Astrid.

"Yeah, but that would imply it's intelligent, that it thinks..." Nilsa said. "I'm not sure I'm comfortable with that implication."

"Let's not be hasty in our conclusions," said Ingrid. "It's one thing to defend itself and communicate with Camu and another thing to be intelligent. The first two might be only spells or enchantments, right, Egil?"

Egil was thoughtful again. "From what I know about enchantments and spells, it's true it could be that. It might be enchanted to serve a purpose, to communicate with anyone who can receive the message and transmit it. It could also be enchanted to defend itself if magic is used on it. That's correct."

"Thank goodness..." said Nilsa.

"But, based on the way it has done so, implies certain intelligence. It hasn't sent messages haphazardly. It only communicated with Camu and guided him. When the orb defended itself, it tried to bend Lasgol's will. I find both events significant. I'd say there is intelligence behind them."

"That's great..." Viggo moaned.

"That makes you think... it might use its magic against us," said Nilsa.

"We must be careful. It could be dangerous and we could suffer an accident," said Gerd.

As soon as he said this, they all felt terrible about his bad luck.

"Gerd is right. It would be better not to interact with the object," said Ingrid.

"Yeah, or we might have another catastrophe."

"We can all agree on that," said Astrid.

Lasgol nodded. He did not want any more trouble with the orb. The only one who looked as if he wanted to go on experimenting with it was Egil. But he had to give in at the general refusal.

"Fine. We'll leave the matter alone," he said.

Chapter 32

The next day Edwina went to see them first thing in the morning, along with Annika. She came into the Cave of Spring when the contenders were already leaving to start their daily training.

"Good morning, Panthers," Edwina greeted them, coming to the bed bunks behind the screen. She stopped to look at Camu, who was not camouflaged.

"Good morning, Healer," Lasgol, who was already dressed and chatting with Astrid and Egil, said.

"So, the rumors were true," she said, staring at Camu with an interested look on her face. "You do have a Creature of the Ice with you."

Lasgol nodded. "This is Camu. He's a special creature."

I very special, Camu messaged to all.

The healer's eyes widened when she received the mental message. Annika also stared at Camu with large eyes.

"The creature is capable of speak... communicating?" Edwina asked.

"He is. He does it through mental messages," Egil explained.

"That's wonderful," said Edwina.

"He's a fascinating creature," Annika said. "Sigrid and Gisli have been studying him, as have Enduald and Galdason."

"If Enduald and Galdason were interested, I assume he must be a magical creature," Edwina guessed.

Annika nodded.

"Extraordinary. I'm not surprised they wanted to study him," the Healer said as she slowly passed her hand over Camu's scales. "He's cold-blooded."

I from Frozen Continent.

"Can I examine you?" the Healer asked Camu. "I've never had the opportunity to be around a magical Creature of the Ice."

Examine?

"You see, I'm a Healer, I have magic that heals," she explained simply so Camu could understand. "I'd like to do a little checkup."

Checkup with magic?

"Yes, if you don't mind. It will be just a moment, and you won't feel anything," Edwina said in a pleading tone.

Healer good, right? Camu messaged only to Lasgol.

Lasgol nodded.

"I promise you it will be just a moment. I'm overcome with curiosity," Edwina insisted.

Okay. I no fear. I brave.

"Thank you," Edwina said with a big smile.

The healer placed her other hand on Camu's right side. She closed her eyes and concentrated. After a moment Lasgol was able to see Edwina's magic in action. A flow of blue energy was coming out of the Healer's hands and entering Camu's body. Once inside Camu, he could not see what the energy was doing, but he guessed it would circulate through Camu's body, exploring it.

Blue energy good, Camu messaged to Lasgol.

"Can you see it?" Lasgol asked, surprised.

I see magic.

"Since when?"

Not know. I see now.

"Interesting."

You see?

"Yes, I see it too."

The Panthers and Annika were staring at Lasgol and had already guessed he was speaking to Camu, although they could only hear Lasgol's side of the conversation.

Edwina studied Camu for a long while. Nilsa, Ingrid, and Viggo were taking care of their gear and weapons while they watched a short distance away. Astrid, Lasgol, and Egil were beside Camu, interested in what was going on. Gerd remained lying in his bunk.

At last Edwina opened her eyes.

"He's an amazing creature," she announced.

I very interesting, Camu messaged.

"Yes, very interesting, like a desert lizard," Viggo replied.

I much more interesting.

"Only by very little," Viggo teased him.

"He is. He's a unique creature, wonderful. I've never seen anything like him," Edwina said.

"Anything out of the ordinary?" Lasgol asked, concerned about Camu.

"I haven't seen anything that leads me to think he's anything but healthy. But I've never examined a similar creature before."

"Well, he's just like a bloated northern lizard," Viggo said.

I not lizard.

"I haven't seen anything that caught my attention regarding illness or any health problems. I think he's healthy. What I have noticed is that he's young. His organs are still at their initial stage of growth," Edwina said.

"He's young, yes," Lasgol nodded.

"Thank you very much for letting me examine you," Edwina said to Camu. "It's been a great experience and I have learned a lot."

No problem, Camu messaged, lifting his head proudly. He looked at Viggo defiantly. Viggo poked his tongue at him. Camu replied by sticking out his own blue one.

"Will you please act like an adult, you idiot," Ingrid scolded.

"The bug started it."

I not bug.

"Here we go…" Ingrid snapped at Viggo.

"Okay, okay, my pretty Blondie, I'll behave for you," he smiled at her with a mischievous gaze.

Ingrid snorted.

"We've really come to see Gerd," Edwina said.

Those words made everyone pay attention to the Healer.

"To see me?" Gerd, who had not moved from his bunk, said.

"Yes, Edwina has come from the Camp expressly to help you," Annika told him.

"I appreciate it," Gerd said, trying to rise with difficulty.

"No, stay down," Edwina told him.

Gerd dropped back down in his bunk.

Edwina and Annika approached while the Panthers watched from a couple of steps behind their backs.

"Here, Gerd, drink this potion. It will help to outline the anomalies in your system," Annika said, handing him a flask containing a dark-blue liquid.

Gerd drank it and made a face that made it clear it tasted horrible.

"Now I'll examine you with my Healer magic," Edwina explained. "Stay calm. It will be like what I just did with Camu. It won't hurt. In fact, you'll feel relaxed and somewhat drowsy. Don't worry about it, it's the effect of my magic. I'll make sure you feel comfortable and don't experience any pain."

"I trust the Healer," Gerd said confidently.

"Will your magic be able to make him well?" Nilsa asked Edwina.

The Healer looked at Nilsa. "I don't know. I'm certainly going to try. There are never certainties with healing magic. It will depend on the seriousness of the damage and whether I have enough skill to perform the healing. What I can assure you is that I'll try with all my being and use the knowledge and experience I have acquired along the years."

"Thank you…" Nilsa said with moist eyes.

"I'm going to lay my hands on your chest and begin to examine you," Edwina said, turning back to Gerd.

"I'm ready," he nodded. He did not look scared at all, which being him was a feat, because he was about to experience magic and uncertain results. Edwina might be able to heal him—this is what Gerd knew.

"No fear, big guy," Viggo encouraged him.

"Don't worry, I'm not afraid," Gerd assured him.

"Well, this is a first indeed," Viggo teased, smiling.

Lasgol was watching attentively. He saw Edwina concentrate and the healing energy leaving the palms of her hands to enter Gerd's body. He wished with all his heart Edwina could find a way to heal him.

"I'm examining his whole body. My healing energy is running through all his organs in search of any problem in them. Once I locate the problem I'll act on it if possible, to heal the affected organ or area."

The Healer was working with her eyes closed, concentrated. Lasgol remembered what Edwina had told him about healing before at the Camp where she had tended to him on several occasions. The Healer had told him that when she healed a patient, she saw all the organs of the body in her mind as her energy went through them. She could appreciate them as if she were painting a picture in different shades of blue which showed the patient's whole system in detail. If an organ was sick or touched by some illness, instead of seeing it in blue it appeared as a purple or greenish tone. This was how Healers visualized non-healthy states as a rule, and the color depended and changed according to the type of problem it represented. Once the point of infection or wound was located, she radiated healing energy to slowly heal it. The manner and amount of energy required for this process depended on the illness and its seriousness. Besides, healing an illness was different from curing an open wound. The latter required a lot of energy to seal the cut, and it had to be done quickly and concentrating great power. A sick organ usually required continued treatment with healing energy until it resulted in a change of tone from lilac or greenish to blue.

Lasgol was wondering whether Edwina had already found the affected organ and if she might have started healing it. The silence they all kept and the seriousness of the situation only increased the tension they were all feeling. Astrid took his hand and Lasgol was grateful; he was so tense and worried for Gerd that he could feel his nerves cramping his stomach and back.

Nilsa was holding back her tears. Egil was holding her arm as he stood at her side. Ingrid and Viggo were watching Gerd with great looks of concern on their faces. They all knew Gerd had much at stake at that moment. If Edwina could not heal him with her healing magic, hope that Gerd might recover completely greatly decreased. At the pace he was going, it would take him an eternity to go back to being what he had been, if he ever managed to.

"How are you doing, Edwina?" Annika asked after a long while of being concentrated without saying a word.

Without opening her eyes and maintaining her concentration, she said, "The body doesn't seem to present any injury, or at least I can't determine where it is. No matter how many times I've gone over his system, I can't find the location of the problem."

"Maybe the problem is mental instead of physical," Annika said. "From what we've gathered, it could be that."

"Yes, I'm leaning toward that option too," Edwina agreed. "I'll go over his body once again—I want to make sure I haven't overlooked anything."

While Edwina continued her examination, Annika told her what they had found.

"We thought the problem had been more mental than physical, since he can't move his limbs or coordinate them and his balance is also affected."

Edwina said nothing and continued sending energy into Gerd's body. He was resting peacefully like a giant baby, breathing deeply. His chest went up and down rhythmically. Camu and Ona had lain down on the floor a little further back and were watching the proceedings. They could also feel the tension.

"I have finished a thorough examination of his body. I haven't been able to find anything anomalous. I will now examine his mind. I don't know whether I'll be able to, since the mind is a complex world and it resists us Healers," Edwina explained without opening her eyes, then she put her hands on both sides of Gerd's head.

"If I can help in any way, let me know," Annika offered.

Edwina nodded and continued sending more of her inner energy to Gerd's head. They all continued watching tensely without missing a single detail. For a long time, Edwina examined Gerd's mind, but from the expression on her face, they could tell things were not going well. They grew increasingly concerned.

"I can't manage… to see… where the problem is in his mind," the Healer said suddenly.

"Can't you get into his mind? Annika asked her.

"I can get in… but I can't pinpoint where the problem is. I can't see any point where there might be a problem…"

"But the problem has to be there," Annika said.

"I know … but I can't see it. The mind isn't like the body—it's difficult to diagnose and even more to treat."

Edwina's words caused great concern in the Panthers. If the Healer could not see the problem, she would not be able to treat it and that would mean poor Gerd was not going to heal with the Healer's magic. His recovery would be a long path of suffering; that was something the giant did not deserve. But all of them were aware that life was not fair. Many times, the worst things happened to the best people. Such was the universe, and they had to accept it. If you encountered bad luck, you had to draw strength and overcome it to keep going. Gerd would pull through, the Panthers were sure of that. It would be a long and difficult road, but he would eventually come through.

All of a sudden, Lasgol had an idea. He was feeling useless, watching Edwina fail when, driven by the desire to help, he had an idea. It probably would not work, but he had to at least try and help his friend.

"Healer Edwina, perhaps I can help," he said.

Everyone looked at Lasgol in surprise.

Edwina stopped the flow of blue energy to Gerd's head and

opened her eyes. She looked at Lasgol with a tired expression on her face. It was obvious the use of her magic was exhausting her.

"Tell me, Lasgol."

"I'm not sure it'll work, but I would like to try something."

"What are you suggesting?" she wanted to know.

"I can't heal the body, and probably not the mind either…"

"But?" Annika encouraged him to go on, eying him with great interest.

"Well… I have two skills that might help."

"Skills with the Gift you mean?" Edwina asked.

"Yes, two skills I've developed with my Talent."

"Please elaborate."

"I've developed a skill I call *Aura Presence,* which allows me to identify a person's auras. In Gerd's case, I should be able to see his body's and mind's auras."

"His mind's aura? Interesting…" Edwina said.

"Yes, I think I can. Additionally, I've developed another skill I call *Ranger Healing* which allows me to cure injuries with my mind. I don't believe it'll work on Gerd, but perhaps… with your help…"

"I think I understand what you want to attempt, and I think it's a good idea. We lose nothing by trying," Edwina said. "Come over and let's try."

"Thank you."

Lasgol went over to Gerd and concentrated. He searched for his inner pool of energy and called upon his *Aura Presence* skill, directing it at his friend as he lay there peacefully. A green flash ran through Lasgol's body. He looked at his friend and saw two auras in Gerd— his mind's aura in his head and the rest of the body's all around him. They both shone with a bright glow. They were a color he could not identify, as if they were made of infinite colors. What he guessed rather than saw was that the two auras were interrelated.

"I can already see the auras of his body and mind," he told Edwina, trying not to lose his concentration and lose his access to the two auras.

"That's good, keep going."

Lasgol focused on Gerd's mind aura and started searching for anything that might be suspicious. He went about it as he did when he was trying to repair the bridge between his mind and his pool of inner power. He began to examine Gerd's mind aura slowly. He was sending his inner energy to his friend's mind's aura and with this energy he began to look around every bit of the aura in search of any tiny spot of a different hue that might be suspicious. He hoped Gerd's problem would appear so in his mind's aura. It might also be a total waste of time, of course. If that was the case, at least he had tried.

He continued examining Gerd's mind's aura for a long time, going slowly as he had planned and trying not to overlook anything. He had known it would take him an eternity, since it took him a long time to analyze his own mind, so examining someone else's he figured would take even longer. He was not wrong. The analysis process of the aura was going extremely slowly.

"I think it's going to take me a long time to examine his aura…" he apologized.

"Don't worry. Keep going," Edwina told him as she sat down on one corner of the bed Gerd was on to rest.

Hours went by, and little by little they all sat down on the floor to rest. Lasgol was still standing beside Gerd with his gaze fixed on him, and by the look on his face it was obvious he was making an important effort. Annika left the cave to go and prepare some restorative potions.

Lasgol went on working, using more and more energy to interact with Gerd's mind's aura, but he was still going slowly. Time passed and there were no results. He began to feel tired and thought about quitting, leaving it as impossible. But he realized he had already examined three quarters of the aura, so he took courage to at least finish the analysis. If he did not find anything he would accept it, but he did not want to stop without finishing the whole examination.

He continued sending energy and doing his examination while his friends and the Healer watched him. At last, he finished the analysis of Gerd's whole mind's aura. It had taken him many hours and he was exhausted, but he had finished. He had covered the whole area of indeterminate color with his own green energy. He sent one last burst of his energy to see the entire aura and something happened. All of a sudden, a dozen purple-black points became visible. Lasgol could not believe it. There they were—he had found the problem.

"I have it!" he cried suddenly, startling everyone. They stood up and came closer to look, although there was little to see, apart from Lasgol staring fixedly at Gerd while the giant slept.

"Did you find the problem?" Edwina asked him.

"Yes, I see the trouble points. There are about a dozen, quite big," he explained.

"If there are a dozen and they're big, this means the problem is troubling. Try to use your healing skill on them," Edwina advised him.

Lasgol called upon his *Ranger Healing* skill. It was the skill he had mastered the least, so he was not confident he could get a positive result. Even so, he was going to try. A green flash ran through his head and the skill activated. Lasgol focused on one of the points he had identified and, using his skill, sent energy and tried to cure the anomaly. He remembered how he had done it when applying it on himself. He would try to do the same thing here. He focused on the point and sent more energy, trying to cure it, to make it change color.

For a long time, he tried. He was sending energy through his skill to the point he was focusing on, but for some reason he could not make any difference. It was as if his energy, his healing skill, had no effect. That seemed weird to him. He could see the problem—he had identified the problem and was sending a lot of energy, with the skill activated it should work. It had when he had applied it on himself. But it did not seem to be having any effect on Gerd.

He began to tire, and the result had not changed. Nothing. Suddenly, he felt a flash in his own mind and realized what was happening.

"I can't use the healing skill on others... only on myself..."

"Are you sure of that?" Edwina asked.

"Yes, now I am. I hadn't known until now. I'm not going to be able to help Gerd..."

"Let's not despair," Annika said. She had returned a short while ago and Lasgol had not even noticed.

"Perhaps there is a way to help him," said the Healer.

"How?" Lasgol asked.

"By combining your skill with mine. I can't find the points to heal, but you can. And you can't cure them, but if I can see them I'll be able to."

"I see..." Lasgol said. "But what do I do so you can see them?"

"Good question... I'm not sure I have the answer," said Edwina. "Only you can see the problems, and only I can heal them..."

"If Lasgol could mark the points somehow in Gerd's mind, you could then see them," Annika suggested.

"Yes, that's a good idea," Edwina agreed.

"I'll try, although I have no idea how I'm going to mark them," Lasgol admitted, scratching his head thoughtfully.

"Don't try to cure them. Try to pinpoint them somehow, make the shine, become visible," Annika said.

Lasgol thought about it. How could he manage to do what they were asking? He had an idea. He concentrated on the dozen problematic points he could see. Instead of sending energy to cure them using *Ranger Healing*, he sent energy so they would stand out. He had found them already, so he sent more energy into seeing them more clearly, not curing them, since he now knew that would not work. To his surprise and joy, the points began to become more visible, more radiant.

"Perhaps now you'll see them," he told Edwina.

"Let's try." Edwina concentrated and placed her hands on Gerd's head. She began to imbue him with her healing energy. A moment later, she announced, "I see them, twelve radiant points."

"Fantastic!" Lasgol cried.

"Edwina, can you mark them somehow so you don't lose them?" Annika asked. "Lasgol looks exhausted. I don't think he can continue marking them for you much longer."

Edwina sent more healing energy.

"There's no need for you to continue showing them to me, Lasgol, Now that I see them, I can locate them. Stop pinpointing them so I can check."

Lasgol nodded and ceased sending energy and stopped his *Aura Presence* skill, which he had kept activated. "Done."

Edwina waited a moment. She ceased her influx of healing energy. She waited another moment and once again sent her healing energy to Gerd's mind.

"I can see them. Once identified I can find them again! I only needed you to show them to me first."

"That's wonderful!" Lasgol said.

"Try to heal them," Annika told Edwina in a hopeful tone.

The Panthers looked at one another—the moment had come. If Edwina could heal Gerd, their friend would recover. If not, the disappointment was going to be terrible after coming so close.

For quite a long while, Edwina said nothing, concentrated on sending her energy to Gerd's mind, trying to cure the problematic points. Nilsa was so nervous she had bitten all her nails and was only holding up because Egil was helping her. The tension was consuming her. Viggo, who as a rule was so cold and acid, was also affected and could not stay still from the tension. Ingrid took his hand and held it hard.

"He'll pull through. Have faith," she whispered in his ear.

Viggo nodded, but his face showed how stressed he was. His jaw looked as if it was going to unhinge at any moment.

Suddenly, Edwina heaved a deep sigh.

"I've managed something…"

"Tell us," Annika asked her.

"One of the points, I've managed to start healing it. It was arduous. I couldn't find a way to do it. I tried with everything I know and nothing was working."

"Then how did you do it?" Annika asked.

"I could not understand the problem. It took me a while to realize what's going on. The points Lasgol have identified and which are the basis of the problem and Gerd's condition aren't points where there's an affliction, infection, or some evil to cure."

"They aren't? Then what is wrong?" Annika asked.

"They're really little holes, like cracks, caused in his mind by an abrupt, deep rupture."

"It would make sense. Yes, it fits in with the symptoms he's showing. There's a rupture between his mind and his body in certain areas, but not in all of them," Annika explained.

"Will he heal then?" Nilsa asked, unable to contain herself.

Edwina answered without opening her eyes. She was still focused on Gerd's mind and the problem she was treating.

"It's too soon to tell, but if I've managed to begin to cure one of the points, I think there's hope."

That's fantastic!" Nilsa cried, and the others joined her excitement with comments and cries of joy.

"Don't get so excited, Edwina needs peace and quiet," Annika told them, making gestures with her hands so they would calm down and let the Healer do her job.

"I'm going to continue a bit longer, until I run out of energy. We'll see what degree of improvement I get."

They all went silent and sat down around the Healer in a wide circle that would let her work unbothered.

Edwina kept going until she was left without a single drop of healing energy to keep treating the fractures in Gerd's mind. She opened her eyes, and Annika hastened to hold her up so she would not fall to the floor from exhaustion. She had made a tremendous effort.

"I couldn't repair much of the first point of rupture," she explained, "but I managed something. The treatment will need time, but I think I'll be able to heal him."

"Wonderful news!" Annika smiled at her.

"That's fantastic!" Nilsa cried.

"Yes, fantastic!" Egil joined in, raising his arms to the sky.

Astrid and Lasgol hugged joyfully.

"He's going to get well!" Astrid said.

"Yeah, I'm overjoyed!" Lasgol replied.

Very happy, Camu messaged to them as he began doing his happy dance, flexing his four legs and wagging his tail. Ona joined him at once, imitating him.

Ingrid kissed Viggo by surprise.

"Double good surprise!" he cried, thrilled.

Happiness and joy overcame them all and they enjoyed the moment. They had all been fearing the worst, and the news was promising.

Gerd woke up in the middle of the uproar and looked at his friends blankly.

"What ...? What's the matter?"

"You're going to get well!" Nilsa cried, and she hugged him tightly with tears in her eyes.

"Wow... that's... that's great," he said.

"Help me carry Edwina to her room in the Cave of Winter—she's exhausted and can hardly walk."

Lasgol went over at once. Ingrid and Astrid did too.

"You were fantastic, Lasgol," Edwina told him, smiling.

"Thank you, Healer."

"Keep working on that Gift of yours. It's stronger and more versatile than you think. One day it will surprise you," she said, and then she fainted, she was so tired.

"Help me carry her. I'll get her to bed and make sure she recovers," Annika told them.

Chapter 33

The following morning, they were all in an excellent mood. Gerd said he did not feel any different from the day before, but everyone else believed in Edwina's favorable prognosis. Gerd left for his daily exercises with Engla and Loke. Annika had recommended he continue with the rehabilitation, since his progress would be greater and improvement would come faster. They needed to combine healing with physical rehabilitation in order to obtain the best results. Gerd agreed on this.

The rest of the group rested and let them work in peace.

At dusk Edwina came back with Annika and Sigrid. The three women examined Gerd.

"How do you feel today?" Sigrid asked Gerd.

"Fine. I really don't feel better or worse, I think."

The reply discouraged the group a little, but they knew Gerd was being sincere and saying what he felt.

"Progress will be slow," Sigrid said.

"I'm going to examine him to make sure I can still visualize the rupture points," said Edwina. Gerd lay down on his bunk and the Healer placed her hands on his head.

They all watched with great interest.

"Does the healer need my help?" Lasgol offered.

Edwina said nothing for a moment; then she shook her head. "I can see the fractures now without any trouble. Thank you, Lasgol. Without you I wouldn't have found them."

"I'm happy to have been of service."

"That Gift of yours seems to be growing," Sigrid said.

Lasgol nodded. "There's still so much I have to learn."

"Always," Annika added

For a long while Edwina worked on the ruptures, the group waiting patiently for her to finish.

The contenders started to arrive and headed to their beds and trunks. They chatted animatedly, making a lot of noise. They were not aware of who was behind the screens or what was going on.

Edwina suddenly opened her eyes. The noise had made her lose concentration.

"I'm managing to heal him. Only a little and slowly, but I'm doing it."

"That's awesome!" Lasgol said, pleased.

"Sensational!" Nilsa cried.

"It might be best to take Gerd to the Cave of Winter to be treated," Annika suggested.

"I think that's a good idea," Sigrid agreed. "There's too much noise in here."

"Yes, I need quiet in order to do my work. The sessions are going to be long and it will take me weeks, if not months, I'm afraid."

"That long?" Ingrid asked.

Edwina nodded. "There are no shortcuts in healing. Body and mind need their own time to recover. I only help them with my magic, but I can't perform miracles."

"It doesn't matter how long it takes, as long as he recovers," said Lasgol.

The others agreed with Lasgol.

"Very well then. We'll continue the treatment in the Cave of Winter, in Edwina's quarters."

"We'll stay outside to be out of the way," said Egil.

Annika nodded, "Thank you, that would be best."

The three women left with Gerd, who nodded to his friends as he left the cave.

"Let's go outside and enjoy the evening, this cave is depressing now," said Viggo.

"For once, I totally agree with you," said Nilsa.

"I think we'd all rather be outside," said Lasgol, and they filed out amid the contenders' looks and whispers.

Camu and Ona were the last to leave, Camu in his invisible state to avoid giving rise to more rumors than there already were. They left the Lair and went up to the Pearl, lying down to watch the clear starry sky. The temperature was warm and the night was beautiful, which was not common in those latitudes.

Ingrid and Viggo seized the chance to get lost on the other side of the Pearl and be alone, which surprised no one since they did this often. Viggo made the excuse that he wanted to get away from the Pearl since it brought him bad memories, but they all knew he wanted to be alone with Ingrid and would use any excuse he could think of.

Camu and Ona lay down on the lush grass in front of the Pearl.

Astrid and Lasgol were contemplating the stars, lying on their backs, holding hands. They were happy about Gerd's healing progress and the help Lasgol had been able to provide. Lasgol was saying it was a pity he was not able to cure Gerd's wounds. Astrid was encouraging him to keep experimenting with his skills and develop new ones. Lasgol had left the Orb he carried everywhere with him beside them on the grass in its pouch to feel more at ease and comfortable.

Nilsa was preparing Anti-Mage Arrows very carefully, a little-ways off. It was a special type of arrow whose basic damage depended on the kind of Elemental Arrow chosen based on the desired effect, but to which an additional effect was added. These arrows were designed to make a loud noise upon impact. As Elder Ivar had taught her, a substantial, unexpected noise puzzled the magi, in turn causing them to be unable to conjure. It was a great way to defend from them; besides, a single arrow could make several enemy magi lose their concentration and stop their spells. This Nilsa had not yet been able to prove, since she had not faced any mage, but she was looking forward to trying. She wanted to see the uproar it caused, plus the elemental effect and whether the mage managed to remain focused enough to conjure or not.

There was little light, so Egil had brought with him a small oil lamp and had lit it. By its light he was reading the tome Sylvia had gifted him, concentrated. What had happened to Gerd had strengthened Egil's idea, even more, if possible, that the group needed a good Healer Guard. The sooner he learned every remedy in the book, the better prepared he would be. Besides, Egil loved the subject.

All of a sudden Camu stood up. He lifted his head, looking at the Pearl.

Call, he warned.

Call? What kind of call? Lasgol half rose, looking at Camu.

"Did anyone hear anything?" Astrid asked the others.

Arcane call, Camu messaged to them.

"That's interesting," Egil said, sitting up.

"Where's it coming from?" Nilsa asked, putting away the arrows she had been working on.

Arcane call come from Dragon Orb.

Oh, the orb? Lasgol transmitted.

"We seem to have a situation," Astrid said, getting to her feet. She pointed at the place where the orb ought to be—it was levitating, and the pouch and scarf that had covered it lay open in the grass.

"Did you take it out of the pouch?" Nilsa asked.

"It wasn't me," said Astrid.

"Me neither," said Lasgol.

"It was the orb itself. It's been activated for some reason," Egil said, staring intrigued at the levitating object.

Be orb. Be using magic… ancient… very, Camu messaged.

"It's been activated… most curious," Egil commented.

"Yeah… it's been asleep until now," Lasgol joined him. "Why has it been activated now?"

"I'd say it's the proximity to the Pearl," said Egil.

"It makes sense. The last time it was also activated here," said Astrid.

"Yeah, and when we took it outside the Shelter it remained inactive. It seemed to enter its unconscious state," said Egil. "It hasn't activated before, has it?" he asked Lasgol.

"No, I only had that bad experience I told you about when I tried to interact with it using my Gift. But it didn't activate like this, that was more a reaction. This seems as if it woke up by its own free will."

"Yeah, it was probably a defensive reaction from detecting magic use on it," Egil reasoned. "This seems different. Besides, it's communicated with Camu. It's calling him. It hasn't called you before, has it, Camu?"

No, not feel call until now.

"Then we should assume there's a reason, and that reason is undoubtedly the Pearl," said Egil.

"Well, then it seems we *do* have a situation on our hands," Lasgol said as he watched the orb, worried.

"Yup, because it seems the orb wants something," said Astrid, also watching the object with eyes half closed.

"What's up?" Ingrid asked as she and Viggo arrived.

Arcane call, Camu messaged them.

"Oh no, the mini dragon in the orb again, no!" Viggo protested, shaking his head as he watched the object levitating and emitting a light-silver gleam.

293

"This is a problem…" Nilsa said, looking at the orb with her hands on her hips.

"What does the call make you feel, Camu? What's it saying to you?" Lasgol asked him.

Feel… be called…

"Called for what?" Ingrid asked, already beside them.

They all watched the Dragon Orb levitate, emitting faint silver flashes. The substance inside the orb and the dragon floating in it seemed to have come alive and swayed as if they were waves in the sea.

"Surely to go somewhere and fall into another trap," Viggo said. "Or have you forgotten what happened the last time we followed the orb?"

"Yes, we all remember. We appeared in a pearl in the middle of the Usik forests and almost didn't come back," Ingrid said, wrinkling her nose.

Arcane call very strong, Camu messaged.

Ona moaned.

"What are you feeling, Camu?" Lasgol asked him, concerned.

Must go. Family in danger. Very important.

"Don't pay attention to that flying sphere, it's tricking you," said Viggo.

"It's dangerous," Nilsa joined him.

"What family? What danger?" Lasgol asked Camu.

I feel… call… help… family great danger…

"What family are you referring to?" Astrid asked Camu.

Family mine.

"But you don't have any family that we know of, do you?" Ingrid asked, looking at Lasgol.

"Unless he's referring to Drokose…" Lasgol said. "Do you mean him? Because we don't know of any more of your relatives."

Yes, Drokose in danger and others family.

"Well, that's strange," Egil commented thoughtfully. "The orb is warning you of a possible danger threatening Drokose and your family?"

Yes. Great danger, for all family.

"One thing, Camu, when you speak of all family… that includes you?" Astrid asked Camu in a troubled tone

Yes. Me too in danger. Serious danger. Urgent.

Wow… this doesn't sound good," Astrid said,

"We also don't know whether what the orb is transmitting to Camu is true," said Ingrid. "It might not be, it might be using him."

"Exactly. Well thought," Viggo joined Ingrid.

"Why would it trick him? What reason could there be?" Egil asked.

"How would we know? There could be thousands of evil, obscure, and twisted reasons," Nilsa said. "There's no way to know."

"Freckles here is right," said Viggo. "We don't know whether the orb is manipulating Camu to obtain something from him, or from us," Viggo said, pointing his finger at them.

"We can't jump to that conclusion either," Lasgol said. "It could also be transmitting the truth. They could be in real danger."

"You're a gullible soul, you'll swallow any lie. You'd be fooled by the village drunkard telling you a sad story so you'll buy him another bottle," Viggo said. "Wake up once and for all. The orb is tricking Camu and wants to trick us all."

"But why?" Lasgol replied. "If you mistrust it, there must be a reason."

"We don't need a reason to mistrust it. It's called common sense. If a magical orb wants your help for something, be suspicious. More so if it's already taken you to some endless forests filled with savages who wanted to kill you."

"That was an accident. It wasn't the destination the orb was looking for," said Egil. "I've been turning this matter over and over in my head, and I think the orb is after a particular goal and wants to go to a specific location, and for that it uses the Pearl's portals."

"We also know it needs Camu to open the portals," said Ingrid. "Otherwise, the orb would've already done it," she said, pointing at the Pearl. "It would've already gotten wherever it needs to go. Therefore, it could be tricking Camu into helping it."

"Exactly," Viggo added. "If it needs Camu's help, it'll trick him. He's a baby after all."

I not baby. Orb not trick.

"We don't know that," Nilsa joined in. "It could very well be tricking you for its own purposes. It's common in humans, and I guess in intelligent Objects of Power with a purpose it is too."

"We have no proof one way or the other," Astrid said, opening her arms and tilting them like a scale. "It could be telling the truth. It could be lying."

"Well, since we don't know, we'll ignore it. Subject closed," Viggo said.

"You've made your stance clear," Lasgol said. "What's not so clear are the repercussions not following this call might have. What if Camu suffers harm for not heeding the summons?"

"And if he suffers harm by answering it?" Ingrid asked. "Our last adventure with the orb turned out to be dangerous. For Camu and for us."

Lasgol nodded. "That's true."

"Let's be sensible," Nilsa said. "Doesn't it seem a little foolish to do whatever a powerful orb asks us to do? Look at it, suspended in midair, pulsating. It's madness. And not only because of the magic— it's just an object, an orb. Think about it."

There was a moment of silence. They were all evaluating the current situation and weighing the consequences.

The orb started to pulsate again with silver flashes.

Feel something new.

"What is it, Camu?" Lasgol asked him.

"Are you feeling all right?" Astrid asked.

Yes, well.

"What are you feeling?" Egil asked him, interested.

Images. Place. Important.

"Is it where the orb wants to go?" Lasgol asked.

Yes, be place where has to go.

"Do you know where that place is?" Astrid asked him.

Not know place. Not know where it is.

"Could you describe it to us, or draw a picture of it?" Egil said.

Camu thought for a moment. He closed his eyes and suddenly flashed with a silver glow. An image started to appear in everyone's minds. It was a place.

"I'm beginning to see an image," said Lasgol. "The rest of you?"

"Me too," Astrid confirmed.

"Close your eyes, it'll reach you better. It must be Camu sending us the vision the orb is transmitting to him," Egil guessed.

"I don't like this at all," said Viggo. "It's in my head, and we all know what happens when we start to see things."

"Are you doing this, Camu?" Lasgol asked to be sure.

Yes, be me.

In the image they began to see a landscape from the sky that showed what looked like a great island in the distance. They could see an intense blue sea and a bright sun in a clear sky. The landscape and the view were from a bird's eye view. It was as if they had become birds, flying toward the island in the middle of an immense blue sea.

"Is anyone else feeling like a seagull?" Viggo asked.

"I feel kind of like an eagle," said Ingrid.

"Flying over the sea in the direction of an island?" Viggo asked.

"I know what you mean, but I feel more like an eagle than a seagull."

"What's the island the image is taking us to? Does anyone know?" Nilsa asked.

"I don't, but by the intense sun I'd say it's not in the north," said Lasgol.

"I couldn't say what island it is," Egil started to say, "but I'm with Lasgol in that it's not a northern island. The weather is too warm."

The image brought them closer to the island. Then the vision suddenly dropped down toward land in large circles above the island as they lost altitude.

"Definitely an eagle. Seagulls don't fly like that," Ingrid said to Viggo.

"Well, then it must be an aquatic eagle," he teased.

"Doesn't anyone recognize the place?" Astrid asked now.

"Nope. It's entirely foreign to me, this strange island," said Egil. "I know the islands to the north and west of Tremia, and it's none of them. It could be from the east…"

The image showed them the vegetation from closer up and they were able to see it was jungle foliage. Plants and trees of an intense green appeared before their eyes. The bird from which they were watching the terrain did several swoops lower and lower, so they could see large clearings of uninhabited jungle. Or at least there were not any signs of civilization.

"The island appears deserted," Ingrid said. "There are no buildings in sight, or cities or even villages. Do you see any?"

"No, nothing. It looks deserted," Viggo confirmed.

"An enormous, deserted island. Why is the orb showing us this?" Nilsa wondered.

"It must be relevant. Let's wait and see what else it shows us," Egil said.

"There must be something on the island that interests the orb," Lasgol reasoned.

"Yeah, because otherwise it wouldn't show it to us," Astrid commented. "Why would it?"

The image kept going down until it brushed the tops of the trees. Suddenly, in a clearing below they saw a great lake into which poured three enormous waterfalls from several plateaus around it. It was amazingly beautiful. The bird did one last swoop over the lake and landed on the ground. It looked toward the east, and what they saw surprised them and at the same time made them understand.

On top of a hill in the middle of the clearing in front of the lake rose a White Pearl.

"This is where the orb wants to go," said Egil.

"The Pearl makes that obvious, yes," Ingrid agreed.

"I'm not going to this deserted island, I'm warning you now," Viggo said.

"There shouldn't be any danger. It's deserted," Lasgol said.

"We don't know if that's true. Remember what happened to us in the Usik forests," said Ingrid. "Just because it looks deserted doesn't mean it actually is. It might be full of indigenous tribes hiding skillfully among the vegetation and that's why we haven't seen them."

"True, and even if it is deserted, why would that be the case?" Viggo asked.

"Because of something bad I bet," said Nilsa.

"Exactly," Viggo confirmed.

The image stayed fixed on the White Pearl, which was identical to the one behind them, only the one they were seeing was in a distant, exotic landscape. A moment later the image vanished from their minds.

"What happened, Camu? Has the orb stopped transmitting the image?" Lasgol asked him.

Yes. I not receive image more.

"How did you manage to transmit the image to us?" Lasgol asked.

Don't know. I receive, then send to all.

"Well, that's an interesting skill," Lasgol said. "I don't remember you having it."

No. Be new. Discover now, call Image Communication.

"That's what I thought," Lasgol said. "I like the name."

"It seems from those images the Orb wants to go there," Egil said. "Can you confirm that, Camu? Is that what you feel? Are we right?"

Feel go there to save family, Camu messaged them.

"Understood," Egil replied.

"When you say family, does that include the orb too? Because you told us you felt like it was family. Or do you mean another family? Drokose?" Astrid asked.

Family all. I, Drokose, orb.

"This bug has a somewhat distorted notion of family. How can the orb be family if it's an object?" said Viggo.

"If he feels like it's family there must be a reason," Lasgol replied with a shrug,

"Besides, the orb is more than a simple object," Egil explained. "We know it has power, that it feels and has intelligence. It's almost like a creature."

"A spherical crystal creature," said Viggo mockingly. "That's not a creature, it's an enchanted object, no matter how much you want us to see a living being," he told Egil accusingly.

"That gives lethal shocks to whoever touches it," Nilsa added.

"Well, at least we know where the orb wants to go," said Lasgol. "That's a major improvement."

"But we don't know why it wants to go there," Ingrid said.

"True. Except that it seems urgent and a matter of life or death," Lasgol said.

"That is if we believe the orb, which I don't," said Viggo.

"What does seem clear is that the orb took us to the forests of the Usik by mistake," said Egil. "The destination it was seeking must have been this one."

"So, it made a mistake about the portal," said Ingrid. "Instead of traveling to the island, we appeared in the forests."

"I wonder how the portals work. How do you choose your destination? Camu, do you know how to do it?" Egil asked him.

No. Not know. Only know how to open.

"That explains why we got lost then," Viggo said, a look of disbelief on his face.

"The orb must know how to do it," Egil guessed. "Although it wasn't able to do it right the last time. There must have been a reason. It also didn't show us an image before, and now it has. It's curious. I wonder how or why."

"Maybe you're not listening to me, but I've already told you, we're not going to travel through the Pearl's portal. No way!" Viggo cried, shaking his head energetically and wagging his finger at them.

Arcane call, urgent. No time.

"Don't rush us, rushing only leads to trouble," Viggo told him. "And don't insist, because we're not going to go through the portal to any unknown island where we have no idea what's waiting for us."

Be not me, be call.

"I don't care—whether it's you or the call or the orb, you won't rush me. No making any hasty decisions and getting into trouble," Viggo said, upset.

"We have to find out what's going on," Egil said, clearly intrigued.

Are you sure you have to go? Lasgol asked Camu.

Yes, arcane call... say go...

"Camu feels like he has to go. I think we'd better go and investigate. Otherwise, I fear he'll go on his own. You know him... when he gets an idea into his head..." Lasgol told the others.

I must go... Camu messaged to all. *Go alone, you stay.*

"No way, I won't let you go alone," Lasgol said adamantly.

"You're not going without us," Astrid joined him.

"I'm with Astrid and Lasgol, you can't go by yourself, Camu," Egil said. "It's dangerous."

Be best. I must go. You not.

"I'm going with him. I can't let him go alone," said Lasgol.

Ona growled once; she was going to come too.

"I'm coming too," said Astrid.

"Count me in," said Egil.

Ingrid looked at Viggo who was shaking his head.

"I'm not going to let them go by themselves. Count me in. I wouldn't forgive myself if anything happened to you," said Ingrid.

Nilsa snorted, "If you all go, I'm coming too."

All eyes turned to Viggo, who was grumbling under his breath and shaking his head.

"I'm coming only to save you all, just so you know, and for no other reason!" he cried. "Because without me you're all going to die!"

"Well then, it's decided," said Egil. "We're going to the island."

Chapter 34

It was the wee hours of the morning by the time the Panthers arrived at the Pearl. They all had full camping equipment, water, and food for several days, and they were armed to face an enemy regiment. They dispersed at a signal from Ingrid to cover a wide area around the Pearl, checking that no one saw what they were about to do. Astrid went to the north, Ingrid to the south, Viggo west and Nilsa east. Lasgol, Egil, Camu, and Ona were beside the Pearl.

They all waited in position for over an hour, and when they were sure there was no one near they gave the sign that all was clear. A special owl hoot came from the four directions, indicating everything was good.

"We're alone. Everything's clear," Egil told Lasgol.

"Let me check one last time," Lasgol replied as he concentrated and called upon his *Animal Presence* skill. A green flash ran though his body and a wave issued from him that swept the surrounding area, seeking animal life. Lasgol detected nocturnal animals but no humans. He called upon the skill again, and this time he made great effort to send it even further so that the wave would cover more land before it vanished. He was surprised to see that his magic responded and the wave traveled further than the first time. His power was growing. It probably had to do with the efforts he was making to repair the bridge between his mind and his inner pool of energy, and the improvement made him happy. He called upon the skill a third time and tried to expand it even more so it would reach further. Once again, he caught the presence of more animals but no humans in the surrounding area.

Seeing it work so well, Lasgol tried again and focused on reaching to where his friends were posted watching. This time he did not get the result he wanted. He was not surprised, as he distance was great. His power was growing and his skills with it, but he still had to keep working on them to take them to their maximum potential. Besides, all skills had limitations, as did all magic, and he would have to find out what the limitation was for his.

"Everything all right?" Egil asked him.

"Yes, everything's as it should be. We can begin," said Lasgol, putting down the pouch which contained the dragon orb. He watched it for a moment, but nothing happened.

He turned to Camu. "Why isn't it activating?" Lasgol asked him, somewhat put off. He had expected the orb to act. It had done so the day before. But when they had covered it with leather it had stopped levitating and seemed to have become deactivated. Lasgol had then put it in the pouch.

"Give it a moment," Egil told him.

And, indeed, after a moment, the orb began to rise out of the pouch. The scarf it had been wrapped in fell to the floor and the crystal surface shone with a silver aura.

"How did you know?" Lasgol asked his friend, looking surprised.

"I guessed it would need a moment to know where it was. If I'm not mistaken, it emits pulses we can't discern in search of objects or creatures of interest," he said, looking at the Pearl and then at Camu.

"To position itself?"

"And to decide whether it wants to activate or not. I'm guessing, of course. I can't know for sure," Egil said with a shrug.

"Camu, can you see the pulses? The ones Egil's talking about?"

Not see, but feel yes. Egil right.

"Am I? Fantastic! I assumed so, but I couldn't prove it," said Egil, raising his arms delighted that his guess had been correct.

"You're right nine out of ten times," Lasgol said, smiling.

"Not so many. Most of the times I'm just using reasoning, working from a certain base knowledge, but still with a lot of uncertainty. I'm not always right."

"Yeah, but you're almost always right," Lasgol said, pointing at the orb as it levitated beside Camu's head, as if it were his pet object.

"Let's see whether my theories are correct now," he winked at Lasgol.

"Yeah, let's. Camu, it's your turn," Lasgol said, turning to the creature,

Open portal? Camu asked. He had been waiting for the moment to do so.

"Yes, go ahead, open it," Lasgol said, nodding.

Okay. I try. Camu closed his eyes and his body emitted a silver flash. After a moment he began to send pulses in the shape of silver waves toward the Pearl using his magic. The Pearl did not react.

"Remember, you need to find the right cadence of pulses or the Pearl won't recognize them," Egil reminded him.

"That's how you did it the last time," Lasgol encouraged him.

Yes, I know. Camu began to send the pulses at a faster pace. The short silver waves impacted on the white surface of the Pearl, but they did not get a reaction.

"Keep increasing the frequency until it hits the right pace, Camu," Egil said cheerfully.

Camu concentrated and went on sending pulses. Following Egil's advice, he was sending them faster every time.

And look for right cadence... pace good...

"That's right. Take your time, you'll get it," Egil told him.

"Easy now, try to feel it," Lasgol recommended, trying to help.

All of a sudden, the Pearl emitted a silver flash in response to Camu's pulses.

Have correct pace, Camu messaged to them.

"Try to memorize it if possible, so later you can hopefully open the portal more easily," Lasgol told him.

I try remember.

Egil began to count out loud as Camu sent the pulses, intending to help him.

"1, 2, 3... 4, 5, 6..."

Think have already

"Very well, open the portal," Lasgol said.

I try.

Suddenly the orb reacted, as if it knew Camu was trying to open the portal. It shone and sent several pulses similar to Camu's, like waves but with different rhythms. The orb's pulses seemed to be more intense.

Orb help open portal, Camu messaged.

Lasgol and Egil could see how the Pearl was beginning to create three circular silver shapes. A circle the same size as the Pearl formed just above it. Then after a moment a second one appeared, oval-shaped and larger, as if the circle had transformed into it. And finally, the shape evolved until it formed a huge silver sphere over the Pearl.

Portal created, Camu messaged.

"Good job," Egil congratulated him.

"Who picks the destination, is it the orb?" Lasgol asked, although he already assumed that was the case.

Orb know destination, I not.

"Can't you tell it to show you how to select the destination?" Lasgol asked Camu.

I ask.

"They're here," Egil said, waving at Ingrid, who was coming at a run. A moment later Astrid, Nilsa, and Viggo also arrived.

Orb feel destination, Camu messaged.

"Can you feel it? Lasgol asked him.

No… can't.

"Well, don't worry about it too much. You'll learn how to use the portal with time and practice," Egil told him. "It's only natural that it seems weird right now."

Lasgol looked inside the great sphere, which seemed to be made of liquid silver. It was as if a silver sea moved in waves inside the sphere containing it. The more he looked at it, the greater the feeling of strangeness. The huge sphere was floating above the Pearl in total silence, without emitting a flash or reflection. Its lower circumference was about four hand-spans above the top of the Pearl, but not touching it. Seeing the two spheres, one above the other, was spellbinding, something beautifully hypnotizing.

"Time to travel," Egil said with a smile, a look of excitement on his face.

"Looks that way," Lasgol said, less thrilled than Egil about the new adventure they were about to jump into, but he knew it was what they had to do to solve the orb's mystery and its relation to Camu and them.

"Everything ready?" Ingrid asked when she reached them.

"Yeah, we're ready," Lasgol replied, indicating the portal shaped like a great sphere.

"Oooh, that portal gives me the creeps," said Viggo.

"Me too," said Nilsa, shaking herself.

"And you'll like it even less when you cross it. It's a most pleasant experience," Viggo added with sarcasm.

"That bad?" she asked with fear in her voice, looking at Ingrid for a real answer.

"Yes, it's a pretty uncomfortable journey. But you recover quickly," Ingrid said, waving at her stomach and head.

"Wow…" Nilsa made a slightly horrified face.

"I want it noted I still object to this journey," Viggo said, raising his hand.

"We know your objections," Lasgol said.

"If you'd rather stay here and wait for our return…" Ingrid offered.

"No way. I'm not going to let you go alone and get killed, which is what'll happen if I don't come with you."

"Is that right?" Ingrid snapped in disbelief, crossing her arms.

"I have to come to protect you. I'm the best Assassin in the kingdom. I'll make sure nothing happens to you."

Astrid cleared her throat loudly.

"You'll have some help…"

"Well, yes, Astrid is a good Assassin too. She'll help me so nothing happens to you," Viggo conceded with a wave of his hand.

"Yeah, thank goodness we're bringing the great Assassin, or else…" Ingrid replied, rolling her eyes.

"Let's get going, the portal doesn't stay open long," Egil urged them, pointing at the sphere.

"Everyone in," Ingrid said.

Camu climbed up the surface of the sphere by adhering to it with the soles of his paws. The orb followed him. He stopped halfway up and waited. Ona ran to the Pearl, took a big leap, hopped onto Camu's back, and with another leap she reached the top. The rest of the group had to help one another climb to the top. Lasgol and Viggo stood below and pushed Ingrid and Astrid up, then Nilsa and Egil. Finally, the two of them grabbed the arms of those already above and were helped up.

Once they were all up, Lasgol gave the order.

"Everyone inside," he said, and the whole group jumped inside the sphere, melting into the liquid silver it seemed to be made of. At once they became unconscious.

Lasgol woke up with a terrible headache and a blinding light penetrating his mind. He felt awful, as if he had been given a beating in the stomach and head. He knew he had vomited from the unpleasant taste in his mouth and the smell that reached him from his left side. From their previous experience he knew it was going to be a while before he recovered, but even so, he tried to open his eyes and get to his feet. Great mistake. He could not. He had to stay on all fours with a terrible headache. The ground he felt was burning. It was rock. He managed to open his eyes and noticed the ground was red rock and intense sunlight was falling from the sky, making the rock burn. He waited until his eyes adjusted to the harsh light and looked around for his comrades. They were on the ground, also trying to recover and get to their feet.

At his back he saw a white Pearl. The portal had shut—there was no silver sphere, only the Pearl.

Camu and Ona had not suffered the effects of the portal and were watching them. The orb was floating beside Camu.

"Are you all well?" Lasgol asked as he tried to stand but was only able to lean on one leg.

"What do you mean by well?" Viggo asked. "A herd of Masig pinto horses just trampled me."

"Don't be a drama queen!" Ingrid had managed to stand and was helping Nilsa do the same.

"I think we're all here and relatively well," said Astrid, watching them all with her hands on her thighs, bent double from the queasiness she was feeling.

"Camu, have we been out for a long time?" Egil asked him.

Yes, enough time. Half day, Camu messaged.

"These journeys definitely don't agree with us," Astrid commented. "I thought it would be easier this time."

Humans bad, Ona and I well.

Ona chirped.

"The orb?" Lasgol asked.

Orb well.

"So, wise guy, don't you have some Healer Guard remedy to help us with the effect of crossing the portal?" Viggo said, already standing but swaying as if he were drunk.

"I'm afraid I don't yet. But I think it's a great idea to start making potions to help us with negative effects like these," Egil said.

"Well, you could've thought of it before, as smart and as good of a planner as you are."

"I'm afraid I didn't have any time. I never thought we were going to use the portal again."

"Oh yeah, as if you weren't desperate to come."

"Don't take it out on Egil," Lasgol defended his friend. "We're

306

here because we all decided, you too."

"I think we have a small problem…" Ingrid said. She had climbed the highest rock and was looking around with her hand shading her eyes to protect them from the brightness of the intense sun.

"What problem?" Viggo began to look around.

They all did. They were on a red, rocky hillock. Around them they saw blocks and peaks of crimson rock in every direction. They seemed to be inside a rocky valley. Above their heads a huge sun of great strength was scorching them with intense rays of light. The heat was suffocating.

"It's curious, this climate is quite arid…" Egil commented thoughtfully.

"Get up here," Ingrid told them, motioning to where she was standing on a higher crest.

They all climbed up to where Ingrid was standing. From that height they could see the entire landscape around them. Their jaws dropped. They were on a great rocky mass with different levels and small valleys inside it. It was long and seemed to go from north to south for several leagues. That was not what surprised them though. What left them speechless was what surrounded the mountain range. An endless desert extended to the horizon in every direction with an infinity of dunes. They were surrounded by a sea of sand.

"I don't know if it's just me, but I think the island the portal was supposed to take us to was surrounded by sea, not by sand. Where the heck are we?" Viggo cried, raising his arms and waving them like crazy.

"I think it's obvious, but I'd say we're in the middle of an enormous desert," Ingrid said in a tone of incomprehension.

"Wasn't the portal going to take us to the island in the vision the orb shared with us?" Nilsa asked, scratching her head and looking dazed.

"Yeah… it was supposed to…" Lasgol said, also confused.

"Well… we seem to have gone a little out of the way" said Astrid.

"A little? A little! We're in the middle of a desert! A desert with no end!" Viggo exclaimed.

"There, to the east, I see a walled city," said Lasgol, who was using his *Hawk's Eye* skill.

"Are you sure? I can barely see more than a speck in the middle of all that sand," Egil said.

"Yes, it's a city, and they have water. There's an oasis within its walls," Lasgol said. He could barely make it out, but it was there.

Camu and Ona were beside the Pearl. The orb was with them Lasgol noticed.

"You already knew that, didn't you?" he asked them.

We know, go out explore when arrive. You unconscious, Camu replied.

Ona chirped.

They all turned to look at them standing below by the Pearl, which was hidden by all the large rocks that surrounded it. From outside the rocky formation the Pearl was not visible, only from inside or above.

"What does the orb say about this place?" Egil asked.

Orb feel this not place.

"Oh, you've got to be kidding me! Seriously?" Viggo cried, waving his hands again. "How did it realize? It wouldn't be all the sand of this scorching desert, would it?"

"Calm down, Viggo…" Ingrid begged him.

"How do you expect me to calm down, it's brought us to a scorching desert. A desert!" he said, pointing at the burning sun above their heads.

"What happened, Camu? Why have we appeared here?" Lasgol asked.

Orb not know.

Viggo leapt down nimbly to the orb.

"Let's see, you brainless piece of crystal! Do you know what you're doing? Or do you really have no idea?"

"Viggo, don't touch it!" Ingrid cried, following Viggo down to prevent him from getting shocked or something worse.

Lasgol, went after them. "Viggo, don't do anything stupid, the orb is dangerous," he warned.

Not threat orb, not good, Camu messaged.

Viggo was close to the orb with his nose almost touching the crystal surface of the Object of Power.

"Oh, don't bug me, and what's it going to do? Send me to the Frozen Continent?" Viggo said sarcastically.

Ingrid arrived at a run and pulled Viggo away from the orb.

Lasgol arrived on her heels and got in between the orb and Viggo.

"Be careful, Viggo. Remember the shock it gave you," Lasgol

warned.

"I remember, okay, take it easy. I've calmed down a little," he told them and kissed Ingrid's forehead. "Thanks for worrying about me," he whispered in her ear.

"Stop being an idiot and you'd make my life a lot better."

"For you I'll do whatever it takes, my blonde princess of the charred deserts," he said and winked at her.

Egil and Nilsa arrived too.

"Camu, can the orb tell where we are?" Egil asked him.

Not know. Know only this not place.

"I understand it doesn't know the reason why we've appeared at this Pearl and not the one on the island it showed us, right?" Egil asked him. "We need to make sure we understand what's going on and that there isn't any other reason why this is happening."

Orb not know, mark correct destination when open portal. Not work.

"Interesting. It either doesn't work because it's not doing something right or because it thinks it's doing it right and isn't," Egil said, thinking out loud.

"Well, while it clears its mind we'd better get back to the Lair. This sun is going to roast us alive, and I'm already soaking with sweat," said Viggo.

"I don't think that's going to be an immediate option," Astrid said.

"And why's that?"

Astrid waved at the higher rocks.

They all looked up.

Surrounding the Panthers from all directions, armed with javelins aimed at them, were about a hundred desert dwellers.

Chapter 35

"Don't make any sudden moves," Ingrid said in a whisper, looking in every direction and being careful not to move.

"Are they wearing turbans?" Viggo asked in a surprised whisper.

"They're wearing red, the same red as these rocks," Nilsa whispered.

"They're dwellers of the deserts," Egil explained, also lowering his voice. "I don't know what tribe or faction, but I guess they're native. And they're not wearing turbans, those are scarves to protect their heads from the intense sun."

I visible. Camouflage? Camu messaged to Lasgol.

"Better not. They've already seen you—if you vanish suddenly before their eyes, they might become afraid and start shooting," Lasgol whispered to him.

"Yeah, best to not even blink," Ingrid said. "This doesn't look good."

Suddenly one of the dwellers began to shout at them in some desert language they did not understand. His skin was darker than the Norghanians' but without being toasted. His hair was long, curly and dark, and escaped from under the scarf on his head. His eyes were strange, the color of rubies. All the men had the same eyes. It was most singular.

"Wow, they do look angry," Viggo said. "They must not like visitors."

"You have to consider that, for them, we've just appeared here by magic," Egil explained.

"I couldn't have said it better," Astrid commented under her breath.

The one who was speaking began to gesticulate and point at the Pearl. Then he made negative gestures.

"I think he's saying they don't like our coming to their Pearl," Lasgol said, interpreting the gestures.

"It might be a hallowed place for them, a place of power," Egil guessed.

"Yeah, that makes sense," said Ingrid. "Now he's pointing at

Camu and the orb. He's angry at them too about something."

"I don't think it's anger, he doesn't like them," said Egil, trying to understand the gestures and shouting. "I guess the orb makes them uncomfortable because it's levitating and emanating that silver aura and they must know it's an Object of Power. Camu surely looks to them like a mythical creature; I doubt there's any animal like Camu around."

"Those not-having-slept red eyes with turbans don't seem too dangerous to me," said Viggo. "I think the best thing is to go after them and solve the situation."

"Don't be a dumbass. They're on an elevated position and entirely surround us."

"Apart from there being about a hundred of them," added Nilsa.

"Well, that makes it a little difficult, but I don't see the problem. I bet they don't even know how to fight. I doubt they can even see us properly with those weird eyes."

A javelin flew at them from the heights and sank in the ground between Viggo's feet.

"You were saying?" Nilsa said.

"Bah, a lucky strike," Viggo said, waving it aside.

"No one make the slightest movement. We don't want a confrontation with these people," Ingrid ordered.

"I'll try to communicate with them," said Egil. He raised his arms high so they could see his hands were empty and slowly turned so everyone could see him. "We're peaceful," he said and set his bow on the ground slowly. "We don't want to hurt you," he said, pointing back at the Panthers and then at the desert dwellers, throwing his axe and knife on the ground.

The one who looked like the chief of the desert dwellers, who had been speaking to them, gesticulated again and shouted what sounded like threats.

"I think he wants us to throw down all our weapons," Egil interpreted from the gestures and shouts.

"No way. I'm not dropping my weapons," Viggo said.

"Stop being difficult and do what Egil says," Ingrid snapped at him. She was already setting her bows on the ground.

"We should drop our weapons, show them we don't mean them any harm," Lasgol said.

"Astrid, talk some sense into them," Viggo said.

"I'm against dropping my weapons as much as you are, but on this occasion, I think it's the best thing to do. Keep your small throwing knife, I'm keeping mine."

"Good idea," Viggo said and did as Astrid told him.

They all put their weapons down and raised their arms.

"If they shred us to pieces, you'll hear from me," Viggo threatened his friends.

"I don't think we'll hear you if we're dead," Nilsa said.

"You know what I mean, smartasses," Viggo snapped, making a face.

Then a man came out from behind the Pearl. He was a desert dweller and was accompanied by a dozen dwellers walking behind him. They were obviously his escort and were armed with a javelin in one hand and long knives at their waists. The man was unarmed and was leaning on a staff. He moved toward the Panthers. He was not wearing a scarf on his head and his age showed. He must have been about seventy. His long curly hair was white. His skin, weathered by the sun, was a light tan and creased. His eyes, like all the others', were a puzzling ruby color. In the middle of his forehead, he had drawn a white circle. He reached the group and stopped, his escort stopping with him.

He asked Egil something in a language they did not understand.

"I'm sorry, we don't speak your language," Egil said, trying to express his meaning with hand signals.

"Are you from the north?" the man asked in the unified northern language, albeit strongly accented.

"Yes, we are. We're Norghanians," said Egil.

The man smiled. "You are quite far from your frozen land," he said.

Egil seized the opportunity. "Where are we exactly? I guess in the deserts of the Nocean Empire, but where?"

"Good guess. You are in the land of my people, the Desher Tumaini."

"Pardon my ignorance," Egil apologized just in case. "I don't know your tribe. I don't think I've ever heard of it or read about your existence."

"It is not ignorance, the Desher Tumaini are a secret desert people. Our existence is not known outside these lands."

"Oh... I see. Where in the south of Tremia are we? If I might ask?" Egil inquired, wanting more information.

"You are in the center-east of the south of Tremia. In the Blood Mountains."

"A proper name, seeing the red rock our feet are on," said Egil.

"It is hallowed rock. Only Desher Tumaini can set foot on it."

"It was not our intention… we didn't know…" Egil tried to apologize.

The leader nodded, as if he already knew they were there by accident.

"My name is Tor Nassor, leader of my people."

"It's an honor to meet you, Tor Nassor, leader of the Desher Tumaini," Egil said respectfully with a deep bow. "My name is Egil."

"I am pleased that you show respect. Will your companions do the same? Who are they?" the leader asked him.

"Introduce yourselves respectfully," Egil whispered to the others.

"My name is Ingrid," she bowed like Egil. One after another, they all introduced themselves. When it was Lasgol's turn, he sent a mental message to Camu and Ona. *Crouch. Camu, don't message the leader or the natives—they'll be frightened, and the situation is already pretty complicated.*

I not communicate with the natives, Camu messaged back as he dropped down to the ground like Ona beside him.

The desert warriors surrounding them cried out to see Camu and Ona crouching.

"I see the creatures that accompany you also show their respect. Surprising," said Tor Nassor, watching them with an intrigued look on his face.

"They show respect like we do," Egil said.

"That creature is a special creature. It is a Hor, a God or a descendant of the gods, since it has no wings," he said, indicating Camu. "He does not need to show respect to anyone."

Egil turned to Camu, who was watching quietly. "He is a special creature indeed."

Tor Nassor approached Camu, followed by his guard. He looked at the creature for a moment and then noticed the orb levitating beside Camu's head.

"He has brought an Eye of Power with him," he said, pointing at the orb.

Egil did not quite know what to say. "Yes, that's right," he replied, although he did not know what the leader meant.

"Welcome to our home, Hor," he told Camu and knelt before him. Following their leader's example, all the warriors knelt too, even the guard and those who were watching from the heights.

I god, Camu messaged to the Panthers.

"That's all we needed…" Viggo muttered.

You're no god, so don't let it go to your head, Lasgol transmitted.

"How fascinating," Egil murmured, watching all the warriors kneeling before Camu.

Tor Nassor stood up and his warriors with him. He turned to Egil.

"Has Hor, your God, brought you here through the great Pearl?"

Egil was puzzled by the question. It appeared the leader of the desert dwellers knew a lot, more even than they themselves did. He looked at Lasgol, and the two shared a doubtful gaze.

Egil nodded, "Yes, the Hor has brought us through the Pearl."

Tor Nassor nodded repeatedly. He addressed his warriors, telling them something in their language which the Panthers could not understand, of course. The warriors started cheering and raising their arms in triumph.

"Apparently they liked what the chief told them," Viggo whispered.

"My warriors are happy and welcome the Hor. We are honored he has decided to visit our lands," Tor Nassor explained.

"It is an honor for us too," Egil hastened to say.

"It would be best if we look for shelter. The desert sun is strong and your northern skins and bodies are not used to it. Come with us," the leader said and gestured for them to follow him.

The Panthers exchanged worried looks, but given the situation their best option was to follow Tor Nassor's instructions and see how things developed, so they did. The leader of those singular desert people led them to a crack between the walls of red rock, right behind the Pearl. Nimbly, Tor Nassor disappeared into the crack which rose several feet between two vertical walls. His warriors followed after him, the Panthers behind them. They all passed through easily, even Camu—the crack was larger than it appeared to the eye. The color red and the overlapping of the rock tricked the eye.

They entered a canyon that went deep into the rocky range. Tor

Nassor sent several of his men to lead the way, the rest placing themselves behind the group. Camu and Ona, who came last, eyed the desert warriors dubiously. But the warriors looked at Camu with devoted looks on their faces. They really believed he was a God. Camu realized this and started walking with his head high.

I more than dragon. I god, he messaged his friends. They all glared at him out of the corner of their eyes.

Don't believe that nonsense and stay alert, Lasgol transmitted to Camu. He did not trust these natives entirely, although the desert dwellers did not seem to want to harm them. It was not a good idea to trust strangers in foreign lands, and least of all without knowing whether they had some ulterior motive.

The warriors at the front led them through a labyrinth of rock at the heart of the Blood Mountains. They had the feeling that these mountains had emerged from large pieces and rocky hillsides sliding against each other while they tried to reach the sun and they were now walking through the empty spaces left inside them.

Suddenly, the leading warriors stopped and before the group there appeared a huge underground lake of reddish water. They were stunned. How was it possible there was a lake in the bowels of the mountain range? They were surrounded by desert in all directions and rock did not produce water. Where was all that water coming from?

"Surprising, is it not?" Tor Nassor asked with a small smile as he noted the group's reaction.

"Really amazing," Egil agreed.

"Where is all this water coming from?" Viggo asked.

"From under the rocks. There are underground springs here," Tor Nassor explained. "They run under the rocks."

"It's an amazing phenomenon, considering we're in the middle of an enormous desert," Lasgol said.

"Yes, the desert surrounds us and extends all along the south of Tremia. But there are oases and water wells. You must know where they are, of course."

"What's the walled city we saw to the west?" Ingrid asked.

"That's a city whose name we do not utter unless absolutely necessary," Tor Nassor replied in a serious tone.

"Oh, my apologies," Ingrid said at once, realizing she had mentioned something delicate.

"There is nothing to apologize for. You are foreigners. You do not know what happens in these lands or what my people suffer."

Several warriors drank from the spring and replenished the leather bags they carried water in. They also saw, at the far end of the cavern on the other side of the lake, a group of women filling water carriers.

"Can you drink that red water?" Nilsa asked, a little taken aback. She went over to the edge and knelt to look at the strange red color of it. "It doesn't look drinkable."

"We can, but you cannot," Tor Nassor told her. "Do not drink, for you will become ill and might die. For you this water is poison. It carries a strong mineral that gives it this red color. We will heat it and treat it so you can drink without being poisoned. We call it water for the impure, since the pure of heart, our people, can drink water like this without first treating it."

"Wow, that's good to know, because I was going to take a swig to see how it tasted," said Viggo, who had knelt beside Nilsa and had his hand in the water. "I'm impure in more than one sense," he said with a sarcastic grin.

"Cut the nonsense and don't drink the water," Ingrid told him.

"This is extremely interesting," Egil commented. "How can your people drink it in its natural state without treating it?"

"Need forces men to get used to extreme situations. We live in the deserts, under an implacable sun and our skin and bodies have adjusted throughout the centuries. We endure the torrid sun and arid climate, the same with this water. Little by little our people drank the water in its natural state and our bodies have acclimatized to its effect. This has happened through generations, it was not from one day to the next, and now we can drink without becoming sick."

"So, you became immune to its negative effects after multiple generations," said Egil.

"Indeed. A long time has passed since my people could drink this hallowed water that gives us life."

"Is that why you all have ruby eyes? Because you drink this contaminated water?" Viggo asked, indicating several warriors.

"Viggo… that's rude…" Ingrid whispered.

Tor Nassor raised one hand and put it down again. "There is no problem, I do not mind answering the question. There are two reasons why my people have eyes the color of rubies. One is indeed because of the water we drink. The other is the place where we live," he said, indicating the red walls around them. "This enters the body too," he said and took a deep breath.

"You don't say," Viggo said and pulled his Ranger scarf up over his mouth and nose.

"The air also carries mineral residues?" Lasgol asked.

"Indeed. The water, the air, the food, everything here carries the Azibo Desher, the red mineral of earth."

"In that case, we'd better put our scarves over our faces," Ingrid said.

Tor Nassor nodded. "It is a good precaution to not become sick, I recommend it."

"We shouldn't eat or drink anything native," Astrid told her comrades.

"We will provide you with food and drink you can consume," Tor Nassor told them.

"We have provisions, but we appreciate the gesture," Egil said with a slight nod.

"Let us continue," said the leader.

Lasgol used his *Animal Presence* skill and noticed there were people following them—the warriors who had surrounded them most likely. He also sensed additional people, and this intrigued him. He felt people in caverns parallel to where they were currently, as well as some at a higher level further along. What puzzled him was that there did not seem to be tunnels or cracks to reach those places. That range must be filled with hidden caverns and passages. It must be a labyrinth of rock with covered passages and areas and even different levels in the open air.

They continued advancing along several irregular tunnels. They went up or down, or turned left or right. Every now and then, they encountered uncovered areas, and the sun punished them with its inclement heat as they crossed them. Most of what surrounded them was the red rock of the mountain range, with a few spaces where the desert came in and covered them with sand. The rock seemed to have emerged from the bowels of the desert and fought to keep it out. Every now and then large stretches of sand appeared surrounded by rock and the natives avoided them. They traveled carefully, circling the sand without stepping on it, as if only stepping on the rock was safe and the sand was dangerous.

"Do not step on the sand. Always walk on the rock," Tor Nassor told them. "It is safer. The sand might swallow you."

"Swallow us?" Lasgol asked blankly.

"It is not safe. Trust my words."

The Panthers exchanged puzzled glances but asked no more.

They arrived at an impressive area. It seemed to be half a dozen concentric, colossal stone rings, one inside the other. They must have been about sixty feet in diameter and stretched ninety feet high. The inner width of the rings looked hollow, as if they had been carved out of rock, and seemed to be over nine feet. All along the rings they saw what seemed like tiny windows facing the interior rings. They could see people through the windows. The sun streamed in through the open upper section and lit up the interior of the red rock rings.

"Those rings must be dwellings," Lasgol guessed, looking with great interest at the amazing architectural monument this place was.

"How did they create those rings? How are there people inside them?" Nilsa asked, looking up in awe.

"I'd say those are communal homes," Egil guessed. "The rings in themselves must be natural rocky formations the natives repurposed as homes."

"And you would be correct," Tor Nassor, who had been listening to Egil, said. "This is one of our villages. Our people live in the bowels of the range. It protects us from the sun and our enemies."

"Are all the villages like this? In the shape of these rings?" Astrid asked.

"They are similar, yes. We take advantage of the mountain's natural shape and we carve out dwellings inside them."

"Do you live all along the range? I ask because there seem to be leagues and leagues of mountains," Ingrid said.

"My people have occupied the entire interior of the Blood Mountains, yes. It is our home, our private world," Tor Nassor said.

"Fascinating," Egil mused.

"I'm not surprised not much is known of your people if no one can even see you," Viggo said.

"It is better this way. We like our privacy," Tor Nassor said. "It also protects us from our enemies."

"You have enemies? There's nothing but desert all around," Ingrid noted.

Tor Nassor nodded with a sad smile.

"All peoples have enemies. We are no different," he said.

"Who is your enemy?" Lasgol asked him.

"Let us sit down to eat. Afterward we will talk about that and other matters."

Chapter 36

These picturesque desert people, the Desher Tumaini, turned out to be kind and hospitable, despite their strange ruby-colored eyes and their mountain range home. They brought the Panthers food and drink, although since the group already had their own supplies, they politely refused the offerings and sat down on the red rock floor to eat and drink what they had brought. The natives did not use furniture, only blankets and cushions they wove themselves, so the group sat on some offered blankets on the rocky floor.

They moved out of the sun that fell through the ring-dwellings and sought the shade. There, protected by the rock and away from the punishment of the burning sun, the temperature was not as high and it was pleasant. It was still stifling for a group of Norghanians, but it was bearable, although they were all perspiring profusely because their clothes were not proper for the desert. Tor Nassor left them for a moment to give instructions to several people. Probably to tell his people about them since they all looked surprised to see visitors. They must not have had many visitors from the outside.

A large number of warriors watched them in silence, forming a circle around the group. They were armed and prepared to act if necessary. The Desher Tumaini might be welcoming, but they remained alert and did not trust outsiders, which on the other hand was natural. The two groups kept apart but near enough.

"It seems they don't trust us too much," Viggo commented with a nod at the warriors while the group ate their travel rations.

"It's only natural, we're foreigners who've appeared all of a sudden in their domain, and we're armed," Ingrid said as she drank some of their own water.

"We certainly don't look like caravan traders who got lost in the desert," Egil said jokingly.

"We look more like a caravan's guard," said Nilsa. "Although we're too white to not raise suspicion. Imagine if Tor Nassor and half a dozen of his warriors suddenly appeared in the middle of Norghana. What would you think?"

"That they were very lost," Viggo commented with irony and

smiled.

"So that's what they must think about us," Lasgol said, watching the natives, who in turn were watching them with great interest.

"They seem to respect us but not entirely trust us," said Astrid, who was watching the warriors while eating a piece of cured meat.

"They respect us because they believe Camu is some kind of god," Nilsa said. "Otherwise, I don't know if they would respect us…"

"We should act cautiously," Lasgol advised them as he looked around. He took a bite of a piece of cheese cured with spices and watched the people who were peeking out the windows of the concentric rings to watch them.

Camu awoke the greatest curiosity. He had laid down in the shade in a clear area, not too far from where the group was sitting, Ona beside him. The orb had stopped levitating and was lying still on the ground as if it were saving energy, although the inner mist the dragon was floating in was still moving, so it looked active.

The children could not stop walking around Camu. They looked at him, pointed at him, ran, laughed, and played around him. Camu was enjoying the attention. Ona not so much because they were pestering her a little. She growled unhappily. The children kept a safe distance from the snow panther and did not come close. Soon several elders arrived and shooed the children away. They looked like the wise men of the place because of their long white hair. Curiously, none of them sported a beard. It must be something cultural. They sat around Camu to watch him, also remaining at a prudent distance. They looked at him with worshipping eyes. They whispered amongst themselves, and some seemed to be calmly arguing. Two of the elders began to draw a depiction of Camu on one of the rock walls with some rustic-looking brushes and paint.

"Hey, look, they're drawing Camu," Nilsa said, waving her finger. "That's funny."

"Camu is very popular here," Astrid commented, smiling.

"Because they think he's some kind of deity," said Lasgol, who did not believe for a moment that Camu was a god, even though he was a very special creature.

"There are cultures where certain animals are considered gods," Egil told them. "They have that status among the natives. Tigers, for example."

Tor Nassor returned from speaking with some of his warriors.

"Is everything all right?" Ingrid asked.

"Yes, everything is all right, nothing we cannot solve," the leader said with a confident, experienced smile.

"Thank you for your hospitality, we appreciate it," Astrid bowed her head before the leader of the desert people.

"We are a hospitable people with whoever loses their way and arrives in our lands. Not with everyone."

"Oh..."

"Who isn't welcome?" Ingrid asked. She wanted to know what the situation was here and the dangers they might face.

"The Jafari Kaphiri people who live inside the eastern walled city," the leader said and spat on the ground.

The gesture caught them by surprise. It was very impolite. Although maybe not for the desert-dwelling people.

"I would like to ask you something and expect you to answer honestly," Tor Nassor began to say, looking at each of the Panthers in the eye, as if making sure they understood it was an important question. "It is imperative."

"We'll answer honestly," Egil told him, speaking for all his comrades, although he looked at Ingrid to make sure the Panthers' leader was okay with him leading the conversation. Ingrid noticed Egil's covert glance and understood the implicit message. She nodded furtively while she ate a piece of bread she had left on the blanket she was sitting on, her legs crossed.

Tor Nassor nodded, a serious look on his face.

"I want to know whether your visit is because of my people, the Desher Tumaini, and whether your intentions are hostile."

They all stopped eating and drinking at the question and the tone it had been asked in, which was serious and concerned.

"I can assure the leader of the Desher Tumaini that our visit has nothing to do with your people and that we do not have any hostile intentions."

"It is my people's custom to give people a second chance to speak the truth, so I will give it to you. Do you maintain that your visit is not because of my people and that your intentions are not hostile?"

The Panthers exchanged concerned looks. Why was he repeating the question? Was there some kind of implicit threat in it? What did he intend? None of them revealed what they were thinking and the group remained calm. They let Egil continue.

"We maintain our position. We are here by mistake and have no hostile intentions against your people or any other."

"Yet you are soldiers," Tor Nassor said, pointing at the group's weapons.

"We are Rangers, a special group of soldiers. A mix of archers, explorers, trackers, and fighters. We defend Norghana from enemies internal and external," Egil explained so the leader would understand.

"I have heard of Norghana and its famous Rangers," Tor Nassor confirmed, indicating the group's members.

"How is that possible? We're on the other side of the continent, at opposite poles," said Egil. "Has Tor Nassor visited our land?"

The leader shook his head. "When I was young, I traveled much. I went to all the deserts to the south of Tremia. Then I traveled up to the green lands. I went west and saw the Kingdom of Rogdon. I spent a long time there training. That is where I learned the language of the west and north. That is where I heard talk about the Norghanians and their Rangers, also about the Masig and their pinto horses, the Usik and their fathomless forests, and the kingdoms of Zangria and Erenal and their continuous fighting. Unfortunately, I could not visit all those lands. I would have liked to very much but I had to come back here, to my homeland, to fulfill my responsibility."

"May I ask what that responsibility was?" said Egil.

"Leading my people. That was why I went abroad, to be a good leader, one well-versed in how the world works and not only these mountains and deserts that surround us."

"A wise choice, to go abroad to learn and return wiser," Egil agreed, nodding.

"All the leaders of my people have done so for a long time. Unfortunately, not all those chosen to lead return. Many die. I was lucky. The world outside these mountains is ruthless and cruel. Two of my sons will follow my same destiny. I hope they return alive," he said and waved at two of the warriors who were watching them attentively. They must have been about sixteen and eighteen. "They will soon leave and make the same journey I made. First, they will travel the deserts and learn who governs the designs of the peoples without water. Then they will go to Rogdon. I have friends there."

"I hope they have safe travels. If they wish to come to Norghana, we can help them."

"The offering is appreciated, but first we must establish a link of respect and trust that does not yet exist between us," Tor Nassor said.

Egil threw his head back. "Of course, I'm getting ahead of myself. I'm sure we will develop that link."

"We will see. I have been tricked by men the color of snow before."

"I am sorry to hear that," Egil bowed his head, ashamed.

"Still, I do believe you are here by mistake or accident," Tor Nassor nodded.

"We are," Egil said with an honest gaze.

"Have you come from Norghana without setting foot in other kingdoms?" the leader asked them.

Egil found the question curious, but since he had no reason to lie, he did not.

"Yes, we have come directly from Norghana."

"Then you have traveled through the Great Pearl. From another Great Pearl in Norghana to this one in our land," the leader said, staring at Egil with distrusting eyes, as if he were trying to find out whether he was lying or not.

"That's right," Egil confirmed; he wanted the leader to trust them.

"But you did not arrive at your destination. You did not plan to come here. This I see and believe."

"That's correct. This was not our destination. How come the leader of the Desher Tumaini does not find this event extraordinary, the fact that we're here?" Egil asked, surprised that the leader would willingly accept that they had traveled through a portal and appeared in the middle of his mountains.

"To answer that question, I prefer you finish eating and then I will show you. Certain truths, certain areas of knowledge, are better understood by witnessing. Words cannot always express the transcendence of the information we try to transmit."

Egil's eyes opened wide and then he looked at his comrades. They shrugged their shoulders unobtrusively.

"Very well," Egil agreed.

They continued eating in silence while the children tried again to get close to Camu without succeeding, since the wise men shooed them off so they would not be a nuisance. By the time they finished eating, the two painters had also finished portraying Camu on the rock wall. In a primitive, tribal manner, it was a perfect drawing of Camu. They were all impressed, Camu in particular.

I very good in painting, he messaged the Panthers.

Yes, they have drawn you well, Lasgol had to admit.

I pretty, easy paint.

Lasgol had to resist rolling his eyes.

You're not pretty and you're not a god. Don't let all the attention you're getting get to your head.

I more than dragon. I God. I pretty, he messaged Lasgol who snorted, under his breath.

When they had finished eating and after refusing some strange dates for dessert, Tor Nassor asked the Panthers to follow him. They did. About thirty warriors followed them, among them the leader's two sons. Tor Nassor led them along several tunnels and once again warned them not to step in the areas with sand, only the rock. They came out into the light of day at several open spaces between the rocks and at once felt the sun's strength. They all pulled their hoods up and put on their gloves to prevent the sun from finding any exposed white surface to roast.

They went by another area where they saw two lagoons, smaller than the one they had seen before but also with that reddish water, synonymous with life for these people. They went on, and a little further ahead they came to a huge lofty cave. The upper part was covered, but it looked like it had been pierced in hundreds of points which let the sun filter in. What surprised them was that the natives had not only poked holes in the ceiling but also the cave's floor. It was moist red earth and thousands of plants were planted in the dirt, all of the same shade of green. They looked like a mix between a pepper and a tomato.

Tor Nassor stopped and showed them the garden.

"My people live off this plant," he told them.

"I've never seen it," Egil said as he bent over to look at it. It surprised him that the red earth seemed to produce a fruit like a small tomato. He also noticed the plants were plagued by white caterpillars.

"It's a native of this place. It can only grow here because it needs the red earth and water of these mountains to survive."

"I'm a student of plants," Egil told him. Being an Expert

Herbalist, he was immediately interested in the plants. "Could I study them? Take one?"

"I am afraid that is not possible. This plant is precious. I do not want the outside world to know of its existence."

Egil was puzzled by the refusal.

"Then why show it to us?" Lasgol asked the leader.

"Because of the link of friendship and trust we are going to establish," Tor Nassor said with a smile.

"Why is this plant so valuable and secret?" Nilsa asked as she looked at it, wrinkling her nose. "Isn't it infested?"

"On the contrary, that is one of its two major properties."

"Those larvae?" Ingrid asked, not seeing their value either.

"These larvae only come out where this plant grows, and as you can see, they come out by the thousands." Tor Nassor bent over and picked up one white larva. He put it in his mouth and ate it with relish. "Exquisite," he said.

Nilsa, Ingrid, and Viggo made disgusted faces.

"It certainly doesn't look too exquisite from where I'm standing," Ingrid said.

"It is a most nourishing food," Tor Nassor assured them. "It feeds my people and is never scarce."

"There are cultures that eat lizards and worms they grow themselves, it's well-known," Egil told his friends.

Camu came over and picked up several larvae with his blue tongue and ate them.

Very good, he messaged to his friends.

Ona chirped twice and moved away from the plants.

Are you sure they're edible, Camu? Lasgol was concerned, although it was too late because Camu had already gulped them down.

Very edible, he messaged back and picked up several more with his tongue and ate them.

"The Hor knows what is good," Tor Nassor smiled.

"Well, it's pretty gross to say the least," said Viggo. "A good steak, on the other hand…"

"A handful of these delicacies is more nourishing than meat," Tor Nassor told him.

"And the plant's second property?" Egil asked, curious.

"It is a plant with healing properties. It fights fever and infections," the leader explained and pulled several leaves off one of the plants. He handed them to Egil. "Smell them," he instructed.

Egil did so and smelt eucalyptus.

"That's curious."

"We call this plant Eshe Baset, and it is fundamental to our survival and prosperity as a people."

"Thank you for trusting us with this secret of your people," Egil said gratefully.

"Follow me and I will show you a special cavern that will no doubt interest you a lot," Tor Nassor said, and leaving the plantation, he led them through two more caverns until they reached one with a ramp. At the top of this ramp at the back they saw several paintings that looked ancient.

"Interesting paintings…" Egil commented.

"Go up and look at the depictions," Tor Nassor invited.

The group went up the ramp, and as they did and saw the great murals painted on the walls. They tried to understand what they were looking at. They looked ancient and as if they were done quite primitively. They resembled the paintings the wise men had just done of Camu, only worn by the passing of time.

Camu was the first to realize what they represented.

Family? he messaged to his friends while they looked at the murals painted on the walls.

Lasgol was studying one of the cave paintings and realized it showed a large sphere in gray over a white circumference in the middle of red rocky walls. It was not hard to interpret. It depicted the portal being used above the White Pearl here in these red mountains. This meant they had known of the portals' existence for a long time. It explained why Tor Nassor was not surprised that they had appeared there.

He went on looking at the rest of the paintings and his surprise grew. In another mural there was a different portal and a creature similar to Camu coming out of the portal, only this creature was much larger and more mature. It reminded Lasgol of Drokose. Was it possible that Drokose had been here? Was it Drokose or some other creature? Were they part of Camu's family? Camu had also recognized the creature in the painting as part of his family.

"This is fantastic!" Egil cried as he studied all the paintings, trying not to miss any detail.

"It seems we're not the only ones to have dropped by," Viggo said, examining another creature in a mural farther back.

"Interesting—there have been more travelers than us," Ingrid said.

"Is it just me, or does that look like another Camu?" Nilsa asked.

"It might be an ancestor of his," Astrid ventured, also examining the painting.

"Or Drokose," Lasgol said beside Astrid.

"It's fascinating!" Egil cried again.

"As you can see, we have already had previous visits of the Hor, the gods," Tor Nassor said, pointing at Camu.

"When was the last time?" Lasgol asked him.

"More than a hundred years ago," was the reply, and Tor Nassor pointed at the painting Astrid and Lasgol were looking at.

"Do you know whether it was a Hor like Camu?" Lasgol asked to make sure.

"It was," Tor Nassor confirmed. "There are other depictions of that Hor in another cave, and he is the same as your Camu but more mature."

"I think it's Drokose," Lasgol said. "I wonder why he would come here?"

"Well, there might be more Drakonians in Tremia we don't know about," said Egil.

"I wonder why a portal was placed here?" said Viggo. "There's only red rock and desert."

"It might have been for its location. We're right in the middle of the south of Tremia. Maybe it was used to shorten the journey," Egil speculated.

"Yeah, that makes sense. Through those portals you can come from the cold north of Tremia to the hot south in the blink of an eye," Astrid said

"Well, Camu and the Drakonians can," Lasgol corrected.

"Not only them…" said Viggo in a mysterious tone as he looked at another drawing.

They all turned to look at him.

"What do you mean?" Ingrid asked.

"I don't think this one here is Camu," he said, pointing at a drawing of a creature above the portal. They all went to look more closely.

"That creature is flying," Ingrid said.

"What is it then?" Nilsa asked, straining her neck to see.

"It has wings, a scaled reptilian body, long tail, huge mouth, and four legs with large claws…" Viggo went on. "I'd say that's a bloody dragon!"

Chapter 37

"Viggo, wait! don't be hasty," said Ingrid, looking at the creature with a frown.

"It's flying, no doubt about that. Its wings are fully extended," said Astrid.

"It could be Camu using his power. Well, a creature like Camu who also had his ability to fly," said Nilsa.

"Could be, only the creature depicted here has a long neck and a fanged mouth, and claws, which don't coincide with Camu's appearance," Egil said, checking the drawing carefully.

Not me. Be family.

"Yeah, I know, but your family is a little weird," Viggo told him. "Aren't dragons part of your family?"

Yes. Dragons family.

"There you go. If it's like a dragon and a relative of Camu's, then it's a dragon," Viggo concluded.

"That would imply the portals we're using are indeed dragon portals..." Astrid said.

"Yeah, I was thinking the same thing," said Egil. "Until now we figured the portals had to do with Camu and Drokose, since they've used them as far as we know. There was no record of a dragon using them."

"Now there is," Lasgol said, indicating the drawing.

"So, we must assume that the portals can be used by Drakonians, and that includes dragons," Egil concluded.

"How nice... it's so reassuring to know there are portals in Tremia the dragons used to move throughout the continent without batting a wing and getting tired," said Viggo.

"They probably used them as shortcuts to reach their destinations faster," Egil said.

"That doesn't matter! It's a dragon portal! Don't you realize what that means?" Viggo shouted at them.

"I'm having trouble seeing it," Ingrid admitted.

"If there are dragon portals, there must also be dragons!" Viggo cried in a desperate tone.

"Let's not be hasty. There's currently no record of dragons," said Egil.

"Yeah, there wasn't of Drakonians either, and look, now we have one with us all the time," Viggo said, pointing at Camu.

"That is a Lesser Fire Hor," Tor Nassor said, pointing at the dragon in the painting they were discussing.

They all turned to him.

"There are different types of Hor?" Lasgol asked him blankly.

"Yes, indeed. He is a Greater Hor," Tor Nassor said, indicating Camu.

I Greater Hor. I powerful. Camu lifted his head, straightened his legs, and shook his tail, showing how long and large he was.

Yeah, yeah, very powerful. Give us a moment to understand this, Lasgol told him.

"That is a Lesser Fire Hor," the leader repeated, pointing at the dragon. "How do your people know what it is?" Egil asked him, intrigued.

"Because it came over a thousand years ago. Our records show it, come with me," he said.

They followed the leader to another cavern deeper in, and there they saw some more archaic drawings. Several of the warriors lit torches since there was not enough light and they could barely see anything. These drawings were simpler, less elaborate and done with paints of lower quality, although they had survived the passing of time. A huge mural depicted three different scenes. The first one seemed to depict a portal forming above the Pearl. The Pearl was in the mountains the Panthers were currently in, since the ancient artists had painted the crest of the mountain in red and a bone-colored sea around them, which clearly represented the deserts surrounding them.

They got closer to look at the second scene, and it clearly represented, albeit in an ancient way, a creature coming out of the portal. Just like the creature they had seen in the other cavern, this one had a long neck, claws, and a fanged mouth, unlike Camu, who shared none of those characteristics. It was shown flying with fully extended wings coming out of the portal. Camu had wings if he used his skill, but it was clear the creature was not the same as Camu.

"Lesser Hor," Tor Nassor said.

"That's another dragon," Viggo muttered.

"It does look like one," Nilsa joined him.

"It's not like Camu. It has a long neck and our Camu has a short one," said Ingrid.

I neck of Drakonian.

Yeah, we know, we're comparing you with the creature in the drawing.

Not Drakonian.

It would seem not, but what is it then?

Be family.

I guess so, but what part of your family?

Dragon.

Well... then dragons are part of your family but they're not the same as you.

No, I more than dragon.

Let me see if I understand it. Then dragons are like your cousins? Or your siblings?

Cousins yes. Siblings not.

And how do you know that?

Drokose say.

I knew you were going to say that.

The third scene showed a creature flying over the red mountains and something that left them all puzzled; something was pouring out of the creature's mouth that was killing the red warriors who were throwing javelins at it.

"That's a dragon without a doubt," Egil said, "and it's spitting fire on the Desher Tumaini, who are trying to bring it down unsuccessfully. It looks like they all burned to death." The depiction of warriors lying down on the red mountains and painted in black did not leave much room for speculation.

"A Lesser Fire Hor did that," Tor Nassor explained.

"Why did your ancestors fight him?" Lasgol asked.

"That Hor was not good. It wanted to kill, eat my people."

"Whoa, nice," Viggo commented.

"It came out of the portal and attacked your people?" Ingrid asked as she examined the scenes closely.

"Indeed. Not all the Hor that come out of the Pearl are good, there are evil ones. This was one of them."

"I find it fascinating that you've categorized them. Why is that a Lesser Hor and ours a Greater Hor?" Egil asked.

"Good question, because that dragon looks a lot more dangerous than this one, with the fire, fangs, claws, and all that," said Viggo, jabbing his thumb at Camu.

Tor Nassor looked at Camu. "Because the magic of this Hor is greater than that one's," he replied, indicating the dragon in the painting.

I more than dragon. Drokose say, Camu messaged them proudly.

Yeah, you've told us that repeatedly... Lasgol replied.

"When did this happen?" Egil asked, scratching his head.

"Thousands of years ago, three or four thousand years, perhaps more," Tor Nassor replied.

"Wow, then your people have been living here for a long time," Lasgol commented. "Didn't the first men arrive in Tremia about three or four thousand years ago?"

"Yeah, as far as we know," said Egil. "Which indicates that the Desher Tumaini are one of the first peoples to populate Tremia."

"Aren't the Norghanians too?" Ingrid asked.

"That's what our history and legends say, perhaps a little later," Egil said. "There's no way to know for sure."

"Then we're with one of the oldest peoples of the continent," Astrid said.

"That's right," said Egil, nodding thoughtfully.

"My people have been here since the time of the first men. When Gods and men fought."

"Gods? What Gods? The dragons?" Viggo asked, confused.

Tor Nassor shook his head. "The Gods that arrived from the sea and finished with the Hor that ruled over the earth and sky. That is what our legends say. It was before my people's time."

"This is fascinating," said Egil. "It corroborates other information we have, that before the era of humans, was one where some Gods ruled over Tremia."

"The Gods of the Sea expelled the Hor from the Skies," Tor Nassor said and pointed his finger up to the ceiling of the cavern.

"It's fascinating, a people that have been here since the time of the first men," Egil said excitedly.

"What happened to the Gods?" Ingrid asked.

"Humans defeated them," Tor Nassor said and pointed at the floor of the cavern. "Thus began the time of men. Our time," the leader said with a wave that included them all.

"How wonderful to be before a people who lived and have records of what happened three thousand years ago when humans first arrived in Tremia. The modern kingdoms don't have this, not in the north or the west. Least of all the east, where all the kingdoms are recently created," Egil said.

"Yes, but there's something that doesn't fit…" Lasgol said thoughtfully. "If the Gods eliminated the dragons, did they expel or kill them? What's the dragon doing in the paintings?" he said and pointed at the creature drawn on the wall.

"True. There's no record that men and dragons ever co-existed," said Egil, "with the exception of what this painting shows. It's fantastic—now there is a record. But you're right, men weren't in Tremia at the same time as dragons."

"It is the last Lesser Fire Hor," Tor Nassor told them.

"There weren't any more?" Egil asked.

Tor Nassor shook his head. "That was the last one. There were no more. They disappeared."

"Wow, that's curious," said Egil. "Then we can assume that this dragon was the last one that flew over Tremia, and he did so here, over these mountains. That would explain why there's no other record of it. At that time, Tremia was sparsely populated."

"What happened to the last Hor?" Lasgol asked, examining the drawing with great curiosity.

"We do not know. One day it disappeared through the portal of the Great Pearl. It never came back," Tor Nassor explained with a shrug.

"Wow, what a pity not to know what happened to it," said Nilsa, also intrigued.

"Perhaps men killed it," said Ingrid.

Tor Nassor shook his head. "Men cannot kill the Hor, they are too powerful."

"Can't they?" Viggo asked, looking at Camu, surprised.

"No, they have powerful magic, and our weapons do not pierce their skin of impenetrable scales."

"Not even with steel from the north like this?" Viggo showed the leader his knives.

Tor Nassor shook his head again. "Steel does not pierce their scales. They cannot be wounded."

"That doesn't seem entirely true. Camu has tough scales, but he can be hurt," said Ingrid.

"That must be because this Hor is still quite young, if my instincts do not fool me. When he grows older, he will become a powerful Hor. He will be indestructible," Tor Nassor prophesized.

I indestructible one day. You see, Camu messaged to them.

Don't go believing all this, because you'll be terribly disappointed later.

"I don't believe Camu will become as tough as steel when he grows older," Viggo said incredulously.

I very tough. You see.

"It would surprise me greatly," Viggo said, putting away his knives.

"And some other kind of Hor? Have there been other Hor who have used the portal?" Lasgol asked, staring at Camu.

"Yes, there have been," Tor Nassor said.

They all exchanged expectant looks.

"Like Camu?" Lasgol asked.

"Yes, some like him. And others not like him." Tor Nassor shook his head.

The answer left them all uneasy. There were different types of Hor and they used the portal, which meant one might appear at the Lair, although there was no record that any had ever done so.

"Have any recently traveled through the Pearl?" Lasgol asked.

"No, only him," Tor Nassor said, indicating Camu.

"Well, that's comforting," said Ingrid.

"Why is Tor Nassor showing us all these secrets of his people and sharing knowledge with us?" Lasgol asked, who guessed there had to be a reason for it. It was one thing to be welcoming and a very different thing to explain secrets that had been hidden for thousands of years.

"Because my people need help," Tor Nassor replied.

Lasgol understood at once—Tor Nassor was going to ask them for something. That was the reason he had behaved so kindly and been so open with them, sharing his secrets. Considering what he had revealed to them, Lasgol was sure the favor was going to be a difficult one to deliver.

"What can we do to help the people of the Desher Tumaini?" Egil offered. "If it's in our power, we'll certainly try."

Tor Nassor sighed deeply. "It involves the city we do not name, the walled city to the east. We need help rescuing a group they are holding prisoner. They are people of my people. My youngest daughter and her two cousins are among them."

"I'm sorry," Egil said. "Why have they been captured?"

"In the city of Jafarika live the people of the Jafari Kaphiri, the people with the stream on the hill upon which they built their great city. We have always been rivals. They want our mountains and their secrets. They are an ambitious people—their King, Mahaes Madu, is at war with our people, continuing the war of his father and his father's father before him, and thus we can go back to the beginnings of both peoples. That is why they have taken our people."

"They've kidnapped some of your people?" Lasgol asked.

"Indeed, when they were fishing in the river Eshe to the far south of the city. My people usually go fishing in that river, always south to avoid the Jafari Kaphiri patrols. Fish is a delicacy we do not have in these mountains. They were captured by a patrol, the three of them and a dozen women and men who were with them. I have tried to negotiate with Mahaes Madu, but it has been in vain. There has been no way to change his mind. They have been sentenced to death in the desert."

"And you want us to take them from the King..." Astrid guessed.

"Indeed, this is what I am asking."

"And if we don't oblige?" Ingrid asked, raising an eyebrow. She was expecting there to be a catch if they refused.

"If the request of the Desher Tumaini is refused, the visitors will be thrown out to the desert and left to their own fate."

"How nice..." Viggo moaned.

"Won't we be allowed to use the Pearl to go back the same way we came?" Lasgol asked in a relaxed tone that disguised how disappointed he was.

"I am afraid you will not be allowed to use the Pearl," The leader said.

"That's not fair, the Pearl isn't yours," Nilsa protested, raising her voice.

"You don't have any rights to it," Viggo said, "and you can't forbid us to use it."

Seeing Nilsa's and Viggo's aggressive attitudes, the warriors who accompanied them became tense and brandished their weapons threateningly. They would not allow any kind of altercation. Their leader made a placating gesture so they would stand down.

"It sounds like blackmail to me," said Viggo.

"It's certainly not very honorable," Ingrid said with a look of disapproval on her face.

"When the need is great and a unique opportunity presents itself, one must take drastic measures. That you have appeared here at this moment of great need is not a coincidence. The Hor of the desert sent us help, and we must accept it with open arms and take advantage of this gift."

"Can't your warriors deal with this? They look like skilled fighters," Ingrid said.

"They are. But Mahaes Madu will be expecting just that, expecting us to come down from our mountains. That is what we must not do."

"And how do you know we'll be able to bring your people back?" Astrid asked.

"My warriors are no rivals for Rangers like you. Just like our enemies' warriors. You are superior warriors with special gifts. You can do what they cannot."

"He's right about that. There aren't any others like us. Well, like me there's definitely not, least of all in the middle of a desert," Viggo said, feigning shaking off some desert dust. "The old man has a good eye."

"Why not ask for our help without conditions?" Lasgol asked. "It would've been the honest way to act."

"Because you would not have accepted. It is not your fight. It is not your problem. You would have left and we would have lost a unique opportunity to save the lives of our own," the leader explained.

"I wouldn't be so sure of that," Lasgol replied. "We help those who need it. But well, now we'll never know how we would have responded."

"My people need help. That is why we ask," Tor Nassor said, and this time his tone was a plea.

"What's the plan?" Ingrid asked. "You must have thought of something."

Tor Nassor nodded. "Tomorrow evening, they will take the group to the Abyss of the Sands and throw them in."

"That doesn't sound good..." Viggo muttered.

"The Abyss is an enormous depression in the middle of the desert between their city and our mountains."

"How big?" Ingrid asked.

"It is a gigantic hole. The depth is unknown, but it is such that the desert cannot cover the great hole," he said.

"I find it hard to picture that," Nilsa said. "It must be humungous."

"If the sand never covers it, it must be," said Egil. "There are geographical anomalies all throughout Tremia, and this must be one of them. Little known, yes."

"Few go near," Tor Nassor said.

"Because of the danger of falling in?" Ingrid asked, looking surprised.

"Not because of that."

"Then why?" Astrid asked.

"Because of the Sand Hor."

Chapter 38

The night was clear in the desert and the crescent moon shone above the endless dunes. The Panthers, accompanied by Tor Nassor and about thirty of his warriors, were walking along the dunes in silence and in single file. The old leader was at the head guiding the group, followed by the Panthers with Camu and Ona right behind. The warriors followed.

Wherever they looked, the Panthers saw only a sea of sand on which the dunes gave the impression of being wide, yellow, immobile waves. The vastness of the arid landscape and the deep silence had them spellbound. They were not used to the desert at all, and the walk from the Blood Mountains to the Abyss of the sands was turning out to be quite hard.

"Sand is getting in everything," Viggo protested as he shook off sand. Unfortunately, the night breeze that swept the dunes made the sand get into and under every item of clothing. They were wearing their full Ranger gear, and although the hooded cloak helped, it made them hot. The temperature was supposed to drop steeply at night, but for now Viggo was sweating with every step and could not manage to get a breath of fresh air.

"Cover your nose and mouth with the scarves, that way not so much sand will get in," Ingrid advised them.

Lasgol felt the scorching heat of the desert climbing up his legs with every step. The feeling of walking in a desert following the crests of the dunes was unique. They would never experience anything like that in the north. It was a most curious sensation.

"The sand is in my boots and the friction is going to give me blisters," Nilsa protested, looking uncomfortable.

"It's difficult to step on this sand and not sink in it," Astrid commented, wrinkling her nose. The sand was up to her ankles, if not the knees, and she was not happy at all. "Making headway is complicated."

"Fighting is also going to be complicated," said Ingrid as she pulled her foot out of the sand and went on taking strides.

"This little nocturnal stroll through the desert is most romantic,"

Viggo commented to Ingrid, "if we weren't heading to an abyss where there's a sand dragon lurking around."

"It is not lurking," Tor Nassor corrected him. "The Great Sand Hor has rarely come out of its lair in a century."

"With our luck, today it'll decide to come out for a stroll like us," Viggo said sarcastically.

"It doesn't matter whether it comes out or not. We're going to its lair, aren't we?" Nilsa asked.

"Indeed," Tor Nassor confirmed. "The Hor lives inside the great abyss."

"I just love the adventures we find ourselves involved in," Viggo said ironically. "And I bet this dragon isn't one of the young ones, it'll be old and have skin tougher than the mountains at our back."

"The Hor is ancient and powerful indeed," Tor Nassor confirmed again. "It arrived through the portal and made its home in this desert."

"Don't know why, but I had already guessed as much," Viggo muttered, raising his arms in the air.

"Then it's a dragon, but not like the one in the cavern paintings," Egil said to Tor Nassor, "since you told us no other fire dragon had come through the portal."

"This Hor is different. This is a sand dragon. It does not have wings or four limbs with claws. Its body is huge and long, round, and covered with scales the color of the sand it lives in. It's like a giant snake, but the head is like a dragon with a huge mouth full of teeth. It has desert magic," Tor Nassor explained.

"Oh okay. Now *that's* reassuring," Viggo said. "You had me worried for a moment there." He waved as if that did not bother him at all.

Nilsa rolled her eyes. "It's going to be a dangerous encounter," she commented with a worried look on her face.

"Best if we do not encounter the great sand dragon," Tor Nassor told them. "It is a god impossible to kill and devours any human or animal it finds in the desert."

"Does it eat meat?" Viggo asked, raising an eyebrow.

"Not really. The dragon feeds off the desert sand. It devours humans and animals for pleasure."

"As I said, charming vermin," Viggo said, shaking his head comically. "We should adopt it to keep Camu company."

No. I have Ona. Not need more siblings.

"Well, this one would be like a grandfather with a bad temper." Viggo smiled.

"Cut the nonsense and keep your eyes open," Ingrid told him.

"Are there any other Hor in this area?" Lasgol asked Tor Nassor to make sure they would not be surprised by any other legendary beasts.

"No, of the Hor that came, only this one stayed," Tor Nassor replied.

"I understand you've tried to kill it so it would stop eating your people, right?" Ingrid questioned.

Tor Nassor nodded. "The best warriors among my people have tried to do so on several occasions. The Jafari Kaphiri have tried too. They could not even wound it. It was not even scratched."

"Understood. We'll have to keep away from this creature," said Ingrid.

"Now that I think about it, is that the reason you didn't let us set foot on the sand inside the mountains?" Lasgol asked.

"Indeed. We teach our people to always walk on the rock. The great dragon of the sand has appeared on occasion in the middle of our mountains in the past and taken some of our people."

"Then it could appear right here?" Nilsa asked.

"It could, but it is not likely. It rarely leaves its dwelling. But it is prudent not to make noise on the sand so as not to attract it. It has superb hearing believed to be amplified by magic."

They all nodded and went on in silence, mindfully imagining what they would find and how they might solve the problem. The enormity of the desert seemed to be swallowing them a little more with every step. The sand blended with the blackness of the night wherever they looked, and a feeling of great loneliness assaulted them.

"We will soon arrive," Tor Nassor told them. "The desert can swallow a man in more ways than one, with its never-ending dunes, heat, immensity or loneliness. People are mere grains of sand in the great desert, and a breath of air can make them disappear."

They stopped to rest and drank from the water supplies they were carrying. They were near and needed to prepare. They checked their gear and weapons. When they were ready they told Tor Nassor, who then led them to the great abyss. They stopped a few paces from the colossal depression in the middle of the desert. They saw a hole even blacker than the night above their heads in the middle of a sea of sand that seemed to swallow the darkness.

"It's fantastic…" Egil murmured with eyes like saucers.

"Vast and fathomless," Lasgol said.

"The size of it… it's enormous…" Nilsa commented, her eyes popping.

"It gives me the creeps…" Viggo said, looking into the Abyss, black as night, that entered the earth without end.

"Its depth and darkness are overwhelming," said Astrid.

All of a sudden, they felt a tremor coming from the great hole.

"Let us not make noise, the dragon might hear us," Tor Nassor told them, motioning them back.

They retraced their steps and took up the positions they had agreed upon, following the plan prepared by Egil with Tor Nassor's help. As they retreated, three warriors erased the trail they had left on the sand with blankets so it would appear as if no one had been there in a long time.

In the distance, they glimpsed a caravan coming from the east over the dunes. They were carrying torches and were divided in two parallel lines. There were over two hundred soldiers.

"Those are the Jafari Kaphiri," Tor Nassor announced. "They are coming."

"Time to get into position and hide," Egil told his friends.

A moment later the Panthers vanished, camouflaged among the dunes. Tor Nassor's warriors also withdrew and hid behind a large dune which covered them entirely. Their enemies could not see them.

Lasgol was watching from his hiding place. He had buried himself in the sand, leaving only a bit of his head sticking out. The soldiers of the city were arriving, and he saw they were armed with spears and small metallic shields with symbols which must be of the Jafari Kaphiri because he did not recognize them. He also noticed they were wearing two-piece armor that covered their torsos and pointed helmets. They certainly looked better prepared for war than the Desher Tumaini warriors, who were not wearing armor or helmets.

Tor Nassor had already warned them that the soldiers of the city made up a strong, well-trained army. They had tried to conquer the Blood Mountains on several occasions, but in that terrain the warriors, using guerilla tactics and hiding in the labyrinth of rock, had defeated the Jafari Kaphiri. But here in the open the Desher Tumaini would lose the battle, and Tor Nassor knew it. That was why he had asked the Panthers for help.

The caravan arrived to the east side of the great abyss and stood in a crescent with their spears and shields ready. By the light of the torches they were carrying, Lasgol was able to see that they indeed looked well-trained. He could make out several officers giving orders to the soldiers, who were taking up their positions skillfully. The prisoners were in the middle with their hands tied behind their backs. They were unmistakable since they were dressed like the Desher Tumaini.

He looked at the end of the caravan. A group of about a hundred soldiers was arriving now. They seemed to be protecting a man he assumed must be King Mahaes Madu since he had remained back, far from any danger. Lasgol guessed he was not going to come any closer and that he would, most likely, watch the macabre spectacle from afar.

A dozen soldiers stepped forward to the edge of the Abyss and started beating great drums with rhythmic cadences that could be heard in the distance. Lasgol did not like this at all, because he knew what they were doing: they were summoning the sand dragon to come and devour the prisoners.

"Brutes!" he muttered under his breath.

The drums called the sand god and the situation began to be complicated. The soldiers led the prisoners to the edge of the Abyss where the monster would appear to devour them. Lasgol identified three women in the middle—they had to be Tor Nassor's daughter and nieces. The poor wretches were fully aware of what was going to happen and were weeping and shaking with fear.

No, it was not that they were shaking with fear, the desert sand was shaking.

Dragon coming, Camu messaged Lasgol.

Can you feel it?

Feel his magic. Much power.

Okay, we'll have to avoid it as best we can.

Okay.

The drums went on beating and the soldiers positioned themselves in two crescents to wait for the dragon to come out for its human tributes. If it did not, there were about thirty soldiers guarding the captives and Lasgol was sure they would throw the prisoners into the Abyss. The ground shook stronger with each passing moment. The dragon was approaching. The soldiers beating the drums withdrew to a safe distance from the prisoners. The tremors were stronger and closer. The soldiers guarding the prisoners also withdrew to a safe distance, as did the two crescents of soldiers. They left the prisoners with their hands tied behind their backs before the Abyss. They were trembling, and several fell to the ground from the tremors and their fear.

Like a nightmarish horror, all of a sudden from inside the Abyss emerged a horrible creature with a colossal snake body and dragon head. The gigantic creature rose, leaving the darkness of the Abyss, reaching over sixty feet to the sky and opening its insane jaws.

Lasgol swallowed. The head of the sand dragon was so colossal it could scoop up a hundred people in a single attack. The prisoners were looking up, waiting for the dragon to fall down and devour them. The dragon finally stopped rising and looked all around as if it were adjusting its sight.

At that moment Astrid came out of hiding a few paces from the prisoners, where she had been buried in the sand. Without hesitation and without a glance at the colossal dragon rising above her, she ran to the prisoners. She grabbed Tor Nassor's daughter and her two cousins and dragged them away. An instant later Viggo came out of the sand and told the rest of the prisoners to run toward the west, to the red mountains, pushing them forward.

It took the scared-to-death prisoners a moment to react, but Astrid and Viggo urged them until they started to move. When the prisoners realized that if they stayed the dragon was going to devour them, they all started running at the moment the dragon's head with its great jaws open was coming down upon them.

"Come on! Run!" Viggo could be heard yelling.

"To the west!" Astrid yelled.

The soldiers soon realized a rescue was being attempted and started to run after the prisoners.

The dragon's jaws closed upon the last of the prisoners who had not reacted in time. Viggo, who was hanging back with them, threw himself to one side to avoid the beast's jaws, which clamped shut, devouring several of the remaining prisoners and the soldiers who were arriving to stop them from escaping. Causing a tremendous tremor, the dragon devoured as many as its jaws could trap.

The soldiers' cries of alarm filled the night.

Astrid was running away leading the group of prisoners, and Viggo, who had already gotten to his feet, finished off a soldier who was running toward him with his spear aimed his way with two knife strokes. A huge group of soldiers that were forming the first crescent lunged in pursuit, following their superior's orders.

As Astrid and the first fugitives were cresting a tall dune, Ingrid emerged from behind it and started releasing against their pursuers, protecting their escape. The great sand dragon rose again, half its body out of the Abyss and the other half inside. It saw the soldiers run past him and went for them, descending upon them, its great mouth open and its teeth slicing the air. The soldiers screamed and tried to avoid the mouth as it fell upon them, but in one tremendous gulp it took soldiers and sand alike and swallowed them all.

The officers were shouting orders to the soldiers, but now confusion and terror had overcome them; no one wanted to die swallowed by that monster. The second crescent of soldiers ran off with their torches high, hoping the monster would not come after them because of the fire. They were waving their torches and yelling in an attempt to scare off the desert monster.

Meanwhile the prisoners' escape continued, Astrid leading them as fast as she could. They went past Lasgol, and now it was his turn. He rose from the sand, picked up his bow, and released at the first of their pursuers, bringing down the soldier. He saw Viggo helping a woman who had lost her footing. The soldiers were almost upon them. Ingrid and Lasgol released to protect them. One lagging soldier jumped on Viggo's back and Nilsa caught him full in the forehead with a long-distance shot from a dune further back.

The sand dragon fell again from the heights, bending its snake body, and its jaws caught another group of soldiers as they chased the fugitives. It devoured them and the dune they were running across. Fire and shouting did not affect the monster—they did not scare it off, on the contrary, it seemed to attract it. The surviving soldiers looked back, undecided, their officers still shouting at them to go after the escaped prisoners. Against their better judgment, they went on with the chase.

Nilsa, Ingrid, and Lasgol were shooting, covering the escape. The prisoners ran over another tall dune and from behind it Egil emerged with his bow and joined in the escapees' protection. Egil's position was the last spot they would have to cross, so they were about to successfully escape. Beside Egil, Camu was camouflaged, and with him was Ona.

Prisoners almost here, he informed the Panthers, who were still fighting.

Let us know when they pass by your position so we can withdraw, Lasgol transmitted.

I warn.

Suddenly the dragon pushed more of its body out of the Abyss and attacked. But it changed its quarry. Instead of attacking the soldiers pursuing the prisoners, it turned to the soldiers in the east. In one sweep that caught the soldiers and with them the officers shouting their orders, it scooped up about fifty Jafari Kaphiri, creating terror and confusion among the troops. The surviving soldiers fled, horrified, before the dragon attacked them again. King Mahaes Madu gave the order to withdraw, and he and his escort fled from the place as fast as they could. The execution of his prisoners had not gone according to plan.

Then the great sand dragon did something no one was expecting. It plunged into the sand, not to attack but to dive in as if it were water. It created an enormous hole while sand flew in every direction as if a whirlwind had struck the desert's surface. The dragon's head started to vanish into the new hole while its colossal body came out of the Abyss to follow the head. The soldiers were fleeing terrified toward their city because the dragon had now vanished under the sand and was slithering under the dunes, seeking more prey to devour.

Astrid, leading the escaped prisoners, passed Egil's and Camu's position.

Prisoners at my position, Camu warned.

Tor Nassor and his warriors were waiting a few paces to the west. Egil signaled the prisoners to run toward them.

They had done it. Viggo was helping two women who had been lagging to catch up with the rest. Ingrid, Lasgol, and Nilsa brought down the last Jafari Kaphiri pursuers. They started pulling back to Egil's and Camu's position.

"We did it!" Nilsa cried excitedly as she hung back in case any of the soldiers got back up.

Tor Nassor hugged his daughter and his nieces tight. The leader's face showed the great joy he felt at recovering them. They exchanged words of love and affection in their language and tears and looks of joy appeared on their faces. The prisoners could not forget the horror they had experienced and their tear-stained faces and haunted expressions were proof of it. The warriors welcomed them and drove the terror away with soothing words; but unfortunately, they had suffered some losses, and those who had managed to escape were in shock by what had happened.

"We are withdrawing to the mountains," Tor Nassor informed the Panthers.

"Go, we'll cover your retreat," Egil told him with a wave telling them to run to safety.

"See, that was easy," Viggo said, arriving last. "I don't know why you worry so much if you have me."

"Oh sure, the rest of us did nothing," Nilsa said as she ran past him to climb the last dune where they all were, getting into position in case they were pursued.

"You only helped a little bit. This sand dragon has been an interesting twist to the mission," Viggo said, beaming and looking up at the group from the foot of the dune.

"Shut up and come to this side of the dune, you smartass," Ingrid told him.

Suddenly, everything started shaking. The sand seemed to open in front of them as they tried to keep their balance and not fall. The dunes flew up in the air. A whirl of sand seemed to emerge from the depths of the desert, throwing sand in every direction. The sand dragon emerged behind Viggo's back from a void in the sand. The force with which it burst out and the sand it expelled knocked Viggo down.

"Viggo! Look out!" Ingrid cried, seeing him thrown to one side.

The dragon's head rose into the starry sky as if it were seeking the moon and then changed directions. It came down again toward the ground, bending its long body.

"Get out of the way!" shouted Ingrid.

"Dodge!" cried Astrid.

Viggo had managed to get back on his feet and saw the dragon descending. It was not coming down on the group that was running for cover—it was coming down on him. He nimbly skipped to one side. The jaws of the great sand dragon followed him, closing over him.

"Noooooooo!" Ingrid cried in despair.

"Viggo! No!" Astrid cried in horror.

The dragon plunged into the sand again and its long, colossal body followed.

There was no trace of Viggo.

The sand dragon had devoured him.

Chapter 39

Lasgol swept the sand with his gaze. Viggo was nowhere to be seen.

Astrid climbed the dune, scanning for him without success.

"It's swallowed him!"

"It can't be!" Lasgol refused to believe the sand dragon had devoured Viggo.

Ingrid ran to the spot where Viggo had vanished. She only found the hole the dragon had made in the sand.

"Viggo! Where are you? Answer me!" she shouted.

Lasgol used his *Animal Presence* skill in case the darkness of the night and all the sand the dragon had upset could be hiding Viggo's body. He perceived the Panthers and the fugitives fleeing west, but of Viggo, not a trace. Lasgol feared the worst. If their friend was dead, he would not feel his presence, his skill only detected living beings.

Can you see him? he transmitted to Camu.

Not see. Dragon eat Viggo.

They felt the sand shaking and knew the dragon was coming for more.

Ona growled loudly.

"It's coming back!" Egil cried.

"Get ready!" Lasgol shouted.

A few paces from where it had plunged in, the dragon's head broke the sand in a whirl of sand expelled in all directions. The head and part of the monster's long body rose into the starry night, and hanging from one side of its mouth they saw a figure.

"Viggo!" Ingrid cried, pointing at him.

"He's still alive!" cried Astrid.

Lasgol saw that Viggo was hanging from the corner of the dragon's mouth which was biting right and left, opening and shutting its jaws, trying to eat its slippery prey without success.

"We have to help him!" Nilsa shouted, arming her bow.

They all nocked and aimed at the dragon.

"Release at the neck and we'll try to make it drop him!" Ingrid yelled.

The arrows flew and hit the great beast that was shaking its head, trying to catch Viggo who was hanging, swaying, but did not fall.

The arrows of all five hit the dragon but none could pierce its scales which were harder than steel. They bounced off without causing it any harm. They released again. They all hit their target but once again the arrows bounced off, unable to pierce the dragon's skin which was harder than armor.

"We can't wound it!" Nilsa yelled.

"Change to Elemental Arrows!" Ingrid shouted.

They did. While they changed, Viggo was already climbing up the dragon's ear, using his knives to secure the climb. The Elemental Arrows hit the dragon in the neck. Fire and Ice exploded on its skin. The arrows did not manage to penetrate the scales, but the dragon noticed that something was going wrong—it did not like the arrows' elemental effects.

"Use Air Arrows!" Egil cried.

They nocked those and released again. The arrows flew while Viggo climbed to the top of the colossal dragon's head. The arrows hit the dragon's open mouth and pierced the tongue and the inside of its mouth. The arrows exploded inside the mouth and the dragon seemed to feel them, because it shut its mouth at once and shook its head from side to side, trying to get rid of Viggo and whatever had attacked its mouth.

Lying on the dragon's head, Viggo was holding on with one knife while he tried to stab it with the other.

"Die, you giant ugly desert vermin!" he was shouting.

The scene was totally absurd. He looked like a mosquito trying to kill a colossal snake. But Viggo did not give up and kept stabbing the dragon's head over and over again with fury.

"Release! The Elemental Arrows did something to it!" said Ingrid.

"Use only Air Arrows, they affect the sand dragon," Egil told them.

The arrows flew, but now the dragon was not opening its mouth. It only continued shaking its head to get rid of Viggo. The creature was over sixty feet tall, and if it managed to dislodge Viggo the fall would kill him. The arrows burst on contact and gave shocks all along the dragon's neck. It felt them, because it lowered its head from side to side and lifted it again fast. Viggo had to hold on tight as he was nearly thrown off.

"We're not hurting it enough!" Ingrid cried.

"We're also not helping Viggo!" Astrid said, seeing he could fall and kill himself.

I help, Camu messaged to them. He climbed a tall dune and stopped camouflaging himself so he was visible.

What are you going to do? Lasgol transmitted, worried.

Viggo in danger. I help, Camu messaged back as he rose above the dune, looking straight at the great sand dragon. Beside Camu the dragon orb was levitating. Camu started to glow with a sliver gleam which became painfully intense after a moment. Lasgol watched Camu with no idea of what he was doing. Suddenly he saw Camu emit an intense pulse in the form of a wave which moved at great speed to the dragon. When the pulse struck the dragon's body, the silver flash went up its scales to the monster's head.

The dragon stopped moving and trying to throw Viggo off and turned to look at Camu. It watched him from the heights with small, bright-black eyes.

Camu sent another silver pulse which again hit the dragon, climbing up the body of the nightmarish creature.

I Camu. Drakonian. I ask you withdraw, Camu messaged the sand dragon.

The monster was staring at Camu from its incredible height and seemed to rise even higher on its own body.

"Don't shoot, let Camu communicate with the dragon," Egil told the others. "He might get somewhere."

They all lowered their bows and watched the scene unfold.

Suddenly a message came from the monster with such strength that Lasgol had to throw his head back. Camu flashed silver and the orb beside him also emitted a silver flash. The message was in a strange language, ancient and distant. Yet, somehow, Lasgol could understand it.

I am Azibo Zuberi, Earth Dragon. How dare you address me? the monster messaged Camu. Viggo was holding on hard and trying to recover his breath. He had felt the jolts as if he were being given a beating.

With respect ask great Azibo Zuberi, Earth Dragon to withdraw and let us go, Camu messaged again.

A roaring sound reached their minds like a burst.

It was the sand dragon, and it seemed to be laughing. *Hahaha, you cannot even speak properly, much less address me,* it messaged Camu with great disdain.

You go. Let us be, Camu insisted.

I am a Sand Dragon, you little inconsequential creature, and this is my kingdom. These deserts are mine. Everything in them is mine and I do with them what I please, it messaged with rage in its tone.

I Drakonian, Camu messaged confidently.

The sand dragon looked at Camu, and its black eyes shone with recognition.

That you are, but still no more than a pup. Your power is insignificant beside mine. Show me respect if you do not want me to end your banal existence before you have even savored what power and life are, the dragon threatened, along with a feeling of great power.

I more than dragon, Camu messaged back without even flinching and with a feeling of superiority.

I am over two thousand years old, you are not superior to me, the dragon responded, along with a great feeling of fury that made Lasgol throw back his head hard.

Yes, be. You leave, Camu insisted.

Your daring will cost you your life. No one speaks to me like that, least of all a creature with such little power, the dragon Azibo Zuberi messaged, along with a feeling of death.

Lasgol knew it was going to kill Camu.

"Camu, no!" he shouted.

The dragon opened its jaws and lunged to devour Camu. Viggo noticed and started plunging both his knives into the dragon's head with all his strength. The head came down at great speed toward Camu. Viggo kept plunging and plunging, but his knives could not penetrate the dragon's scales.

"Camu, move away!" Egil cried, seeing the attack.

At that instant the dragon orb emitted a potent silver pulse which hit the dragon as it attacked. Azibo Zuberi changed its descending plunge and rose again at great speed.

Leave. Go back to your home, now, they heard another voice say, much more powerful and much deeper than Azibo Zuberi's. Lasgol fell on his back from so much power.

The sand dragon stared at the orb for a long while with bright eyes.

Everyone was expectant.

So it will be done, Azibo Zuberi replied suddenly, and with an enormous leap it came entirely out of the sand to plunge head first into the great abyss it had come out of.

"Viggo! No!" Ingrid cried, seeing the sand dragon carrying Viggo with it into the depths of the Abyss.

"It's taking him!" Nilsa cried with a look of horror on her face.

Viggo jumped off the head just when the dragon plunged into the Abyss, but the hole was so large he could not reach the edge and fell inside.

Camu reacted and ran to the edge of the Abyss, the end of the sand dragon's tail was vanishing. Without a second thought, Camu jumped into the Abyss.

"Camu! Don't!" "Camu, no!" Lasgol and Egil shouted at the same time.

They all ran to the edge of the Abyss. The orb and Ona were just beside the spot from where Camu had leapt.

"We've lost them both!" Nilsa cried, horrified, putting her hands to her head.

"Can anyone see anything?" Ingrid asked, staring into the blackness with a look of tremendous frustration.

"I can't see a thing, it's absolutely black. The darkness is impenetrable," Egil said.

"We have to do something!" Ingrid said desperately.

"I'm afraid there's not much we can do," Astrid replied with great sadness.

"I refuse to believe they're dead," said Lasgol.

They were all silent, contemplating the horrendous possibility. The blackness of the Abyss had swallowed both.

Ona was moaning in anguish. Lasgol went over to stroke her in an attempt to calm her but could not. The snow panther was desolate.

"What did Camu throw himself in for?" Nilsa asked.

"Because he wanted to save Viggo…" Astrid replied.

"And he's a brave creature," Egil said.

"They can't have died. We have to get in there," Ingrid said, making a move to jump into the Abyss.

"Don't even think about it," Astrid said as she lunged at Ingrid and knocked her down.

"You can't jump in there. We've already lost Camu and Viggo, we

353

can't lose you too," Lasgol told her.

"I'm not going to stop looking for Viggo. If I have to throw myself into an abyss, I'll do it," Ingrid said, struggling to rid herself of Astrid's grip, who had her on the ground.

"Nilsa, help Astrid, don't let Ingrid jump," Lasgol told her.

"Coming," Nilsa said, leaving her bow on the ground and helping Astrid hold Ingrid down as she struggled to get free. Both women were grunting from the strength they were exerting, one to free herself and the other to hold her down.

"What do you think, Egil?" Lasgol asked him with a horrified look on his face. He feared the worst.

"I need to think. We can't jump into the Abyss, that's suicide. With some time, I might find a way..."

Lasgol noticed that the orb had stopped levitating and was coming down onto the ground. It was no longer shining. It seemed to have turned off.

"Let me go after them!" cried Ingrid, who kept struggling against Astrid and Nilsa to get free. "I have to save him!"

Ona was moaning and Lasgol did not know what to do.

At that moment, a light shone inside the Abyss.

"Look, a light!" Egil cried, pointing inside the gaping, fathomless hole.

They all stared at the light. Ingrid stopped fighting, as did Nilsa and Astrid.

"What's that light?" Astrid asked, squinting to try and see what it was.

The light was so bright in the midst of the absolute darkness of the Abyss that the more it shone, the less they could tell what it was. It was an intense silver light radiating in every direction. Suddenly the light emerged from inside the Abyss and flew past them to rise toward the sky.

The dragon orb began to levitate.

Ona gave a long shrill whistle.

They all watched the light rise, and against the stars and the night sky they were able to see what it was.

"Camu! It's Camu!" Lasgol cried, overjoyed.

"He's flying with his wings spread!" cried Astrid.

"And on his back... that's Viggo!" Ingrid cried.

"Viggo's holding onto Camu's back!" cried Nilsa.

"This is fantastic!" Egil said. "Camu has used his skill to fly. Look at his magic silver wings!"

"Viggo's alive!" Ingrid sobbed, raising her arms to the sky.

Camu was rising with Viggo holding onto his neck. Since he only knew how to fly upwards, flapping, that was what he was doing. They were going up vertically.

"You can stop going up, we're climbing too high," Viggo told Camu.

I go down.

"Yeah, but not into the Abyss, I know you."

Glide?

"Yes, you should glide, but do it away from that blasted hole."

Camu started to glide down. But the gliding went a little too wide. He tried to turn to lose altitude and managed to, but the movement was not very good and he accelerated his descent. He tried to turn again and in so doing went even faster.

"Up! Up! We're going to crash!" they could hear Viggo yelling.

Camu tried to turn but it was too late. They hit the tip of a dune and the impact sent them crashing headlong into a larger dune further ahead. The blow was hard. They struck the dune with their heads and half their bodies buried in the sand.

"Come on! They've landed," Lasgol shouted.

"Quick, before they drown in the sand!" Egil shouted too.

"We have to help them!" cried Ingrid.

They all ran toward Camu and Viggo. They arrived at the dune and pulled on Viggo and Camu, who, half-buried in the sand, could not breathe. They pulled them out by their legs, shifting off the sand on top of them.

"Will you please do me the favor of learning how to fly before you kill someone!" Viggo shouted as he spat the sand out of his mouth.

Very funny land on sand, Camu messaged to them all while he came out from under the mountain of sand with Astrid's and Lasgol's help, who were pulling on him while Ona and Egil swept the sand off him.

"Funny? What do you mean by funny! You bug!" Viggo cried, almost outraged.

"Viggo! You're alive!" Ingrid threw herself on him, knocking him down in the sand to cover him in kisses.

"Of course... I'm... alive...." Viggo muttered while Ingrid kissed him over and over.

"You scared us to death!" Astrid told him.

"How did you manage to get out?" Egil asked, intrigued.

I fall in hole until reach Viggo.

"He weighs three times my weight—he was falling like a rock," said Viggo.

Then call upon skill Drakonian Flight.

"Yeah, the one you don't know how to use," Viggo protested.

Viggo grab me. I come up.

"Fascinating," Egil was nodding excitedly.

"Well done, Camu, you're awesome," Astrid congratulated him.

"Yes, this numbskull owes his life to you," Ingrid said.

"Well, there's no need to exaggerate. I bet I could've gotten out by myself."

"Yeah right, not in a thousand years!" Nilsa corrected him.

"You were both amazing!" Lasgol told them.

"Well, except for the part of climbing onto a dragon's head," Ingrid said.

"Yeah, what an idea," Nilsa joined her.

"We thought you were a goner!" Astrid told Viggo.

"Because of that little dragon? Pshaw! I had everything under control," Viggo said, shaking the sand off his shoulders.

"Yeah, under control," Nilsa said, laughing out loud.

Viggo funny. Can't let die.

You did very well, you're very brave.

I brave, I fly.

Well, when it comes to flying, you still have much to learn.

I know how learn fly, Camu messaged only to Lasgol.

How? Over the desert?

No. Better. With water. Much water around.

Well, that's a very good idea, Lasgol transmitted to him with a smile.

"Now, I'll tell you one thing. Those dragons have very tough heads," Viggo said, showing them his knives. They were completely bent from the blows he had delivered with them.

"You don't say!" Ingrid said.

"How about getting out of this desert?" Nilsa asked them.

"Yeah, before a giant scorpion comes out and my daring numbskull decides to go riding on it to play the hero," Ingrid said, her voice dripping with irony.

They all laughed. A moment later they were heading toward the red mountains.

Chapter 40

The next morning, the Panthers were making preparations to leave. They were going over their gear in front of the Pearl in the southern part of the Blood Mountains. Beside them were Tor Nassor and two dozen of his soldiers, as well as his daughter.

"It makes me sad that our guests must leave," the leader of the Desher Tumaini said.

"We'd like to stay, but we must resume our responsibilities in our lands to the north," Ingrid replied as she gathered her bows.

"We have a great debt we will never be able to pay back," Tor Nassor said with a wave at his daughter.

"As long as you don't attack us if we appear here by accident again, that'll be enough," said Viggo.

"The great hero, the tamer of the dragon of the desert, and his comrades will always be welcome in our lands. The victory achieved is already being depicted in our caverns. The next generations will hear about the day when a handful of northerners arrived with the Great Hor and one of them bowed down the great desert dragon, riding on its head," Tor Nassor said, very impressed. He pointed at Viggo and said something in his own language.

The warriors gave shouts of victory.

"Well, it seems I'm already a legend here," Viggo commented, puffing up like a peacock.

"Don't let it go to your head…" Ingrid whispered in Viggo's ear.

"Make sure they depict me properly in these paintings. Handsome and lethal. I know the paints and surface you use aren't much, but well, do what you can," Viggo told Tor Nassor.

"You will be depicted on top of the dragon, lethal and good-looking," the leader promised.

Ingrid rolled her eyes.

"Let my legend spread throughout Tremia," Viggo said, making a gesture with his arms of utter happiness.

"Are you sure the Hor and his companions of the north do not want to stay for some time with the Desher Tumaini?" Tor Nassor insisted.

Egil looked at Lasgol, who in turn looked at Camu and asked him.

This isn't where the orb wanted to go, right?

No, this not it, Camu messaged back, the orb levitating beside him.

But it still wants us to go somewhere, right?

The arcane call continues, yes. Want go another place.

Do you know why or what for?

No, not know. Only feel arcane call.

And it's coming from the orb, isn't it?

Yes, call coming from orb.

"No, we can't, we must return home. We arrived here by mistake," Lasgol explained.

"A mistake we thank the Hor for," Tor Nassor said.

"We'll come back one day, or at least I will," Egil promised, "There's so much to study and learn here. The legends, the mythology, the Hor, the paintings, everything your people know. As soon as I have the chance, I'll come back."

"You will always be welcome," Tor Nassor said, bowing his head.

"What will happen now with King Mahaes Madu and his people, the Jafari Kaphiri?" Egil asked, concerned.

"What has been happening for generations—they will continue trying to conquer our mountains and our secrets, and we will fight to stop them."

"That's not good at all," Nilsa said, saddened.

"Such are ambitious kings and peoples. They seek to expand their power at the expense of those weaker than them. But we, the Desher Tumaini, are a proud people and fearless. They will not be able to defeat us. We will resist them like we have been doing thus far."

"I wish I could help you…" Lasgol said.

"This is not your fight. It is the fight of my people. Do not worry. You have already helped us more than enough," Tor Nassor said.

"We don't like injustices, we fight them," Astrid told him.

"We'll drop by to see how you're doing in the near future," Ingrid promised.

"We will?" Viggo asked her blankly.

"Yes, we will," Ingrid nodded. "As Astrid said, we don't like injustice. If the Jafari Kaphiri continue in their intent, we'll have to see what we can do about it."

"And here I was thinking we were leaving the desert forever…"

Viggo said resignedly. "This climate is just terrible for my skin."

Ingrid threw him a look of incredulity.

"I agree, we should come back to see how the situation evolves," said Nilsa. "I don't like bullies, be they kings or peoples. And yes, I know our own people and our own king are too…"

Ingrid nodded. "Unfortunately."

"We'll return," Lasgol promised Tor Nassor.

"It will make my soul happy if you do," Tor Nassor replied.

"Do you think you'll have trouble with the great sand dragon again?" Ingrid asked.

"The sand Hor has gone back to its shelter, forced by the hero Viggo and his comrades. It will not come out for a while. That is what my people hope."

"Let us all hope that is the case," Lasgol said.

"If you need me to get rid of that little dragon, you only need to call," Viggo said, as if he could handle the great monster single-handedly.

"We hope it will not be necessary," Tor Nassor said.

"Yeah, let's hope so," Ingrid shot a look at Viggo that meant 'shut up'.

"It has been a pleasure meeting the Desher Tumaini," Lasgol said to Tor Nassor.

"The pleasure has been all ours. It is not every day a Greater Hor appears in our mountains accompanied by great heroes who save our people."

The Panthers said goodbye to Tor Nassor and his warriors.

"Camu, let's go back to the Lair," Egil told him.

"And make sure it's not some other lost corner of Tremia," Viggo added.

Do you think the orb can return to the Lair? Can you communicate with it? Lasgol transmitted to Camu.

I ask.

Lasgol waited for a moment, expecting to receive some message from Camu or the orb. None came.

Nothing? No communication? he transmitted to Camu.

No, not respond my messages.

That leaves us in an awkward situation. We can't travel blindly.

I try another way, Camu glowed with a silver pulse. The orb seemed to react to the pulse and glowed back with another pulse.

What's the orb saying? Lasgol asked him.

Message feeling yes.

Wonderful, then let's go back, Lasgol said.

Camu went up to the Pearl and started sending silver pulses to the great object in a rhythmic manner, searching for the right cadence. They all watched Camu as he worked to open the portal.

After a moment the Pearl emitted a silver flash in response to the pulses Camu was sending to it.

Pearl respond, Camu messaged.

"Go ahead, Camu, open the portal," Lasgol told him.

Camu emitted a flash. *Ask orb help open portal,* Camu messaged.

The orb flashed in reply. It joined Camu and emitted several more-intense pulses in the form of waves with different cadences.

Above the Pearl the three silver circles they were beginning to be familiar with, started forming. First the same-sized circle as the Pearl appeared on top of it. Then the second circle was formed, oval-shaped and larger, as if the circle had turned into an oval. Finally, the shape became a huge silver sphere.

Portal open, Camu messaged.

"Good job," Egil congratulated him.

"To the Lair, right?" Ingrid asked Camu, pointing at the orb as they climbed into the portal.

Camu flashed and the orb flashed back.

Yes, Lair.

"Everyone in," said Lasgol.

"It's been a pleasure!" Egil spoke for all of them.

Amid chants of farewell to the gods of the people of the red mountains, the Panthers entered the portal.

The awakening was as bad as on the journey out. All except Camu, Ona, and the orb were left sick on the ground after losing consciousness for several hours.

"Are we… at the Lair?" Ingrid asked, since she was the first to start recovering from the negative consequences of the journey through the portal.

Lair, yes, Camu messaged to her.

"Thank goodness…" said Lasgol, who was also beginning to

recover. He had managed to get on one knee and was trying to stand.

"I don't like this way of traveling at all, I just vomited my guts out," Viggo moaned on all fours.

"I'll try… to make a tonic that'll help…" said Egil, who was unable to get up and was lying on his stomach.

Astrid was helping Nilsa, who was feeling very dizzy.

"It's like we had just come out of a tornado," the redhead said.

"Something like that, yes…" said Lasgol.

"Luckily, it's well after midnight, so no one has seen us arrive," Ingrid said, looking around.

"What should we do?" Nilsa asked, feeling a little better.

"Let's sleep, act like nothing's happened here," Ingrid said.

"Won't they question us?" Nilsa said.

"Sigrid has granted us permission to come and go as we see fit. She said we didn't need to give her any explanation, so we won't," said Ingrid.

"Yeah, because the explanation would be long and difficult," Egil said with a smile.

"You don't say. I'd like to see you explain my heroic actions with the sand dragon," Viggo commented.

"We'd better not say a word," Ingrid replied.

"Yeah, that would be best," Lasgol agreed.

Once they had recovered, they went into the Lair and headed to their bunk beds. The following morning, they told the whole adventure to Gerd, but only to him. The giant could barely believe what his friends were telling him, especially everything about the great sand dragon, which fascinated him. As Sigrid promised, there were no questions about their comings and goings. Gisli dropped by to greet everyone, as did Ivar, and they chatted animatedly with both Elders.

The next day they accompanied Gerd to his rehabilitation practice with Engla and Loke. It was once again the exercise of catching an apple in the air, the simple exercise Loke had thought of and which frustrated and made Gerd despair since it betrayed how damaged he was. Even a child could have done the exercise without any trouble. On this occasion Annika and Edwina were also present, so adding the Panthers they made up a whole crowd for poor Gerd. He looked embarrassed and he had not even started.

"Relax. Concentrate and you'll do just fine," Loke told him.

"I'll try," Gerd said uncertainly.

"Then it will be my turn, so we'll share the embarrassment. Don't worry," Engla said, trying to cheer him up, since she knew they would fail the exercise and be left looking ridiculous in front of their audience.

Loke threw the apple simply as he always did from a short distance so Gerd would have a chance to catch it, something he and Engla had not managed to do yet. They always got close but never caught it. It was as if their movements were too slow, for some reason, for them to even have a chance.

Gerd saw the apple leave Loke's hand, and as always, he tried to catch it. His mind gave the order and he started to move his arm. He knew his hand would almost reach it in time but that he would not actually catch it.

He was wrong.

His hand closed on the apple and he caught it in mid-flight.

"He did it!" Nilsa cried joyously with a look of incredulity on her face.

"He caught it!" Viggo was staring at him with eyes like saucers.

"Fantastic!" Egil cried, clapping his hands.

Gerd was looking at the apple in his hand in absolute disbelief.

Annika and Edwina were smiling and nodding happily.

"I… I caught it…" Gerd muttered, unable to believe it.

"It looks that way," Loke smiled.

"Have him do it again. It might have been luck," Engla said.

"Are you ready to try again, Gerd?" Loke asked him.

"Yes… throw it again, please."

Loke took the apple from Gerd's hand, stood in position, and threw the apple. Against all odds, Gerd caught it again.

"Impressive!" Lasgol cried, clapping his hands excitedly.

"He caught it again!" Engla said, unable to believe her eyes.

"It has to be because of Edwina's healing," Gerd said, looking at the Healer.

"And your hard work," The Healer replied.

"Let me try," Engla said eagerly.

The Elder stood in position and Loke threw the apple. Engla could not catch it. She tried twice more and failed both times.

"Perhaps you should follow Gerd's example and let Edwina heal you," Annika advised her.

Engla looked at Gerd, then at the apple on the ground.

"If you would be so kind, Edwina, could we start the healing?" she asked her.

Edwina nodded. "Of course, Engla, it would be my pleasure."

"Thank you, Edwina" Engla replied.

"Lasgol, I will need you to find and mark the points to heal for me" Edwina told him.

"Of course. I will help" Lasgol said with a nod.

"When you're done here, please come see us and help me."

"I will," Lasgol assured her.

Engla congratulated Gerd and left with Edwina and Annika toward the Lair.

"I'll have to come up with a more complicated exercise," Loke told Gerd with a wink. "Great job," he added and left.

The Panthers lunged to congratulate Gerd amid cries of joy and affectionate hugs.

"You're going to get well!" Nilsa cried, weeping with emotion.

"He's definitely going to recover, and a lot sooner than we thought," Viggo said with a big smile and hugged Gerd.

"It has to be Edwina's healing magic," Gerd said, still in shock.

"Yes, it is," said Lasgol. "Her magic is powerful and she can heal many wounds. I know from experience."

"Let her continue treating you and you'll be amazed how soon you recover," Egil told him. "From what she told me on the way here from the Camp, she thinks she can heal you completely with some time."

"And she is," Ingrid said, patting Gerd's back.

Nilsa broke into tears, covering her face with her hands.

"Don't cry, it's great news," Gerd said.

"Yes... the Healer's magic is working miracles..." Nilsa said, sobbing.

"It looks that way. I'm so happy," Gerd smiled.

Nilsa nodded repeatedly. "Never again will you hear me criticize magic. I'm done blaming magic for my father's death. Magic isn't bad—what's bad is whoever uses it to do bad. Magic can be good, very good," she said, looking at Gerd with tears of joy and hope in her eyes. "I've been so wrong. I won't fear magic anymore. I'll defend those who use magic for good. I'll pursue those who use it for evil."

"Well said," Egil smiled at her. "As it should be. We should all treat magic that way."

"She's stubborn, the redhead is, but it seems that with enough time, things sink into her head," Viggo joked.

"Well, no matter how much time passes, I'll never stop thinking you're a numbskull," she replied with a comical gesture, wiping away the tears.

"I think we can all agree on that," Ingrid said, and laughter returned to the group.

Their joy at Gerd's improvement and hope for his recovery had the group enjoying each other's company for two more days. Lasgol helped Edwina and he managed to mark the problematic points so that the Healer could start healing them.

The third day, Sigrid called them.

"Royal Eagles, a message has arrived from our leader Gondabar. Your presence is required in the capital," she informed them at the entrance to the Lair.

"Understood," Ingrid said at once. "Do we need to leave right away?"

"That is correct," Sigrid confirmed. "Say your goodbyes to Gerd. We will continue his rehabilitation with Edwina here in the Shelter. I will keep you posted on his progress."

"We appreciate that, Mother Specialist," Lasgol thanked her respectfully.

"It is good he has been improving—Engla accepted being healed once she saw Gerd's progress."

"We are all happy," Nilsa said.

Sigrid nodded, "Go, and good luck. The Shelter will always be open to you."

The Panthers bowed to the Mother Specialist respectfully and left. They were expected at the capital, in all likelihood for a new mission.

Chapter 41

A few days later, the Panthers were in the capital waiting to be given their next mission. Gondabar had already informed them it would be for King Thoran and of the utmost importance. Preparations were being made, but they knew nothing more so far. While they waited for the order to leave, Ingrid and Nilsa practiced with their bows while Astrid and Viggo did the same with their knives. They trained and made preparations for their upcoming mission.

Ona and Camu were resting in the Royal Eagles' shared room in the Rangers Tower. They had noticed it was the best and largest in the whole tower—apparently their growing status came with some benefits. Camu instantly took advantage of the space to try and improve his Drakonian Flight skill. The room had a lofty ceiling which allowed him to rise up to it, although he continued to struggle on the descent. He had already broken two chairs and a bed. Luckily the falls had not hurt him too much, and since he was very stubborn, he went on practicing, despite everyone telling him to stop until they could find a better place to do it, preferably somewhere with lots of water.

Lasgol and Egil were using the time before their new mission to try and gather some more information about the two mysteries bothering them: the end of the era of men and the mysterious dragon orb. They were all too aware how little time they had left before they would have to leave, and they had focused on searching around the capital. It was a big place where you could find information if you knew where to look and paid in gold, particularly the latter.

Egil had gone to see Remus Imalsen, a collector of exotic objects he had heard might have some information about an orb of power a great Norghanian Ice Mage had used in defense of the kingdom. It was unlikely the information would be relevant for their present situation, but even so Egil did not want to leave any stone unturned in their search for information about the dragon orb and its inner workings. After what had happened in the desert with the sand dragon, it was more important than ever to understand the Object of

Power.

They had all heard, or rather felt, the dragon orb order the great sand dragon to go back to its home. If that had seemed weird, the fact that the haughty and mighty dragon had obeyed the orb had been even weirder. That had generated another thousand questions they had no answers for. How had it done it? Why had it intervened and helped them? Why had the sand dragon obeyed the orb when it had ignored Camu? What was the relation between the orb, Camu, and the sand dragon? And so many other questions the Panthers had no idea how to process.

Lasgol was walking along the main goldsmiths' street with a tome under his arm. He was returning from paying a visit to Rufus Fildensen, one of the city scholars in matters of Norghanian religious orders and secret societies. To Lasgol's surprise there were more than he thought, and of all kinds besides, something that had quite puzzled him. The conversation with Rufus had been lengthy since the scholar enjoyed giving long explanations, probably because few were willing to listen and he had finally found a friendly ear in Lasgol. It had become late and night had already fallen over the city. That was the downside of listening to an old man talk about religious orders obsessed with the apocalypse or other dubious and dark objectives. Lasgol had not been very lucky with Rufus, who had told him many things that did not seem to have any relation with what they were investigating.

He hoped Egil had had better luck than him in his search about orbs with dragons. Lasgol could feel the arcane Object of Power under his cloak, in the pouch tied to his Ranger's Belt. He carried it with him everywhere. Since they had left the Shelter, the orb had gone back to a sort of hibernation state. It did not communicate, pulsate, or glow, and the inner substance the dragon was floating in barely moved. It appeared asleep. Egil believed the orb only activated in the proximity of a Pearl. Lasgol shared this theory. The arcane call Camu had felt had also ceased, so they had all been left out on a limb, unsure what to think. The orb was a mystery.

Lasgol continued walking and turned a corner at the next street. He realized he was a little lost. He did not know that area of the city, and at night many of the streets were similar. He studied the surrounding buildings—they seemed familiar, but he did not exactly know where he was.

"Never mind, I have to go north, to the upper part of the city," he muttered to himself.

That was the advantage of living in a tower of the Royal Castle: it was impossible to miss. From his current vantage point, he could not see it because the street was narrow, but the moment he turned onto a wider path he would see the castle towers. He took the next turn and there they were, in the distance above the other buildings. It was a little far, but the night was peaceful and warm and the walk would do him good. It would clear his mind after hours of listening to Rufus' stories and theories. Lasgol smiled, the old man was nice, albeit a little crazy with his conspiracy theories. According to the scholar, there were a great number of brotherhoods and secret organizations in Tremia with obscure goals. Some even worked for the monarchies of certain kingdoms. Lasgol found everything he had been told quite unlikely.

He continued along the street and a woman appeared around a corner. She tripped on the cobblestones and fell on her face. Lasgol hastened to help her.

"Are you okay?" he asked as he bent over to help her.

"Yes... how clumsy..." the woman muttered as she turned around on the ground.

"Let me help you," Lasgol said, offering her his hand.

"Thank you very much, what a stupid fall," she said as she took Lasgol's hand.

Lasgol tried to pull her up, but the woman dragged him to the ground using her own weight.

"Ma'am..." Lasgol started to say when he saw something out of the corner of his eye. He saw it an instant too late. Something hit him on the head hard.

A burst of pain filled his mind and he fell sideways on the cobblestones, completely stunned.

A man appeared armed with a truncheon. Lasgol tried to see who it was but he felt dizzy and found he could not focus.

"You may go, this is none of your business," the man told the woman, who stood up and ran away.

Lasgol knew he had fallen into a trap. He tried to turn over and received a second blow with the truncheon on the head, hard and dull. He was left almost senseless. A terrible pain burst inside his head—he was going to faint but resisted, struggling to stay conscious.

Two men appeared behind the first one. The three figures stared at him lying on the ground.

"Is it him?" the tallest one asked.

"It is," the one who had hit him replied.

"Does he have it?" the tall one asked again.

"My quill marked him two days ago. I've been following him ever since."

"Let's see if mine does," the third one said. He looked like the most veteran.

Lasgol was able to make out that the three men were dressed alike, each wearing a long gray robe with two circles, one inside the other, embroidered in silver on their chest. They almost looked like clergymen or some sort of religious group, but they were armed with short swords and long daggers. They looked like weapons from the kingdom of Erenal. Lasgol recognized these men—Astrid had described them to the group. They were her uncle's men.

One of them took out a long metal rod and put it close to Lasgol. The rod started to vibrate. It did so with a silent rhythmic movement. After a moment it began to emit a shrill whistle. The vibration increased at the same time as the shrill whistle.

"The quills do not lie," the veteran said.

"We have been searching a long time," the tall one said, triumphant.

"And now the search comes to an end," said the one who had hit him.

"Search him. He must be carrying it," the veteran said.

They opened his cloak and found the pouch with the dragon orb.

They took it and set in on the ground to one side.

"Let me check," said the one who was holding the quill. He put it close to the orb. The vibration increased so much he had to move it away from the object.

"We have it!" the tall one said, undeniably pleased.

"At last, after all this time!" cried the one who had hit Lasgol. "We must take it to our master."

"That's not going to happen," said a powerful, somber voice.

Lasgol was about to faint, but he followed the origin of the voice with his gaze and saw two men. The first one, the one who had spoken, was wearing a bright silver robe with a long hood, his face hidden. The other man seemed familiar to Lasgol. He was in his thirties and had short chestnut hair and brown eyes. Where had Lasgol seen him? He was carrying a two-handed sword, and on his wrists, he had two silver bracelets. Lasgol remembered then—the Zangrian spy at the inn, after Orten's mission, the one who had been watching them.

The three men beside Lasgol scrutinized the new arrivals. The one who had the quill put it away and the whistling stopped. He reached for his weapons. The veteran grabbed the pouch and tied it to his own belt at his waist. Then he brandished his weapons. The third one did the same. It seemed there was going to be a confrontation.

"The sacred object is ours. It belongs to our master," the veteran said.

"I'm afraid you are gravely mistaken. That object belongs to me," the man in the silver robe said.

"Who are you?" the veteran asked while his comrades moved apart and stood in an attack position with the short sword and long dagger in their hands. They did not seem to have any intention of surrendering the orb.

"My name is Drugan Volskerian, but I doubt you have ever heard my name before," said the man in the silver robe.

"No, we have not," the tall man who was one of Astrid's uncle's men said.

"That is because I have been away from this kingdom, in foreign lands."

"You may return to wherever you came from. You will not take the sacred object."

"I'm afraid I cannot do that, since I have come precisely to get this object. You see, it is very precious to me."

"Last warning. Leave and you will not die," the veteran said. "We will deliver the object. It is our sacred duty."

"I'm sorry you are so dedicated to your sacred cause. It will only lead you to death," the stranger warned, and his tone was one of certainty.

The three men exchanged glances.

"For the sacred quest!" they shouted suddenly and attacked.

The man with the two-handed sword took a step forward, bearing the brunt of the attack, and delivered a tremendous round blow with his sword against the two men who were lunging at him. The first one blocked the stroke with his sword and dagger but was sent flying backward from the strength of the blow. The second one delivered a stroke which the warrior blocked following his vicious swing.

Drugan Volskerian took out two short swords with dragon-head pommels and, pointing them at the veteran who was approaching to kill him, murmured some magic words. As the attacker's sword rose to fall in a lethal stroke, an intense flame burst out of one of the swords, which hit the man carrying the orb full in the chest.

Lasgol tried to stand but could not. He watched helplessly as the wretched veteran burned completely, and with him the pouch and the orb.

The man with the two-handed sword cut off the tall man's head with one tremendous stroke. The other attacker delivered a stroke that grazed the warrior's supporting leg.

Lasgol heard some arcane words. The man with the two-handed sword stepped back. His opponent searched for the source of the words and saw Drugan's other sword pointed at him. He was out of reach of the sword but not its magic. A flame came out and caught him fully. The poor wretch burnt to death.

The man in the silver robe was either a powerful warlock or sorcerer, and Lasgol knew he should run, but he was so stunned he could not even stand.

The warlock approached the man who had been carrying the orb and was still burning. He pointed one of his swords at him and cast a spell. From the burning leather pouch at the wretch's waist the orb emerged, rising. It rose free from the pouch, flashed with a silver gleam, and drifted to the warlock's head.

"Come with me, my lord," the warlock said to the orb, which levitated to where the warlock was and remained at his side.

"Shall I finish him?" the man with the two-handed sword asked the warlock, pointing at Lasgol.

Lasgol knew he was lost. He tried to use his magic, but the pain in his head prevented him. He lay on the ground, helpless.

"No, he is of the blood. Let him live so he may witness the new dawn approaching, the new era."

Lasgol made one last effort to get up, and in the attempt he finally fainted.

Chapter 42

Lasgol regained consciousness a while later. His head was pounding, but this was not the first time he had been struck there and he knew he would be fine. He was surprised to find that the three dead men had vanished. He checked the ground for evidence of the fight and soon saw the bodies had been taken. There was a trail of blood and two more of burnt flesh that led to the eastern streets. He thought of following them, but Astrid's uncle's men had most likely taken their dead and already left the city to avoid problems with the guard.

"I better get back to the castle," he said and headed up the street to the north.

He went to the Ranger Tower without further incident and headed to the room they shared. He found the whole team preparing for bed.

"You're finally here, I was getting worried," Astrid said, coming over to embrace him. She hugged and kissed him and in so doing realized something was wrong. "What is it?" she asked, looking into his eyes.

"I was attacked…" he replied.

They all stopped what they were doing and turned to Lasgol.

"What do you mean you were attacked?" Astrid asked, looking frightened.

"Where? Here in the capital?" Ingrid asked him, jumping to her feet and leaving her weapons on the bed. She had an upset look on her face.

"Yeah… in one of the streets, when I was coming back from visiting Rufus," he said and showed them the book he had with him.

"They attacked you and robbed you? A Ranger? In the capital?" Nilsa asked, also upset. She left the anti-mage arrows she had been preparing to one side.

"Who was it? They'll pay!" Viggo cried, his knives already unsheathed and ready to attack.

"Oh they'll pay all right! How are you? Are you hurt?" Astrid asked him, frantically looking Lasgol up and down for any wounds.

You okay? Camu messaged, full of concern.

"Well…" Lasgol started to say. He did not know which of the questions and shows of affection to address first. His head still hurt a lot.

"Perhaps we should let the victim explain what's happened to him," Egil suggested. "Also, that way I'll find out whether he needs me to prepare some cure or potions for him."

"Of course! Tell us, Lasgol, what happened?" Astrid said, leading him to his bed, where Lasgol sat down.

He recounted what had happened with as much detail as he could remember. While he recalled the experience, his friends listened intently, holding back their questions. Once he had finished telling them, Astrid examined his head, worry written across her features.

"You have two huge lumps!"

"That's good, it means they couldn't crack his head open," Ingrid said.

"Let me examine him," Egil said as he went over to determine the seriousness of the blows his friend had sustained.

"My uncle's men did this to you?" Astrid was furious. She reluctantly moved back to make way for Egil. Her fists were clenched in rage.

"I think it was them, yes… from your description of their clothes and weapons…" Lasgol said while Egil checked his head.

"I'll kill them all!" Astrid cried.

"You can't kill your uncle… or his men," Egil said soothingly, trying to calm her down.

"I don't see why not. I'd be delighted to help you," Viggo told her.

"You're not helping…" Ingrid whispered into Viggo's ear.

"Attacking a Ranger and robbing him is punishable with death," said Nilsa. "We need to inform Gondabar. Measures will be taken."

"Let's not be hasty…" Lasgol said. "We need to think this through. I think… what happened to me has multiple implications…"

"These are two well-delivered blows. Whoever struck you knew what they were doing," Egil told Lasgol.

"Well, he won't be doing it again…" Lasgol said with a look of pain.

"Luckily, they don't look concerning. I'll prepare a couple of healing tonics, one for the swelling and the other for the pain. That should help."

Lasgol well? Camu messaged, distressed.

"Yes, everyone be at peace, he'll recover. All he needs is rest. He has a tough head," Egil assured them as he went to the trunk in front of his bed to look for the ingredients to prepare the medicines.

"We already knew that, not even a great Norghanian war axe could crack the weirdo's head," Viggo said jokingly.

"I'm going to talk to my uncle right away and demand an explanation for all this! And he'd better have a good one, or he'll pay dearly!" Astrid snarled.

"Let's not go down the path of taking justice into our own hands… it's a path with no return…" Ingrid told her.

"I said answers, I'm not going to hang him," Astrid corrected herself.

"It would be best to go to Gondabar. This is a crime against the Rangers," Nilsa insisted.

"That way we can find out what happened," Egil said as he prepared the tonics.

"Yeah, I also want to know what's going on here," said Lasgol. "I need to know why I was attacked and why they stole the dragon orb."

Orb stolen? Camu asked sadly.

"Yes, they took it from me…"

Orb family…

"Don't get started about your dysfunctional family, bug. That orb isn't your family," Viggo told him.

Orb family. It have be with me.

"I think being rid of the orb is great. The two lumps they gave you don't seem like much for freeing us of that infernal thing," Viggo said. "Or do I need to remind you of the trouble it's gotten us into?"

"Huh, I have to agree with Viggo on that," said Nilsa.

Not fault of orb, Camu defended it.

"Of course it's the orb's fault, it's more lost than a northern bear in a desert," Viggo retorted.

"A desert with a sand dragon," Nilsa supported him, nodding.

"Let's not forget the important question," Egil said.

"Which is…" Ingrid said, coming closer to hear what Egil had to say.

"They attacked Lasgol to steal the dragon orb. That means they knew we had it and that Lasgol was carrying it. They waited for him to be alone and stole it from him. Why? What for?"

"Because they're a crazy religious sect obsessed with the apocalypse?" Viggo said.

"How did they know Lasgol had it? I never mentioned anything about the orb to my uncle. I didn't even know he was interested in the object..." Astrid said, trying to make sense of what had happened.

"They knew I had it because of the quills... they vibrate near the object," Lasgol explained.

"The Quills of the True Blood?" asked Astrid.

"Yeah, two of your uncle's men had them and they checked the object with the quills to ensure it was what they were looking for."

"Well, they must have been combing the city until they found it," said Ingrid, frowning.

"That's what I think. They had been looking for the orb for a long time from what they said," Lasgol said.

"Do you think the orb is what my uncle was searching for? Could it be the orb?" Astrid asked them.

"Well, if it was the orb, your uncle's quest has been a total waste of time, because it's been stuck in ice for over a thousand years," Viggo said, chuckling.

"Not a bad hypothesis," Egil commented as he continued working on the tonics. "It could well be, and that's why he hadn't found it until now, after it thawed out and we had it."

"What I can tell you is that with the quills you can follow its trail and find whoever has it," said Lasgol.

"I wonder what my uncle wants with the orb?"

"To go on holiday to an island he doesn't know how to get to?" Viggo said with sarcasm.

"Do you think they know about the Pearls and portals?" Ingrid asked.

"We have no way of knowing if they do or don't," said Egil. "Only that they wanted the orb for some reason. We have no idea why or if it has anything to do with the portals."

"Well, I'm going to ask my uncle as soon as I lay my hands on him," Astrid said angrily.

"As I said, let's not be hasty, there are many questions to this situation," Egil said. He had finished preparing the two potions and he gave them to Lasgol. "I'm afraid they don't taste nice," he warned him with an apologetic smile.

"Never mind," Lasgol replied, gulping them both down.

"At least you're all right.... It could've been much worse... I don't even want to think about it." Astrid stroked Lasgol's face lovingly.

"Yeah, you're a 'goody two shoes.' How many times have I told you not to be such a good person?" Viggo chided him. "Who else would help a stranger at night in a dark lonely alley? You're too good for your own good. Always distrust, I've told you a thousand times..."

"Yeah... I know..." Lasgol felt terrible for falling into the trap.

"I'm more worried about that new warlock who suddenly appeared..." Ingrid commented with a look of disgust.

"Yeah, a powerful mage according to Lasgol's story," Nilsa commented. "Throwing fire with his swords is frightening."

"And he seemed to know you, didn't he, Lasgol? How could that be?" Viggo asked.

"I've no idea," Lasgol shrugged. "I didn't recognize him, but I saw his warrior at the inn we stayed at in the village of Olouste near the Zangrian border after Orten's mission."

"Zangrians?" Nilsa asked blankly.

"I don't think so. They didn't strike me as spies," Lasgol shook his head.

"If he was there and has reappeared at the scene now, we must conclude it's no coincidence," Egil reasoned. "You already know my theories about coincidences."

"Yeah. In a nutshell, coincidences don't exist," Viggo said.

Egil smiled. "In a nutshell, yes. Two events considered a possible coincidence have an established relationship we aren't capable of seeing in the moment and that's why we rule them as coincidences. That man was in the inn watching us and has appeared with his lord to act and take the orb."

"Yeah, that's what I think also," said Lasgol.

"Then we have two different groups interested in the orb?" Ingrid asked.

"Three, if we count us," Egil stated. "But yes, the warlock wants the orb for some reason. Maybe the same one your uncle wants it for,

Astrid, although it might also be a completely different reason. Only they know for sure."

"Well, I want to know those reasons," Astrid said, still fuming.

"Me too," Lasgol nodded, prodding his lumps carefully.

"One thing we do know. The warlock knew you since he let you go. After robbing you he let you live," Ingrid said.

Lasgol shrugged. "I don't have the answers. I only know he said he was letting me live so I could witness the new dawn coming, the new era…"

"That's very similar to my uncle's message," said Astrid.

"If we analyze it coldly," Egil said, trying to arrive at some conclusion, "we have two groups or organizations, probably religious or arcane. They both want the dragon orb for something—the orb is obviously important, given the time and means employed to getting it. We've also heard references to a new era, not man's, from the two groups. And other preachers too, I should add. Therefore, I assume they're referring to a possible apocalyptic event."

"So now you do believe those apocalyptic theories had some truth to them?" Lasgol asked Egil.

"Yes, I think they must have some truth in them," Egil nodded.

"And you think they're related?" Ingrid asked to make sure.

"Yes, they must be. If as I suspect they are true, then they are related since they might be one and the same, interpreted in different ways."

"Which brings us to the orb," said Lasgol. "The object the two groups have been looking for and fighting over."

"The orb is key to solving this problem. What I can't fathom is what part it plays in it," Egil commented.

"An important one it seems, if they're willing to shed blood for it," said Astrid.

"Yes, that's what it seems," Egil nodded. "I'm beginning to see we have an important mystery on our hands, one of unfathomable importance…"

"So, we have no choice but to solve it," said Lasgol, "because we're in the middle of the whole thing."

"Yeah, we need to find answers before there's a catastrophe," Egil said in a worried tone.

"Like the end of the era of men?" Viggo asked sarcastically.

"Exactly," Egil replied.

"Well, I can foresee this is going to be a wonderful adventure," Viggo said.

"We'll solve the mystery and stop whoever's behind all this," said Ingrid.

"We'll have to be careful," said Nilsa.

"Oh, we will," Lasgol said. "Tomorrow we'll start seeking a way to solve it."

"Hmmm… I'm afraid it won't be tomorrow," Nilsa said.

"It won't? Why not tomorrow?" Lasgol asked blankly. He wanted to start solving the mystery as soon as possible.

Nilsa brought out a parchment and handed it to Lasgol.

"It arrived while you were being attacked."

Lasgol read the orders.

"We leave on a mission. Tomorrow at dawn's first light," he commented as he read.

"Yeah, those are the orders," Ingrid confirmed.

"Mission to the east, from King Thoran himself," Lasgol said, surprised.

"We'll be given the details at dawn," Ingrid told him.

"For once I'm glad we're being sent on a mission. That way we'll forget about mysteries and the end of the world and all the messes you're always getting us into," said Viggo. "Besides, with a little luck, we're being sent to steal the crown jewels of some eastern kingdom."

"If that's the case, you can already forget about keeping them. And I mean right now," Ingrid snapped at him.

"Of course—what a party-pooper you are!" Viggo smiled from ear to ear. "Let the kingdoms of the east prepare. Here comes Viggo, the best Assassin in all Tremia!" he cried, raising his arms.

The Panthers could not but smile, all except Ingrid, who rolled her eyes. Then she kissed Viggo so he would stop speaking nonsense.

At dawn the group would set out on a new adventure, one filled with excitement.

The adventure continues in the next book of the saga:

Note from the author:
I really hope you enjoyed my book. If you did, I would appreciate it if you could write a quick review. It helps me tremendously as it is one of the main factors readers consider when buying a book. As an Indie author I really need of your support.
Just go to Amazon end enter a review
Thank you so very much.
Pedro.

Author

Pedro Urvi

I would love to hear from you.
You can find me at:
Mail: pedrourvi@hotmail.com
Twitter: https://twitter.com/PedroUrvi
Facebook: https://www.facebook.com/PedroUrviAuthor/
My Website: http://pedrourvi.com

Join my mailing list to receive the latest news about my books:

Mailing List:
http://pedrourvi.com/mailing-list/

Thank you for reading my books!

Other Series by Pedro Urvi

THE ILENIAN ENIGMA
This series takes place several years after the Path of the Ranger Series. It has different protagonists. Lasgol joins the adventure in the second book of the series. He is a secondary character in this one, but he plays an important role, and he is alone…

THE SECRET OF THE GOLDEN GODS

This series takes place three thousand years before the Path of the Ranger Series

Different protagonists, same world, one destiny.

You can find all my books at Amazon.
Enjoy the adventure!

See you in:

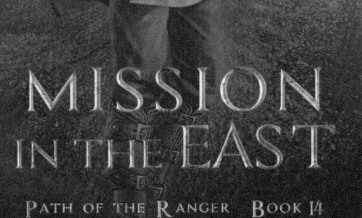

PEDRO URVI

MISSION
IN THE EAST

PATH OF THE RANGER   BOOK 14

Made in the USA
Middletown, DE
31 August 2024

60084705R00215